ALL I DESIRE

Other Avon Books by
Rosemary Rogers

BOUND BY DESIRE
THE CROWD PLEASERS
A DANGEROUS MAN
DARK FIRES
THE INSIDERS
LOST LOVE, LAST LOVE
LOVE PLAY
MIDNIGHT LADY
SURRENDER TO LOVE
SWEET SAVAGE LOVE
THE TEA PLANTER'S BRIDE
THE WANTON
WICKED LOVING LIES
THE WILDEST HEART

ROSEMARY ROGERS

ALL I DESIRE

AVON BOOKS  NEW YORK

This is a work of fiction. Names, characters, places, and incidents either are the product of the author's imagination or are used fictitiously. Any resemblance to actual events, locales, organizations, or persons, living or dead, is entirely coincidental and beyond the intent of either the author or the publisher.

AVON BOOKS, INC.
1350 Avenue of the Americas
New York, New York 10019

Copyright © 1999 by Rosemary Rogers
Published by arrangement with the author
Visit our website at **http://www.AvonBooks.com**

ISBN: 0-7394-0113-0

Printed in the U.S.A.

ALL I DESIRE

Part One

Prologue

1867

1

Even though it was early April, Angela Lindsay shivered in a cold wind that blew icy air into her bedroom and banged the loose shutter in a loud clatter over her window. Fierce gusts blew her hair into a coppery tangle over her face as she leaned out to grab the shutter, and she muttered a curse she had heard her cousin Simone use. *"Merde!"* What a wretched night, not fit for man nor beast.

Stretching farther, at last she succeeded in wrenching the shutter away from greedy fingers of wind to fasten the latch firmly. Then she pushed the hair from her eyes and into a clumsy twist on the nape of her neck, and moved back to stand before the welcoming fire. What cold winds. Every winter into spring they swept down from the Vosges Mountains near the border between France and Germany, cutting to the bone and making her long for the warmth of summer.

She stared into the flames, her violet eyes narrowed against the bright glare. The wind rattled the shutters in a relentless *rat-a-tat-tat*. Curling her arms around her slender body, she stood shivering on the small hearth rug. A glimpse of her blurred reflection in the polished brass firedogs showed a distorted image that seemed all red-gold hair atop bare feet. Her toes curled into the warm wool of the rug, and her fine cambric nightdress shifted around her body as she held out her hands to heat them at the fire.

Oh, it is so *cold* here, she thought. I would much rather be in the soft sunshine in the south of France where the sea winds blow off the ragged rocks and over my face . . . they will smell of salty water and adventure, of places I have not seen and may never see. Oh, there is so much I want to see and do in life, yet I have always been so isolated from the world. . . .

It was true. The school she had attended was remote and secluded, set in France's Lorraine countryside that was so beautiful but so desolate at times. And the good sisters of the convent were very strict with their pupils; daughters of good families were exposed to the refinements of religion and classical studies. Angela spoke three languages and even a smattering of Greek; had studied philosophy, geography, and world history; and yet she still felt naive and untutored.

After leaving school, she had discovered just how naive she was when she was allowed a holiday in Paris with her Tante Marie and cousins. In the city there were so many different places to go! And one afternoon when Tante Marie napped, Angela made the startling discovery of another side of life she had never dreamed existed. It was Cousin Simone who suggested the reckless exploration, and Angela and her cousins had slipped from the house for a daring venture into the haunts of Paris. Simone was older by two years, and quite intrepid; it had been her idea for them to go into a cabaret escorted only by her younger brother, Paul. Of course, they had not remained long, but long enough for Angela to be intrigued by what she saw inside.

It was a revelation.

There was an entirely different way of living than what she had known, and since that day she felt as if she had only scratched the surface with her few travels beyond the quiet village of Saint-Dié.

Why had Maman chosen to come here to live? But she knew the answer to that, of course. It was revealed in the recent letter she had received. It was still wrapped in a square of linen and kept close, for she cherished the letter greatly. But since it had come, her life had altered in finite ways that she did not quite understand.

It was a complete mystery to her why her mother refused to speak of her father, why she had never talked of the land across the ocean where she had lived so briefly and where Angela had been born. During the years, Angela's questions had remained unanswered, and always she had felt a vague sense of displacement, as if she should be somewhere else. But perhaps the answers were in the letter after all, for John Lindsay had seemed to pour his heart into the inked words. Oh, the reasons were not stated plainly, of course, but they were there nonetheless, between the lines of bold flowing script that her father had written to her.

When first she had read his last letter, she had been filled with excitement and had run to her mother with it to beg to be allowed to visit him in America. Mignon Levasieur Lindsay's reply had been a curt and unqualified refusal.

"It is far too unsafe there, Angelique. Everywhere, there are dangerous men—heathens and criminals who are no better than wild animals—

and I was afraid the entire time I stayed in that horrible land. No. You will not go, for you are far too young.''

"I am almost the age you were when you visited New Orleans and met my father," Angela had pointed out, but it made no difference to her mother, as she had known it would not.

But it was true. And her father wanted to see her now, for he had not seen her since she was a baby. Did he not promise to keep her safe? To see that she had everything she needed? He would have sent for her much sooner, he wrote, but until recently there had been a civil war fought in America and it was too dangerous for her to come. Now the war had ended and it was safe again, and the country was growing more prosperous than ever. He lived on a beautiful estate in the foothills where it was very warm, with miles and miles of open land ringed by mountains. Oh, it sounded so beautiful, so wonderful, and she wanted badly to go.

"Cousin Angelique?"

Angela turned, smiling as Simone opened the door a crack and peered inside. She beckoned an invitation. "Come stand by the fire and tell me all about your handsome Jean-Luc, Simone. You had best not let Tante Marie know you are seeing him."

"Sh." Simone closed the door softly, her face a mixture of delight and guilt as she joined Angela in front of the fire. "He is so handsome, is he not?"

"Decidedly. But you are to wed Monsieur Picot, and if Tante Marie should discover you are seeing Jean-Luc, she will be very angry. You should be more careful, Simone. Monsieur Picot is very rich, you know, and you should not risk losing him as a husband."

"Ah, you do not understand, Angelique."

"Angie. Call me Angie."

"Bah. Angie is so . . . American!"

"Yes, I know. That is why I wish to be called by that name. It is how my father wrote me . . . 'Sweet Angela, my darling Angie. . . .' I will go to see him, for I am eighteen now, and soon I will be old enough so that Maman cannot stop me."

Simone stared at her with rounded eyes and open mouth. "You will leave France for that barbaric land?"

"It is where I was born, remember."

"Yes, but you have never lived there. Always, since you were only an infant, you have been here, in France, where it is civilized and painted savages do not roam the streets maiming and killing women and children."

"You do not know they do that."

Simone nodded so vigorously her dark ringlets shivered against her cheek. "But yes, I do. Tante Mignon said it was so, that she saw it herself when she lived there. She said she will never go back."

Frowning, Angie bit her bottom lip. How vexing that Maman should be so set against it. She looked at her cousin with a toss of her head, and loose coppery curls bounced against her shoulders. "I will go. You will see."

"Good God, I know that expression! Like a wicked little fox, heh? Always, you get your own way when you set your mind to it, though I am certain I do not know how you manage it." A sly smile curved Simone's mouth. "Since you are so clever, little cousin, I want you to help me meet Jean-Luc later tonight. Oh, do not look at me that way, for you know you want to help!"

Laughing, Angie nodded. "Very well, I will help, but you must not blame me if it does not succeed. And you will help me with Maman when I ask it of you, yes?"

"But of course, cousin. Why would I not? We are like sisters, and I will always come to your aid when you need me."

But later, when Angie stood outside the garden house as a sentry to warn Simone and her lover of intruders, the wind blew cold around her body and she shivered almost uncontrollably as she thought of New Mexico and how warm it must be. John Lindsay said the sun was bright and hot there, and that the land stretched for miles under a cloudless blue sky.

Yes. One day she would go there, where it was warm. She would manage it despite her mother's objections, for it had always been her dream. In America, it would be exciting, an adventure, a new land that was growing prosperous, as her father had said. And she would be a part of it. Oh yes, she must talk her mother into going, for she could not bear the thought of staying here forever and ending up like her cousin, promised to a man she did not love but must marry even when her heart belonged to another.

In America, she had read, everyone was free. And it was warm. One day, she would go there and see it for herself. It would be so lovely to bask in the warmth of the sun and gaze at miles and miles of land empty of people. . . .

2

Jake Braden's blue cavalry uniform had lost its crisp lines in the suffocating July heat that pressed down like a giant hand on the New Mexico hills. Here in the shade of a cottonwood it was cooler, and in the distance a purple haze hung on the horizon to seam sky and land together with the promise of a bearable evening. Molten heat still seared the air, tasting of dust and straw chaff—and irritation.

Damn her, where could she be? This wasn't at all what he'd had in mind when he'd come to the Double X to buy beef, and if Rita wasn't the daughter of a friend, he'd let her come back when she was good and ready instead of waste his time looking for her.

His mount shifted restively and shook its head in a metallic jangle of curb chains. Overhead, a hawk soared with a keening cry that drifted downward, but there was no other sign of life in the barren landscape.

But Rita had grown up on the Double X and knew this land, and all the places on it to hide, well. Jake swore softly as he removed his army hat to shove back damp, clinging strands of black hair from his forehead.

If it was up to him, he'd tan her little backside for her, but of course, John Lindsay would never harm a hair on the head of his precocious daughter. That was a large part of her problem: Rita Lindsay thought she was above rules and restrictions. At nearly sixteen, she was turning out to be quite a handful, and Lindsay had better do something about it before it was too late.

But that wasn't Jake's problem. Neither was looking for her, but with Lindsay so weak from illness and still in bed, it had seemed the only way to keep the rancher from exerting himself too much. Every Double X cowhand that could be spared was out scouring the range for the girl.

By God, she'd better hope they found her instead of him, Jake thought grimly, because he was likely to put her over his knee. It was inexcusable for her to run off like this, especially in light of the recent Apache raids.

Narrowing amber eyes against the reflected glare coming off the rocks, Jake studied the foothills that rose sharply against the horizon, rugged edges chewing at the blue bowl of the sky with jagged teeth. Nothing moved. Where was she?

"Hell, she just took off, Jake," Lindsay had muttered weakly as he struggled to dress. "I don't know what's the matter with that girl lately. Mad 'cause I won't let her go to a dance in town with some trail trash—"

"I'll find her, John. You stay here and help my men cut out the beef you're selling to the fort. Rita will probably see us looking for her and sneak back. When she does, do us all a favor and take a birch limb to her, will you?"

Grinning, John Lindsay had shrugged with obvious relief. "I shoulda done that a long time ago, I know. She's gotten outa hand."

It was an understatement.

As he regarded the arroyos and brush-studded slopes, Jake remembered that the housekeeper, Concha, had once told him that one of Rita's favorite refuges was an old shack in Mimbres Canyon. "She says she goes there to think, *Señor* Jake, but I think she meets that hombre, Matt Peña. He is bad, but she will not listen . . ."

Reining his bay around, Jake left the spreading shade of the cottonwood and spurred toward the crusty slash of the Tierra Blanca Creek, which flowed from the foot of the Mimbres mountain range. The shack near the meandering creek was little more than a few rough boards thrown together, meant to offer a night's shelter for cowhands out looking for mavericks. When he reached it, Rita's horse was tethered outside, and beside it was another. Concha had been right in her suspicions.

Jake dismounted and ground tied his bay. Drawing his pistol, he moved quietly across the sun-scorched earth toward the shack. A hot wind blew loose dirt in a spiral, and Rita's horse lifted its head to nicker softly, ears pricked forward. It was enough to alert those inside, and when Jake kicked open the door, the man with Rita was already spinning off the cot and reaching for his gun.

Cocking his .45, Jake said softly, "Throw down and I'll kill you. Back off easy now."

With a hand hovering over the butt of his pistol, the man hesitated, then seemed to sag. His hand shook slightly as he held it away from the weapon.

"All right. I'm backin' off."

"Kick the gun toward me and step back." Jake looked at Rita

sprawled in half-naked abandon on the bare mattress of the cot, and told her to dress. "You look like a goddammed *puta* lying there like that."

"Maybe I am, Jake." Her mouth curved into a mocking smile as she stretched languidly. Bare breasts thrust up in impudent defiance from the open bodice of lacy underpinnings and she crossed her long brown legs without moving to dress.

He ignored her as he scooped up the pistol and stuck it into his belt, then kicked the man's pants toward him with a contemptuous shove of his boot. "You Matt Peña?"

The man looked surprised, but nodded as he reached cautiously for his pants. "Yeah. What of it?"

"I hear you've been warned to stay away from her before. You hard of hearing or just plain stupid?"

A deep flush rose in Peña's face and stained his neck as he retorted belligerently, "I ain't neither one. This wasn't my idea. She's the one who said to meet her here."

"And you're as innocent as an altar boy. Put your damned pants on later. Get out now. I'll keep your gun."

"Leave my gun? Hell, I paid twelve dollars for that gun and I ain't about to leave it with you!"

"Then we'll bury it with you if you're that attached to it." Jake cocked the hammer on his Colt, and Peña blanched.

"Never mind. Christ Almighty, I shoulda known better than to listen to some damn fool female . . ."

"Yes, you should have."

When Peña was gone, leaving the shack door swinging crookedly from the remaining hinge, Jake eyed Rita with a detached gaze. "I told you to get dressed. Unless you want to ride back to the Double X in your drawers, do it now."

"Why?" She smiled, watching him through narrowed lashes as she drew a fingertip down over her bare breast. Her skin was dusky brown, the nipple a dark beaded rose. He could see the faint track she made with her circling finger through the misty sheen of perspiration that dotted her torso. Her arms bent to lift her long dark hair away from her face, the motion jiggling her breasts. "It's so hot now, Jake. We can wait until it's a little cooler to go back, can't we?"

Twisting her slim body as if trying to burrow into the thin mattress of the cot, Rita smiled up at him with obvious seduction and said huskily, "I can see you want to stay, Jake. Why don't you come and lie down with me?"

"Why don't you get that pretty ass of yours up off that bed and get dressed like I told you." Jake retrieved her blouse from where it had been flung onto the floor and tossed it to her. "*Now*, Rita. I don't have time to waste out here playing games with you."

She laughed. "But you'd like to. Oh, don't pretend you haven't noticed me. You have, the same as I've noticed you." She sat up in a lithe twist of her body to perch on the edge of the cot, but made no move to dress or get up. "I noticed you the first day you came to the Double X, three years ago. Remember? I thought you were so beautiful, with those gold eyes like a mountain cat's . . . you were dark and dangerous and so sure of yourself. I wanted you even then."

"You were twelve years old, for Christ's sake."

Slender bare shoulders lifted in a shrug, and she swung a foot idly. "Old enough. My mother wasn't much older than fifteen when she came to live with my father. She had me when she was only a little past sixteen. Out here, women have to grow up quick or we don't get a chance to live."

There was a distant light in her dark eyes for a moment, as if she was thinking how short life could be, then she leaned back with her arms braced behind her, her breasts an open invitation and temptation. White cotton drawers trimmed with lace ended at her knees, and her legs and feet were bare. Slowly, she let her thighs fall apart, and the open slit in the crotch of her drawers parted to reveal the lush femininity beneath.

Angry now, Jake crossed to the bed in two steps and grabbed her by the arm to jerk her up. "I've had enough. I don't give a damn if you play the whore with someone else, but not with me. I'm taking you back to your father."

She flushed with angry chagrin. "Do that and I'll tell him you raped me."

Jake's eyes narrowed. "You think he'll believe you?"

"Yes. He always believes me." She laughed angrily and pulled loose from his restraining hand, but curled her fingers around his forearm to hold him. She shook back the dark, tangled hair from her eyes to gaze up at him. "Why wouldn't he? Papa doesn't really know you *that* well, and I'm his daughter. You're only some army captain who comes out here to buy beef and warn us about Apache renegades."

Jake didn't reply for a moment. This wasn't the first time she'd tried to get him alone, and he was getting tired of it. For Rita Lindsay, life was a constant battle. She defied her father and convention with supreme indifference, and because her mother had died when she was only two, John had always let her get away with it. Guilt, maybe. Or because it was easier to let her have her own way than to argue with her. Whichever it was, he was regretting it now.

As she stared up at Jake with a smug smile curving her pretty mouth, Jake reached for her, and he saw her eyes widen with anticipation and triumph. It was short-lived.

Instead of kissing her, as she obviously expected, he pulled her to him and flung her over his shoulder. Her breath was forced out in a harsh whoosh of air, and she began immediately to kick her feet and pound on his back with her fists.

"Put me down, Jake Braden! Let me go or so help me I'll tell everyone you forced yourself on me . . . Papa will take a bullwhip to you for it, and then you'll hang . . ."

Her threats were somewhat diluted by breathless, choked pants for air, and Jake ignored her as he left the line shack with her over his shoulder. The sun was going down, and purple shadows hazed the rough-toothed line of the mountains. By the time he put her atop her horse, she was sobbing with fury and chagrin, and looked down at him with streaming eyes. He stared back at her, and she seemed to crumple as she buried her face in her palms and wept like a thwarted child.

For the first time, he felt a spurt of sympathy for her, and shook his head. "Look, Rita, I know you've had a hard time of it out here, but this isn't the way to get what you want."

"How would you know what I want?" she muttered sullenly, and scraped a hand over her wet face to stare at him through spread fingers. "Men don't have to pretend like women do. If I laugh, it's too loud. If I want to go into town, I'm being irresponsible. If I smile at a man, I'm a whore. Always, there are so many rules, and Papa is never here. Until lately, that is, and now . . . now he's dying and I'll be all alone!"

Her lower lip trembled, and Jake saw past her defiance and outrageous behavior to the fear she tried so hard to hide. "Hey, *chica*," he said softly, "you won't be alone. Fort Selden isn't that far away. As long as I'm stationed out here, I'll make sure you're all right."

Lifting tear-drenched eyes to his face, she studied him for a long moment with childish vulnerability in her quivering mouth and frightened eyes. Then she smiled sadly. "You won't always be here, Jake."

"Maybe not. But by then you'll be grown up and married and won't care where I am. You'll be safe enough."

This time when he handed her the discarded blouse she took it, thrusting her arms into the sleeves and buttoning it slowly as she watched him through her lashes. After propping the broken door back in its frame, he gave her the rest of her clothes and mounted his bay.

Rita did not comment as they rode along the banks of the creek, then east toward the Double X. The valley floor heaved upward in gradually sloping hummocks of land dotted with mesquite bushes. Delicate green leaves hid lethal thorns amidst the foliage, but the beans provided meals for beast and man at times. Beyond the swales where yucca plants grew in groves of ten-foot stalks lay the alkali flats, where only the hardy greasewood could grow. Neither spoke as they rode up an incline thick with tall grama grass, and dusk slowly blanketed the foothills that reached the knees of the mountains. Miles of prickly pear, and rabbit brush spread around them, filled with the wakening predators of night.

There was a sharp yip that sounded like a coyote, and then another, and Jake reached for his rifle. If it was Apaches, they'd attack before dark, fearing night spirits more than the white man.

Yet even with the threat of danger, the night held intense beauty. A full moon rose slowly, spreading silvery light over the lonely, whispering wilderness. Rita crowded close. She was native to this savage land and recognized the signs of danger.

"Jake, I'm afraid," she whispered, and he nodded.

"Stay close to me. Do what I say and don't argue. It's not far now."

But it was far enough if those coyote yips were human instead of animal, and Jake laid his Winchester across the pommel of his saddle in readiness. When the lights of the Double X came into view and they saw the ranch buildings nestled below in the cup of sloping hills, he reined in behind a clump of ocotillo. Nothing moved below them. There was only a calm quiet, with not even a breeze to sway the long, snaky arms of the ocotillo. Greenish fur covered the slender wands, each one tipped with a long finger of scarlet that dangled from the fronds.

"It looks all right," Rita said softly, but anxiety made her voice quiver. "Not even a jackrabbit out."

He grinned, and in the soft silvery gloom, saw her uncertainty as he said, "I'll race you . . ."

For a moment she looked only startled, then she laughed, and digging her heels hard into the sides of her horse, took off at a dead run down the familiar slope into the valley. Jake was hard behind her, and they were almost to the gates of the stone walls enclosing the ranch when they heard the first wild yips and shouts.

Easing his rifle up, he waited until he saw the dark silhouette of a rider before he took aim, and the rifle bucked in his hands as he fired. There was a choked cry, and a riderless horse careened out of the shadows and in front of them.

Rita screamed, and Jake shouted at her to keep going as he slowed a bit. Men appeared atop the Double X walls, and the gates swung open to allow Rita inside as she drew near. More shots were fired now, and in the pale glow of the moon that hung like a huge silver dollar low in the sky, he saw that the unexpected resistance had turned away the raiders. They scattered into the night beyond the ranch, disappearing up into the surrounding hills.

When Jake reached the ranch a short time later, it was dark. John Lindsay came out to meet him as he dismounted by the corral, and the rancher's face was creased with pain and worry. "You all right, Braden?"

"Yeah. I just stopped to take a little souvenir."

He held it up and heard Rita's soft cry of revulsion. She clapped a hand over her mouth, staring at the length of short brown hair and bloody scalp dangling from his hand.

"It's not really mine, though I've taken a few scalps in my time," he said in a soft drawl, and saw from John Lindsay's eyes that he knew what he meant. The scalp was fresh, and the Apache had tied it to his belt . . . Jake wondered if Matt Peña had made it back or if this was his scalp he held, but he wasn't about to bring it up in front of Rita.

It wasn't until much later, when John had retired for the night and Jake stood on the low front porch smoking a thin cigar, that Rita came to find him, coming up behind him almost as quietly as a cat in the dark.

"Jake?"

He blew out a stream of smoke, then dropped the cigar to the dust and ground it out with the heel of his boot as he turned to look at her. Moonlight silvered her face, and she wore a high-necked dressing gown that covered her from chin to toes. He smiled slightly.

"Yeah?"

"I just want to say that I'm sorry about today. I was wrong. I . . . I don't know what gets into me at times. I just act all crazy, when all I really want is to feel safe. To be loved."

"Your father loves you a lot, Rita."

"Oh, I know. But that's not enough." She leaned against the support post and crossed her arms over her chest as if chilled, dark eyes staring beyond the ranch into the hills rimmed with pale light. "I wish I could go to a big city to live, where there are people and linen tablecloths and gaslights . . . the theater and opera houses, where no one worries that at any moment a band of renegade Apaches is going to swoop down and slaughter them. . . . I hate it out here."

Jake didn't answer for a moment, but surveyed the stark land silently. Then he turned to look at her again.

"This will all be yours one day, you know."

"Maybe. Maybe not."

He lifted a brow. "Who else would your father leave it to? He'll leave it to you, and you'll get married and stay here with your husband and children, and one day there won't be the threat of Apaches hanging over your head. It will be a paradise then, Rita."

Her laugh was bitter. "Like the garden of Eden? No, you make it sound wonderful, but that will never happen, Jake. You see, my father never married my mother. He is still married to his first wife. I'm a bastard, and bastards don't inherit."

For a moment he didn't reply, then shrugged. "John Lindsay is not the kind of man to worry about that. He'll leave it to who he wants."

"Oh, yes. He'll certainly do that." She drew in a deep, shaky breath, and her voice was almost a whisper. "He's not leaving it to me, Jake. He's leaving it to his first child. Oh, he's made it quite clear that I won't be left out, and if for some reason she doesn't want it, then it will default to me. But there you have it—I'm only a replacement, after all. A substitute heiress."

She turned to look at him, and moonlight filled her eyes with wet, silvery reflection. "Will you wait for me to grow up, Jake? Please? In spite of how I act and what I've said, I really have loved you since the first day I saw you. Marry me and take me away from here . . ."

When she leaned into him, it seemed natural to let her, and he put an arm around her shoulders to hold her lightly. After a moment, he said softly, "I'm not the marrying kind, *chica*. I'd only make you miserable. But I'll hang around until you find the right man, and I'll make sure he's the one who will make you happy. All right?"

"Maybe if you hang around long enough, you'll be the right man."

He laughed. "Don't count on it. Besides, when I leave the army's payroll, I'm going to live on my own land, and it's even more remote than the Double X. You'd hate it there more than you say you hate it here."

"Not if you were with me." She tilted back her head, and her eyes gleamed with soft light as she smiled up at him almost wistfully. "My garden of Eden would be where you are, Jake. You'll see. One day I'm going to marry you. And then we'll travel, and you may not want to go back to your ranch to live. We'll go to Paris, London, New York . . . even New Orleans. It would be fun seeing those places for the first time together, don't you think?"

Jake didn't bother telling her he'd been to all those places already. That had been years ago, another life for him. A life before all the trouble came, before he'd lost everything in this world he cared about. He knew just how Rita Lindsay felt. She wasn't the only one who had been replaced and robbed of an inheritance, and he could well understand the hatred she must feel toward the interloper.

He felt it himself, but for a different person and a different reason. One day, he would take back what was his. The right time would come.

Part Two

The Beginning

1870

3

It was Angela Lindsay's first full day in New Orleans. Royal Street sprang into vibrant life in the early hours of the morning, and now the street was filled with vendors hawking their wares, shouting inducement in a mixture of French, Creole, and English that she found most intriguing as she brushed aside the flimsy gauze curtains to open the window. A warm May breeze carried enticing scents upon the gentle currents, smelling of hot bread and the burned-sugar candies called pralines. She had eaten one the day before and found the sweet sugar-and-nut confection delicious—as was everything in this bustling city.

A smile of satisfaction curved her mouth, and her violet eyes tilted slightly at the corners so that she looked as content as a well-fed cat. She was here. At last. It was about time. In the past three years she had practiced her English diligently, certain that the time would soon arrive for her to go to America. And it was as wonderful as she had always dreamed it would be, though sadly, part of her dream had been dashed upon their arrival with the news that John Lindsay had died a few weeks before. She had so wanted to meet her father . . .

"Angelique! What are you doing?" Mignon Levasieur Lindsay leaned over her daughter and yanked closed the flimsy curtains over the window. "You make of yourself a spectacle, displaying your face to all those rude barbarians in the street."

Angela turned away from the hotel window with a shrug, and leaned back on the fat cushions of the horsehair settee to gaze at her mother with a smile. "I refuse to be shut in today. It's so wonderful here. And I thought we would never arrive—such a long journey, and that ship was so small and cramped and damp—but at last we are here."

"Yes, so we are." Mignon gave her daughter a pinched smile. "But

I do not intend to stay long in America, so do not grow too attached. Since he is dead, we will stay only long enough to receive your inheritance, then we go back to France, where life is civilized instead of so crude.''

"Do you think America is crude?'' Angela glanced back at the window, hidden now by folds of gauze that filtered the bright light. "I think it is terribly exciting. Is this not where you met my father?''

"Yes.''

Mignon did not elaborate, but Angela could not subdue the curiosity to know more about her father. After all, now it was too late to meet him, a crushing blow. Oh, the few letters had been a link with him, but not enough. More often were the letters from his bankers in New Orleans, not from John Lindsay. He had sent money for her care and education, but it was not at all the same; no, not at all . . . what had he been like, this man who was her father?

She looked up at her mother. "Tell me about him, Maman.''

"If you mean John Lindsay, I prefer not to think of him.''

Angela's chin came up, and she wound a coppery curl of her hair around a finger, her foot tapping against the floor with rapid irritation as she studied her mother.

"But I must know,'' she said finally, her soft tone not meant to hide her determination. "Never are you willing to speak of him. But he was my father, and you must once have cared about him or you would not have wed him so long ago. It was here, was it not—in New Orleans— where you met and married him? Was he handsome? Dashing? Gallant? Why did you fall in love with him if he was so terrible?''

"Foolish child. You are too young to know about such things.''

"Maman, I am twenty-one years old, well past the age of knowing about such things. You did not think I was too young with Capitaine Poirier. Or the Belgian consulate we met in Strasbourg, Monsieur Beaulieu. Or—''

"Enough, Angelique.''

Angie recognized that tone from her mother and subsided at last, though still determined. Her chin squared, and she tapped her fingers against the small cleft in the center as she regarded Mignon with appraising eyes. How *long* could one hate? And how could one hate someone she had once loved enough to marry?

Swinging one foot idly, she remarked, "The barrister said we must stay in New Mexico a year for me to receive my inheritance. Do you think you will be so unhappy there?''

"I have no intentions of staying in America an entire year, *ma petite,* so do not distress yourself unduly. We will do what must be done, then return to France with enough money to live properly, instead of as peasants.'' Mignon's smile was cool as she tucked a blond hair back into place and smoothed an imaginary wrinkle from the pearl-gray silk of her gown. ''There are always ways to get around certain unpleasantries, and I am confident I will be able to do so this time.''

''But what if I want to stay, Maman? I may like New Mexico.''

''You will not. It is hot and barren, with nothing of the kind of life you enjoy. There are no soirees, or galas for you to attend, no handsome young beaux to dance attendance upon you—oh no, *ma chou*, you will not like it at all, I assure you.''

But Angie thought that perhaps she just might, after all, like New Mexico very much. America had an air of raw excitement that she found intriguing. Just riding several blocks in an open barouche from the New Orleans docks to the St. Louis Hotel, she had seen much that interested her.

The avenues of the *carré de la ville* were lined with brightly colored houses laced with wrought iron and dripping with a profusion of flowers that she found most charming. And earlier this morning, she had awakened to the lyrical calls of vendors on Royal Street, their accents as exotic as their coffee-colored skin and the bright cloth turbans the women wore that were called *tignons*.

Surely, if New Orleans was so exciting, New Mexico must be even more so, Angie thought, for it was far newer to civilization, far more primitive. And she had grown so *bored* in France, where it was expected that she meet insipid young men who seemed to think they were so irresistible and wonderful—an opinion she had not once shared. No, they were too confident, too haughty. And she was not a fool, however much they might wish it. She had grown quite weary of hearing how they admired her so, when she knew quite well they only wanted stolen kisses in the arbor or some secluded corner away from the watchful eyes of her mother or Tante Marie.

Had she not learned well the lesson poor Simone had suffered at the hands of a heartless roué? *Oh, yes.* She would not forget that men wanted only what they could not have, and once it was given them, they no longer wanted it. Poor Simone. It still grieved Angie that she had not been able to help her cousin, despite all. It had also forged a great determination in her not to suffer the same fate.

That determination had been strengthened even more by an overheard conversation between her mother and Tante Marie one afternoon:

''Perhaps she should be betrothed to Monsieur La Tour after all, Mignon, for he at least is wealthy and will provide well for her.''

Maman's response was abrupt: "Angelique refuses to wed him, and I do not blame her. He is fat and old."

"So? What did marrying a young, handsome man do for you, my dear? Nothing. Ah, Mignon, you should have wed Pierre Chaveau instead of your Americain . . . but no, nothing would do but you marry in that far-off land, and now look: Here you are, back in France, married but without a husband."

"Yes," Maman had replied softly, "that is true, I know. But the reason I would not divorce John is to save myself from being forced into another marriage and the attentions of a man who disgusts me. No. I will not force Angelique to marry a man like La Tour, but I will encourage her to marry well. I have several advantageous offers that I am seriously considering."

Listening, Angie had realized for the first time how tenuous her life must really be. Never had she thought of it before, assuming with girlish naïveté that all would continue as it always had. Not long after that revelation had come the letter from America saying that John Lindsay was sick and must see his daughter before he died, that he wanted her to have her inheritance, but with a stipulation:

To claim it, she must come to America.

For Angela, it was a dream come true. But Mignon had fumed angrily that it was all a trick to get her back to that savage land and that she would not go, even if it meant a great deal of money. Finally, Angie had stated her decision to go, reminding her mother that she was old enough to travel without her permission and that Lindsay had made all the necessary arrangements, including passage on a ship across the Atlantic and an army escort from New Orleans.

"I would like for you to accompany me, Maman, but if you choose not to go—"

Angie's shrug had decided Mignon at last, and now they were here in America. When they were greeted in New Orleans with the news that John Lindsay was dead, Mignon made immediate plans to modify the will so that they would not have to remain in America.

And Angie struggled with new, unsettling emotions.

She did not know her father, so it was difficult to feel abject grief, yet there was a certain . . . regret . . . that she had never known him and now he was gone. Worse, she could not help a growing feeling of resentment that her mother had not let her visit him before, and now that it was too late, she did not seem at all disturbed, but relieved.

"Angelique," Mignon said as she shook wrinkles from a stylish gown, "you should rest more, for tonight we attend a fete in our honor.

It is so kind of Monsieur Gravier to plan such a welcome for us, and we dare not seem unappreciative.''

"But it is only noon, and I am not tired. I would rather see more of New Orleans than rest—''

"Angelique, do not be quarrelsome. It is important that we socialize, and that we make a good impression on Monsieur Gravier's friends as well. The governor of Louisiana will be in attendance, and we may need his help untangling the terms of your legacy. So do as I say, eh? I will have Bette press your gown while you rest.''

A little annoyed, Angie kept her comments to herself as she complied, and lay down upon the bed clad only in thin cotton pantalettes and beribboned chemise. Sunlight slanted through the wooden shutters over the windows, and bars of light penetrated the gauzy curtains with relentless determination in this sunny clime. She wriggled her bare toes with a resurgence of anticipation.

Oh, it would be so different here, so new and exhilarating, that she would soon forget all the worries that had plagued her on the tiresome voyage from Calais. Stretching, with her arms above her head as she gazed up at the ceiling, she smiled. Yes. All would be well. And tonight she would dance and be gay, for her future lay before her like a bright, shining gold coin. Why, there could be anything ahead of her in this new land, and she had her father to thank for it.

She was still thinking of him when she drifted into sleep, and a slight breeze that smelled of burned sugar and jasmine wafted over the open transom and belled out the sheer curtains.

Mignon peeked in at her, and frowned a little as she saw the open transom and Angela's scantily clad form sprawled across the bed. How difficult she had become since her last birthday. It was her age, of course, and her new found maturity. Ah, she was so lovely, so innocent for all her pretense at being worldly. Had it been twenty-one years ago, Mignon wondered, that her daughter was born in his rough, raw land?

There were times when she thought of those days with a shudder— and at other times, with regret. Oh yes, she had loved John Lindsay as only the young and foolish can love, with all her heart and soul and every fiber of her being.

It had nearly destroyed her.

No, that would not happen to Angelique, not to her precious daughter, who meant all. She would save her from such a fate, for the years had been so unkind to Mignon since she had last been in New Orleans.

A faint smile curved Mignon's mouth. So long ago now, that time a distant memory, yet so clear. Tante Gabrielle had begged that she come to New Orleans for a visit, for she missed France so in those days, and insisted Mignon would help her adjust. The visit was intended to be brief, but fate had deemed otherwise, in the form of John Lindsay.

And yet . . . and yet she could remember the handsome, dangerous young man who had stolen her heart at a ball here in New Orleans as if it had happened only yesterday; she could still hear the husky timbre of his voice as he asked her to dance. Ah, he had been so gallant, combining an exciting blend of danger and mystique with New World charm and brashness, and he had swept her off her feet. She must have been mad to think she would be happy in America, for it was so different from her beloved France. And New Mexico—oh, how it had frightened her! Wild savages, barely clad and descending in the night to ravage settlements; and the Mexicans, to the south, who still claimed New Mexico as theirs even after a war had wrest it from them—never a day without danger, never a night without fear that not even love could ease.

No, she had not been able to bear it, and John had never forgiven her for it.

But that was behind her now. John was dead.

Closing her eyes, Mignon allowed herself a moment's grief for him. Angelique was wrong—she had never hated John Lindsay. Even after leaving him, she had loved him, so much that she could not seek a divorce or love another man. But he would not leave his land, and she could not live in it.

So here she was again, twenty years later, reluctantly bringing their daughter back for an inheritance that would kill her if she claimed it. But she would not allow that. No, she would fight tooth and claw to keep Angelique from being so foolish as to risk all to live in such a hostile land. And she would see that her daughter received the legacy that should have been hers long ago. They would return to France with enough money to live well, instead of on the sufferance of her relatives, always regarded as poor relations, though Angelique had not suffered any stigma. No, she had gone to the best schools and been well educated, and had attended the most fashionable functions and been received by those who really mattered. But it was not enough. Now, at last, there was hope for her future.

With this in mind, Mignon decided to ignore the social convention that said they were bereaved and so they must wear black, for after all, few would know that Angelique was supposed to be in mourning, would they? Instead she chose a gown for her that was suitable—if one considered her innocence. She was still so young, really, though she seemed to think she was much older than her years at times. And at times it was very disturbing when men looked at her daughter as they had once looked at her, with eyes bright with admiration and longing.

No, it would never do to have Angelique appear too sophisticated.

She shook loose the flounces of the gown she had chosen for Angelique, an ivory grosgrain that set off her delicate porcelain skin and red-gold hair. Such unusual coloring, with flaming tresses and large eyes that reminded Mignon far too much of John Lindsay, a lustrous blue that often deepened into violet. Ah, Angelique was very much her father's daughter, whether she knew it or not, for never had John Lindsay allowed himself to doubt his own abilities, and neither did Angelique. Yet Angelique was herself very American, though she had been just an infant when they left for France. How did it happen? Mignon had been so careful not to talk of America. Yet Angelique had been fascinated with it since childhood, insisting upon using the Anglicized version of her name—and even the horrid, informal *Angie*.

It was the wild blood of her father in her that must be tamed, Mignon thought with growing determination. She could not allow Angelique to ruin her life by staying in this uncivilized, dangerous land. She would see to it that they returned to France as quickly as possible.

4

The St. Louis Hotel was located in the heart of the *carré de la ville* and favored by the Creoles for fashionable balls. It was here in the rotunda, a circular apartment with a high, domed ceiling in the very center of the hotel, that political meetings were frequently held. The ballrooms were on the second floor, with separate entrances on both Royal and St. Louis Streets.

And tonight, it seemed only natural for those attending a meeting in the Rotunda to gravitate to the ballroom, where music played gaily and beautiful women swooped over the polished floors in elegant gowns.

Angie paused in the doorway, more to survey the room than for effect, but nonetheless she caught the attention of several young men. Mignon leaned close to murmur in her ear, "Keep your shoulders straight, *petite*. You will ruin the lines of your gown if you slouch."

Though she automatically straightened her shoulders, Angie could not help a flash of resentment at her mother's direction and moved forward swiftly to avoid more unwelcome strictures. As she crossed the floor, she caught a glimpse of her reflection in one of the long, mirrored doors flanking the ballroom, and thought with despair that she looked far too ingenuous. Another battle lost—she had wanted to wear the sleek, form-fitting gown of lustrous blue that she had bought in Paris, sewn by Worth, but Maman had insisted Angie wear what she had chosen for her. It wasn't at all the impression she wanted to make. She felt more like a child than a sophisticated young woman.

Her long flounced skirt of ivory grosgrain was trimmed with three pinked flounces of the same material. The overskirt of point lace was a delicate lilac tint, draped behind by means of two grosgrain ribbons of ivory, and tied in a bow. The low bodice opened in front over a white lace underwaist and was clasped with an amethyst brooch the same color as her eyes. The jeweled pin winked with pinpricks of reflected light from the overhead chandeliers. Atop her crown, she wore a delicate wreath of tiny violets nestled among sprigs of lacy florets, and Bette had combed her hair into a cluster of ringlets that dangled down her back. Amethyst-and-gold earrings swung from her pierced ears, and around her neck she wore only a simple gold locket.

Despite Mignon's urging, she wore no gloves—a small victory—and her arms and shoulders were bare, gleaming under the flickering light of gas lamps and candles. She carried a small ivory-and-lace fan in one hand, tied to her wrist by a ribbon—an affectation in France, but here in the sultry heat of New Orleans, a necessity.

Unsettled by the clothing dispute with her mother, Angie defiantly took a proffered glass of champagne punch as a waiter paused with a silver tray. She sipped the cool, bubbly liquid slowly, surveying the ballroom over the gold-trimmed rim of the goblet.

"Do you think that wise, *petite*?"

Angie did not look at her mother as she shrugged her shoulders. "It is only one glass of champagne."

"Yes, but too much goes to your head, and you must not behave foolishly tonight."

"I have been drinking champagne for several years, and know when to stop." She sounded petulant and she knew it, but she was quite weary of having her every move judged and condemned. Why must Maman still treat her as a child? And she felt so *foolish* in this lacy confection of a gown, when she should be garbed in a stylish garment such as Mignon wore.

Mignon, at forty, was still a beautiful woman. Her pale blond hair was swept from her face and piled atop her head in a bounty of artful curls. The black gown she wore set off her fair coloring; it was close-fitting and sleek, a satin train trailing behind her as she walked. Diamonds glittered at her throat and in her hair, and over elbow-length gloves, she wore a diamond bracelet. She was a vision of cool beauty: sophisticated and stylish, and desirable.

Beside her, Angie felt gauche.

She took another sip of champagne, and Mignon's mouth tightened the slightest bit. Not too much, for it would cause aging lines, of course. "Here comes Monsieur Gravier, so do be on your best behavior, Angelique."

"He is a toad."

"*Angelique!*"

It was true, but she refrained from more comment as the portly Creole reached them and bowed gallantly from the waist. Monsieur Gravier took Mignon's hand and kissed her gloved knuckles, murmuring in French that he was honored to have so beautiful and gracious a lady in his presence once more and that he hoped she would favor him with a dance.

"And your daughter as well," he added, looking up at Angie with a smile that she found much too assessing and disturbing. "It is true that beautiful mothers have most beautiful daughters, I see. I am the envy of all the men in New Orleans tonight, with such belles as my guests."

"You are too kind, Monsieur Gravier," Mignon replied so coolly that Angie thought she must dislike him, too. "It is we who are honored that you have gone to so much trouble to assist us in our hour of need."

"But of course! Why would I not? My father spoke of you so often and with such admiration that I would be shamed were I not to offer whatever assistance I can in your situation." His black eyes glistened, and he stroked a finger over his full mustache in a manner that Angie detested as he smiled at them. "Already I have set in motion the events that will gain your desires, madame. You will not be sorry you came to Raoul Gravier with your problem, heh? Now come. The music begins, and I was promised a dance by the most beautiful woman in all of France, and now that you are here, in all of Louisiana as well."

Angie followed as Monsieur Gravier led her mother across the ballroom floor, feeling a little awkward as she pretended not to see his outstretched arm for her to take. If Maman wished to dance with him, it was fine, but she would not feign an interest she did not feel. Especially not when there were so many other intriguing gentlemen in the room now, dark-eyed Creoles and Americans standing elbow to elbow.

It was easy for her to differentiate between the Creole and American men, for the Creoles bore an air of inbred arrogance that was easily discerned. Although the Americans were more casual, they seemed no less arrogant, even a little dangerous, and she wondered with a faint smile if her imagination had run amok. No doubt they were all ordinary businessmen such as bankers and clerks, or perhaps merchants, not the untamed, feral men her mother had always said were so uncivilized and frightening in America.

Ah, perhaps it was true that she had far too romantic a nature, as Mignon often remarked with disapproval. None of the men who had courted her in France had piqued more than mild interest, seeming far too insipid and boring to her. Always, she had felt a sense of vague dissatisfaction, as if there was something waiting just around the corner for her.

Yet now she was here, where often she had dreamed of being, and the men looked all too familiar to her, with either vacuous expressions or faces showing intense impatience.

But still, it was a warm May night and the music was playing and the champagne was delicious, and she allowed herself to be coaxed into a dance by one of the young Creoles she had met upon her arrival the day before.

"I have received permission from your maman to dance with you, mademoiselle. Perhaps you do not remember me?"

Fluttering her fan, she gazed at him over the lacy pleats. "Of course I remember you, Monsieur Delacroix. You were with Monsieur Gravier when he came to meet us at the docks."

"*Oui.*" He bowed over her offered hand, looking up at her with deep, dark eyes. "And you are even more beautiful today than you were the first moment I saw you, though I thought then that no woman could be as perfect. I see that I was mistaken in that assumption, for you are unrivaled tonight."

Angie left her hand in his and swept with him onto the dance floor, her belled skirts swaying about her ankles as she put her hand lightly upon his broad shoulder. He was tall and slim, with dark hair and eyes and a small mustache that was neatly trimmed over his upper lip, and he did not try to hold her too closely as they waltzed. He was quite handsome, she thought, though far too fervent for her tastes. Still, the flattery was nice to hear.

Delacroix gazed at her with ardent admiration. "I am very pleased you have come to New Orleans, Mademoiselle Lindsay. You are the fairest flower to yet grace our city."

"You are too kind, monsieur." She moved with automatic grace in the steps of the waltz, and her attention drifted from the young man holding her with cloying attention and flattery to focus upon those in the crowded ballroom.

"But no! I am only truthful. Never have I seen such glorious hair or lovely eyes . . . like jewels, they shine."

"*Merci,*" she murmured, frowning a little as his arm drew her a bit closer to him. He smelled of hair oil and a vague, musky scent, and she deliberately pushed him back to a proper distance that only elicited more comment.

"Ah, your beauty is like the sun, too bright to gaze at for long without going blind, mademoiselle. Dare I say that I am already smitten with you?"

Crossly, Angie wondered what she was supposed to say to such effusive adulation. It always left her discomfited, for she never knew quite what to reply.

But then there was no need for comment, for he began to tell her of his important position in New Orleans, and that his father was one of the most respected—and wealthy—men in the city. "I am just come from a political rally in the rotunda, and now that control of our city is being slowly returned to the proper citizens after the fiasco of the war and Reconstruction, we have high expectations and hopes for Louisiana. For far too long, New Orleans has been run by carpetbaggers and unscrupulous profiteers who nearly ruined our lovely city. But at last we have regained control in the Senate. It is hoped I will soon take a seat in Congress."

"How intriguing." Her polite response only invited more information about his rising importance in New Orleans, and Angie's attention waned rapidly.

At last the waltz ended and Monsieur Delacroix escorted her to a long, linen-covered table bearing beautiful ice sculptures and crystal bowls of champagne punch. Creamy, fragrant magnolia blossoms were strewn over the lacy linen, nestled amidst large, shiny green leaves and spicing the air with a sweet, almost lemony fragrance. Thin slices of orange floated in the crystal bowl of champagne punch, and a waiter dipped out a liberal portion for Monsieur Delacroix.

As the Creole turned to give her the cup of punch, he smiled. "Perhaps you will find New Orleans too lovely to leave soon, Mademoiselle Lindsay. Dare I hope that you will allow me to call upon you while you are here?"

Despite his flowery phrases and courteous manner, she was growing annoyed with him. Oh, he was handsome enough, but must he be so *attentive*? Perhaps she was being silly, but she could not help the feeling that men who were *too* polite and gallant hid ulterior motives. Had it not been proven before, in Paris, when she was there with Tante Marie? Oh, yes, and Monsieur Beaulieu had shown his true nature when he had her alone, despite his perfect manners in public. It had left her wary of men whose gallantry exceeded the usual.

So though she smiled and gave the expected replies, she did not let Monsieur Delacroix cajole her onto the balcony overlooking Royal Street, nor did she allow him to remain too long at her side before she politely requested that she be escorted back to her mother.

Mignon smiled when Delacroix swept her a bow and kissed her hand, and after he departed, she bent a speculative gaze upon her daughter. "Monsieur Delacroix seems quite charming, Angelique. He is very wealthy, I am told, and has important connections in Paris. And it is plain he is taken with you."

"He is even more taken with himself." Angie spread the pleated fan wide and did not look at her mother, though she could feel her frowning gaze. "It is stuffy in here. I think I shall step onto the balcony for some fresh air."

"In a moment, Angelique. Monsieur Gravier wishes for us to be introduced to Governor Warmoth, and we must make an excellent impression upon him. Ah, there they come now. Do stand up straight, *ma petite*."

As the two men approached, Angie flashed her mother a glance of resignation and dipped into a graceful curtsy when the governor reached them.

"What a pretty gesture," Governor H. C. Warmoth remarked with a smile. When Angie returned his smile, he chuckled. "Lovely, lovely. Why, Gravier, I can certainly see why you feel you must lend aid to these ladies, for they are quite the most exquisite creatures to grace New Orleans in my memory."

He spoke with a booming rhetorical flair, and Angie saw several heads turn in their direction. A rather pompous man, she thought with distaste, and very full of self-importance. He seemed the sort who would not mind lining his own pocket at the expense of others.

As Gravier introduced them, Mignon offered her hand, and Warmoth bent graciously over it, looking up at her with a broad smile as he straightened. "It will be my pleasure to assist you, Madame Lindsay. My most special pleasure."

"Indeed, Governor, I look forward to it." Mignon did not remove her hand from his, but allowed him to hold it far longer than Angie deemed necessary. Finally, she withdrew it and turned to Monsieur Gravier. "Have you informed His Excellency of our specific needs, monsieur?"

"*Oui, oui,* of course, madame."

"It is something we must discuss more privately, madame," Warmoth interjected. "Of course, you understand."

"Of course." Mignon turned to Angie. "My daughter would rather remain here, I am certain. Monsieur Gravier, perhaps the young man who was with you when you met us at the docks would be so kind as to be her escort while the governor and I discuss when to meet?"

"Monsieur Henri Delacroix . . . yes, of course, madame. I know that Henri is most taken with Mademoiselle Lindsay. He will be quite happy to escort her until our business is concluded."

It rankled Angie that no one bothered to ask her if she would be happy to have Delacroix as her escort, but she did not comment. Indeed, she was rather relieved that Mignon would be away from the ball, even if for only a short time.

Delacroix came at once, his handsome face creased in a smile as he escorted Angie across the ballroom floor. She put her hand lightly upon his sleeve, only partially listening as he spewed more flattery.

"Monsieur Delacroix," she said at last, breaking into his comparison of her to the moon and stars, "would you be so kind as to fetch me some more punch? I feel a bit warm in here, with the press of so many people around us."

"But of course, mademoiselle. Would you like to go out onto the balcony, perhaps?"

"No, just a cool drink will suffice."

He left her by a tall potted palm, and she idly waved the ivory-and-lace fan to stir up a breeze. She had not lied. She *was* flushed, as much from irritation at the situation as from the champagne and the exertion.

She leaned against a slender column of faux marble by the potted palm to watch the dancers. The musicians had been playing a stately waltz but suddenly halted, and silence fell as the dance floor cleared. It was then Angie noticed a young girl garbed in a crimson skirt and blouse standing by herself at the edge of the polished floor. She reminded Angie of a Spanish Gypsy as she moved forward with innate grace, bare feet slapping confidently against the smooth wood.

Fascinated, Angie watched as the dark-haired beauty just stood in the center of the dance floor. A throbbing beat began. The girl's fingers snapped in time to the pulsating tattoo of a small drum, then as the guitars picked up the melody and increased the cadence, she began to dance, slowly at first, her body swaying with seductive agility. Slender bare arms lifted over her head, and suddenly her bound hair fell free, spilling down her back in a cascade of ebony curls to her waist. The hem of her skirt swirled higher and higher, revealing bare brown legs amidst a froth of black lace petticoat. The music had a pulsing beat that was somehow erotic, and those in the ballroom had grown quiet as they watched the girl.

Angie found herself thinking that she would like to dance like that, with carefree abandon and sensual grace, much like the Spanish Gypsies she had long admired.

Henri Delacroix had come up behind her, and his voice was soft in her ear. "Her name is Eugenié. She is a mulatto but passes for a quadroon. I have seen her dance before."

"She's beautiful. What nationality is Mulatto?"

He laughed quietly. "It is not a nationality but a race. One parent is black and the other white. A quadroon is the child of two mulattos, with very light skin."

Puzzled, Angie glanced around at him, but he was staring fixedly at the supple body of the dancer. "I do not understand. Is she not American?"

"*Oui*. But not as we Creoles are American, or as Anglos are American. It is different here, mademoiselle. There are class distinctions that are quite defined, much as in old France, though not based on aristocratic blood but race. It is the same all over the world. Always there are those who are different, their station lower or higher."

"I thought that it was different in America, that here all people are the same. Are mulattoes not free now?"

"Yes—and no. It is true that since the war people of color can rise above the station they were born to and that slavery has been abolished, but not everyone is the same. A man must make his own opportunity, yet for some . . ." His eloquent shrug was indicative of skepticism. "Pinckney Pinchback, who was elected to the state senate two years ago and is leader of the Fourth Ward Republican Club, was born a free Negro but has risen to power. Before the war he would not have been able to rise so high. But he is an exception."

"Then they are still oppressed."

Delacroix laughed softly and indicated the dancing girl. "She does not seem to mind, no?"

Frowning, Angie focused on Eugenié. Her face was shiny with perspiration beneath the heat of the lights, and her tawny skin glowed like polished amber. She was very beautiful, with delicate features and curling jet hair, and it was plain to see that every man there would love to be with her. It was written on the avid faces watching her. And it was obvious Eugenié knew it, for she smiled slowly, her eyes half closed and her mouth parting to reveal white even teeth like pearls between her red lips. She swayed, first toward one side, then the other, arms lifted in supplication as if offering herself to them, then she bent from the waist as gracefully as a ballet dancer, her long hair sweeping across the polished floor before she stretched upward again, her lissome form enticing and rejecting at the same time as she whirled away.

Some of the men tossed flowers to her as she danced; red roses and white littered the floor at her feet. Stepping nimbly over them, she bent in a supple glide to pluck one from the floor and hold it in her teeth. She lifted her skirts to her knees, then tossed her head so that her hair waved behind her in a silken tangle down her back.

With sultry allure, she undulated over the gleaming boards of the dance floor as the music kept up a relentless beat, to pause in front of a tall man leaning against one of the faux marble columns. He did not move, but only gazed at her with narrowed eyes and one corner of his mouth slightly tucked into the faintest of smiles. His arms were crossed over his chest, his posture indolent, yet there was a wary watchfulness about him that struck Angie at once.

While Eugenié swayed with the single red rose in her mouth and her eyes fastened on his face, Angie studied the object of the dancer's attention. His skin was almost the same tawny tint as the girl's, his black hair worn long enough to graze the top of his low collar. Dressed in fitted buff trousers, a black cutaway coat, white shirt and short tie, he appeared quite stylish.

Yet there was an air about him of a coiled spring, a tension like that of a cat poised to strike though there was no reason for it that she could see.

Angie realized suddenly that her heart was beating furiously and that the steady, pounding beat of the drum had escalated. Eugenié's hips rolled to the rhythm, and her feet slapped against the floor as she danced with suggestive proficiency. Angie thought then of that narrow avenue in Paris where she had gone with her cousins and seen the girls who danced with flying legs and bare skin. Many men visited the cabaret, most to choose from among the lovely girls for a mistress. Oh, yes, she knew about such things, was quite aware of how men took young women under their protection for a time, showered them with gifts, money, and even houses until they tired of them. In France, there was no shame attendant upon such arrangements.

"That man," she murmured to Henri Delacroix as she took the cup of punch he held out to her, "is he Eugenié's protector?"

Delacroix laughed, but there was no humor in the sound. "No, he is not. Not, at least, in the sense you must mean, mademoiselle. I knew him during the war, when he was here as part of the occupation forces. I have heard he is still with the U.S. Army instead of pretending to be a gentleman."

"Is he? He does not look as if he is in the army."

"Because he wears no uniform? That is only a charade. He shows no weapons, but he is no less a danger for all of that. Jake Braden is not a man I would care to meet alone on a dark street, or even in a public hall, and I cannot think what he must be doing here tonight, unless he wishes to make an assignation with Eugenié—*Bon Dieu!* Pardon, mademoiselle. I forgot myself in speaking of such tawdry subjects to you. I should not even mention a man like him to a lady, for after all, he is little more than a half-breed libertine with only a thin facade to hide his lack of scruples."

"Half-breed? What does this mean?"

With a shrug, Henri explained, "It is said that he is the product of a union between a Comanche squaw and a Mexican, though that is only a rumor. No one has ever dared ask him if it is true, and of course, he would not want it bandied about publicly if it was, so would not answer the question anyway, I am certain.''

"Of course," she replied, intrigued despite herself. "A Comanche is one of those Indians that abound in the West, is it not so? Are they not regarded as primitive, or—"

"Savages, yes. But I suppose his father's blood has diluted the heathen blood in him enough so that he is capable of *behaving* as a gentleman when it suits him.''

Now her attention was riveted on Jake Braden. How dangerous he must be—and Henri Delacroix thought so, too, if his comments were any indication. This, then, was a man like those her mother had always spoken about so bitterly.

Yet Mignon had never mentioned that they could *seem* so civilized, garbed in expensively tailored garments that lent an air of propriety. Perhaps it was only a facade after all, and her imagination was again running amok.

Yes, that must be it, for Jake Braden seemed quite civilized as Eugenié teased him with the rose. Her feet kept time to the music as the velvet petals raked across his chest in a lingering glide, and her skirts whirled around her long, slender legs in a frothy billow of petticoat. He remained motionless against the column when she finally danced away from him with a sultry smile and an inviting glance from exotic sloe eyes.

While Eugenié finished her dance, Angie sipped her punch, staring across the ballroom floor at Braden, oddly intrigued with the man reputed to be so dangerous. Without moving, he suddenly seemed to be staring straight at her, and Angie's heart skipped a beat. Was he looking at her? No, of course not. He must be looking at Monsieur Delacroix, for they were acquainted.

"*Sacré bleu!* Such insolence!"

"Monsieur?" She glanced around at Delacroix, startled by the vehemence in his tone. He smiled stiffly, but there was outrage glittering in his dark eyes as he stared across the dance floor.

"Pardon, mademoiselle, it is nothing. Old offenses should be forgotten. Tonight, I should be thinking only of you, nothing else.''

Bemused, she looked back, but Jake Braden was gone. She felt suddenly as if some of the excitement had gone from the evening. Perhaps she was searching too hard for the elusive danger she had often dreamed of encountering in a life far too mundane and boring. No doubt if she did encounter real danger or a man who was truly menacing, she would not be so enamored with the idea of it. But she had not, so it still retained an allure for her that was tantalizing.

"Mademoiselle, did you find her dance intriguing?"

Delacroix's query brought her back to the moment, and she wondered with a little dismay if it was so obvious that she had. But she shook her head disdainfully.

"No, I do not find that sort of dance at all intriguing. It is degrading for a woman to be so exhibited."

"But of course, you are right. You must be shocked by our little entertainment for the evening, but in New Orleans one grows used to such displays. Come, and I will escort you back to your maman, for I see her returning with Monsieur Gravier and Governor Warmoth."

As Angie accompanied him across the ballroom, she could not resist turning to see if Eugenié had been joined by her handsome lover, but there was no sign of either of them. No doubt he was with her and Angie would never see him again, which was certainly for the best.

But still, she could not help feeling a small twinge of disappointment that the first hint of excitement should be so quickly ended.

Oddly deflated, she pleaded a headache when she joined her mother, and Mignon frowned but said of course she could return to their room.

"Shall I go with you, Angelique?"

"No, I do not want to take you away from such charming gentlemen. I will be fine, Maman. Bette is there, and she can make a tisane for my head."

"Very well. It is all the excitement after such a long journey, I am sure."

The gentlemen expressed regret for her affliction and hopes for her swift recovery, and Angie escaped the muggy heat of the ballroom gratefully. It was much cooler in the wide corridors as she descended the stairs to reach her room on the first floor, and her steps slowed.

An open door stood wide to allow in cooling breezes from a veranda, and impulsively, she stepped through it to stand outside under a leafy arbor of tangled vines and fragrant blossoms. A stone fountain with a carved fish spewing water into wide basins stood in the center.

Moving to stand by the fountain, she drew in a deep breath of air that smelled of jasmine. Light from a lantern on the wall played over the splashing water in fitful patterns. It was quiet here, though she could still hear faint strains of music from the ballroom above, a familiar nocturne by Liszt. A small songbird perched among the leaves and flowers looped over the arbor, its song a haunting accompaniment to the nocturne. Evening shadows deepened in the small enclosure, gathering around her in soft shrouds. For the first time since she had arrived, she felt at peace and welcomed by her father's homeland.

When the musicians began to play a popular tune, she sang along softly, the words to the sweet ballad coming easily to her lips. "Believe me, if all those endearing young charms that I gaze on so fondly today, were to dim and all fade away . . ." She sang softly, and the songbird twittered in the arbor as if joining in, a duet of peaceful pleasure that no doubt both enjoyed equally. Then the song ended, and the bird flew away with a final chirrup, leaving her quite alone by the fountain. For several moments, she stood silently listening to the tinkling of water falling from tier to tier, reveling in the solitude.

Beneath the arbor against the far wall was a wrought iron bench, and she crossed the veranda to sit upon it, bunching her skirts in both hands to arrange them so the ribboned flounce in the back would not be crushed beyond repair.

As she seated herself, she glanced up, and her heart suddenly leaped into her throat as a tall shadow detached from the wall and moved into the hazy pool of light. She would have screamed, but her throat closed on the sound as she recognized the intruder.

Jake Braden. . . .

5

"Sir! You should have announced yourself. . . ."

"And miss such a charming performance?"

She held her breath as he stepped closer, shocked as much by her own reaction as his sudden appearance. Her heart thudded painfully against her ribs, and her hands shook so that she tucked them into the gauzy folds of her skirt.

Jake Braden loomed over her, distinctly more dangerous in the murky light than he was on the ballroom floor. His dark face was barely illuminated by the single lantern on the wall, revealing rakishly slanted eyebrows over leonine eyes. Those eyes gazed at her from beneath the shadows of his long black eyelashes, narrowed a little as he regarded her with a stare that was far too bold.

That brought her indignantly upright, and she rose to her feet with her chin lifted. "I think it would be best if you were to leave here at once, sir."

"No. I think not." A wicked smile flashed when she gasped angrily at his cool refusal. "Sorry to disappoint you, ma'am. It's obvious that you're used to having things your own way all the time."

"And it is obvious to me that you are a rude barbarian, sir!"

"If that's supposed to reduce me to the same quivering lump that you've made out of Henri Delacroix, then you're about to have your second disappointment of the evening."

His words came out in a soft, sardonic drawl, not at the courteous tones she had come to expect from the men she met, and Angie stared at him in the gloom. Mixed with the outrage she felt at his rudeness was an inner agitation that she did not quite understand. It confused her, leaving her breathless and taut, as if waiting for something to happen.

But what? And how *dare* he be so vulgar as to stare at her as he was doing—why, as he had stared at the Gypsy girl!

"You are quite wrong, sir. You have not disappointed me, but only reinforced my opinion of you as a mannerless boor. If you will not leave, I will. Please step aside so that I might pass."

She half expected him to refuse, but he moved aside with casual deliberation, as if mocking her. Angie swept past him toward the door, feeling his gaze on her as she did. At the door, she paused, glancing back, and saw him watching her still, his face half in shadows with the light above him.

When she turned back around, she came face-to-face with Eugenié, and jerked to a startled halt. The girl looked at her, then at him, and flushed with anger.

"Is this what you wished to tell me? *Espèce de salaud!* What are you doing with her when—"

"Be quiet, Eugenié. The lady was just leaving. We are not the only ones who find this veranda a quiet spot for retreat."

Though he spoke softly, there was an edge of menace in his voice that could not be missed, and Eugenié instantly calmed. She glanced back at Angie with a lifted brow and tossed her head as she commented in French that she should have known he would not be interested in such a pale, docile creature. "But I will dismiss her so that we can be alone, my love," she added, and turned with a counterfeit smile for Angie as she switched back to accented English.

"Pardon, mademoiselle, for I have mistaken you for someone else. It is so dark." Her accompanying shrug was meant to placate, but Angie was in no mood to be appeased.

"It is too bad that your nature is not as charming as your dancing," she replied in French, and was only slightly mollified by the dusky flush that rose in the girl's face. "I can only hope that we never meet again, in light or the dark. Good night."

She heard Jake Braden laugh softly when Eugenié gasped with outrage, then he said sharply, "No, do not even think about it, Eugenié, for I am not as certain as you that she is so docile. Let her go, or you will have all the hotel in an uproar."

Angie did not turn around to look, but she sensed that the girl meant to resort to violent retaliation. She did not hurry, but forced herself to leave at a sedate pace, as if completely unconcerned. Her heart beat rapidly and her mouth was dry as she returned to her room, and she was grateful that Bette was still up and awaiting her.

"Are you well?" the little maid asked anxiously when Angie

slammed the door shut behind her and took a deep breath to calm herself.

"No, I have a headache. Too much champagne, perhaps. Will you kindly prepare for me a tisane, Bette?"

As the maid went to brew the concoction that would ease her headache, Angie paced restlessly. Music drifted through open doors over the low balcony, and a slight breeze swelled the gauze curtains. She moved to the doors and pushed them wider to allow in more air, and leaned against the frame to stare into the fragrant night.

How enraging that the girl should be so insulting. And how dare she? She might be beautiful and talented, but she was still only a mistress. And the mistress of a man whose reputation was hardly unsullied, if Henri was to be believed.

Perhaps America was not so very different from France after all, for there seemed to be unexpected prejudices of all kinds. Pale and docile? Eugenié was definitely wrong on that assessment, for whatever Angie might be, she had never been regarded as docile in all her twenty-one years.

With a frown, she moved to the mirror to gaze at her reflection. She *was* pale, though. Except for the two bright, angry spots of color on her cheeks, she looked as white as a sheet. Was it so very unattractive? Eugenié thought so—did Jake Braden? Apparently he preferred women with dusky skin and dark eyes, or he would not have made an assignation with Eugenié, as Henri Delacroix had said he would. She did not care about that, of course, for the opinion and morals of a man like Jake Braden did not matter to her at all.

Still, it was so annoying that the girl had been rude enough to speak of her in that disparaging fashion, as if Angie was too obtuse to perceive that she had been insulted. Even if she had not understood most of the patois Eugenié used, she would certainly have understood the disdainful tone of voice and the haughty toss of the girl's head as she dismissed Angie with a shrug. Yes, her contempt was meant to be understood.

It was not as if Angie had actually gone there to meet him, after all; it had been an accident that had taken her to the secluded alcove where he waited on his mistress to join him. It was ridiculous—why would Eugenié think Angie would be even remotely interested in Jake Braden? He had intrigued her only because he was reputed to be dangerous, one of the *barbarians* Maman insisted abounded in America. There was no other reason to stare at him as she had.

Indeed, she found him to be rather a sordid man, though with a certain undeniable attraction. Not that *she* was attracted to him. No, not at all. But just because she found him personally repugnant did not mean that she was blind to his physical features, which were, after all, quite passable.

If one considered a feral smile and thick black hair worn a bit too long on the neck so that he looked like a pirate attractive, perhaps it was true that he was handsome. It was certainly true that he was very male, very assured and overbearing in his manner. *No* man had ever spoken to her in such a fashion, with a drawling amusement that left her feeling somehow deficient in some way—no, not ever.

Perhaps he was as Henri Delacroix hinted, a half-breed who was not quite tame and not quite wild. But why did she even continue to think of him? No doubt she would never see him again, for soon they would leave New Orleans. If Maman had her way, they would return to France, but Angie intended to prevail. She wanted to see New Mexico, wanted to see the home her father had carved out of a dangerous wilderness. If fate had denied her the chance to meet him, perhaps she could find a bit of John Lindsay in the things and places he had loved.

But it would never do to try to say that to Maman, for Mignon harbored an ancient resentment—and yes, even hatred—for John Lindsay. If not, surely she would not have stayed away from him all these years. Oh, it was so frustrating to feel as if she could not discuss openly with her mother the things that concerned her, but whenever she had tried, Mignon grew too agitated to continue. So, Angie had learned not to bring up the subject.

But now she was old enough to make her own decisions, and she knew what she wanted. It had nothing to do with money, and everything to do with discovering what life had to offer. There had to be more than just marriage to some dull, overweight man with a dour disposition and exacting expectations, and much more than the girl Eugenié had—selling her soul and her body for elusive protection from a man who might not linger once her beauty faded. Oh, yes, Angie knew well what she wanted, and she intended to do all in her power to get it. Not for her the life of her mother—a bitter woman with ancient resentments. But neither did she want a life such as women like Eugenié, who risked all and gained nothing. Even poor Simone was to be pitied, for though she had married well, she was miserable. Her so-handsome lover had not wanted marriage but only a casual alliance, and had left Simone devastated. On her wedding day, Simone had wept copious tears as she walked down the church aisle in an exquisite gown to be wed to the man waiting for her in front of the altar, and it had amazed Angie that no one seemed to notice they were tears of grief instead of joy.

But she had known.

Before the wedding she had listened to Simone's misery many a night, and had known then that she would not put herself in the same position and that perhaps it was best not to love a man at all, for always one got hurt by displaying such open, vulnerable emotion.

"Never fall in love, little cousin," Simone had said through her tears, "for it is a cruel, cruel disappointment."

Angie listened well. No one had to hit her with a stick to impress upon her the disaster inherent with loving unwisely, and she did not intend to put herself in that position ever. No, never.

Another burst of music drifted from the open windows of the ballroom, and Angie recognized the strains of a stately waltz. She turned away from the mirror just as the door opened and Bette returned with the tisane in a white china cup.

"Shall I undo your laces for you, mistress?" Bette asked as she carefully placed the tisane upon a lace-covered table in the center of the room. "You must feel confined with them still tied too tightly."

"Yes, please," Angie replied with a murmur. "I do hate corsets so, and hope that one day they will be unnecessary for ladies to wear."

"That will never happen, I think. But you are so small that you do not need tight stays. Why, your waist is tiny, quite perfect, and I never have to pull hard on your laces to tie them." Bette worked swiftly, her nimble fingers managing the buttons of Angie's gown, then the silken knots in the laces of her corset.

As the undergarment was removed, Angie took a deep breath of relief at the easing of constricted ribs. When the frame of flounced crinolette was removed as well, she flopped down in a chair wearing only her long drawers, stockings, and silk chemise. The latter clung to her skin, and she lifted it away with a frown.

"It is so warm here. Of course, all these layers of clothing do not help to keep me cool. One day I shall refuse to wear such things, Bette. It is ridiculous that a woman should be forced to endure such barbarous torture in the guise of fashion. Perhaps I shall be a grande dame and set the styles . . . yes, that is what I shall do when I am older, be the supreme arbiter of fashion."

"Ah, perhaps your future husband will not agree that you should do so," Bette replied with a laugh. "Not many men wish to part with their money so easily for a woman's stylish clothing."

"And perhaps I will not marry, but be a courtesan instead. They have much more freedom." She smiled at Bette's gasp of shock. "Oh, do not look so horrified, for I only speak idly. But still, if you think on it, I am right. Wives are confined and restricted by codes of behavior so strict that it is like being a child. Or a slave. Yes, that is it. A slave. But courtesans . . . ah, they choose from many men for their lovers, allowing them to lavish jewels and money on them in return for a few hours of pleasure. And when they tire of them—*phhht!* They dismiss them for other, more exciting lovers, who are perhaps even more generous. Is it not so? Of course it is."

Bette laughed softly. "If you say so, mademoiselle."

"I say it." Stretching, Angie lifted her arms over her head in a luxurious easing of taut muscles, finally relaxing a bit from the strain of the evening. While she spoke mostly from idle conjecture, there was a grain of truth in her words that struck her with possibilities. Not that she would seriously consider being a courtesan, of course, but there was no law that said she *must* marry. Not now. Now she had an income of her own, thanks to John Lindsay, and would not have to be dependent upon anyone, man or woman.

It opened up an entirely new world to her, and the thought of the future grew more exciting with each passing hour. Oh, she could not wait to leave New Orleans and travel to her new home! What would it be like? Wild and hot, with open skies everywhere she looked . . . she knew that much, for her father had described it in such glowing terms. And of course, it would not be as untamed as it had been when her mother had last been there, for after all, that had been twenty years before. Much could change in so long a time. No doubt the wild savages that had roamed freely were now subdued for the most part.

Swinging a stockinged foot, she thought suddenly of Jake Braden, and wondered if he was really part Indian, as Henri claimed. He had certainly *looked* savage enough in the dim light of a single lamp, though he had seemed civilized in the ballroom. Perhaps it was only a thin facade, as Henri had said so sarcastically.

Ah, *bon Dieu!* she should stop thinking of him. No, she should be thinking of her future instead of the tiger-eyed man with the wicked smile and husky drawl, for he no doubt had not given her another thought since their unexpected and uncomfortable meeting.

But Angie was wrong in that belief, for at that very moment Jake Braden was giving her a lot of thought, though he was not even aware she was the same girl.

After their brief meeting and his strained farewell from Eugenié, he was running late for the meeting with Governor Warmoth and Monsieur Gravier. Eugenié had reacted as he'd anticipated, with tears of rage and feigned grief at his rejection of her, but he had hoped she would be like the usual *un fille de joie,* and look upon their relationship as it had truly been—a physical relationship in return for generous payment. Apparently, he had misjudged her.

He took the back stairs, and met them in a small alcove near the ballroom. Gravier seemed irritated, and the lady with them was coolly composed though obviously upset, while the governor was oblivious to the undercurrents in the cramped space behind heavy velvet draperies. Cigar smoke hung heavily in layers that barely dissipated when Jake left the draperies open to clear the air.

Madame Lindsay greeted him with cool courtesy when they were introduced, and Governor Warmoth added slyly, "Captain Braden is most experienced in Indian fighting, Mrs. Lindsay, and is the perfect man to escort your daughter west."

Mignon Lindsay regarded the governor with barely concealed hostility. "As we have discussed, Governor, it is my wish to avoid such an arduous and dangerous journey."

"Yes, yes, so you have said." Warmoth heaved an expansive sigh. "But unfortunately, your late husband's will is most specific about the terms. Without a codicil, or perhaps a later will, my hands are tied. You realize that I have no jurisdiction in New Mexico. But I agree with you. While there is the offer of a small amount of money should she decide to go back to France instead of New Mexico, there is a lot of money involved in this legacy if she accepts the terms."

"And if she does not? Tell me, sir, if you will, what happens to the estate if Angelique should decide to return to France? Is it sold to provide her with the money you say she will get, or does it revert to the government?"

"Ah, such details are still uncertain at this time. Of course, without an owner, the land could not just sit there unused. There is no provision set up to hold it in trust, you understand. It was left to your daughter. You may remain here in New Orleans while she goes to New Mexico, if you prefer. I will see to it that you are most royally entertained in her absence."

Jake noted that Mignon was well aware of the reason behind Warmoth's refusal to aid her, for her eyes flashed with wrath and her mouth thinned into a taut line that did nothing to diminish her beauty.

"I am grateful for your generosity, Governor, but if my daughter must risk her life, I will not allow her to do it alone. I will accompany her, of course."

"There is no need for that, Mignon—I may call you that?—for the U.S. Army is at her disposal. Captain Braden is the most competent guide and scout now in New Orleans. He was stationed here after the recent civil conflict, but only recently returned from New Mexico. It is your home, is it not, Braden?"

Arms crossed over his chest, Jake nodded curtly. He did not like

Warmoth, had never liked him, and thought even less of the burly, overbearing man now than he had before.

"Yes, Governor, but don't expect me to say it's safe for Madame Lindsay and her daughter to travel through Indian country. It's not. Right now, there are renegade bands of Apache and Comanche roaming the land who are likely to attack anyone they consider a threat, and that includes women and a baggage train. I told you before I don't like the idea of it, and I'm telling you again—it's too damn dangerous right now."

"Balderdash, Captain. Have you forgotten the peace treaty signed by Comanche, Apache, and Cheyenne at Medicine Lodge?"

"That was over two years ago," Jake pointed out, "and that treaty was broken by General Custer's massacre of a Cheyenne chief and village on the Washita River a year after it was signed. Believe me, the Apache haven't forgotten how well the white man keeps his word."

"Perhaps not, Captain Braden, but even as we speak, sixteen war chiefs are in Washington for a conference. Once they are convinced of our invincibility, all hostilities will cease, I assure you."

"If you believe that, you're a bigger fool than I already thought, Governor."

Warmoth bridled with barely restrained fury. "Your opinion is uninformed and unneeded. The savages will calm down once the army stops coddling them. And you might remember that you take your orders from Colonel Patterson, who happens to be a very good friend of mine."

"I take orders from the colonel, not you. That's the only reason I'm here, and Patterson said nothing about lying to this lady about the risks. It's not a good time for any white man or woman to be traveling through Indian country."

"Now see here, Braden," the governor began, his fleshy face reddening with anger and his brows lowering over his eyes, "you have your orders, and—"

"And they don't include arguing with you, Governor. Good night, ma'am."

Jake strode from the alcove without looking back, but he could hear Warmoth sputtering with rage and Gravier attempting to soothe him. A faint smile curled his mouth.

"Captain! A moment, *s'il vous plait.* . . ."

Halting, he turned to wait for John Lindsay's widow, and as she approached, he thought that she did not look as if she could have changed much in twenty years. She still looked young and vibrant, the only indication of her age the very faint lines at the corners of her gray-blue eyes.

"Madame." He waited politely for her to begin the discussion, and moved aside with her when she indicated she wished to speak with him more privately.

"Captain Braden, I very much appreciate your frankness just now," she said softly when they stood out of sight of Warmoth and Gravier. "It is important to me that the governor understand the risks inherent in this journey, and that he agrees to aid me in my desire to change my late husband's will. In Angelique's best interest, of course."

"Before you continue, maybe I should tell you that I don't intend to help you change John Lindsay's will. He was a friend of mine, and I know he wanted to see his daughter before he died. But neither do I want to be responsible for getting her killed on the way out there, and the way things are right now, it would be best if she takes the lesser money and goes back to France. I'm not as optimistic as Warmoth, and will tell you quite plainly that it's unlikely the Indians will calm down anytime soon."

"My sentiments exactly, Captain. Of course, the will must be revised to reflect this change in the situation, which is why—"

"Excuse me, ma'am, but I don't agree. If this is all about money, then you're talking to the wrong man. I don't give a damn who gets the land or the money. But John Lindsay did. At least your daughter wants to fulfill the terms of her father's will, which is more than I can say for you."

Mignon Levasieur Lindsay studied him for a moment without speaking, then unexpectedly smiled. "You are blunt, Captain. *C'est bon.* I can be blunt as well. It is always better when the truth is known, *n'est pas?*"

"Sometimes. And sometimes it's a lot more comfortable to keep it to yourself, ma'am."

She laughed softly. "I see you are a man who puts his cards upon the table. Very well. So will I. I have no intention of going to New Mexico if I can possibly help it, nor do I intend to do anything as ridiculous as stay there an entire year. Angelique might have some romantic notion of living there, but only because she has never experienced the harshness and cruelty of the land. Forgive me if I offend your homeland, but I was reared gently, and so was she."

"Since we're being so blunt, maybe I should remind you that you aren't involved in this. It's your daughter's decision to make. She's old enough to decide what she wants to do, and needs to be told the risks."

Mignon sucked in a sharp breath, and her eyes narrowed a bit as she studied him for a moment. Then she shrugged. "That is so. Perhaps if you say to her what you just said to the governor about the inadvisability of traveling to New Mexico, she will listen. Would you do that, or would it compromise your great friendship with my late husband?''

Impatient now, Jake shrugged. ''I'll tell her that it's dangerous, but that's all I'll do. If she has any sense at all, she's probably figured that much out for herself anyway. She understands English, I presume.''

''Of course. Angelique is not uneducated, Captain, though far too gently reared to be subjected to the rigors of the journey John Lindsay has tried to foist upon her. It is a crime, this stupid will he wrote, and I warn you that I fully intend to have it overturned.''

''Lindsay was no fool, madame. I wish you luck in that endeavor. I have five minutes to spare you, if you want me to advise your daughter to forget going to New Mexico. Otherwise—''

''Now? But of course—Angelique has retired to our rooms for the evening, but is most likely still awake. We are on the first floor overlooking Royal Street, so you—''

''Lead the way.''

With a sidelong glance at him, Mignon gave another eloquent shrug of her shoulders and moved gracefully to the staircase leading below. Thick carpet muffled their steps as they approached the door to her rooms, and she gave a sharp rap on the painted wood.

''Angelique? Bette?''

There was soft laughter, then a bolt being slid back as a young girl with dark hair and eyes swung open the door. Mignon swept past her into the room, leaving Jake to follow. The girl gasped softly when she saw him, and threw a hand up to refuse him entry.

''*Non, non*, monsieur, you must not,'' she began, and when Jake looked past her, he saw the reason for her distress.

A barely clad young woman was lurching upright from a sprawled position in a chair, reaching for something to cover herself as she exclaimed, ''Maman! I am not dressed!''

He immediately recognized the girl he had met earlier on the veranda, though she looked older without the yards of frilly lace and ribboned bows. Maybe it was because she wore so little now that he could see the evidence of her maturity in the ripe, upthrust curves of her breasts and in the shadowy forms of her legs beneath the filmy linen drawers.

Mignon scooped up a dressing gown and flung it toward her, saying tightly in French that she should know better than to lie about the receiving room so scantily clad. Then she turned to Jake with a brightly flushed face.

''Be so good as to turn around, Captain Braden, while Angelique suitably covers herself.''

With a shrug, he did, though he had already seen an admirable exhibition of Angela Lindsay.

"Miss Lindsay and I have already met," he drawled, and heard the girl's choked comment that it was not a memorable occasion. He grinned. "I thought it very memorable, though I admit, this is even more so."

The maidservant, Bette, dimpled at him and put a hand over her mouth to hide her laughter as he winked at her.

"Captain!" Mignon sounded outraged. "I am certain that as a gentleman, you will of course repeat none of this to anyone. It would only sully her reputation needlessly, if a man such as you cares about that kind of thing. You may turn around now."

He swung back around, his amusement fading under the lash of Mignon's tongue. Angela was wrapped in an ivory silk dressing gown that reached to her ankles, and her pale complexion was prettily colored as she met his gaze defiantly. He cocked a brow at her.

"Miss Lindsay, your mother wanted me to repeat to you what I said to the governor earlier, so I will: This is not a good time to go to New Mexico, no matter what you might have heard. It's dangerous. Your mother is right. You seem very unsuited to the rigors of life in New Mexico and wouldn't last a week out there. Take the money you've been offered and go back to France where it's safe and civilized instead of wasting your time and mine."

Violet eyes regarded him coolly. "Really? Captain—?"

"Braden," he supplied, and watched her with narrowed eyes as he recognized the signs of rebellion in her mutinous expression.

"Captain Braden, while I appreciate the fact that my mother has obviously gone to a great deal of trouble to find someone who will agree with her, I should inform you that I fully intend to travel to New Mexico at the earliest opportunity to claim the lands that my father left me. I have no idea how or why my mother decided to involve you in our private business, but I assure you that your opinion is of little or no interest to me. Good evening."

Lifting a brow, his mouth curled in a cynical smile. He had known she would be a contrary little fire-eater. He'd guessed that much on the veranda, when she had met Eugenié's tirade so coolly. He shrugged.

"I'm sorry to hear that, ma'am. Maybe your mother decided to involve me when she was informed that I've been assigned to escort you to New Mexico. Since you insist upon going, be ready one week from today. You will be allowed one trunk each. No more. I have no intention of being bogged down with a lot of useless baggage on a wagon train through hostile country. Good evening, ladies."

As he closed the door behind him with a decisive snap, he heard Angela Lindsay make a very unladylike comment, and laughed softly to himself. If she intended to go, fine, but he would do his best to see that she changed her mind before they got to Texas.

6

Music from the St. Louis Hotel wafted across the street on a light breeze that finally cooled the air a bit. The night was dark above the street lamps, with clouds that hid the moon and masked the light. Jake stood in the shadow of a balcony suspended over the banquette that ran parallel with the street, cursing softly to himself as he lit a thin cigar. Damn it. Ringgold was late as usual. Too bad Logan was held up somewhere and he had to deal with this new man he wasn't too sure about. Ringgold had been hired because he was fast with a gun and available, but he was proving to be undependable.

Now he was running late, and too much time had already been wasted arguing with contrary women. He squinted against the curl of smoke in his eyes. Why had he been so certain they would be smart enough to see reason? He should have known better. Obviously, he'd underestimated Lindsay's daughter, and he had the wry thought that John would have been proud of her. She was as stubborn as he'd always been.

Unfortunately, her stubborn determination might well get her killed, and he sure as hell didn't want *that* on his mind. A carriage passed, wheels rumbling loudly over the cobblestones of the street, and soft laughter drifted through an open window of the brougham's interior.

Angela Lindsay was nothing like what he had expected her to be. He wasn't quite sure what he had expected, but he did know it wasn't a dainty beauty with pale skin, copper hair, and violet eyes that slanted seductively at the corners. Nor had he expected the cat-eyed girl he'd seen with Delacroix in the ballroom—and more closely on the veranda—to be the daughter of his old friend.

Christ. It complicated things. How had she hooked up with such a villainous crew as Delacroix, Gravier, and H. C. Warmoth? He knew

Lindsay would never have done business with men like them, and suspected that it was Mignon who had hired them. She was as ruthless and determined as John had said she would be, and quite obviously had her nose out of joint because Warmoth was proving more stubborn than her charm and beauty could vanquish. If it wasn't frustrating, he'd find it amusing.

But the mother's ambition was driving her daughter in the opposite direction, and neither of them was thinking clearly. What a stupid irritation. And he had Jim Patterson to thank for sending him here to deal with it.

"It's perfect timing, Jake. It's the best excuse for you being in New Orleans that I've been able to come up with, and you know it. Don't look so angry. You know you want to get these bastards who've been selling rifles to the Apaches as much as I do."

"Yes, but I'd rather do it my way."

"Your way is liable to get you executed for murder," the colonel had said dryly. "You may be a scout, but you're still officially on the army payroll, and there are certain rules we have to follow to keep our asses alive and out of trouble."

"There are rules out there, too, and those include not being fool enough to tip your hand to the enemy. Going to New Orleans to bring back two women won't do anything but make us targets, and I won't be held responsible for what may happen if I can't convince them not to come."

"Fair enough. Just meet the informant in New Orleans. He said he'd talk to you, but only you. I don't trust that, but we don't have many choices. Jake—be careful. These men are playing rough."

So here he was, and tonight he was supposed to meet the secret informant who promised to tell him who was behind the illegal selling of weapons to renegade Apaches.

"Jake . . . *mon cher, s'il vous plaît. . . .*"

Swearing softly, Jake turned as Eugenié flew across the street and onto the banquette and into his arms, catching him off guard. "What the hell are you doing here?" he grumbled.

"Oh, Jake, I had to see you again. Do not be angry with me, yes? I know that you said you are leaving, but you are not gone yet, and I cannot bear to part with you so soon—oh, do not look so angry at me, *cher*, for I cannot help the way I feel."

Her impassioned outburst was muffled by his shirtfront, and he put her back a step, gently but firmly. "Eugenié we went through this already. I told you I'll be too busy the rest of my time here to give you the proper attention you deserve. It's not as if you have no other admirer to pass the time and buy you expensive gifts."

Lifting wet eyes, she shook her head, and her voice broke on a sob. "But it is you I love, *mon cher* . . . no one else."

When she leaned into him again, he put his arm around her, and it seemed only natural to kiss her when she lifted her face to his with an open, eager mouth. Passionate little creature. He would really miss her sweet body and unbridled ardor, but this was inevitable.

Breaking off their kiss, he tilted her face upward with a finger under her chin. "I have never lied to you and pretended that I would stay, Eugenié. You knew from the first that it was only temporary."

"*Oui,* it is true, that, but I thought—hoped—that you may change your mind and stay in New Orleans. Or you could take me with you, Jake—I would like New Mexico, I know I would. And there, perhaps I could pretend I was your wife, and no one would know, for do I not look much like one of the aristocratic Creoles?"

"Christ, that has nothing to do with it." He felt the racing thud of her heart against his chest, and the anguish in her eyes was all too real. "Eugenié, you are one of the most beautiful women I have ever seen, but you want a man who stays home. I'm not the one. I'm not the kind of man who likes sitting beside a safe fire at night."

She wrapped her arms around his neck and leaned into him with another passionate kiss, and after his initial resistance, he kissed her back, a little angrily but with rising desire. He was tempted to lift her skirts and take her there in the shadows against the brick wall, but even if he had time it would only make matters worse and he knew it. Besides, she would consider it a rekindling of an affair he had ended, and there was no point in it.

This time when he put her back and away from him, he kept a hand on her shoulder and his voice was cold. "Enough, Eugenié. Go home."

Though she was trembling she collected her composure at last and met his gaze with dark, wet eyes and a firm chin. "I see that it is no use. You will go. Just remember that I will always be waiting for you on Rampart Street when you return to New Orleans. *Au revoir. . . .*"

He watched as she crossed the street to the St. Louis Hotel under the light from the street lamps. Her black hair was briefly lit, then she passed into the shadows of a balcony and was gone from sight. When he started to turn away, a flicker of movement caught his eye, and his gaze shifted to the source.

A pale shimmer was backlit by light from one of the rooms, and his eyes narrowed with amusement as he recognized Angela Lindsay standing on the low balcony outside her room. She would have to be blind not to have seen his meeting with Eugenié. No doubt it would only reinforce her already low opinion of him, and that could be to his advantage if she decided he would make an unsuitable escort to New Mexico.

Laughing softly, Jake stepped back into the shadows and moved down the street. He had more important things to do than think about Angela Lindsay right now. If he delayed much longer, the informant might get nervous and leave before he got there. He'd have to meet up with Ringgold later. He'd already waited too long for the gunman, who always seemed to lose track of time and show up late.

It was a dozen blocks from the riverfront to the Swamp, where Jake was to meet this mysterious informant. When he reached the notorious Swamp, an area of New Orleans that only the most desperate and dangerous cutthroats frequented, Jake paused in the shadows along Girod Street. It was noisy, with raucous laughter and a few angry shouts splicing the air, mixed with a medley of discordant tunes from a variety of off-key musical instruments.

He stood in the shadow of a low-gabled building built of cypress and leaning precariously to the east. Inside, the bar consisted of planks laid across two kegs, with a few rough stools for the patrons. Faro and Hazard were the games of chance usually played in this part of town, with the odds always on the side of the house. Those few who managed to win a few coins were relieved of them once they left the establishment, often at the cost of their lives.

Save for Gallatin Street, the Swamp had gained the reputation of being the favorite haunt of the villainous and rough flatboat men who came down the river on their flat-bottomed boats. It was without a doubt the most vicious area of New Orleans, abounding with ruffians who practiced the art of mayhem to a fine degree. The only law here on Girod Street was that of the fist, knife, or gun. For the past twenty years, no officer of the law had dared to set foot in these half dozen blocks of saloons, dance halls, gambling dens, and brothels.

It was the perfect place to meet an informant, if one lived to pass on the information.

Jake moved quietly along the darkened street, ignoring some of the bolder whores who loitered about and called out to him to join them in one of the rickety bordellos.

"*Un beau gosse* . . . For only a picayune, you can have a bed, whisky, and a hot woman, monsieur." A woman bolder than the rest swayed toward him. Her dyed red hair was glaring even in the cast-off light from a lantern, her ample breasts displayed in a low-cut gown that had seen better days.

"Mille graĉes, mais non." He wasn't tempted. For six cents' worth of rotgut, a flea-ridden bed, and a diseased woman, the man who would accept that invitation risked his life in one of those murder holes. He'd be safer in a nest of rattlesnakes.

Jake turned a corner at Cypress and South Liberty Street, and moved toward the misty gloom of the Protestant cemetery. It was quieter here, though the noise from the Swamp was still audible. A metal gate swung slightly in a noisome wind that swept up from the river and carried with it the foul odors of rotting fish and decaying humanity, and he stopped in front of the entrance. The gate moved on rusty hinges as it swayed forward with an eerie screech like the howl of a banshee.

Premonition trickled down his spine, and he drew his loaded .45 from beneath his expensive coat. There was no moon, only scudding clouds that filtered the silvery glow and kept it from being pitch-black; the air smelled of imminent rain. He kept to the shadows of the stone buttresses that supported the gate, and slipped past the swinging metal and into the cemetery. A cloying smell drifted toward him as he moved down the gravel path with only a slight scrunching of the rocks beneath his feet. He knew that smell, and it wasn't one that should be in the cemetery tonight.

In the dark, he felt his way to a high, gleaming mausoleum with winged cherubs perched on each side of two shallow steps that led up to the interior of the tomb. A studded iron door was open, and the cloying smell was strong here.

Swearing softly under his breath, Jake lit a match and in the brief flare saw all he needed to see. As the light extinguished in the wind and gloom, he knew that whoever the informant was, he wouldn't be giving out any information. Not in this life.

A flutter of something white caught his eye, and he bent and picked it up. It was distinctive, a hawk feather with familiar markings. He knelt there in the dark, and as his eyes adjusted to the absence of light, he saw another feather, and a knife with more distinctive markings. It wasn't until he lifted it that he realized the marks and paint were imitation Apache. Mescalero, from the looks of it. Christ. He glanced at the body again, and even in the dark saw the rampant butchery.

"Braden . . . are you in there?"

Turning, still kneeling, he saw the tall shadow step up onto the tomb steps with gun drawn. "Yeah, Ringgold. You're late."

"I was delayed—Jesus! Is that who we're supposed to get information from? It should be difficult for him to tell us much without his tongue, don't you think?"

"Look." Jake stood up and held out the bloody knife, and Ringgold took it with a frown.

"Is this supposed to be Apache?"

"Supposed to be. Notice anything different about it?"

"Yes, very different. It is not authentic. Why is it here, or do I assume that this man's gruesome death is to be blamed on an indigenous people a thousand miles distant from here?"

"That's my thought. I just don't know why anyone would bother. Killing him is one thing. Doing this to him can only mean someone wants to put the blame for his death on the Apache to stir up trouble. You know how high sentiment is running these days, with all that's happened in Texas and New Mexico."

"True." Ringgold's shoulders lifted in a shrug. A shaft of moonlight broke through the clouds and silvered the ground outside, throwing Ringgold into silhouette and illuminating the ugly scene inside the tomb. Shadows wavered over the cemetery, and Ringgold shifted uneasily. " *'Facilis descensus Averno . . .'* I have a bad feeling about this, Jake. Perhaps we should leave before we end up involved in it."

"Too late." Jake inclined his head toward the tomb's opening and rose to his feet as the shadows outside formed into the uniformed shapes of policemen. "We've been set up, Johnny."

Angie heard about the arrest of Captain Braden early the next morning, when her mother awoke her with the news.

"It is impossible now, of course," Mignon said as she sipped her morning coffee with her usual cool composure, "for us to go to New Mexico. Monsieur Gravier has said that this Captain Braden is the only man really qualified to take us there, but he will no doubt be executed for this terrible murder."

Wide awake now despite the fact that she had spent a very restless night, Angie shivered, and pulled her dressing gown more snugly around her. No, it could not be true. Why, she had seen him last night with Eugenié—would he have left his mistress to go murder a man in a *cemetery*, of all places? Oh, it must be true or he would not be arrested, but it seemed so unbelievable.

"Are they certain it was Captain Braden who did this terrible thing, Maman?"

"Monsieur Gravier says that he and an accomplice were caught at the scene, so I imagine they have the proof." Mignon's delicate brows dipped into a faint frown. "It was a particularly violent murder, and as it is rumored that the captain is part Indian and the dead man was killed in a most brutal way favored by Indians . . ."

She did not finish the sentence, and Angie looked away. It should not matter to her. Indeed, she should be grateful he had shown his true nature before they left New Orleans, but she could not help feeling an overwhelming sense of dismay and disappointment that was only exacerbated by Mignon's calm reasoning.

"See, *ma petite*, I was not exaggerating when I told you that there are dangerous men everywhere in this country and that one cannot trust them not to do horrible things. It is even worse in New Mexico Territory, for there is no law out there. It is too wild, too vast for there to be proper laws enforced—but you have discovered for yourself a small bit of what I mean."

"Yes. I suppose I have." Agitated, Angie rose from the small table that was cluttered with pots of the dark, thick coffee favored here, and flaky pastries nestled in baskets by china plates piled high with fresh, succulent fruit. She moved to the French doors that led to the balcony and pushed aside the gauzy curtain to gaze outside.

It was across this street that she had seen Jake Braden standing on the banquettes with Eugenié, and known what they were doing. She had seen them making love, seen the captain kiss the girl with evident hunger, and had watched even though she knew she should not, that it was a private moment she should not witness. But she had not turned away, and thought briefly that if it was meant to be so private, he should not be kissing her on a public street as he was—

"Angelique? Are you unwell? Or is it just this sordid news that has so distressed you?"

"Yes." She turned away from the doors. "That is it. I find such events very . . . distasteful. We shall discuss other things, I hope, and put this behind us for now."

"And later? What will you decide about that dangerous journey you were advised not to take?"

Angie bit back a harsh retort and resorted to a shrug of her shoulders instead. She would *not* be drawn into that topic right now, not when she was so shaken from this news and the doubts that had kept her awake long into the night. Why, she could barely concentrate on anything at the moment and did not know what she would do. Who could tell? So many things were happening so quickly, and she was at such a loss as to what would be best . . . yet she hated the thought of just giving up, of letting go of her dream.

Oh, *damn* that Captain Jake Braden for being so stupid as to murder someone and get caught! Perhaps it was selfish, but at the moment, she was too frustrated and upset to think of the poor murdered soul.

Instead, she could think only of her shattered hopes and dreams of being independent, of living in a land of warmth and sunshine where she would not have to always yield her wishes to those of another. Independence was even more elusive now than it had been when she was still a schoolgirl in France, expected to be dutiful and obedient to the wishes of everyone else.

If she did not pursue the dream of independence now, she was ever doomed to remain under the thumb of her mother or future husband— an intolerable prospect.

No, she could not bear that. She would find someone else to guide her to New Mexico. She had to.

7

It had been four days, and the chief of police, A. S. Badger, was losing patience. Weighed down with wrist and leg shackles, Jake was summoned from his small six-foot-by-six-foot cell and led up a flight of stone stairs. Damp gray walls changed to painted wood as he was taken into the light, and he squinted against the unaccustomed glare.

Badger drummed his fingers against the smooth polished surface of his desk and motioned for the guards to leave. He scowled at Jake from beneath bushy brows. "You are too stubborn. A man is dead, and you were found with the knife that killed him. Do you still say you do not know him?"

"It was a little hard to recognize him with his face gone." Jake shifted, and the clank of chains was muted against his legs. "By law you cannot charge me with a crime. I'm under military jurisdiction."

Badger glared at him. "So your superiors have informed me, but I am not yet ready to release you to them. Our experience with the army in New Orleans has not been the best, you understand."

When he did not respond, but stood silently, Badger in exasperation sent him back to his cell "to think about the unpleasant prospects" if he did not cooperate. Jake wondered about Ringgold. He had not seen him since they'd been arrested, and wondered if he'd been charged as well. It wasn't likely that Badger would tell him anything. If they were going to charge them with murder, he wished they'd go ahead and do it. He hated the waiting, the long hours spent in a windowless cell that seemed to close in around him with each passing minute.

Not even the books that Eugenié sent did much to relieve the interminable boredom that dogged him. She came to see him and was refused permission to visit, but every day she sent fruit or more books. He heard from no one else, but hadn't really expected to. Who else would care?

At least the long hours of incarceration had given him some time to think, though he wasn't too sure that was good. He thought of too many things in the past, remembered too many things he couldn't change. Strange, how memories that had not returned in years haunted him now in the dark hours of night. Maybe he should think more about what he'd once been told by a wise man he had met in Ceylon. Then he'd been too young to dwell on it, but now he thought of it again.

Chabhi—meaning "key" in Hindi—had offered him a new way of thinking: Unless a man could know himself, all else that he might learn in life would be of no use. "It is the inner man that is most important, that provides the strength necessary for life. And in life, it is the journey that is the most important, not the destination."

Well, he certainly had time now to acquaint himself with the inner man Chabhi had talked about, but he still found it difficult to focus. Other memories, less idealistic ones that conflicted with the inspirational principles he had heard from Chabhi, kept intruding. If he let himself dwell on them too long, the old rage would build, so he closed his eyes and thought instead of the small bit of land that was his in New Mexico. It was peaceful there, tucked beneath the shelter of the San Andres Mountains. It was all that was left to him now, except the memories.

He was still thinking of his land when footsteps paused outside his cell and the grating sound of a key in the lock brought him to a sitting position on the narrow jail cot.

"Braden, you've got a visitor. Don't get too excited. It ain't that pretty little gal that comes around every day to see you."

A little surprised that they didn't shackle him again, Jake went with the guards to Badger's office. The chief of police was scowling, and jerked his head toward the window, where a man stood with his hands clasped behind his back.

Jake couldn't hide his surprise as he recognized the slouchy hat and fringed coat. "Cody?"

Swinging around, the blond frontiersman swept off his battered hat and grinned. "The same. Heard there was a bit of trouble with some Apaches here in New Orleans, and couldn't resist checking it out. Damn fool police. That knife looks like a child painted the markings on it."

"Now see here, Mr. Cody," Badger protested. "We have it on expert authority that the murder weapon is quite genuine!"

"A genuine fake, sir. Do you question my judgment?"

"Well, as a matter of fact—"

"I thought not, since I've been employed as chief of scouts for the army far longer than you've been a chief of police in this river town.'' Cody smiled, but there was a bit of granite in the showing of his teeth that silenced Badger for the moment.

Cody turned his attention back to Jake. ''As I was sayin', I heard about it from a friend of mine who knew I was here and thought I could help out.''

''What are you doing in New Orleans? I thought you were in New York since Buntline made you famous in the *Weekly*.''

Cody reddened a little but grinned widely. ''Ain't that the damnedest thing you ever heard? Hell, I been busier than a one-legged man in a kick fight since he started writing those tall tales about me and getting them published. That's why I'm here—the editor of the *Picayune* invited me to speak at a meeting of journalists. Not bad for an old boy whose main schoolin' was learned while ridin' for the Pony Express, I'd say.''

''The way I hear it, Buffalo Bill Cody is getting more famous than President Grant these days.''

''Damn, Braden, let's talk about you instead of me. The chief there is liable to think I'm pulling rank on him.''

Badger snorted rudely. ''No, you've already done that, Mr. Cody. Or more precisely, Colonel Patterson has managed it. When the police followed Mr. Ringgold to the scene of the crime, Captain Braden was found kneeling over the body with the knife in his hand. To me, it's implicit evidence. But to the army—Bah. I wash my hands of it!''

Jake eyed the irate official. That explained why Ringgold hadn't been charged but not why he'd been followed. He didn't comment while Cody explained that it was a military matter, and since Braden was officially listed on the army's payroll, though in a mainly civilian capacity, the army would handle this in its own way.

''Colonel Patterson's by way of being an old friend of mine. We've done some fighting in our time, and I can tell you that those markings on that knife are nothing like what would be on a killing knife. Hell, Badger, that's a damn imitation ceremonial knife. No self-respectin' Apache would take a scalp with that.''

Badger rose to his feet and said tightly, ''As Braden has already been released by my office, there is no need for further discussion, Mr. Cody. You are both free to go, though while you may go on to your luncheon with the fine editors of the *Picayune,* Captain Braden is invited to leave our fair city within forty-eight hours. I suggest he secure passage aboard the next packet or pack mule out of here.''

''I don't think he'll mind that too much.''

When Jake walked out into the May sunshine with Cody, he blinked against the unfamiliar light. "Damn dark in that jail cell. I'm glad to be out. Thanks for coming to my rescue, Cody."

Cody grinned. "I said much the same thing to you once, if you remember. Only that time, it was Apaches who had me pinned down, not some idiot civilian who wouldn't know a war knife from a toothpick. Look, Jake, I don't know what's going on here, and Patterson didn't mention it in his telegram, but if you stay in New Orleans, there'll be trouble."

"I was going back anyway." Jake dusted his hat against his leg and squinted at the Customhouse Street signpost. "I guess I've got some orders waiting for me at my hotel."

"You can be sure of it. Patterson's thorough, even if he is a stickler for the rules. If you care to join me later, I'm going down to the river after this damn meeting. There's a steamboat race—the *Robert E. Lee* against the *Natchez*. Coming down from Memphis under full steam. My money's on the *Natchez*."

"Think I'll save my money for my own steamboat race out of New Orleans. I may need it."

Cody grinned and shook his head. "Never can tell, but my money would be on you."

After they parted company, Jake returned to the St. Charles Hotel, where he was staying. It was a grand hotel, still beautiful even after Union occupation during the Civil War. General Benjamin Butler had stayed here as commanding officer of the Union army, using the elegant quarters on St. Charles and Common Street for his command post until after the war ended and Reconstruction began. Any evidence of that occupation had been mended by careful attention, and the hotel with its Corinthian portico and immense dome could once again be compared to St. Peter's in Rome and the czar's palace in St. Petersburg, as it had been before the war.

As he stepped into the lobby, an elegantly garbed lady stood and came toward him, and Jake's eyes narrowed as he recognized Mignon Lindsay even with her face concealed by a veiled brim on her fashionable bonnet.

"Captain, a word with you, *s'il vous plait.*"

"I don't have much time right now, Mrs. Lindsay, so maybe later—"

"Captain. Please." She sounded faintly desperate, and he relented, moving aside with her to a secluded area of the lobby filled with only potted plants and an empty settee.

He waited, and in a moment she said softly, "I come to you to plead for your cooperation in the matter of this journey to New Mexico. My daughter is determined to go, it seems, and will not be dissuaded from her decision.''

''Ma'am, I've already talked to Miss Lindsay about it. Nothing else I say is going to be any different than the last time.''

''Oh, no, Captain, you misunderstand.'' The black veil over her face fluttered when she laughed softly. ''This time I come to ask you to agree to take us. If I engage you as our guide in light of the recent . . . events . . . that have occurred and been reported in the daily news, Angelique will perhaps decide that she does not want to go after all. As she has not found any other guides who are even remotely suitable, she may realize that this is not a propitious time and be sensible enough to listen to reason at last.''

''I see.''

''I knew you would.''

He'd taken off his hat upon entering the lobby, and now he slapped it against his leg in irritation. ''I don't feel much like playing games right now, ma'am. I've had a busy few days, and I'll be leaving New Orleans as soon as I can. You'll have to find someone else to keep tally.''

''I hardly think it would cause you problems to do as I request, Captain. As you claim you are an old friend of my late husband's, I had thought you would do what you can to keep his daughter safe. It seems I have misjudged you.''

''Yes, ma'am, you sure have if you think I'll be bludgeoned with guilt into doing what you want.''

''Then there is nothing more to say.''

He nodded shortly. ''That's right.''

As she left, her steps angry as she stalked through the lobby to be met outside by a liveried coachman and a handsome chaise, Jake couldn't help but think that she was just as John Lindsay had once said—ruthless as any Apache squaw in getting what she wanted.

''Christ, Jake,'' he'd said wryly, ''I've made a mess of things. You probably don't remember my wife. Never did get a divorce—Mignon. Beautiful creature. Elegant. Hated it out here. Thought it'd be civilized like New Orleans, where I met her.'' His eyes clouded over, and he'd held his cigar for a long moment without smoking it, staring at the mountains as if seeing the past. Then he'd continued softly. ''I was too damn bullheaded to give an inch back then. Told her to go on back to France if she hated it here so bad. So she did. Took our child with her. I sent money all these years, but never have seen them since. God, it was so long ago . . . guess I let time pass without making enough effort. A few letters here and there, but hell, I'm not much of a hand at that.

But now I've got a chance to make it up to her. I'm leaving her the ranch, Jake.''

"To your wife? She didn't like it then, and New Mexico hasn't changed much in the past nineteen years.''

"No, I'm leaving it to Angie. She's got my blood in her. Hell, she's got her mama's blood, too, and Mignon can be as ruthless as any Apache squaw you've ever seen, trust me on that.'' Taking another puff of his cigar, he blew out the smoke slowly, while the ash grew longer and dropped into the dust. "Rita hates it here and would sell it right off. I want to leave all this to my own blood. Maybe Angie will like it out here. She's young enough to give it a chance.''

Who knew? Maybe she would like New Mexico Territory, for there was enough of John Lindsay in her to meet fire with fire, that was for sure.

Right now, he was glad he wasn't anywhere near Angie Lindsay. He wanted a drink, a bath, and a woman, in that order. The past few days had been pretty unpleasant, and he was in no mood for more conflict. He wanted uncomplicated female companionship, not another battle.

With that in mind, he summoned a young boy and pressed a few picayunes in his hand to deliver a message.

"Tell her to be discreet,'' he added, and the boy nodded and grinned, his black eyes shining at the newly acquired wealth in his palm. White teeth flashed in his dark face.

"I will, and I will be quick, like a rabbit!''

"Not too quick. I need a bath first.''

As the boy sped off on his errand, the desk clerk hailed Jake with a sealed telegram. Jake took it to his room to read, then swore softly. It looked as if he wouldn't be leaving Angie Lindsay behind after all, but he was damned if he liked it. She was too volatile, too fiery, and they were bound to cross each other soon enough.

I hope to hell Patterson knows what he's doing, Jake thought in disgust as he wadded up the telegram and threw it atop a table. And I hope to hell Angie Lindsay has enough sense to go back to France.

Somehow, he doubted it.

8

The fire that Jake saw in Angie flared high when her mother informed her coolly that she had engaged the captain to be their guide.

"He is the most qualified, after all, Angelique, and I see no reason not to use him since he has been released of all charges in this murder."

"No reason! After all that was in the papers about him? A man was brutally murdered—hacked to death with a knife as if he was no more than a piece of meat, and now you say that there is no reason? I do not understand you at all, Maman, and I do not think I ever will."

It's too much, Angie thought, torn between anger and defeat. Why was Mignon suddenly so enthusiastic about Jake Braden when before she had been so set against him? It was not at all like her mother to change her mind, and it set Angie's teeth on edge that she chose now to do it. Why couldn't everything be as simple as it had promised to be when she decided to come to America? But no, nothing had gone right since she'd gotten off the boat in New Orleans. Now this.

"There is nothing to understand, *ma petite.* You said you were going to New Mexico whether I went or not, and I am only trying to help. Captain Braden is very qualified."

Angie's eyes narrowed slightly. Mignon had used that ploy before, and now suddenly Angie recognized the ruse in the tone of her voice, the too-casual shrug, and the small, secret smile that curved her mouth. Oh, no—she had almost been fooled by her mother, but now she knew better!

How absolutely *devious* Maman can be! Why, she did the same thing when she thought I wanted to leave school early! I have been so foolish—then I let her trick me into staying when I hated it so, arranging for me to be so bored that I would *beg* to go back to the convent—but now I see through it, and I will not let her be so clever this time.

"Perhaps you are right, Maman," she said with a little sigh that made her mother look at her closely. "I should learn to be more flexible now that I am in America, after all. Yes. Perhaps since Captain Braden is so qualified, and I have not been able to find anyone else as qualified or who does not look as if he would murder us the first night out, I should reconsider. Yes. I will go and talk to him again, and tell him that I agree with your hiring him to guide us to the Double X. After all, we do not know the details of this crime he is supposed to have committed, do we? It could be that it was in self-defense. . . . Yes, you are right, as always. I will reconsider."

"Angelique—but no . . . where are you going?"

Smiling brightly as she picked up her bonnet, Angie said, "To talk to Captain Braden, of course. If he is to be our guide, I must be certain we are ready in time, no?"

It was sweet triumph to hear her mother's choked protest, and sweeter still to savor the success as she took Bette with her and had a rented hack brought to the front of the St. Louis Hotel. The paper had said that Captain Braden was staying at the St. Charles Hotel, in the American section of New Orleans, and the driver nodded and set the horses off at a swift pace through the narrow, angled streets.

"But are you so certain this is wise?" Bette asked in a whisper, looking more excited than reluctant. "To go out alone like this?"

Iron balconies dripped with brilliant blossoms and shiny green foliage growing in pots and up the walls, and an onslaught of intriguing scents washed over them as the open hack jolted over the cobblestones.

"Yes, of course it is, Bette." Angie hoped she sounded more confident than she felt. What had been sweet vengeance a few minutes before was mounting reservation now. Always, she let her temper get the best of her. But perhaps she could still brazen this out, and no one would be the wiser once she announced her decision to use another guide instead of the captain. "We are merely going to the lobby, after all. No harm will come to us there, in full view of half of New Orleans."

She held up a long veil she'd tucked into her reticule and gave it to Bette. "Not that I am completely unaware of the impropriety in visiting a man like Braden at his hotel, however. Here. Help me put this on over my hat so that we will not be recognized."

Giggling, Bette complied, and with a conspiratorial wink, she soon had Angie's face satisfactorily concealed behind the gauzy veil. Angie wished she could see how she looked, for she had chanced to see the veil lying on a bombé chest and snatched it up in a hurry as she left their room, angry that her mother was so deceitful. But it did not really matter, did it, how she looked? No. It was only Jake Braden, and she did not care what he thought of her.

When she asked the clerk behind the front desk of the hotel to summon Captain Braden to the lobby for a visitor, the man directed her politely to another room. "It is down that hall and to the left, miss. Captain Braden left word that he is waiting on your arrival."

"Waiting on me? Are you certain?"

"But of course. It is the second door on the left."

How *infuriating!* Had Maman known she would fly off to see him at once? Oh, how *irritating* it was to have one know how she would react . . . perhaps she had misjudged her mother after all, for apparently Mignon knew quite well what Angie would do. But she was here, and as it was no doubt expected that she would leave in a huff, she would at least do the unexpected and save what little dignity she could.

"Come along, Bette. This will not take long at all," she said over her shoulder, and turned down the hallway indicated by the clerk. The darkened corridor was lit by a single lamp, but the light from the bright lobby did not reach here as she peered through the folds of her veil.

Angie hesitated in front of the closed door before straightening her shoulders and rapping briskly on the smooth wood. "Really," she muttered, "this is so ridiculous. Perhaps we should just go, Bette, do you not think?"

She half turned, and was slightly startled that the little maid was not in sight. At that moment, the door opened quickly and a hand came out to grab her by the arm and pull her into the darkened room. The door shut loudly.

Too surprised to protest, she thought angrily that it was just like Jake Braden to behave so imperiously, and opened her mouth to tell him exactly what she thought of him. But she found herself jerked forward and into his harsh embrace, heard him mutter that he hadn't meant for her to wear a goddammed veil, for Chrissake, and then it was shoved up and his mouth came down over hers with brutal possession.

Angie had been kissed before, many times, but never had a man kissed her as Jake Braden was doing! No, and never had a man *dared* hold her as close as he was, so that she felt the entire length of his hard frame pressed so tightly against hers it was as if he was welded there . . . it was an outrage!

He held her with his arm around her waist, while his other hand moved beneath the clingy veil to cradle the back of her head in his palm so that she could not move her head or twist away from his kiss. A little dizzily, Angie felt him bend her back so that she thought she would be snapped in two—then his tongue slipped between her parted lips to explore her open mouth, and she began to whimper soft protest.

Why was he doing this? And oh God, why didn't he stop? His mouth was so hard over hers, bearing down with a fierce pressure that conveyed need and impatience and primitive boldness. Angie's legs went boneless. He tasted like heated wine, strong and aromatic—intoxicating. Insanity to yield, but an odd lethargy stole through her veins to render her immobile, to leave her weakly sagging in his embrace while her breath came faster in her lungs and her heart beat so loudly she wondered why he did not hear it.

Worse, an erratic pulse began to throb low in the pit of her stomach, then spread to her thighs and between her legs so that her entire body felt afire with the raging heat that coursed through her in pulsating waves. It was the first time she had ever experienced this reaction, this— this overpowering sense of *urgency* that filled every part of her. It beat inside her with growing fervor, a clamoring insistence that bewildered and excited her, made her yearn for some mysterious culmination that yet eluded her. Oh, why was he doing this? And exactly *what* was it he was doing that left her so . . . so agitated?

As Jake's tongue explored her mouth, she twisted her hands, but they were trapped between her body and Jake's, and she could not free them. It was then she realized that beneath her curled fists were bare skin and hard muscle, and the shock of it dissipated the enveloping heat like a dash of icy water in her face.

Somehow she found the strength to push him away, wrenching her mouth from his and forcing him back a step. He still held her firmly, his arm like a steel band behind her as he began to untie the gauzy chin straps of her hat.

"Let's get this stupid thing off, Anna," he muttered, "before you put out my eye with it."

Anna! Oh, she would *like* to put out his eyes, but not with so soft a thing as her hat, she thought then, fiercely now with the return of her resistance and the lessening of the strange lassitude that had claimed her so briefly.

With the return of resolve came fury, and as he loosened the hat ties to remove her scoop bonnet by the wide brim, she lifted her hand with swift purpose and slammed her palm against his face with a loud, cracking sound. There was a brief look of angry surprise on his face before he grabbed her by the wrist, and as her hat fell to the floor and he turned her with a sharp twist of his hand that brought a gasp of pain from her, the light from a lamp fell across them and into her eyes. She blinked as he swore softly.

"Christ! You? What the hell are you doing here in my room, Miss Lindsay?"

Despite her anger, she was a little frightened by the ferocity of his demand and the cold fury in his eyes as he stared down at her.

"I am in your room because you pulled me in here!" Her voice rose with suppressed rage and apprehension. "If I had known you meant to . . . to *attack* me, I would have sent the police instead! How *dare* you treat me as if I were one of your Gypsy girls . . . you should still be in jail instead of out here assaulting innocent women, luring them to your room so you can—"

He dug his fingers harshly into the tender skin of her wrist. "Be quiet or you'll have the entire hotel in here."

"I don't care!" She drew in a shaky breath that was perilously close to a sob. "Let them all come and see what a—a *felon* you are! I hope they shoot you. . . ."

"Keep that up and you might get your wish." He released her, and his dry tone conveyed more amusement than fear. "I don't think it would do your reputation any good to be found in here alone with me, but if you want a crowd of witnesses, just keep shouting like that."

Was he trying to threaten her by implying scandal? Oh, she *should* scream, she really should, just to show him that he could not bully her! But common sense intruded when he eyed her with narrow speculation, and she knew that he would no doubt turn things around and make it seem as if it was her wish to be here. No, she could not create a scene, not when he stood there half dressed.

His gaze narrowed even more when she took a deep breath and looked away from him, unwilling to be caught staring at his bare chest visible beneath the open shirt.

"It seems there has been a mistake here, Miss Lindsay. I thought you were someone else."

His drawling voice was amused, and she shot him an angry glance as she rubbed sullenly at her aching wrists.

"Is that why you called me Anna? Do I look like some Gypsy girl?"

"No, but with that ridiculous hat on, I couldn't see anything but that you were female. Now, answer my question—what are you doing here in my room?"

"The clerk at the front desk told me you were waiting for me here. I thought you knew I was coming to see you."

"Ah. I see. Well, you're both wrong. I'll ask again—what *are* you doing here? At this hotel?"

"There has been a mistake. It's true I came to see you, but not for the reason you obviously think I did."

"You have no idea what I think, Miss Lindsay, and if you did, you'd do more than slap my face, I assure you. Ah ah, don't get any ideas," he drawled when her head snapped up and she began to sputter angrily. "Why do you want to see me? Morbid curiosity?"

"No. Nothing like that." She felt foolish suddenly, and realized it had been a terrible idea. He would not help her at all. But she was here and might as well try; she looked up to meet his eyes. "My mother does not wish to go to New Mexico, as you are certainly aware. Yet I do. In light of your recent . . . troubles . . . you are no longer suitable as a guide, of course. So I would like for you to recommend someone to conduct me there."

"Would you?" He looked wary, his eyes very gold in the dim light of the lamp behind him that left half his face in shadow. "Why?"

Exasperated, she glared at him. "I should think it would be obvious to you that I want to get to New Mexico as safely and quickly as possible. Monsieur Gravier informs me that if I wait too long, the heat will be debilitating. I would like to leave soon, and I would like to have someone competent and experienced as a guide to get me there."

When he did not reply at once, she added, "And do not think I will be cheated, for I know what the rates are for guides, and I will pay only what's fair."

"So you came to ask *me* to recommend someone."

His mouth twisted in a faint, mocking smile that made her want to slap him again, and she drew in an angry breath before exhaling it sharply when he agreed.

"All right. I'll recommend a scout who will get you there in one piece. He knows the route and the danger, and he won't be distracted by a pretty face and flirting eyes."

Angie held tight to her strained temper and folded her arms across her chest. I will *not* be goaded again, she thought, and managed a cool nod of her head.

"Excellent. I will have Bette restrain herself with him. Who is this paragon you would recommend for my guide?"

He moved forward, a smooth glide that made her think of a prowling cat, and the white shirt shifted away from the rigid muscles and bronze skin of his chest as he came closer. She felt the heat of him again, forceful and so very male and intimidating, and her throat tightened as the rapid pulse began again in the pit of her stomach.

Through the thudding beat she heard him say, "Me."

For a moment she could not speak, could only stare up at him. But— surely he did not mean that, for he was not at all suitable . . . oh no, he was much too dangerous a man to even consider his suggestion, and she shook her head.

"You? Why would I want *you* to be my escort?"

"What you want doesn't matter. It's already been arranged, unless you'd rather go back to France. That's your other option."

"How *dare* you! You have no idea what my options are, Captain Braden!'

"I'm afraid I do." His eyes narrowed a little, glinting like a panther. "I knew your father, and I scout for the man who arranged your passage to America and your journey to New Mexico. It was settled before you ever got on the ship."

He sounded so certain that she did not reply for a moment. Was he right? All the arrangements had been made for them by her father, so he was probably telling the truth. But how irritating!

"I'm not at all certain I want a . . . a murderer to be my guide, Captain Braden!"

She had the brief reward of seeing a flash of anger light his eyes, then his hand was on her arm again and he held her in a fierce, steely grip.

"Miss Lindsay, you've got a sharp tongue that's going to get you in trouble one day if you don't learn to curb it. There are folks who take real exception to insults, and it won't matter to them if you're a woman or a man. You could end up looking down the barrel of a pistol for being stupid enough to voice your opinions."

"Are you threatening me?"

"No, ma'am. Just warning you."

She drew in a shaky breath. "Let go of my arm, Captain, or I will be forced to scream for help."

Instead of releasing her, he leaned forward, his body a lean threat as he pushed her back against the wall. Her heart beat so hard that she could hear it, and she pressed her shoulder blades against the wall behind her as if she could escape him that way. He frightened her, but not for her life—there was something else in his eyes as he stared at her in the dim light that frightened her.

His mouth slanted up at one corner in that knowing, cocky smile that always made her feel as if her blouse were open or she were somehow deficient.

"You're beautiful, Miss Lindsay, but it's obvious you know that. Don't get to thinking you can use it out west. It's a harsh land, and a pretty face won't save you. It's more likely to cause you problems."

There was a grim certainty to his tone that gave her the strength to push him away, and this time he did not hold her.

"I hardly need any warning from *you*, Captain Braden. And if you find me so repugnant, perhaps you can explain why you kissed me!"

"I told you I was expecting someone else," he said in an impatient tone of voice that grated on her temper. "How was I to know you'd come here? Besides, Miss Lindsay, you should know better than to come to a man's room, even in such a ridiculous disguise."

It was true. Chagrined, she forced herself to hold her tongue as she reached for her hat. Braden picked it up for her and held it out, and she snatched it from his hand with a less than graciously muttered thank-you.

"I suppose I'd better leave before your . . . *friend* . . . gets here, then."

"Yes." He looked amused as his hard, reckless mouth slanted upward in a mocking smile. "I'd hate for her to think my taste in women has changed."

Furious, she jammed her hat down over her head and tied the ribbons under her chin, aware of his sardonic regard as she fumbled with the clingy veil.

"Yes, there is no point in letting her think you've actually *improved* your taste, since it seems to run to Gypsy dancers."

"Somehow, I'm not too sure she'd be able to tell the difference between you and Eugenié."

She gasped with outrage. "What do you mean by such an insult! I am *nothing* like that . . . that cabaret dancer!"

"No? Maybe not in looks. And maybe I'm wrong. At least Eugenié is honest about what she wants and how she feels."

"If you are implying that I have any interest in you, Captain Braden, you are wrong. I do not. I find you quite repulsive."

He shrugged. "You can lie to everybody else, but if you did find me so repulsive, you wouldn't have kissed me back a few minutes ago."

Because he was right, and because she had no intention of admitting how he had made her feel, Angie lifted her shoulders in as careless a shrug as he just had.

"I have kissed a lot of men, Captain. It was just an experiment. Do not flatter yourself that it meant more than that."

When she left, exiting the door with what she hoped was consummate dignity, she knew he was watching her, standing in the open doorway to stare after her as she found Bette and they left the hotel.

What an infuriating man! And if it was true that he was to escort them all the way to New Mexico, she wasn't at all certain she would be able to endure it.

9

It was bad enough that Jake Braden was to be their guide to New Mexico, Angie fumed after their confrontation at the St. Charles Hotel, but he also had been right that it had been planned all along. Indeed, when she'd returned to her hotel after leaving his, a telegram awaited her from a Colonel Patterson in San Antonio who recommended Captain Braden as the most efficient and trustworthy scout the army had on its payroll.

"Braden's recent arrest is a regrettable error," the colonel had wired, "and he should be considered the best man to get you safely through unpredictable terrain."

Patterson had known her father, and it was the colonel who had arranged for Braden to be her escort, not—as she had first thought—John Lindsay. She was to leave on a steamer to Galveston and then on to Corpus Christi in just a few hours, with Jake Braden as her escort.

She should be glad that she was getting her wish, that she was going at last to New Mexico, but she was not. Oh, it was because of Jake Braden, of course, that she felt so uncertain, so . . . *awkward*. That was it. Awkward. Because of what had happened in his hotel room, because he had kissed her so thoroughly and she had yielded, even responded.

It was the last that left her burning with shame and indignation, and she hoped fiercely that he had not guessed how he'd made her feel. The memory of it had kept her awake most of that night. But she had no intention of revealing her momentary weakness to anyone, and so when she met him again, she would be coolly indifferent. That should be enough to convince him that she was not at all affected by him or anything he did.

How she despised him! He'd made her feel gauche and childish and foolish, when it was his fault she had been treated with such effrontery.

"Are you ready, Angelique?" Mignon rapped sharply on the bedroom door, then swung it open to peruse her daughter with a set expression. "The porter is here to collect our baggage. It is not too late, however, to change your mind should you have come to your senses about this foolish notion of some mythical quest for your father."

Stung by her mother's disdain, Angie's chin came up. "I hardly think that claiming my inheritance qualifies me as in pursuit of a mythical quest, Maman."

"No? Perhaps not." Mignon looked disgruntled. "At any rate, the porter is here. Monsieur Gravier has kindly consented to allow us to store the rest of our things with him until we can send for them or return for them. It is ridiculous, being confined to taking only one small trunk apiece. I cannot imagine how Captain Braden thinks we will be able to manage."

"No doubt Captain Braden wears the same clothing from day to day and does not consider a change of garments a necessity. Anyway, Maman, he is probably right. It will be a difficult trip, if what Captain Braden says is true, and we should travel as light as possible."

"You begin to sound like him, Angelique. How droll that we are in New Orleans less than a fortnight and you begin to sound as American as if you had lived here all your life."

"Well, I didn't. I was never given the opportunity to make that decision, was I?"

Angie moved past her mother before Mignon could reply, a little disconcerted by her continued animosity. Perhaps Angie should suggest that Maman remain here. It would be such a long journey, and she dreaded the thought of having her mother constantly harping at her the entire time. There were times when she wondered if she really knew her mother at all, for she could be so cold and aloof, so distant when Angie needed reassurance.

But it had always been that way. Now should be no different, though they were in a different country.

The unsettled feeling lasted even after the steamer pulled away from the docks and chugged out into the river. She had glimpsed Jake Braden only from a distance, but he was somewhere on the packet with them, no doubt gambling in the huge room she had seen as she went to her stateroom.

Bette, up and busy since early morning, lay down across the narrow bunk and fell instantly asleep. Her dark hair fell across one cheek in a damp tangle, and Angie sat in the silence and listened to the noises of the crew getting the steamer under way. It was a noisy boat with huge smokestacks that belched black clouds of smoke, and the floor beneath her vibrated as the engines worked. Mignon was in a small room next to theirs, and had no doubt done exactly what Bette was doing. Only Angie was filled with fitful energy.

Restless, she decided to go above deck to stand on the observation area and watch the shoreline slip past. It was with a bit of regret that she saw New Orleans recede in the distance, for she had truly been enthralled with the wicked, elegant city that was rather like a bawdy aristocrat.

As she moved to stand at the rail where no one else crowded close, a wind blew over her that smelled of coal smoke, fish, and stagnant river scents. High, chewed banks that were ragged with waving grass edged the muddy river that flowed in small whirlpools and swirling eddies. An occasional house or building perched near the river's edge, with moss-hung trees like lace-shawled ladies swaying in the wind that blew off the water.

Angie stood there a long time, even after the other passengers drifted away and the afternoon shadows began to grow longer. She was vaguely surprised that Bette or her mother did not come for her, but it was so pleasant standing there by herself where she could think that she did not tempt fate by dwelling upon it for long.

Then she heard a familiar voice and turned slightly to stare with wide eyes as she saw Jake Braden escort Mignon to the rail and stand with her. They spoke softly, and neither of them seemed to notice her standing in the curve of the rail. But how infuriating! After all Maman had said, for her to allow him to escort her above deck was astounding!

After a moment, Jake Braden glanced up and saw her, and he must have said something to Mignon, for she turned, her face a little flushed when she saw Angie standing there. She beckoned, and Angie was tempted to ignore her, but she knew it would look spiteful and childish if she did, so she moved along the rail with the careful steps of someone unaccustomed to walking aboard a ship until she reached them.

"Good afternoon, Maman. Captain."

If Jake Braden was discomfited by her presence, he did not show it, but merely nodded politely and stared across the rail at the last bit of land edging the Gulf of Mexico.

"We will dock in Galveston sometime early in the morning, madame. I will have you escorted to your hotel, and we will leave for Corpus Christi the next morning."

Angie stared at him. He had spoken in fluent French, and Mignon was actually *smiling* at him! Not only that, but he was attired in quite expensive clothing, and the cut of his jacket was perfectly tailored to his broad shoulders and lean hips. As tall as he was, he still managed to seem unobtrusive, leaning casually against the rail on one elbow, his posture as indolent as a great, arrogant cat's.

"That will be excellent, Captain Braden," Mignon replied in the same language, and glanced at Angie. "I know my daughter is anxious to reach New Mexico, and now that I have begun this journey, I admit to a certain impatience as well."

A slow smile touched the corners of his mouth as he nodded, and finally looked directly at Angie. She lifted her chin in cool disdain.

"Miss Lindsay," he said in drawling English, "enjoy this part of the journey while you can. Once we leave Corpus Christi, there will be no more comfortable beds or clean clothes until we get to San Antonio."

"If you are trying to discourage me, Captain," she said sweetly, "do not waste your time. I am well aware that there will be a lack of conveniences on this journey, but you will find that I am much hardier than you assume."

"Glad to hear it, ma'am."

Her eyes narrowed. He was trying to goad her, but she would not let him. It was apparent he and Mignon had banded together to dissuade her.

"You might remember, Captain, that you are being paid to escort me to New Mexico, so I find it a bit odd that you would attempt to prevent me going. Was it not your decision to accept my offer?"

"No." He smiled at her little hiss of anger. "It was my commanding officer's decision that you have someone escort you, since you're so determined to go. He seems to think I can get you there alive. I'd rather leave you here."

"Then I am certain you and my mother have a great deal in common, for she is also of the opinion I should give up my inheritance. But it is mine. It is all I have of my father, and I will not allow anyone to stop me."

For an instant, she saw what looked like a gleam of approval in his eyes, but it was gone so quickly she might have been mistaken. He gave a brief shrug of his shoulders and uncoiled his long body from its indolent sprawl against the smooth wood of the ship's rail.

"I admire your tenacity, if not your judgment, Miss Lindsay." He turned to Mignon. "I look forward to seeing you at the evening meal, ma'am."

Angie watched him go with an irritated frown knitting her brows together. He was much too arrogant, and the dislike that had formed the first night she'd met him grew stronger. It was true that she did not care

for men who fawned, but it was also true that the opposite end of the
spectrum was hardly acceptable either. There must be a compromise, a
blending of characters that would combine the gentle nature of one with
the strength of the other.

But of course, such a paragon most likely did not exist, and in truth,
she should not expect it.

"You are so quiet, Angelique," Mignon observed, and a faint smile
played at the corners of her mouth. "Are you unwell? The motion of
the ship, perhaps?"

"No, I am not at all unwell. Surprised would better describe my
feelings at this moment. I thought you detested Jake Braden."

"I see we are being brutally honest. Very well. It is true that I usually
find a man such as Captain Braden to be abhorrent, but as he and I
share the same concern for you, we have . . . met on common ground,
you could say."

Mignon looked so coolly composed, even with the brisk hot wind
tugging at her blond hair and fluttering the ties of her hat. Angie felt
rumpled and unkempt beside her, and frustration lent a tart edge to her
words.

"I see. How charming that you and a complete stranger should be so
compatible while you and I have never been."

"Do not put words into my mouth, Angelique. It is only that I have
made inquiries of my own and learned that it is Captain Braden's very
reputation that will safeguard you most. Monsieur Gravier assured me
that since the captain is regarded as something of a professional gunman,
very few outlaws will dare confront him. He was once enlisted with the
army and is now a scout for them. Yet because he has such a fierce
reputation, it is a matter of pride with such a man that he protect those
who pay him."

"Perhaps you trust him, Maman, but I do not. And I do not understand why you must insist that we continue with this man when there
are others who would do just as well."

"None that we have found are willing to risk their lives as you are,"
Mignon said sharply, then more softly, "*Ma cher*, you know it is only
my love for you that prompts me to agree with Monsieur Gravier. Do
you doubt?"

Yes. *Yes*, Angie doubted it; she thought it was more an issue of
control than love that made her mother determined to have her own
way. But this time Maman would not prevail. This time, Angie thought
defiantly, *I will succeed!*

She shrugged, and turned to stare across the steamer's rail at the
fading coastline. Twilight seamed sky and water together into a collage

of dark blue and crimson, with the sun's lowering reflection mirrored on the erratic surface.

Mignon, watching her, was well aware of the conflicting emotions driving her daughter, could see in her expressive face the struggle. She understood it and feared it.

Ah, Angelique was maturing so quickly, growing away from her and becoming so stubborn . . . how could she convince her that life was not the exciting adventure of the books and glowing letters she had read? It was not. No, there were devastating disappointment and disillusion awaiting those foolish enough to ignore the warning signs, for she had experienced all the crushing defeats herself and knew them well. It could have been *her* standing at the ship's rail with such eager anticipation, just as she had done twenty-two years before. . . .

The hopes and dreams and all-consuming love that had obliterated common sense and cast her into an abyss of dark fear and screaming nightmares were behind her now, but she remembered them with excruciating clarity.

Willful girl—considering how clever she was, Angelique could be so obtuse at times. She was a frustrating blend of perception and imagination that kept her in continual conflict with her own nature. She had too much of her father in her, an idealistic fascination with the unattainable, the same foolish illusion of independence and self-sufficiency that had fueled John Lindsay's determination to dwell in a harsh land with no compensation but the knowledge that it was an accomplishment just to survive.

Ah, dear God, how could she protect Angelique from herself when the child's very nature was the enemy? It was too difficult, but she must manage it somehow, must bring her to see that she was too refined and civilized to risk all for the limited reward of survival in a hostile environment.

And if she had to use Jake Braden to manage it, she would. She would use what weapons she could summon to her disposal to save them both, for if Angelique failed, so would she. Their destinies were entwined, and she had thought once that she would never have to face her old fears again, never have to return to the land of her nightmares . . . it was agony that she was here again, when she had fought so hard against this very thing. Did no one realize how difficult it was for her to return? But no, her fear had been something she had found difficult to discuss all these years, saying only that it was a dreadful land with hostile savages and she would never go back.

Mignon wanted to laugh at the cruel twist of fate and John Lindsay's Machiavellian mind that had brought her back against her wishes. She could have stayed in France, could have remained in New Orleans, but then she would have lost all. He would have won.

That she could not bear.

So here she was, returning to face old nightmares. It was the only way to triumph, to defeat them once and for all so that she would never have to encounter them again. And she would do anything she had to do to triumph.

It was gratifying that Braden also felt that it was it far too dangerous for them to go to New Mexico. He had other reasons, of that she was certain, but it did not matter as long as he would do what he could to dissuade Angelique from continuing her journey. In that, she would lend him all the assistance she could.

When the evening meal was over, and Angelique rose from the table where they had dined with the steamer's captain and Braden and murmured a polite excuse that she needed fresh air, Mignon said nothing about a proper chaperon or the need for her to be careful, but watched her leave the dining hall alone.

"It is a beautiful night, Captain Braden, do you not think?" she said a few moments later, and gazed at him over the rim of her wine goblet. "I have always considered the moonlight on water to be so lovely."

Braden, who had been unusually taciturn during the meal, met her gaze with a lifted brow. "I'm expected at a poker game with Captain Sorenson, ma'am."

"Really? How depressing that you should have to while away the night in a small room filled with cigar smoke and pasteboard cards. But I suppose that one must do what one feels best."

Captain Sorenson laughed. He was quite handsome, with white hair and rugged features that were appealing, but he was a bit too ebullient for her tastes.

"Madame Lindsay, we would far rather remain in your charming company, of course, but Captain Braden wants a chance to win more money from me. The last time we met, he managed to clean me out, and I want my vengeance. You would not begrudge me that pleasure, I hope!"

"No, of course not, Captain Sorenson. Do what you must."

But she watched Braden from the corner of her eye and wondered if he took her blatant hint. There was no sign he had as he shrugged his shoulders and drank his wine. He surprised her, this rough American, for he spoke fluent French and was much more civilized than most men here. He was very handsome, in a rough, ruthless sort of way, though far too aggressive for her tastes. Still, he was the kind of man who would be an asset in deterring Angelique from her resolve to linger too long in New Mexico. She was sure of it.

And when Captain Braden rose at last from the table with a polite withdrawal, she watched the eyes of every female passenger follow him as he left the dining cabin and went out onto the main deck. He paused, then moved away in the direction of the poop deck, where passengers were allowed to stroll, and she smiled to herself. Perhaps he would be able to end this adventure before it began.

"More wine, Madame Lindsay?" the steamer's captain leaned forward to say, and she looked up and smiled at the admiration gleaming in his eyes.

"Why, yes, Captain Sorenson. You are too kind."

10

Moonlight silvered the swirling water in a wide path and made black lacy silhouettes of trees on the far bank. The constant hum of engines and rushing currents provided a lulling noise as the steamer toiled through the vast waters of the Gulf of Mexico and toward the Texas coastline.

Jake found Angie Lindsay alone and leaning on a wide rail on the poop deck, at the ship's stern. Dark shadows cloaked her, but light from a single lantern on the wall of the deck housing cast a hazy, wavering glow that reflected off her red-gold hair like molten copper. He watched her for a moment, studying her delicate profile and slender curves that looked far too frail to withstand the rigors of a dangerous trek across hostile-infested country. He should order her to stay and tell her why, but it wouldn't do any good.

Angie turned then and saw him standing behind her. She drew in a sharp breath. "Really, Captain Braden, must you sneak up so quietly?"

"I didn't have to sneak. The engines make enough noise to drown out a herd of buffalos."

With a self-conscious gesture, she pushed the hair from her eyes where the wind had tangled it. "I suppose that's true enough. Did my mother send you for me?"

"Are you expecting her to?"

"Why can you not just give me a straight answer instead of another question? You sound like a lawyer!"

He grinned at her irritated comment. "I once studied to be a lawyer. Guess I forget that you're not on trial."

She eyed him in the gloom of night shadow and reflected light that made her eyes a deep purple. "Really? Somehow, I never suspected you to be a man who cares about the law."

"We all have our dark secrets." He moved to stand beside her at the rail. "Once I thought knowing the law would make a difference."

"Now that you're well acquainted with it, you prefer to break the law, is that it?"

"If you're referring to that little incident in New Orleans, I'm not the man responsible. If I was, I wouldn't have been stupid enough to leave him where anyone would find the body."

She shivered and tugged at the lacy shawl around her shoulders. His gaze dropped to the low-cut bodice of her gown and the creamy swells of her breasts that had caught his attention more than once during the course of the evening. This Angie Lindsay was very different from the girl he had seen that first night dressed in an ingenuous gown that had made her seem very young and innocent. Tonight, she looked every inch a mature woman.

He thought briefly of his mistake at the St. Charles Hotel. If he hadn't been so impatient, maybe he would have noticed sooner that it was definitely not Anna in his arms. Anna Crews was an acquaintance from the time he'd spent in New Orleans right after the war ended, always willing to oblige with eager enthusiasm. She was an uncomplicated woman who needed no emotional ties or reassurance, nothing but the pleasure of a few hours of satisfying sex. It was the kind of relationship he preferred.

Now Angie looked up at him with a slight frown. "But you did not do it, did you? I received a telegram from your commanding officer, and he assured me that you had nothing to do with that horrible murder."

"I've never known Colonel Patterson to lie." Jake's eyes strayed to the curves and hollows of her body, amply displayed in the deep blue gown, especially with the wind playing havoc with the lacy fringe meant to camouflage the swells and valley of her breasts. The material was cut in a curve almost to her nipples, with only the pleated lace to preserve her modesty. A very daring and provocative gown, and he was surprised that Mignon had not forbidden her to wear it.

But Angie Lindsay was headstrong, and no doubt would have refused any attempts to govern her choice of garments.

Now, as if aware of the direction of his gaze, she put a hand on the bare skin of her throat, fingers idly toying with the gold necklace she wore. A single, square amethyst hung from the gold links, not large, but the same color as her eyes and striking in its gleaming simplicity.

Jake's eyes narrowed, and when he looked up at her face, he saw her watching him with a kind of wary fascination. The tip of her tongue came out to scrub over her bottom lip, a pink flash that sent a spear of heat through him at the implied intimacy. He thought of how she had felt and tasted, and when she drew in a ragged breath, he knew she must be thinking of it, too.

For a brief instant, she held his gaze, then she veiled her eyes and looked away, biting her lower lip.

"Angie—Miss Lindsay—" He put a hand on her shoulder to regain her attention, intending to tell her that she should postpone her trip for her own safety, but at that moment a sudden lurch of the steamer to the starboard caught him off balance and threw him against her. Automatically, he put out his arms to brace himself against the rail and found them full of female.

It was one of those moments that felt too natural to be wrong, and when her head tilted back and she stared up at him with startled eyes and parted lips, his head bent and he kissed her. She did not protest or struggle, as he half expected, but yielded with sweet fire, returning the kiss and surprising him with her response. It was definitely not the kiss of an adolescent, but of a passionate young woman.

It caught him off guard, and he kissed her as he would have kissed any woman, with fierce hunger and rising desire that he took no trouble to conceal. He leaned into her, pressing her back against the rail with his weight until he felt her go limp and heard her soft moan. The swell of one of her breasts was beneath his hand, and he could feel the hard little pucker of her nipple against his palm. He cupped her breast, teasing the beaded, satin-covered rosette with his thumb and finger.

A flash of heat scored him when she gasped and arched her back so that she was even closer, and for a moment he forgot his own resolution and where they were as he caressed and kissed her. Soft, heated flesh, the sweet scent of her so close, and the desire she had ignited in him previously coalesced now into rousing need. Her unexpected surrender only fanned the flames.

Still kissing her, Jake angled his body so that he was pressed fully against her and could feel the soft swell of her stomach against him in stimulating pressure. For a brief instant he was tempted to see just how far she would go with him.

Then lucidity returned, and he broke off the kiss to step back and away from her, swearing softly under his breath at his own faulty judgment. Stupidity to even consider it, despite the circumstances and her brief yielding.

Her breath came in swift pants as she stared up at him, and her eyes were clouded with confusion and turmoil.

"I should slap you for that," she said then in a voice that was anything but angry, and he shook his head ruefully.

"No need to. I'm sure I'll regret it a lot more than you do."

She recoiled as if slapped herself, and drew in a sharp breath that thrust out her breasts. He reached out to pull the edges of her shawl over her, ignoring the wild swipe of her hand as he did. His jaw set.

"What did you expect from me, Miss Lindsay? Apologies ain't my style."

"I don't doubt that." A trembling hand rearranged her disheveled bodice and pulled her shawl over the tempting cleavage. Then she looked up at him with a faint frown. "To be perfectly honest, I don't know what to expect from you. You . . . you aren't like any man I've ever met before. I don't know how to categorize you. Most men fall into one of two categories, boring or dangerous. You've been both."

"I'm flattered."

His wry comment put an angry flush in her cheeks. "You mock me, but I'm very serious. I want to trust you. I *have* to trust you since my life will literally be in your hands on this journey, but you—you frighten me at times. Are you a man capable of brutal murder? *Should* I be frightened of you?"

"Yes." He saw the sudden shock register in her eyes at his harsh reply, and shrugged. "If you want it sugar-coated for you, you'll have to go elsewhere, Miss Lindsay. I could tell you what you want to hear, but it's not the truth. When the occasion calls for it, I do what I have to do, and if that means killing a man, I do. If I want a woman, I take her, as long as she's willing and knows that it won't be anything more than that. I may want you, Angie Lindsay, but it won't be moonlight and roses once it's over. I'll go my way and you'll go yours. That's as blunt and honest as I can make it. It's your choice. If you say yes, we'll go to my cabin right now, but in the morning you won't be anything more to me than the woman I've been hired to get to New Mexico."

She stood trembling in the cool wind of the Gulf waters that washed over the steamer and lifted a loose strand of her hair in a flutter of copper silk. Then she looked up at him again, her voice soft.

"What if I say yes?"

Shocked by her unexpected response, Jake said harshly, "That's not what you want, Miss Lindsay."

"You don't know that. Maybe it is what I want. Maybe I need to discover for myself what it is I'm not supposed to want." Her brow arched. "Men prefer simple, uncommitted arrangements—is it so impossible for a woman to do the same?"

"For Chrissake, you're just a virgin playing at passion. You have no idea what you're talking about."

"That is precisely my point, Captain. Knowledge is power. If I knew what makes men want women so badly, and why women yield so willingly, perhaps then I would understand it better."

"So you think that's what you want? Maybe we'll just see about that."

Before she could react, he pulled her to him with ruthless determination and jammed his mouth down over her parted lips in fierce possession. No tenderness, no holding back; he kissed her with savage ferocity that surprised even him. His arms went around her and he moved her into the shadows of the deck housing. Using his weight as leverage, he pinned her against the wall with his body while he plundered her mouth thoroughly.

Her arms rose to twine around his neck, the motion bringing her breasts against his chest in an erotic glide of satin and pebbled nipples. Half angry at her reckless response, he lifted one hand to spread his fingers in her hair and loosen it to tumble down her back. Still kissing her, his mouth muffled her soft moans as he pulled down the lace bodice to cup her bare breast in his other hand. A tremor went through her at his touch, and he expected her to pull away, but she didn't.

Instead she leaned into him, a dangerous surrender. He bent to kiss her breast, tongue teasing the pouty pink nipple into a tight knot. Impatient now, he ignored her halfhearted protest and trailed his tongue over her sweet-scented skin to her other breast; her hands held his head, fingers curled into his hair to hold him.

"Angie . . . Christ!" he muttered harshly, and it came out a groan.

God, he wanted to put himself inside her, feel her soft heat close around him and ease the driving hunger she'd sparked with her artlessly naive experiment. Damn her.

"Jake . . ."

His name was a soft, heated whisper on her lips, her breath warm against his face. He drew her nipple into his mouth and heard her gasp. Her hands tightened in his hair and she sagged into him. If he wanted her, she was his. All he had to do was take her and he knew it.

But it would cause more problems than it would solve, and he knew that too. Deliberately, he pushed away from her before he forgot himself and went too far to stop.

"Guess that should help explain why women yield, Miss Lindsay."

For an instant she looked confused; desire still hazed her eyes and flushed her face. Then, as she realized that he'd pushed her away, she recoiled.

"Yes, in a way, I suppose it does." She stepped back, returning to the rail and barricading herself behind dignity and a lacy shawl as she pulled it around her. When she turned her face away, he saw the brief quiver of her lower lip before she firmed it. "I assume this is when I'm supposed to thank you for the lesson in deportment."

Her obvious chagrin flattened his lips in a smile. "Maybe not right now."

"I'm not a fool. I know you're trying to scare me off, but you needn't have bothered. I told you that I was curious, and that's all." She flashed him a quick glance from shadowed eyes. "But I wonder, aren't you ever tempted to try emotion instead of such a primitive reaction?"

"No." He stared at her coldly. "Most of the women I've been with know what to expect and don't want the extras any more than I do. There's no time in my life for moonlight kisses and slow seduction, Angie Lindsay, and if you know what's good for you, you'll stop this little flirting game. I'm not interested in what you want, and you don't know enough to run like hell from what I want."

"Thank you for your pithy lecture in morality or the lack of it, Captain. I'll keep it in mind."

She averted her face so that it was hidden from him by wind-whipped curls. After a brief pause, he shrugged and bid her good-night, then left her standing at the rail.

He glanced back once; she was gazing at the infinite horizon of water and sky bound together by the silver gleam of reflected moonlight that made it seem as if there was no beginning and no ending to the night. It was somehow fitting that she should be a part of the immeasurable night.

As he went to join the poker players in the captain's cabin, the taste and feel of Angie Lindsay lingered. She was different from any woman he had ever met. Somehow, she would make a difference in his life that he would certainly regret. It was a hunch, and he always trusted his hunches.

But he had never walked away from trouble before and he wouldn't start now.

Dave Logan, Tom Spencer, and Captain Sorenson sat in a thick haze of smoke and half-full liquor bottles around a small table that had been bolted to the floor of the captain's cabin.

Logan looked up when Jake came in, then hooked a chair with his boot to drag it from under the table and kick it toward him. Jake acknowledged the gesture with a sardonic lift of his brow, and chair legs scraped loudly as he pulled out the ladder-back chair and dropped into it.

Texas-born Dave Logan had known Jake Braden since they were raw kids with restless feet and a yen for adventure. During the intervening years their paths frequently crossed, and they often worked together, as they were now. He guessed he knew Jake better than most, and he recognized that something had got under his friend's skin pretty good tonight.

Chewing on a half-smoked cigar, he squinted against the thin curl of smoke and drawled, "Reckon squirin' two pretty ladies all the way to New Mex Territory ain't put you in too good a mood, Jake."

The only reaction was a quick flick of Jake's eyes and a casual shrug, and Logan grinned.

"Yeah, I heard that you argued against it."

"That's right."

Spencer dealt the cards. "Ante up, Braden."

Dave Logan grinned and said laconically when Jake looked up at him, "I'm ready to start playin' cards."

"I bet you are. Didn't lose enough to me last time, Dave?"

Sorenson pushed a couple of coins forward into the pile in the middle of the table. "Captain Braden was a bit busy with a beautiful young woman earlier. Perhaps if we're lucky, he'll be too distracted to concentrate on cards."

Jake lit a cigar and ignored Sorenson's gibe. The captain perused his cards, but his benign expression didn't mask his intensity. They played silently for a while, then Sorenson broke the quiet.

"I have a message from Patterson. He's waiting on you men in San Antonio."

"Any news?" Logan asked in his usual terse manner.

"You know the colonel wouldn't tell me what he knows. He'll wait to tell you. He did mention some reservations about one of the men who was hired recently."

Jake glanced up at that. "Ringgold?"

"Yes." Sorenson discarded one card, drew another, and bet a gold eagle, then waited expectantly as Spencer threw in his hand in disgust and Logan drew three. Jake stood pat, and the steamer captain bet another gold eagle coin, then said, "I believe he has some concerns about his suitability. Call."

"Two pair. Deuces and eights." Logan spread his cards on the table.

Jake spread out three jacks and a pair of tens. "Full house."

Sorenson heaved a sigh. "Four of a kind—read 'em and weep, gentlemen."

As he pulled in the pot, Sorenson glanced up at Jake again. "Patterson said he'd trust your judgment on it."

"Ringgold's calling himself Ringo now. He's a quick draw, but I don't know if he'll make the long haul. He's too restless."

"Do you trust him?"

"No." Jake shrugged. "He's young, college educated and likes to show it. Ruthless when it's not necessary. He's got something gnawing at him, and it makes him edgy. He's the kind who's liable to shoot first and ask questions later. I wouldn't turn my back on him."

"That figures." Logan's comment was dry. "You know who hired him as scout, don't you?"

Jake looked up, and something flickered in his amber eyes. "Gravier."

"Right. Said two hired guns would be better than one on this trip."

"My bet is Gravier's in it with the governor, and you know who Warmoth works with."

"Your uncle."

Jake's mouth flattened into a grim line. "A dirtier pair of bastards have never been seen. Leave it to them and New Mexico Territory will belong to Mexico again."

"You still think that's who's selling rifles to the Apache and Comanche?" Logan shook his head, frowning. "It doesn't make sense."

"Not to us, maybe. But there's a plausible reason behind it, you can bet on that. Too bad they got to the informant first. Poor bastard probably figured he'd be safer in New Orleans than Santa Fe, but he figured wrong."

"Ever find out who it was?"

"No, but I've got a good idea. If I'm right, then I can get to the truth."

"Think Ringgold's in on it?"

"Maybe. If he is, he'll show his hand quick enough. He's liable to cash out before we leave San Antonio. I've got two other men working for me, scouting sign in Texas. I'll meet up with them soon enough and see what they've found out."

Sorenson frowned and reached for his cards. "It's somebody big who's in charge of this. No small fish, but a big one who has the men and connections necessary to start another war. Lately I've begun to think he might just succeed. Another war so soon would be disastrous for the United States. Our resources are still depleted from the last, and I'm not at all certain we can count on our allies in Europe to help us against Mexico." His mouth tightened. "After we gave all that aid to Juárez, *el presidente* has chosen not to reward us in the way we hoped."

Logan flicked a quick glance toward Jake, but Jake's face was impassive. It was no secret where his loyalties lay, but Dave often wondered if it didn't cause him some inner conflicts at times. It would have to.

"How many?" Spencer had dealt out the cards, and he looked up at them with a half smile. "Dealer stands pat."

"Christ." Logan threw in his hand in disgust. "I don't know why I bother playing poker with you sharps. I always leave broke."

"Maybe you should play with the ladies."

Logan grinned at Jake's drawling comment. "I'll leave that up to you, Braden. You're a damn sight better at riskin' your scalp with irate females than I am."

"Not better," Spencer put in, "just a lot slower at learnin' not to tease tigers."

Logan laughed, and Sorenson looked up at that and smiled slyly. "Yes, I do admire your sense of initiative, Captain Braden. I'm rather glad I won't be along on this journey. It promises to be . . . volatile."

11

Galveston was nothing like New Orleans, and nothing like Angie had expected. She waved a lace-and-ivory fan vigorously to stir up a breeze, but the muggy heat enveloped her like a steam bath. Perspiration beaded on her face and trickled down her sides beneath the gown she wore, so that she felt hot and sticky and very uncomfortable.

A little wryly, she thought of how she had once longed for the heat instead of the cold winds of France. Now she complained! Thank God they were to stay here only one night, for she did not think she could bear much more than that.

Nothing Mignon had told her had really prepared her for this sweltering heat, but she refused to admit it when her mother gave her an ironic glance as she sat in the shade of a tiled patio that faced the sea. Palmetto fronds shifted slightly in a hot breeze that swept up from the Gulf.

"Are you enjoying Texas, *ma petite*?"

"It is very exotic, rather like India, I would think."

"No doubt." Mignon's gray-blue eyes narrowed slightly, and her fan moved with lazy deliberation back and forth so that loose strands of her pale hair shifted at the current generated. "Here, however, the tigers are two-legged instead of four, *n'est pas*?"

Her mother's glance beyond the hotel patio to the street drew Angie's attention, and she saw with a little frisson of disquiet that Jake Braden was there talking to some men. They were all garbed in rough clothing, and with another shock she saw they all wore weapons, even Jake. A leather belt slanted across his lean hips, and a holster hung at an angle, with the butt of a pistol lethally evident. It was more evidence of the expected dangers of their journey, and she shifted uneasily in her chair as she watched them.

"I thought we were to be escorted by the army," she murmured, and Mignon laughed softly.

"Army scouts. There is a huge difference between them, for the scouts are only on the payroll, while soldiers are bound by certain rules of conduct. But of course, since you are so determined to continue, it does not really matter, does it? I mean, Captain Braden is said to be very efficient so it does not matter if he is not bound by the same rules as the soldiers, does it?"

Another subtle dig at her, and Angie's lips tightened as she tried to ignore it. It should matter. It *did* matter, but she would not admit that to her mother. No, she had made her decision, and even if she had occasional doubts, once she was safely at her destination all of this would be forgotten.

Yet she could not help but think of the night before, when Jake Braden had held her so hard against him, his mouth ruthless and exciting, stirring unfamiliar emotions in her. Oh, he confused her so! She had thought for a brief moment that he must care something for her, but then he had bluntly informed her that he did not. And yet—and yet, she had recognized his desire for her, and she wondered if he was only being wary, as she had been.

Worse, she wasn't at all certain what she wanted from him. He left her feeling oddly restless inside, with that strange, aching need that nothing appeased. She knew all about sexual desire, but this felt different from what she had supposed it would be. Had she not observed Simone? Her cousin's encompassing passion for Jean-Luc had been disastrous from the beginning, an obsession that Angie certainly did not feel for Jake Braden.

Yet she had to admit he intrigued her at times.

Maybe it was because he was such a contradiction, an exciting blend of gentleman and rogue that she found inexplicably fascinating. Perhaps it was the turmoil he had stirred in her with his touch, the strange, feverish ache that had coiled in the pit of her stomach and between her thighs to render her incapable of protest or resistance, leaving her weakly yielding and simmering with restless need. Twice he had affected her like that, yet since last night he had barely even glanced at her.

This morning, when they were still aboard the steamer, he had been indifferent to the point of rudeness and all but directly snubbed her. Chagrined by his obvious rebuff, her first rush of wounded emotion slowly evolved into an angry humiliation that he would behave as if she did not exist.

Indeed, even now, when he glanced up toward the hotel and the patio enclosed by a low stone wall and greenery, he did not acknowledge her but turned back to the men with him. Burning with suppressed rage and embarrassment, Angie sipped at the glass of chilled orange juice a waiter brought her and vowed that she would not be so easy again. No, Jake Braden had best keep his distance from now on, for she would not allow him such liberties in future.

It was a little cooler when the sun set that evening, and clouds stacked up on the horizon in towering masses. Angie went up to her room immediately after dinner, leaving her mother and Bette to sit out on the patio.

There was no sign of Jake Braden, though his companion, a pleasant, polite Texan named Dave Logan, brought her a message from him, standing at her door as he delivered it.

"We'll meet you at the docks in the morning, ma'am," he said, smiling a little. "Everything will be ready for you, and we'll be in Corpus by tomorrow night. We'll go on from there to San Antonio."

"Mr. Logan, isn't it?" Angie returned his smile, though she was still irritated that Braden would send someone else instead of come himself. "Well, Mr. Logan, tell Captain Braden that I expect him to keep me better informed than he has been doing. Since I am paying his wages, I must be made aware of his plans."

Looking a little uneasy, Logan nodded slowly. "Yes, ma'am, I'll give him your message."

"Good. Please have the captain make all the necessary arrangements for our stay in Corpus as well, so that there is no delay."

Logan shifted from one foot to the other; he was tall and lean, and looked to Angie as weathered and tough as well-tanned leather. His brow creased in a slight frown.

"Ma'am, Captain Braden is no greenhorn at this. He'll take good care of you."

"No offense meant, Mr. Logan, but it's wisest not to depend upon the fallibility of others. I like to reassure myself that all details are attended to before I venture into unknown territory."

For a moment, it looked as if Logan would protest, but he just lifted his shoulders in a shrug and nodded. "Yes, ma'am. I'll pass along your message."

With a polite farewell, he tugged his hat back over fair hair that was still a little damp from the heat, and left. Spurs clinked softly as his steps faded away, and she closed her door and leaned against it. Why did she feel such a desire to needle Braden? It was futile and probably foolish, but it rankled that he was avoiding her so pointedly. As if *she* had done something wrong!

Left alone with her thoughts, Angie changed into a white lawn nightdress with no sleeves and a slender thread of violet ribbon gathering the bodice, cool and comfortable in this suffocating heat, then went to sit at the window that, thankfully, looked out over the Gulf and enjoyed a cool breeze through the open shutters. Lights spread out in a glittering necklace to form an arc along the streets below her hotel room, evidence of a thriving nightlife. Galveston had a certain charm to it, she thought, for the town itself lay like a Mediterranean cluster of whitewashed buildings staggered along the coastline.

If not for the rather rough-looking saloons such as the one directly across the street from the hotel, she might have thought herself in the south of France. Yet even the air was different here, the atmosphere charged with a raw tension, almost anticipation, that she had never found in Europe. Was much of America like this? So brash and new? New Orleans had seemed rather like a decadent, gracefully aging lady, but Texas was abrasive and fresh, a vibrant land teeming with promise.

She knew she could be content here, where the past was forgotten and the future was dazzling and exciting. It was what she had always dreamed of, after all, an independent land that would allow her to grow.

She sat at the window for a while as the night closed around the town and the breeze cooled her room, until finally she grew sleepy. Her room was small, so Bette slept in the adjoining room with Mignon, leaving Angie in cherished solitude. She was grateful for it. This would be the last night for several weeks that she would be able to enjoy such privacy.

She had turned out the light and gone to bed when a sudden burst of laughter drifted in her window to shatter the silence. Angie turned her head on the pillow. Voices wafted into her room from below, clear in the night air that had grown silent. A little annoyed, she debated whether she should close the window, but as she sat up, one of the voices was all too familiar.

"Hell, Johnny, it's your call. It won't be an easy ride."

"Maybe not, but after that trouble in New Orleans, I feel like I owe it to you."

In a little harder tone: "You did leave me holding the bag, I reckon."

"Well, it hardly seemed like the appropriate time to point out to the authorities that we were already well acquainted. I knew you would understand."

Angie could almost feel Jake's careless shrug as he replied that he understood it very well. "It was the easiest thing to do."

The faint, acrid smell of cigar smoke drifted into her open window, and she realized that the two men must be standing almost directly below her room. She slipped from the bed and moved softly to stand at the window. Even on the second floor, she could hear them as clearly as if they were in the room with her.

The man named Johnny spoke softly. "You know Benton is looking for you. He's been at the saloon all day drinking and bragging that he intends to kill you this time."

"He's welcome to try. I already warned him that if he throws down on me, it will be the last thing he does."

There was a lethal certainty in the drawling comment that took Angie's breath for a moment. Jake Braden sounded so . . . so deadly and unemotional when he talked about killing a man.

"I told him that you wouldn't back down, Jake. I don't think he believes me. In light of your recent problem with the law, I could take care of him for you."

"That was in New Orleans. This is Texas. I don't need anyone to fight for me."

"Aw, hell, Jake, I know that. Just thought I'd offer. It's been hard keeping the others from getting in it. Two of our men got into a scuffle with some of Benton's cowhands. Rod Jones and Sam Mason ended up in jail for the night."

"I should have settled this a long time ago. It's his tough luck he showed up in Galveston right now. I'm willing to let bygones be bygones, but not if Benton braces me."

"If it comes to that, don't wound him. Shoot to kill."

"I always do."

Angie could hardly believe her ears. Was he really talking about killing a man so coolly and casually? And this was the man who had embraced and kissed her, touched her so intimately . . . dear God, what had she been thinking?

There was a prolonged moment of silence, then: "Ah, hell, Johnny. I'll see you later."

"Where are you going?"

"Didn't you say Benton was across the street in the saloon?"

"He was."

"Then I might as well get this over with tonight."

"You going to throw down on him?"

"No, but I'll be available if he wants to give it a try. I'd rather do it now when I'm ready than have him come up on me when I'm not."

Pressing her palms against her flushed face, Angie felt slightly sick. Once, the thought of men who courted danger had been remotely exciting, but this was different, far different, from what she had thought it would be. This was killing he was talking about, not a chivalrous defense of his life or a heroic act. Murder—an ugly word for an ugly act.

She backed slowly away from the window, uncertain she could bear to hear any more. But then she knew they were gone, for the silence that fell was almost deafening despite the muted noise of laughter and music that came from across the street.

Sagging to her knees, Angie clung to the wide sill of the window and peered out. For a moment she saw nothing, then, as her eyes adjusted, she saw two darkened silhouettes outlined by the light from open doors across the street. The wood floor where the thin carpet did not reach to the wall was hard and oddly cold beneath her bare knees, but she did not want to leave the window to retrieve a chair, and so hung there straining in the darkness to see.

She recognized Jake's tall, lean frame as he was briefly illuminated by the light streaming out the door, then both men disappeared inside the saloon. Her heart was pounding painfully hard against her ribs, and her throat was dry. She wanted to call out, to scream for help before the devastating sound of bullets and death could occur, but she did nothing.

It seemed an eternity passed as she knelt there on the floor by the window. A tinny tune still plinked on a piano, and muffled laughter came from down the street. There was the smell of rain in the air, and the wind coming off the Gulf carried a salty tang. Her eyes began to hurt as she strained to see inside the half doors of the saloon, but she saw only a blur of light and shapeless forms.

Maybe this Benton had backed down. Relief began to seep through her when there was no uproar or gunfire, and she shifted position and rose slowly to her feet, stretching the cramped muscles in her legs. Thank God. What if Jake Braden was killed? She might not think very much of him at the moment, but she still did not want him dead. If for no other reason than because she needed him to guide her to New Mexico. Yes, of course, that would be the best reason to fear for him, for how would she—

The sudden staccato burst of gunfire startled a scream from her, and she whirled around to the window again. Oh, God, no! But as the shots faded into silence and even the piano stopped, she knew that whatever the outcome, there had been a confrontation. The smell of burned powder carried on the wind, stinging her nose. Voices floated toward her, and the sound of men running on wooden boardwalks was loud and excited.

Pushing aside the curtains, she leaned far out the window but could still see nothing. Then she heard a rapid, insistent pounding on her door and her mother's voice.

"Angelique! Are you all right? Answer me—"

"Yes. Yes, Maman. I am fine."

"Open the door. There were shots—"

"Yes, I know. I'm all right, I told you." She flung the words over her shoulder, and when she turned to look back outside, she saw Jake Braden and his companion exit the saloon and stand for a moment in a bar of light that fell across the boardwalk. There was a brief flare of light before a cupped hand shielded it, but not before she had seen Jake's face briefly illuminated.

Slowly straightening, she let the curtain fall back over the window. Then she walked to the door to open it for her mother as if she were in a dream, feeling dazed and sick.

Part Three

The Journey

San Antonio, Texas

12

Dust pervaded everything, insidious and constant, seeping into food and water and under Angie's clothing to leave her with a continuously gritty feeling that she was eager to wash off. A bath! A *real* bath in a big copper tub with hot water and thick towels, and food that was properly cooked instead of charred over an open fire or boiled in a pot. Tonight she would not have to worry about scorpions or other creatures crawling into her bedroll, or hearing the clicking warning of a rattle-snake and waiting apprehensively for it to strike! No, she would have a bath, and proper food, and a room with no desert creatures in it!

Yes, those were the first things on her list now that they had reached San Antonio at last, and as they rode through the rutted streets lined with a profusion of false-fronted wooden structures built almost on top of the more sturdy adobe buildings, she was impatient to reach their hotel.

As badly as she wanted the comfort of a bath and decent food and a real bed, she wanted to get away from Jake Braden.

Only once on the hot, long trek had he spoken directly to her, and that was when she didn't obey his orders. The scene had sparked lin gering resentment in her and left her smarting from the sharp lash of his tongue.

"I don't have time to mess with a spoiled brat, Miss Lindsay," he'd said flatly, to the amusement of his men and her great chagrin, "and if I have to put you over my knee to keep you from doing anything else stupid, I will."

"I wanted a bath, Captain," she had managed to say with all the dignity she could muster, but of course, he had completely ignored that.

"There's Indian sign all around us, and if you wander off alone from camp again, I'll make sure you regret it. From now on, everywhere you go there will be a man with you. And don't bother telling me again that you pay my salary, because you don't. I draw my wages from the U.S. Army, and that's who hired me to get you to New Mexico.''

Furious, she had realized that to continue the argument with him would only make her look foolish and contrary, and so she had shrugged with feigned indifference. But she had not forgotten it, nor had she forgiven it.

For the duration of the exhausting journey overland from Corpus Christi to San Antonio, she had focused instead upon the charming company of one of the cavalry officers with them. Tempe Walker was handsome and attentive, and had been the only man to offer even a partial apology for the brusqueness of the scout.

"He may not be very tactful, but he's a good scout and Indian fighter, Miss Lindsay. If Braden said there's Indian sign around, you can trust there is. And I'd hate for anything to happen to you out here.''

"Yes, Lieutenant, I agree that I should not have gone off as I did, but after all, I was almost in sight of camp and within shouting distance. I did not think it would hurt anything if I tried to clean off some of this dust.''

Grinning a little, Walker had betrayed his sympathy, but he'd only shaken his head. "Next time, ask me to stand watch for you. You won't have to worry about me seeing what I shouldn't. Just ask, Miss Lindsay.''

"Angie," she'd said then, smiling at him so warmly that a flush had spread from his neck to his eyebrows, making his eyes very blue. "Please call me Angie.''

Tempe Walker was her almost-constant companion from that moment, and if Jake thought anything of it, or even noticed, he didn't betray by word or action that he did. Indeed, he was rarely with their little caravan of two wagons and twenty riders, always going ahead to scout for sign of the Apache or riding with one of the other men.

A frown creased Angie's brow as she slanted a glance toward Jake and thought of that night in her hotel room in Galveston. She had heard the next morning that a man named Benton had been killed, just as Jake had warned he would be. Oh, she wished she hadn't overheard them, for then maybe she would not feel so . . . afraid. But she had, and it left her uncertain.

Now Jake rode just ahead, and a man introduced to Angie and her mother as Johnny Ringo rode beside him; they looked like part of their mounts, riding with the curious grace of men well accustomed to long hours in the saddle.

Johnny Ringo was an enigma, too, an educated young man who exchanged gibes in Latin with Jake—another shock!—yet was reputed to be an expert gunman. Still, in Galveston she had heard how casually he spoke of killing, as casually and indifferently as Jake Braden. They were both frightening men, but she had not mentioned to her mother why she was so uneasy. After all, she had insisted upon continuing and would not admit that she might have made a mistake.

At this moment, though they had finally reached San Antonio, where they would linger for a few days to rest and get new supplies, she was beginning to wonder if she *did* have what it would take to stay in this hot, arid land where danger lurked behind rock and hill—and even under stunted brush. Rattlesnakes lay coiled in the scant shade of odd-looking plants with spiked foliage, only the *brrrrt!* of their clacking coils sufficient warning before they struck.

Though there had been sign all around them—if Jake Braden was to be believed—there had been only one sighting of Indians, and those a scraggly band of Tonkawas more interested in food and blankets than scalps. Yet it was the tension, the constant expectation of danger and death, that she thought the most wearing on her nerves, and so it was with relief that they were finally in a town of sufficient size to feel safe for a while.

Angie was pleasantly surprised by the elegance of the accommodations in this combination frontier town and hub of the cattle industry; when they entered the lobby of the Menger Hotel, across the alley from the Alamo, where so many men had died defending Texas against the Mexican army, she felt as if she had stepped into a European hostel.

Equally delighted, Mignon—who had borne the trials of the journey with remarkable complaisance—announced that she did not intend to leave the city until she had a decent meal and a surfeit of clean linen.

"It is so charming here," Mignon observed with obvious relief, "and before we continue our journey, I must have sufficient repose. I have not slept well."

The stark white of the hotel's outer walls concealed unexpected luxury inside, with marble floors in the lobby, paneled walls, an exquisite rotunda with gold-and-white Corinthian columns, and two mezzanines boasting enormous paintings of western scenes and religious depictions. Overhead was a superb stained-glass ceiling that allowed prisms of colored light to dance across the floors.

"I can certainly understand why this is said to be the finest hotel west of the Mississippi River," Angie remarked when she and Bette were shown to the room they would share and she had collapsed on a four-poster bed hung with gauzy bed curtains. Ornate velvet-upholstered and marble-topped furniture filled the room, and the entire atmosphere was one of luxury and opulence.

Closing her eyes, she forgot for a moment the cramp of muscles long strained by hours and hours of riding in a roughly jolting wagon that not even a night's rest could ease. Had she ever had a moment without aching muscles? It didn't seem so right now. But after a hot bath—then she might feel human again, might feel as if she could go on.

It seemed that she had just closed her eyes when Bette was shaking her gently, saying that it was time to get ready to go down for dinner, that madame would be waiting.

"Oh, my—have I slept that long?" Angie rubbed sleep from her eyes but smiled as she stretched languidly. "I suppose I needed it—Bette! Is that a hot bath?"

Bette nodded, her dimples flashing as she held up a towel. "I knew you would want to soak a little before you must go downstairs, yes?"

"But yes, of course!" Delighted, Angie lost no time in peeling off her dusty, wrinkled garments and slipping into the tub, sliding down into the mounds of bubbles and hot, steaming water with a sigh of utter contentment. What absolute luxury, not only elegant rooms but bathrooms complete with hot water and bath salts . . . she might decide to stay here, she thought then with a slow smile as she lifted a puff of bubbles in her palm and blew gently.

It was rejuvenating, and even when she regretfully left the tub and slipped into a dressing gown, she felt the return of energy as she allowed Bette to style her hair.

"I like it up like this, yes?" Bette deftly twisted a loop of hair and pinned it with a jeweled comb, leaving artful curls to dangle in front of Angie's ears and over her wide, smooth brow. Angie turned her head to gaze at her reflection in the gilt-edged mirror.

"Yes, that looks quite sophisticated, Bette. I don't know what we would do without your talents. I am glad you decided to come with us."

The little maid smiled as she finished arranging Angie's hair, her small hands swift and efficient as she tucked pins and curls into place, then reached for Angie's corset.

"I am glad to leave France and come here, for it is an adventure. And perhaps one day I will go back home and marry André, if I have enough dowry."

"Are you betrothed?" Angie was surprised, for Bette had never confided in her, but the maid laughed softly.

"You will not be shocked if I tell you, but André was my lover. We did not have enough money to marry, so when I came with you here, it was to earn enough for my dowry. When I go back, we will marry in the village church, and I will look so beautiful and André will be so handsome.''

She held up the hated corset. ''Are you ready to dress now?''

Angie frowned. ''No, not the stays tonight, Bette. It is too hot here, and I feel as if I'm suffocating when I wear that thing. Will the gown fit without it?''

''But of course. You are so small, the envy of every woman who must wear stays to get into a gown at all. Here. I will show you.''

As Bette worked the buttons of the gown, Angie asked, ''What is it like, to love a man enough to take him as your lover?''

Shrugging, Bette fastened the last button, then smoothed the sleek lines of the gown and stood back to admire her handiwork and smile approval.

''Love is not always part of it. André was not my first lover, and he will not be my last. Oh, I love him, yes, but until we wed, I will please myself, as he does.''

A little shocked but unwilling to admit it, Angie lifted her shoulders in a casual shrug that mimicked Bette's gesture. ''My cousin should have thought as you do, and then she would not have been so wounded when that wicked Jean-Luc refused to marry her. Instead, she wed another man she did not love, and is miserable.''

''And you? What will you do? Have many lovers and enjoy life, or marry to be miserable?''

Angie laughed. ''Neither. I will do as I please, whether it is take a lover or marry, but if I do marry, it will be only to a man I love, not because I am forced into it.''

With a sly glance at Angie, Bette said in a dreamy sigh, ''Me, I would like to be with the so-handsome Captain Braden, if only to see if he is as strong and wild a lover as he looks to be.''

''Captain Braden!'' Angie's eyes narrowed. ''Why on earth do you want him?''

''You do not think he is handsome?''

''Oh, yes, I suppose he is good-looking . . . in a rough, crude sort of way . . . but much too offensive. Besides, he is a dreadful rake with tawdry taste in women.''

''Do you think so?'' Bette tugged at the lace edging of Angie's bodice, and a small smile touched her lips. ''Yet I have noticed him watching you at times. Yes, it is true. And once I heard him say to that nice-looking Lieutenant Walker that he was to stop sniffing after you like a dog . . . oh, do not laugh! It is true. He sounded jealous when he said it, so I think Captain Braden likes you.''

"If he does, he certainly has an odd way of showing it. Oh, no, Bette. I will not need the shawl tonight. It is already too warm."

Was it the truth? *Did* Jake Braden like her? Not that she really cared about that, of course, but still, it was interesting to know. She shrugged lightly, as if dismissing Bette's comments.

"Captain Braden cares only about his own needs, Bette, and no one else's. I would not like to be one of his casual mistresses. Besides, when I take a lover, it will not be a man who is so crude. And I may wait until I find the man I want to marry before I have sex anyway."

For a moment Bette did not respond, then she smiled a little wickedly. "Perhaps it is best to have both a lover and a husband, then you do not worry, heh?"

Though she laughed, Angie was still thinking about Bette's advice when she went downstairs to join her mother in the dining room. Why should she wed at all? Perhaps she *could* be daring and modern, and just take lovers. Once a woman married, she yielded all to her husband, her name and her independence, and became little more than his property, with no rights of her own. Even in America Angie had heard the protests of women as they struggled for rights that men took for granted. It wasn't just the vote they demanded, but the rights to their own bodies, and there were those intrepid females who commanded—and received— public attention for the injustice that was often visited upon women.

Angie had no desire to be one of those rather strident women who repulsed men and espoused the cause of equal rights for their sex, but she would join in the struggle and demand that laws be changed to reflect the changing times and roles of women in society. And why not? It was illogical to keep women downtrodden and at the mercy of the whims of their husbands.

"Angelique . . ." Mignon beckoned to her from the doorway of the dining room, and Angie crossed the marble floor of the lobby to join her.

"You look very lovely tonight, Maman," she said, and it was true. Mignon wore black again, but the gown did not at all resemble widow's weeds. It was sophisticated and sleek, and fit her closely so that she turned several male heads as they entered the dining room.

A little slowly, Mignon murmured, "But not as lovely as you do, *ma cher.* Without the modesty of the shawl, every man here is staring at you in that gown."

A becoming flush rose in Angie's cheeks, and she was glad that her mother had not reproved her for wearing it. The deep blue gown with the low-cut bodice was the one gown for evening that she had brought with her; she had filled the rest of the single trunk she was allowed with more sensible day dresses and undergarments that would be much more practical on the journey. Once they reached New Mexico, she could send for the beautiful gowns she had been forced to leave behind in New Orleans.

It was easy to imagine herself back in France tonight, Angie thought, for the dining room was elegantly appointed with snowy linen and heavy china tableware. Crystal goblets were kept filled with chilled champagne by unobtrusive waiters, and the food was superb.

Soon, all of the territories out here would be as civilized, Angie thought as she sipped her champagne, and then perhaps Maman would not be so unhappy. If San Antonio was already refined with such elegant hotels, she asked her mother, would not New Mexico be so as well?

"Not necessarily," Mignon replied with a shrug. "This city was settled over a hundred and fifty years ago by the Spanish, who have become quite adept at creating an oasis of civilization in barbaric lands."

"But is not New Mexico as settled? There was the war with Mexico for it, just as in Texas."

"Yes, but as in Texas, there are vast areas that are still primitive. You saw the land we traveled through as we came here, Angelique. Now it is still relatively flat, though arid, with predators and danger of attack by hostiles. There are entire regions ahead of us that have nothing but high mountains and ravines, where there is no grass and no water, and only the hot sun beating down—but you will soon see for yourself."

Angie frowned, then gave a little jump when a masculine voice behind her drawled, "Still trying to scare her out of going, ma'am? She's too stubborn to listen and it's too late to turn back now anyway."

"What would you know, Captain?" Angie looked up at him, and her eyes narrowed with anger. How dare he be so rude as to join their table without an invitation? And to mock her so openly? Why, he looked like a . . . an *outlaw*, appearing in the elegant dining room garbed in dark cord trousers and a gun belt instead of proper evening clothes. Over a red shirt he wore a vest of supple black leather. Gleaming silver buttons reflected candlelight, and though he held his hat politely in his hands, nothing could lessen the allusion to danger he embodied.

Angie's fingers tightened around the stem of the crystal champagne goblet, and her voice was tight.

"If you are afraid to continue the trip, please, by all means tell us now, sir, and we will replace you. That might be for the best, anyway, as I feel you are a disruptive presence."

Instead of being intimidated, Jake Braden shrugged.

"Suit yourself on that, Miss Lindsay. I'm sure you can find someone in San Antonio willing to escort you to New Mexico. You can always ask Lieutenant Walker.''

So. He *had* noticed! Bette had been right.

Angie smiled sweetly and murmured, "That is an excellent notion, Captain. Perhaps I shall discuss it with Tempe.''

Ignoring that, he turned to Mignon. "Ma'am, I came to tell you that Colonel Patterson would like for you to join him on the patio when you have finished your meal.''

"Colonel Patterson? He is here?'' Mignon looked a little flustered, but her voice was cool and composed. "Thank you, Captain Braden. Please inform Colonel Patterson that we accept his invitation and will join him when we are through.''

"Yes, ma'am. I'll tell him.'' His amber eyes narrowed slightly, making Angie think of a wolf as he looked at her. "While I don't want to scare you ladies, I'd like to suggest that you remain at the hotel and not go out. San Antonio can be a little rowdy at times, and it's not exactly safe on your own.''

"Really, Captain, you are in no position to tell us what to do while here,'' Angie said sharply. "We are hardly children to be constantly supervised!''

He studied her angrily flushed face for a moment with one brow lifted and his mouth twisted in a sardonic smile. "Then you ladies have a pleasant evening,'' he drawled.

"Oh, I am most certain we will, Captain, for we'll have a rest from your tyranny for the first time in a week!''

"Angelique . . .''

Mignon's gentle admonition only reinforced her irritation, but Braden did not even seem to notice Angie's comment as he politely inclined his head toward Mignon.

"Good night, ma'am. Miss Lindsay.''

As he walked away, Angie stared after him furiously. It was as if she hadn't spoken, for he'd looked right through her again, with the same polite indifference that he'd exhibited since Galveston. But at least she had *made* him look at her once, and he had been forced to speak directly to her, even if it was just to give her a veiled order.

She could feel her mother staring at her as she lifted her glass, and in a moment Mignon said softly, "That was very rude, Angelique.''

"Yes, it was meant to be. I am sorry, Maman, if it upset you, but there are times that man is so provoking.''

"I understand.''

"I'm glad you do, because I certainly do not know if I will be able to bear his company much longer. Surely there is another guide in San Antonio who can get us safely to New Mexico."

Mignon's brows lifted the smallest bit. "Yes, there is no doubt another escort available. Perhaps Colonel Patterson will have some suggestions."

Angie clenched her teeth. Why had Maman agreed to meet with this Colonel Patterson? But of course, probably so that he, too, could warn her about all the dangers on this trek to New Mexico. Oh, it was all so infuriating.

But when they were through with their meal and had joined Colonel Patterson on the lovely patio with lush tropical plants and hanging lanterns that bobbed small pools of light on the tiled floors and over comfortable chairs, he was exceedingly polite—and, to Angie's delighted surprise, most encouraging. After greeting her mother, he turned to her with a broad smile.

"How nice to meet you at last, Miss Lindsay. I am delighted that you are so eager to accept the responsibility of John's ranch. I admired your father greatly, you know."

"No, Colonel, I was unaware you knew my father." Angie took the seat he indicated while her mother sat on his other side, then met his smiling gaze with a blunt question: "So you approve of my decision to claim my inheritance?"

A lean, spare man with iron-gray hair and a neatly trimmed mustache, Patterson nodded.

"I do, indeed, Miss Lindsay. Ah, I realize that there has been some discussion about the advisability of your move to New Mexico, but I think you are a strong young woman quite capable of handling the rigors you may face. Captain Braden speaks highly of you."

That surprised her, and her brows lifted. "I cannot imagine that he would know too much about me."

"Perhaps not, but he did observe you on the journey from Corpus Christi, and he seems to consider you suitable for the occasionally rigorous life in the territory."

Again, she was surprised—and speechless. Mignon leaned forward to gaze steadily at the colonel.

"Colonel Patterson, we are flattered you have such faith in us, but perhaps you are unaware that Angelique has been gently reared. I fear for her safety once we are left alone in the primitive wasteland of New Mexico Territory."

Steepling his hands, fingers end to end, Patterson smiled indulgently at Mignon. "Fort Selden is not very far from the Double X, Mrs. Lindsay. I do not believe it was built when you were last there. New Mexico has changed in many ways. Have you heard of the Santa Rita? No? Though the copper mine is not as productive as it once was, it is still quite active. There are plans to enlarge it and make it the largest copper pit in America. Before you know it, all of New Mexico will be as civilized as New Orleans, maybe even Paris.''

Mignon's smile was taut and disbelieving. ''Forgive me, Colonel, if I seem rude, but I must inquire about this rather abrupt switch in views. Not too long ago, it is my understanding, you were against Angelique's going to New Mexico. Now you are all but saying the streets are paved with gold. May I ask why this sudden change of mind? What advantage to you will it be for us to be in New Mexico?''

''Maman!'' Angie stared at her mother. But Patterson only smiled again, a little wryly this time.

''I see that you are as blunt as ever, Mrs. Lindsay.''

''Did you think I would change so much in only twenty years, Colonel?''

Did Maman *know* the colonel? But of course, she must have met him before, when she lived here.

''No,'' Patterson was saying softly, ''I never thought you would change, and I was right. You are as lovely as ever. It is as if you have never been gone.''

A strange current passed between them that Angie did not understand, and then Mignon looked away. Two bright spots of color stood out on her high, sculpted cheekbones.

''You are as forward as ever, Colonel.''

''Not as forward as I should have been at times.'' His tone was a little harder now, and he flicked a glance at Angie before smiling slightly. ''Do not be alarmed by our conversation, Miss Lindsay. A long time ago, I tried to convince your mother not to leave. I was unsuccessful, so I cannot say I am sorry she has returned.''

Mignon's head turned back, and her voice was sharp. ''Then it's your fault we are here? Did you arrange things so that we would be forced to come? I refuse to be manipulated, Colonel Patterson!''

''No, this is no manipulation. I did my best to delay your arrival—though, if you want honesty, I think your daughter is doing the right thing by going to New Mexico. Despite the danger with renegade Apaches and Comanches still raiding and so unstable, the territory is a vital part of this country. It will be much safer soon. For everyone.''

''I find that difficult to believe.''

Colonel Patterson inclined his head, and his voice was softer now. ''I can well understand that. What happened so long ago was . . . difficult.''

Angie stirred uneasily. Her mother's hands were trembling, and she looked very pale except for the bright spots of color flagging her cheeks. There was much more that Angie did not know, that she had never suspected.

"Maman?"

"Angelique, if you would not mind, please give us some privacy. I have some things I wish to say to the good colonel that I would rather you not hear."

"But Maman—"

"Angelique! If you please!"

A little awkwardly, Angie rose from her chair, and she murmured assent as she left the patio. How strange that she had never really known her mother, but Mignon must have gone through things that still haunted her.

How could she have not known? But she could not have guessed that Patterson and her mother had shared things in the past. Disturbed, she moved inside and down the corridor, pausing, a little confused, when she did not recognize anything, and retracing her steps. Once more back in the lobby, she hesitated in front of an unfamiliar corridor to get her bearings.

"Miss Lindsay?"

Startled, Angie turned, and was relieved to see Tempe Walker in her path. The young officer smiled.

"You look kinda lost, Miss Lindsay."

"Yes, I suppose I do. Where am I?"

He grinned, and she thought how very handsome he was in his blue uniform. And his light blue eyes were so warm, smiling at her instead of being cold and analyzing. A groove deepened in his cheek when he grinned as he did now.

"This is the bar. Best in San Antonio, but a little crowded right now. If you'd like, I could escort you to the patio for a cool drink—"

"No. No, not the patio." She smiled to hide her stinging resentment that Maman was so secretive. Why could she not confide in Angie? Would it be so terrible to tell her daughter the truth that haunted her?

When Walker stared at her curiously, she managed a bright smile and a careless shrug of her shoulders designed to hide her dismay.

"Is there another place that we could go, Lieutenant? I have never been here before, and San Antonio seems like such an exciting town."

"Well . . ."

When he hesitated, she said quickly in a coaxing tone that rarely failed to work on susceptible men, "Oh, but I would so like to see something different, something uniquely American—nothing in Europe is like this, you know. It's so different here. . . . I want to go to a part of town that is exciting and gay, where there are lots of people and music and dancing—is there a place like that you can take me?''

Tempe looked like a man caught on the horns of a dilemma, and Angie smiled her prettiest smile at him, letting her eyes sparkle. He capitulated with an answering smile.

"Yes, I suppose there is. But perhaps you should bring along a chaperon as well, Miss Lindsay, for it won't look very proper if we go off alone.''

"Tut! I am a modern woman, Lieutenant, and do not need a nursemaid. If you do not want to take me, just say so.''

"No, no, that is not it at all. I just thought—never mind. Of course, I will be delighted to be your escort.''

Shut out by her mother, and in turmoil caused by doubts that going to New Mexico was right, Angie gave in to the reckless urge to act impetuously. Why should she always do what was expected of her? Besides, she would be leaving San Antonio in a few days. Why not see all she could?

Putting her hand on Tempe's arm, she looked up at him with her most provocative smile. "Good, for I feel *very* daring tonight. We must go where there is laughter and dancing. And we will stay out all night and dance until the sun comes up!''

"Miss Lindsay, I would like nothing better.''

As Tempe Walker escorted her from the elegant lobby of the Menger and out into the soft, warm night, Angie thought of Jake Braden's warning and dismissed it with a defiant toss of her head. He might know the trail and the terrain, but Jake Braden knew absolutely nothing about her.

Tonight, she would do as she pleased, for she was tired of everyone's telling her what she should and should not do. No one ever *asked* her what she wanted, or why. No, it was always a command, a warning, a rejection.

Well, not tonight.

And if Jake Braden thought his warning mattered, he would learn soon enough that it did not. Not to her. It would do him good to learn that she did as she pleased and that other men found her desirable. For even though Tempe stole glances at her bodice, cut so low over her breasts, she knew she would be safe with him, for he would never treat her as Jake did—nor did she want him to.

Angie found herself wondering what Jake would say when he found out that she had gone off with Tempe Walker, and if he would look at her differently then. A slow smile curved her mouth. Oh, yes, he would. She knew he would.

13

San Antonio had been settled by the Spanish in 1718, and though it was now an American town, Spanish influence was still evident in its red-tile roofs and white adobe buildings. As a hub of the cattle industry and a mail route center, it was a thriving town that lured a variety of visitors, not all of them respectable merchants.

In this section of San Antonio—a swath of one-story saloons and shabby hotels—gunfighters rubbed elbows with dusty trailhands, gamblers, and buckskin-clad frontiersmen all looking for the same things— strong whiskey and loose women. Music and laughter sounded harsh, a cacophony of sounds that filled the air.

Johnny Ringo leaned casually on a well-worn bar with a drink in his hand. Eyes that looked far too old in his young face surveyed the crowded saloon with idle reflection.

"Why is it that one sees the same faces in different saloons all over the West?"

"You talking about anyone in particular?" Jake asked.

"No, just a generality. See them?" He swept an arm out to indicate the room. "A teeming mass of humanity—and inhumanity."

Jake lifted a brow and shrugged. This was a part of the young gunman that he'd not grown used to, this tendency to moralize. Usually he didn't mind it, but tonight he was in no mood to get into one of the lengthy discussions of philosophy and morality that Ringo favored.

Ringo downed his whiskey in a single gulp and quoted, " 'When my love swears that she is made of truth, I do believe her, though I know she lies, that she might think me some untutor'd youth, unskilful in the world's false forgeries . . .' Shakespeare's third sonnet from the *Passionate Pilgrim.* Or part of it, at any rate."

Slamming his empty glass on the bar, Ringo motioned for the barman to fill it again. Then he looked at Jake with red-rimmed eyes and a scowl. "You don't drink fast enough, Braden."

"I do all right."

"Yeah." Ringo emptied his glass again in a single gulp, then wiped his hand over his mouth. "Guess you do at that. Tell me about this extra pay I'm supposed to get if I find who you're looking for."

"Patterson is authorized to offer a thousand dollars to the man who finds Nick Cooley. If you want to give it a try, report to Patterson."

"Yeah, I might just do that. That kind of money would come in pretty handy." Ringo frowned. "Why aren't you interested in going after him?"

"I've got something else in mind."

There was a moment of silence while Ringo studied the bottom of his whiskey glass, then he shrugged.

"I know I signed on to go all the way to New Mexico, but you don't really need me and I'm getting a bit restless. This isn't what I thought it would be. When Patterson first asked, I suppose I thought there would be more action. All we've done so far is play nursemaid to two French ladies who can't stand the sight of either one of us. Or of me, anyway. I think I'll give this Cooley a look-see."

"No problem here. I've got enough men signed on to get the ladies to New Mexico."

It was as Jake had figured it would be, and he wasn't sorry to see Ringo go. The young man was too explosive to keep a cool head under fire. He'd seen him go off half-cocked one too many times, usually when he was drinking as he was now. It had been Ringo who had precipitated the gunfight in Galveston, mocking Jack Benton until Benton lost his temper and went for his gun.

That mistake had cost Benton his life.

Jake preferred avoiding unnecessary gunplay for the simple reason that it was usually needless when threats or quiet intimidation worked just as well.

John Ringgold—or Johnny Ringo, as he preferred to be called—was too young or too reckless to consider either option.

Looking a bit relieved, Ringo shook his head. "Glad you don't object. I'd hate to get on your bad side."

"I don't have a bad side. Patterson doesn't pay me extra for that."

Ringo grinned. "I heard that after you mustered out a couple of years ago the troubles with the Apaches got worse, and Colonel Patterson convinced you to ride scout for a few weeks. The situation with the renegades must be worse than the papers back east report. Any truth to the rumor that white men are selling the Apaches those new rifles they're using to plunder half of Texas?''

"They're getting them from somewhere.'' Jake shrugged when Ringo looked at him quizzically. "Reckon one of us should just ask the next renegade we see where he got his fancy new Winchester and see what he says.''

Ringo laughed softly. "You do that. I'd be most interested to hear his answer.''

After finishing his drink, Ringo said he wanted to leave the saloon, and Jake walked out with him to stand outside in the night air.

"You going back to the hotel, Jake?''

"No. Not now. There's an old friend of mine in a little *cantina* that I want to visit while I'm here.''

"I'd bet a gold eagle it's a female friend, and I'd bet two gold eagles she's not old.''

"You might lose that wager.''

Shaping his hat between his hands, Ringo grinned and shook his head. "Maybe . . . but two weeks ago I would have bet that ten-dollar gold piece that you and Miss Lindsay would end up between the sheets, too.''

"That would be a sure loss.'' Jake eyed him coolly. "As you said, Miss Lindsay can't stand the sight of me.''

"That's just what she pretends. Hell, a blind man could see that all it would take from you is a word or two. I've seen that look in a girl's eyes before. Once, I saw it directed toward me. But that was a while back, before . . .''

Ringo's eyes narrowed, and his mouth thinned into a taut line as he glanced up the street. Light slanted across his face from inside the open saloon door, and he shrugged and pulled on his hat as he looked back at Jake.

" '*Odi et amo.*' Right now, hate's at the top of the list. I'll see you in the morning, Jake.''

As Ringo walked away, Jake stood in front of the saloon and listened to the noises around him. Beyond the lights it was dark; he could smell the San Antonio River only a short distance away. He stood at the edge of the boardwalk that was no more than a collection of rough planks that would be washed away by the first good rain, then moved down the street to a familiar *cantina*.

As he drew near the music grew louder, and out on the open patio next to the *cantina*, shouts and laughter rose to mingle with the throbbing beat of a guitar. Dusty vines thickly covered an open lacework of crossed willow limbs to form a roof over the patio. Fragrant white flowers spiced the air and looped over the edges of the roof.

Jake pushed through the low gate and went onto the patio to stand just inside the small enclosure. It was more open here than it had been in the closed-in atmosphere of the saloon, where the only women were dance hall girls or whores. In the *cantina*, matrons garbed in modest skirts and blouses sat beside young, dark-skinned girls with low-cut blouses and bare legs.

Jake made his way to a rickety table in the corner that afforded him a view of the patio and entrance.

A fiery brandy, *aguardiente*, was brought to him by one of the serving girls, who said her name was Juana and gave him a sultry glance along with the drink.

Jake smiled when Juana bent low, displaying her breasts beneath the gathered top of her *camisa*. He gave her a generous tip, and she scooped it up quickly to tuck into the waist of her skirt.

"Muchas gracias, señor."

"De nada." He looked around, then back at the smiling girl to ask in Spanish, "Is Lupe here?"

She lifted her shoulders in a shrug. "Perhaps."

Jake held out another coin, and when she reached for it, he leaned forward to tuck it into the top of her *camisa* between her breasts. "Tell her that Diego is here to see her, pretty one."

With a languid smile, she moved away from his table and disappeared into the adobe building next to the patio. Jake settled back in his chair, tilting it on the two rear legs as he propped a boot against the table and sipped his drink. The music had grown loud. Guitars throbbed with the familiar ecstatic music that he'd always known. Beyond the crowded tables, he glimpsed several dancers.

One of them seemed new at it, and a little clumsy. A long *rebozo* swathed her from head to foot, so that all he could see was her back as she stood laughing on the hard-packed dirt floor. His gaze shifted to her companion and his brow rose as he recognized Tempe Walker. One of Patterson's men, the lieutenant was adept but too cautious. If they'd run into any real trouble on the way from Corpus, that hesitation could have caused some problems.

As he sipped the potent liquor, Jake's gaze shifted back to Walker's companion, and this time his eyes narrowed with recognition. The voluminous cloth *rebozo* had slipped a bit, and beneath the folds of draped material he saw lamplight glint off copper curls. Dark blue satin flashed, and the fringed shawl slipped even lower as the girl turned in a graceful twist of her body.

Angie Lindsay . . .

A flash of fury ripped through him. The little fool—and what was Walker thinking, to bring her here!

Laughing, Angie accepted the offer of a drink from a thick brown bottle, recklessly lifting it to her lips as did the others, choking a little on the fiery liquid. Walker was immediately at her side, solicitous and much too friendly as he put an arm around her shoulders and bent to whisper in her ear.

Whatever he said was rejected, for Angie only tossed her hair and gave Walker a sly glance as she shook her head in obvious refusal. Combs holding her hair had loosened, and long tendrils dangled around her face and down the nape of her neck. She was flushed, and looked a little drunk, whether with excitement or whiskey, Jake wasn't at all sure. Whichever, he'd better get her out of here before she did something she would regret.

Jake pushed away from the table and rose to his feet just as the guitars began a lively melody and a black-eyed young man began to stamp his feet in the dirt. It was the *jarabé*, a peasant dance from Mexico, and apparently Angie had been learning the steps, for the man pulled her into the center of the small area and urged her to dance.

She stood still for a moment, glancing around her, then lifted her shoulders in a shrug and laughed. Slowly, her young, slender body moved to the impetuous strum of guitars as if she had been born to the music of the Spanish gypsies. Dancing in the center of the patio, her hair alone would have defined her in the crowd of dark-haired observers, but even more striking were her soft, pale skin and the curves displayed by her French gown. It was the same damn gown she'd worn on the steamer, much too provocative for the modest ladies in Texas. But then, Angie Lindsay was much too provocative. With her parted, seductively curved lips and the unsophisticated yet sensual rhythm of her body, she appealed to every man there, and they all watched her with rapt, intent fascination.

The wild, pulsating music switched to a *corrido*, and as her feet found the rhythm her arms curled upward over her head and her body swayed in a tantalizing rhythm; violet eyes half closed, there was a dreamy expression on her face. She danced with utter abandon, irresistible, sinuously writhing, and there wasn't a man there who didn't want her.

Including him.

He glanced at Walker; the man looked as if he had been poleaxed, standing and staring at Angie as if he'd never seen her before, and there was a look in his eyes that Jake knew well. Angie Lindsay was playing with fire, by God, and either didn't know or didn't care what she started. She looked as if she had been dancing the *corrido* all her life. She looked as if she waited for the arrival of a lover. Damn her, he thought without rancor.

As the primitive, earthy music soared, the young man began to dance with her, his smoldering gaze fastened on Angie's face and body as he moved with limber agility under the light from flickering lanterns. Silver glitter sparkled on the lapels and collar of his short jacket, and a snowy white shirt emphasized his dark skin. He moved around her warily, feet stamping with loud accentuation against the floor, and Angie swayed toward him, then away. Her pale arms twined upward to touch the Mexican lightly on his shoulders, then she whirled away in teasing rejection. The steps were a barnyard ritual, the mating dance of two animals, a seduction and invitation.

Jake's eyes narrowed. Damn little tease. In a few minutes, one of the hot-eyed Mexican men watching her would accept her blatant invitation, and Walker, being the gentleman he was, would protest in defense of her honor. The result would be inevitable, and the situation could have only one ending if he didn't stop it.

Angry now, as much at himself for allowing her to go this far as he was at her, he moved through the crowd. After a glance at his face, the spectators parted to allow him through. The next time Angie whirled around, her face flushed with damp heat and her hair tumbled into her eyes, he snared her by one arm.

Halting with an angry gasp, her eyes widened when she recognized him.

"How dare you—release me at once!"

"So you can continue making a fool of yourself? Come quietly and everyone will think leaving is your idea."

She tried to jerk free, but he held her arm above the elbow and tightened his grip so that she gasped with pain and rage as he escorted her from the dance floor under the curious eyes of those watching.

High spots of color flagged her cheeks, and she hissed through her teeth, "Let go of my arm or I'll scream!"

"Is that the only threat you can think of, Miss Lindsay? It's gettin' kinda old."

"I'm getting tired of you following me, Captain Braden! Is that all you have to do? If you'd wanted to be included in our company tonight, you should have just asked us. I'm certain the lieutenant would have been able to find a more polite excuse to refuse than I could!"

Ignoring that, he pulled her with him toward Tempe Walker. The lieutenant had the good sense not to protest, but a muscle leaped in his jaw when Jake told him curtly to go back to the hotel and report to the colonel.

"Patterson might be interested in hearing your reason for bringing Miss Lindsay into the *barrio* like this, Lieutenant Walker."

"He might." Walker's tone conveyed more than just irritation. "I'll escort Miss Lindsay back to the Menger before I report to Colonel Patterson."

"I think you've made enough bad decisions for one night. Patterson should be at the Cattlemen's Rest by now. Report there."

Walker bridled. "Look, Braden, you're not in the army and I'm not on duty. You don't need to be giving me orders."

"You take orders from me or answer to Patterson. It's your choice."

For a moment, Walker looked as if he'd say more, but then with a tight jerk of his head, he turned to Angie. "Miss Lindsay, Captain Braden will escort you back to your hotel, it seems."

"No!" Angie wrenched free from Jake's grip, and he didn't try to hold her. She flung herself at Walker and put her arms around his waist as if she was used to being with him. The lieutenant's arm went around her shoulders, and she gave Jake a smug smile before tilting back her head to look up at Walker. "I have no intention of being left with *him* when I came here with you, Tempe."

"I'm afraid I'm outranked at the moment." Walker shot Jake a hostile glance. "My orders were to obey commands from Braden, and if I don't, I'm liable to be court-martialed for disobeying my commanding officer. I have no choice."

"That's ridiculous! I shall talk with Colonel Patterson myself, and tell him just how high-handed and *unreasonable* Captain Braden is being."

Her eyes glittered with fury as she turned to him with her hands on her hips, and Jake cut her off before she could begin what was obviously going to be a tirade.

"Make a scene here, Miss Lindsay, and you'll wish you hadn't. I promise you that."

His flat warning had the desired effect of silencing her. Though she glowered with banked fires in her eyes, she did not protest when Walker pivoted on his heel after a curt nod and little bow in her direction, then stalked from the *cantina*.

"So what are you going to do now, Captain?" Angie demanded tartly when the lieutenant had gone. Her chin thrust upward, and her eyes were bright from the liquor and anger. "After all, you cannot arrest me. I cannot be court-martialed like Lieutenant Walker, nor can you control me."

"I wouldn't be too sure of that."

Angie gave him a quick, uncertain look. "I'm growing weary of your threats, Captain."

"Too bad. Get your *rebozo*. You're leaving."

He saw the storm clouds gathering in her face and in her eyes, and cut her off again.

"You can leave willingly or unwillingly, but you will be leaving here, Miss Lindsay."

Her eyes sparkled dangerously. "You brute! Do you think it makes you more of a man to order me around? It doesn't. It only proves that you are a tyrannical bully, as I've said since the first day I met you."

"Ma'am, it doesn't matter to me what you think as long as you do what I tell you."

He handed her the woven *rebozo*, but she shoved it away. "It's not mine. I borrowed it when I became chilled."

Impatient now, Jake growled, "Then give it back to its owner so you can leave."

She arched a brow and gave him an infuriating smile. "Certainly."

When she turned to hand the shawl to a young woman sitting nearby, Jake heard his name called, and looked back over his shoulder to see Lupe coming toward him.

"Diego! Ah, Diego, it has been so long since you were last here . . . and look at you now, so handsome! It is too long since you have come to see Lupe!"

She spoke in Spanish, and he replied in that language, grinning at the large, matronly woman he had known most of his life. Streaks of gray flecked her dark hair in places, and her round face and dark eyes beamed with pride and love as she embraced him.

"And you are still the most beautiful woman in my life, Lupe. When will you leave that worthless husband of yours and marry me?"

Lupe laughed hugely, and kissed him on the cheek before she drew back a little to look up at him. "Always, you have asked me that, and my answer is still the same—when you ask me and mean it!"

"I always mean it."

She cuffed him on the arm playfully, then her glance moved past him to Angie, who had come up behind them and stood waiting with obvious resentment.

"Ah, is that why you have come back to see old Lupe, to bring me your wife and make me happy?"

"No, she is not my wife."

"Diego, you must not let her get away. She is pretty, it is obvious, but also sweet, eh?"

"Until she opens her mouth." He glanced at Angie and saw the bright spots of color in her cheeks. "But we are being rude, Lupe, for she does not speak Spanish."

In English, he said, "Miss Lindsay, this is a very good friend of mine, Lupe Martinez."

"How do you do, Mrs. Martinez."

Angie's polite stiffness was waved away at once by Lupe. "We are not so formal here, Miss Lindsay. Please, call me Lupe. You both must eat—no, no, I insist. I have not seen Diego in too long, and I cannot let you leave before Carlos comes back. He has not gone far and will be back soon, eh? Now come. What shall I feed you? You have grown too thin, Diego. I can see your ribs."

"Miss Lindsay has to return to her hotel right now, Lupe, but I will return later to visit with you and Carlos."

"Ah, Juana, you slow girl," Lupe said in Spanish when the barmaid passed them, "tell Rosario that I want a bottle of our best wine brought out, and he is to take special care with the food, for this night we have a special guest."

Juana's gaze slid past Lupe to Jake and lingered. A slow, sultry smile curved her mouth, dimming a little when she chanced to meet Angie's narrowed glare. With a lift of her brow and a toss of her dark head, she dismissed Angie.

"Yes, I met Diego earlier. He is very special."

Jake grinned back at Juana when she smiled at him with bold impudence. "And you are very beautiful, love," he replied in Spanish.

"Bah, Juana, you stay away from him. Can you not see he is with a beautiful woman?" Lupe scolded.

A little sulkily, Juana lifted her shoulders in a shrug. "She is not so very beautiful. I think she is too pale, like goat's milk. Besides, if she is not his wife, she cannot be very proper or she would have a *dueña* with her, is it not so? No unmarried woman goes out without a chaperon unless she is a whore."

"Juana! Go to the kitchen and do what I tell you. Have Rosario prepare his finest food, you wicked girl. And do not keep making eyes at Diego like that or I will tell your papa where you go at night when you leave here, eh?"

With a sly glance at Jake, Juana said as she left, "Perhaps later I will tell *Diego* where I go at night. . . ."

Lupe fired a volley of reprimands at the dusky-skinned girl that seemed to be largely ignored, then turned to say in English, "Forgive my niece's rudeness. I will return. If I do not go and tell Rosario myself what I want served, it will not be done. But you will come back later to see me, Diego, yes?"

"Yes, of course."

Lupe's gaze shifted to Angie, and though there was uncertainty in her eyes, she said with innate courtesy, "You are welcome to return tomorrow, Miss Lindsay. A good friend of Diego's is always welcome in my home and my heart."

A wicked gleam lit Angie's eyes as she smiled. "Diego will want to visit with you alone, I am certain, but it is so pleasant here, and the music is lovely. Perhaps tomorrow I shall accept your kind invitation and return."

Lupe beamed. "*Bueno!* Then come tomorrow to see me."

Jake walked Angie across the crowded patio and through the gate, then halted at the edge of the street to spin her around to face him.

"What the devil do you think you're doing, Miss Lindsay?"

"Accepting a charming invitation, of course. We are going to be here for a few days, are we not?"

"That doesn't mean you can wrangle an invitation under false pretenses."

"Excuse me, *Diego,* but you are the only one I know who is acting under false pretenses by using the wrong name."

His jaw set. "Diego is Spanish for James, my given name."

"Is it? How intriguing. Yet you go by Jake—an alias, perhaps?"

"A nickname, Miss Lindsay. Like Angie for Angela."

Violet eyes smoldered up at him with resentment. In the soft light of the hanging lanterns, she looked beautiful and desirable. Her hair shone with vivid copper lights, and the smooth, pale skin of her throat and shoulders gleamed with ivory translucence.

She had the mouth of a courtesan, a tempting swell of lower lip emphasized by the shorter upper lip to give her a sultry sensuality. He found himself remembering how she had tasted, and the soft texture of her skin beneath his mouth, like heated velvet.

Damn Patterson for allowing her to come out here. Angie Lindsay was a woman who belonged in Paris, New York, maybe even San Francisco, but not out here, where it was dangerous and too unstable. If he had any sense, he would ignore the colonel's command and send her back east.

Angie's chin tilted upward, squaring so that the cleft in the center deepened with stubborn rebellion.

"If you will just procure me a rented hack, I will get back to the hotel on my own," she said shortly. "I do not need an escort."

"You don't know what you need."

"And you think you *do* know what I need?"

"Don't tempt me to say what's on my mind, Miss Lindsay. You won't like it."

"You are always coming to conclusions about me, but you are rarely right. I'd like to know why you think you know so much!"

"Observation."

He steered her across the street, his fingers around her arm above the elbow. They were halfway across when she pulled away from him to whirl about in the middle of the hard, rutted street. Light from open doors and windows slanted across the road and glinted off her hair.

Anger radiated from her, somewhat diluted by a curious vulnerable quiver of her lower lip.

"You don't know anything at all about me, Jake Braden. Nothing."

"Don't I?"

"No. No, you don't. You think you do. Oh, yes, I see it in your eyes and hear it in your voice, but you don't know *anything* about me, about what I want or why—so don't presume to tell me I don't know what I want."

"Then tell me—what the hell *do* you want?"

She stared at him, while behind them music and shouts of laughter thickened the night air. Tension vibrated between them, heavy and rife with silence. She made an aborted motion with one hand, lifting it, then shrugged her shoulders helplessly.

"I don't want to fight with you. Since we're going to be so close together in the coming weeks, couldn't we declare a truce, or just stop quarreling all the time?"

Jake moved toward her again, taking her by the arm to pull her with him to the side of the street and into the enveloping shadows that loomed under the overhanging eaves of a two-story building. He stared down into her upturned face with narrowed eyes. She was shivering, and her eyes were huge dark pools in her pale face.

"This isn't the place for talking, Miss Lindsay, and it isn't the time."

"No." She drew in a ragged breath. "No, it isn't. But you should not treat me as a child. I'm not a child, I'm a grown woman, with the emotions and perceptions of a woman."

"Then you need to act like one. A grown woman doesn't pout like a child when she doesn't get her way."

Her mouth set in a taut line, and she made no comment when he took her by the arm again to walk her down the street. It was late at night, and no rented hacks came into this section of San Antonio—not surprising, since it could be dangerous. He'd take her to his hotel and get her a hack from there to the Menger.

"Where are we going?" she demanded sullenly when they passed through a narrow alley near the river. A cool breeze washed up, smelling of dank, musty air. She shivered. "This is not the way Tempe brought me down here."

"Maybe not, but it's the way you're going back."

She said nothing else until they reached his hotel, an out-of-the-way hostel on a back street that he preferred to the more crowded lodgings where the others were staying. It was small but clean. Whitewashed adobe walls rose to a red-tile roof, and tubs contained bright flowers that spilled over in fragrant profusion. A rectangle of light streamed through the open door onto the wood-planked boardwalk outside. Music from a *cantina* next door played, softer than that in the *barrio* but just as wild.

Jake hailed a one-horse hack, and it pulled up in front of the hotel and stopped. He turned to Angie, who stood with her arms folded over her chest and her chin squared.

His eyes narrowed. He'd thought the brisk walk in the cool night air would sober her up, and it had. But she was no more tractable than she'd been before.

He opened the hack's door and held it for her.

"This hack will get you back to the Menger, Miss Lindsay. I suggest you get some rest."

Raking her with a critical eye, he frowned when she made no move toward the vehicle.

"I have no intention of returning to my hotel this early, Captain. I have been cooped up in a jolting wagon for the past week, forced to eat dust and drink tepid water and listen to your insults at every mile. I wanted a night out in San Antonio so I could forget that you exist."

"Then you should have chosen the place and companion more wisely."

"Should I? If Lieutenant Walker is so unacceptable, why did you hire him as my escort all the way to New Mexico? Ah, I see that you have no answer for that." Her mouth curved in a mocking smile. Music from the *cantina* next to the hotel grew louder, a soaring melody. She glanced toward it, then back at him. "I'm too restless to sleep tonight. I want to listen to the music and I want to dance. I don't want to go back yet."

He knew it was a mistake, but he was tired of arguing with her. Besides, maybe it would do her good to exhaust herself. After the long day they'd had, it shouldn't take much more to tire her. Jake relented with a shrug.

"All right. But when I tell you it's time to stop for the night, I don't want any argument."

A genuine smile curved her mouth. "Why would I want to argue with you, *Diego*?"

14

Why shouldn't she have a good time? Angie thought with mounting rebellion. Especially since it irritated Jake Braden. Oh, it had been all she could *do* to hold her tongue earlier, when he'd said such insulting things to Lupe about her—but worse were the things that bark-faced girl, Juana, had said. Incensed, Angie had pretended she did not understand Spanish, for she would have told that sluttish girl *exactly* what she thought of her!

Perhaps she should have gone back to the hotel, but it was so obvious Jake was in a hurry to return to his little slut that perversely, she'd insisted upon staying. What surprised her was that he'd agreed.

Sliding a glance toward him where he sat with his back to the wall and facing the door, she wondered what he was thinking. Beneath the brim of the low-crowned black felt hat he wore, his face revealed nothing. It never did. Only his eyes ever gave away what he might be thinking, and they were so unreliable. The harsh angles and planes of his face reflected only what he wanted her to see. Most of the time he was so cold and aloof that she never knew how to react.

Even now, he seemed closed in on himself, his eyes wary, as if he waited for her to do something unexpected. Perhaps she should end his wait.

Rising from the table, she wasn't surprised when he moved swiftly to grasp her wrist.

"Where are you going, Miss Lindsay?"

"I can't see the dancers from here. Isn't that why I came? Besides, you won't let me drink anything but water, and you're just glowering at me, and this is hardly what I had in mind when I said I wanted some excitement."

Swearing softly, Jake rose to his feet. *"Mierda!* All right. Stick to watching. I don't want to have to fight off any overzealous admirers."

Angie didn't answer, but when they reached the circle of dancers, she deftly eluded Jake's grasp and stepped into their midst. She glanced over her shoulder at him and laughed softly. So he still would not react? Instead he watched her with an ironic smile touching the corners of his hard mouth.

It was only when she met his narrowed gaze that she read the warning there and turned away with a shrug.

Angie was welcomed into the circle of dancers. It was a Mexican waltz, the *chiapanecas*, and she took an inside position in the double circle. Joining hands with the man next to her, she put her free hand on her hip as she saw the other dancers do. It took a moment for her to learn the steps, but she mimicked the dark-haired girl in front of her and was soon stepping and swinging her feet in time to the music.

Stamp, step, swing. They kicked and clapped their hands, and her partner grinned as he introduced himself.

"I am Pablo Ortega. You learn quickly, *señorita*—"

"Lindsay, Angela Lindsay."

"Ah, it is as if you have always danced."

"I have, but not like this."

A little breathless, she allowed him to grasp her around the waist and swing her into the next position, and caught a glimpse of Jake Braden's face. He was watching closely, leaning against a post that held up the low roof. One hand rested on his hip, the thumb tucked into his belt, and his shoulder was braced against the post that was nothing more than a shorn tree trunk. He held a drink in his free hand, and though he looked relaxed, there was an air of coiled tension about him that betrayed his annoyance.

Reckless, still stinging from his earlier comments and the insults directed at her, Angie ignored him with blithe unconcern. Let him stew. What could he do? Besides, it was not as if she was in danger, and everyone here was having a good time. Why shouldn't she?

"Caramba!" her partner exclaimed when she tossed her hair and stamped her feet with greater enthusiasm. "You are too beautiful to be here alone. Are you with that man?"

"Yes. But don't let him bother you. He means nothing to me."

Dark eyes gleamed appreciatively as he smiled at her, and his teeth were white in his dark face. "He does not bother me, *señorita,* but I had to ask. He looks so fierce at you that I thought he must be your husband or *novio.* I do not want to be shot by your husband, no?"

She laughed and glanced at Jake. "I am not married."

"*Bueno!* Husbands can be jealous. And me, I would be jealous of you whether you were my wife or not. You are the most beautiful woman here."

There was an intensity in his face and voice that put her on guard, and she avoided his eyes and focused instead on the steps of the dance. When the *chiapanecas* ended another dance began, this time the lively *jarabé* that she had learned before.

At once, Pablo pulled her into the center of the dance floor, and as if in a dream, her feet found the rhythm and her body moved to the driving tempo. She thought of the mulatto girl, Eugenié, who danced with such divine grace and sensuality, and who had kept all the men at the St. Louis Hotel in New Orleans entranced with her beauty and fire.

This dance was earthy, primitive, as old as wine and just as intoxicating. She felt drunk with the feeling of power it gave her, saw the shining admiration in the eyes of the men and women around her as she turned and twisted, her loosened hair tumbling down around her shoulders in a fiery mass that reflected the light from lanterns.

For the first time, she understood why the Gypsies danced, why they cast off all inhibitions and put such emotion into their music and its pulsating rhythm. It was a release, an expression of the soul put to music. She felt like an artist with an empty canvas . . . the compelling need to create, to share the beauty, obliterating everything but the moment.

Her body moved of its own volition while her feet kept pace with the rapid, thrumming beat of the guitars. Now the rhythm of the *corrido* soared into the air, and she moved as she had seen the others do earlier, her body swaying and her arms curling upward over her head, alternately teasing and rejecting. With eyes half closed, her face damp from heat and effort, she danced in the very center of the crowd, her mouth curved in a sensual smile. Her movements were uninhibited, provocative, and enticing.

"*Dios mío,*" Pablo muttered, and his black eyes glittered with hot lights as he gazed at her hungrily. "You are too beautiful! A goddess!"

Angie heard him as if from a distance. At first she had danced to irritate Jake, but now it was for the dance itself, the wonderful release gained from moving her feet and her body, losing herself in the throbbing beauty of the music. Why had she not known? Perhaps it was this land, this wild, untamed, savage land, that had given her the courage and the need to respond with such primal emotion. For she could forget everything when caught in the spell of the music and the dance, and concentrate only on the driving urgency of the guitars and the growing awareness of her own body.

Her glorious hair was like a living flame around her pale shoulders, and the deep blue of her gown was a vibrant blur as she turned and twisted, her breath coming in short pants for air.

At last the dance ended, and she paused for a moment, her face flushed with misty heat as she struggled to regain her breath. Then she saw Jake, his dark face impassive as he moved toward her.

"It's time to leave, Angie."

She heard him in a blur, but shook loose his hand when he took her arm. "No. I am not ready to leave. I'm having fun, and the night is still young."

"I have somewhere else to go, and you've had enough fun for the night."

He sounded impatient, the cold indifference clipping his words and infuriating her with the reminder that he had to go back—to meet Juana, perhaps? Angrily, she shrugged.

"Then go on! Leave me here. You're not my keeper."

"No, but I am responsible for you. Leaving without you is not an option. Christ, I knew better than to let you talk me into coming in here, but I thought you'd keep your word."

Chagrined, and feeling a little guilty, she pushed the hair from her eyes to look up at him. His eyes were narrowed and hard, like pieces of yellow flint, and she flinched from the contempt in them.

"I didn't actually give my word."

It was the wrong thing to say, and she hadn't really meant it. Her promise had been implied, and she knew it. But before she could retract her careless statement, his hand shot out to grab her by the arm again, and this time he jerked her from the dance floor in a single angry tug.

"I would not do that, *señor*," Pablo stepped in to say softly and with definite menace. "The lady has said she does not want to go."

When Angie turned, she caught a glimpse of Jake's face and was frightened by the violence she saw there. There was a cold warning in his eyes that anyone could see, yet the man Pablo was ignoring it. Her heart thudded with dread.

"No, no, it's all right." Angie looked at Pablo with an uncertain smile. "I want to go with him—"

But Pablo put out his hand to her, stopping when Jake caught his wrist and held it. Their eyes clashed, black with gold, both fiercely intent.

"This is none of your business, *amigo*. Go back to your *aguardiente* and leave the lady to me," Jake said softly.

Angie shuddered. Though he hadn't lifted his voice, it held the same dangerous threat in it that she had heard that night in Galveston, the ominous warning that the man named Benton had ignored. Now this man was ignoring it, and she wanted to scream a warning at him to retreat before it was too late.

As Jake released his arm, Pablo shot her a dark look. "Is he your brother? Your *novio*?"

A little desperately, she shook her head. "You don't understand. I came here with him."

"But he is not your husband, no?"

"No, but that does not matter. Please—"

"Angie." Jake pushed her to the side, his voice low and impatient. "Get out of the way."

The two men faced each other like . . . like predators, or like wary wolves circling stiff-legged before a fight, and panic rose in her that something terrible was about to happen. Jake looked so calm, but there was a taut wariness in his lazy posture that contradicted his composure.

In an almost casual gesture, Pablo's hand dropped to his side, his palm resting on the butt of a pistol. His mouth twitched beneath his mustache, and his voice was a soft challenge.

"She has said she wishes to stay, *señor*. She may stay with me, but you will leave."

"When I leave, she goes with me. And I'll shoot the first man who tries to interfere."

The music had stopped, and Angie could hear the faint shuffling of feet and a few gasps at Jake's words. For an instant no one at all moved, then chairs were overturned and the dance floor cleared as those watching got out of the way.

Oh, God, she couldn't move, could only stand as if mesmerized as they stepped apart, bodies braced and legs slightly bent at the knees, both men looking dangerous and deadly. Why didn't somebody stop them?

Pablo stared at Jake, his black eyes narrowed slightly and his body tense. Angie wanted to scream but was afraid to distract either man. The tension stretched unbearably, until she thought she would snap with the strain of it.

Why didn't they *say* something? Or why didn't someone interfere and halt this before it was too late? God, she had underestimated Jake Braden, never thought he would actually challenge this man as he was doing—and it was obvious Pablo Ortega had not expected it, either.

A faint tremor ran through Ortega's body as he returned Jake's cold, hostile stare. He licked his lips, and his hand quivered above the butt of his pistol in nervous indecision. Doubt flickered on his face, followed by chagrin.

Then Pablo slowly straightened, and as if someone had pulled a cord, the tension evaporated. He stepped back with a glance at Angie, and shrugged.

"If she is yours, *señor*, you need to take better care of her. Another man might not see reason."

Jake took Angie by the arm. His muscles were corded beneath the red cotton shirt he wore, his hand hard on her.

Without a word, she allowed him to escort her from the *cantina*. She stood shivering in the suddenly chill night air outside that smelled of dust and damp.

"Jake—Captain Braden, I didn't mean—"

"You meant every bit of it, Angie Lindsay, and don't bother trying to deny it." He was furious; she saw it in the taut slash of his mouth and the opaque glitter in his eyes. "It would have suited your vanity just fine to have two men draw on each other because of you, wouldn't it? Never mind that one of them would most likely be killed, because you're just looking for some fun tonight. Would that have been entertainment enough for you? Should I go back in there and call him out? He may have backed down once, but he probably wouldn't back down twice. His pride wouldn't let him. Is that what you want—more fun?"

"That . . ." She licked suddenly dry lips, frightened by the ferocity in his eyes and words. "That isn't fair. That's not at all what I wanted, and you know it."

"No, I don't know it. All I heard was you whining about how you wanted to have fun tonight. I was right about you. You're a spoiled brat, Angie Lindsay. I'm glad John isn't alive to see it."

Without thinking, she whipped around and slapped him, a hard blow that left the white imprint of her fingers against the dark skin of his cheek. The sound seemed to reverberate in her ears, but Jake didn't move or flinch. He stared down at her with silent fury. His eyes froze into chips of ice, and his gaze raked over her from head to toe, making her instinctively cringe.

Suddenly she wanted to run, afraid of what he might say or do, but there was no place she could go, and he would catch her anyway if she tried. She lifted her chin.

"Leave my father out of this."

"You ever hit me again, and you'll regret it," he said softly. "That's twice. Don't push your luck."

She believed him. Her anger dissolved as quickly as it had flared, and she stared up at him with her thoughts in turmoil. It was true that she had taunted him this evening, still piqued by his rejection of her. Perhaps it was the strong drink. And now she cringed at the thought that she had behaved so childishly and petulantly. It wasn't a very flattering image she had of herself at the moment, and she tried to regain some of her dignity.

"I shouldn't have hit you. . . ."

"No. You shouldn't."

Shadows flickered across his face as the door to the hotel opened and closed. Music had started in the *cantina* again, and a dog barked somewhere close by.

"Jake, I'm sorry. I was wrong tonight."

The words tumbled out before she could take them back, and she realized that she wanted to say them. It was true, and honesty compelled her to the admission.

"I behaved badly, and you have a right to be angry."

He looked surprised and a little wary. "It's late, Miss Lindsay. Your mother is probably worried about you."

"Maman is already in bed, I am certain. Bette gives her medicine every night to help her sleep."

She stood awkwardly, and unbidden came the memory of how he had touched her that night on the steamer, his hands and kisses ruthless and demanding. Despite the wary distance he kept between them, he had not been able to hide the fact that he wanted her—and wanted to do more than just kiss her. He'd said harshly, "I may want you, Angie Lindsay, but it won't be moonlight and roses once it's over. . . ."

She should run, but instead she felt weak and strange, shivering more with reaction than because of the cool air that swept up from the river. It was frightening, losing control of her emotions as she did with him, to want his touch, his mouth on hers, and the heated turmoil he created when he caressed her as he had . . . yet she craved it, wanted to hear his husky voice in her ear again, muttering her name as he held her so tightly.

Her heart pounded with fierce reaction, and her throat was suddenly dry. Every nerve in her body tingled; she felt a sharp awareness of him and of her own vulnerability, her own need. The tension between them was so thick it was almost palpable, and she wondered distractedly why he did not feel it, too.

"Jake . . ."

He reached for her, and there was a taut set to his mouth. "Don't say it. For Chrissake, Angie Lindsay, I'm as close to the edge as a man can get. Do us both a favor and get as far away from me as you can, because I don't make any promises about being gallant and gentlemanly if you don't. Ah, *Christ*!"

She leaned into him, undone by the suppressed violence in his words and tone, by the raw need she saw in his face. His arms went around her. She should retreat, she knew it, but she felt the thudding race of his heart beneath her palm and the tension in his strained muscles as he held her against him, and didn't.

Then it was too late anyway, because he was taking her with him into the hotel. They passed through the empty lobby that was little more than a foyer, and down a shadowed hall lit by a single dim lamp on the wall.

It was warm and stuffy in his room, shrouding them both in intimacy and shadows. Jake lit a small lamp and turned to look at her. She felt his eyes move over her, and wondered awkwardly what she should do now.

A little dazed, she regarded him with shy hesitation. "Jake, I—"

"Hush, Angie." He came to her, his hands oddly gentle as he cupped her face in his strong, brown hands and looked into her eyes. Her heart thudded loudly. His eyes were so warm, like molten gold, with dark pupils that reflected the faint glow of the lamplight. Smoothing his thumb over her mouth, he bent to kiss her, and she closed her eyes.

Blindly, she returned his kiss. He kissed her for a long time, until some of her tension eased and she kissed him back. His hand moved to the back of her neck, fingers tunneling through her unbound hair to lift it from her nape and drape it over her shoulder, gentle and caressing. Then he kissed her again, this time with his tongue easing between her lips to explore her mouth.

It was potent, heady, the heat and the taste of him stealing through her body to render her pliant and yearning. She wanted what he would do to her, needed to feel him hold her, and needed to feel his strength against her. From the very first, when she had seen him across the ballroom floor in New Orleans, she had somehow known that he would be the one to make a difference, to remove the barriers of caution and reserve that had always kept her so indifferent to the seduction of others.

It was as if she had waited for him all this time.

And now he awakened her with his hands over her breasts and down the curves of her body, caressing her through the thin satin of her gown until he finally grew impatient.

"Let's get this off you," he muttered, and unfastened buttons and hooks with the deft expertise of a lady's maid.

Angie's arms were still around his neck, and she shivered as he peeled away the gown to let it puddle to the floor at her feet. She wore only her shift beneath, and it clung damply to her skin so that she felt exposed.

When he took her with him across the room to the bed, she thought suddenly of Cousin Simone and how desperately in love with Jean-Luc she had been. All those stolen hours alone, and later Simone had come back to whisper to her of the things they had done, things that then had sounded far too ludicrous to be true. Surely no one did that sort of thing, and she had tried to envision Maman allowing a man to touch her in the places Simone had claimed men liked to touch, but had not been able to manage it.

Now she was allowing Jake Braden to touch her there, to lie beside her on the mattress and touch her breasts through the thin silk of her shift. She might just as well have nothing on, for the sheer material clung to her as if a second skin, hiding nothing.

Jake's dark head bent, and he covered her nipple with his lips, drawing it into his mouth with heated pressure. A spear of heat flashed through her, coiling in her belly and making her strangely restless. She whimpered softly, but he did not stop, and oddly, she didn't want him to stop. It felt—it felt as if there was much more to come, as if the fire he ignited would consume her if he did not continue, and she arched toward him, her hands moving to tangle in his hair and hold him to her.

Wet silk cooled when he lifted his head, and when she would have murmured protest he moved to her other breast, his tongue circling damply around the taut, beaded nipple beneath the silk. The fire was hotter and higher, and a pulse throbbed between her thighs with urgent insistence.

Oh, God, what was happening to her? She wanted something but didn't know what would ease this restless, driving need that filled her, and her hands moved aimlessly over him, skimming the cool leather of his vest, touching the crisp black hair on his neck, then curling into his shirt to hold him.

He sat up suddenly, and she could hear that his breath was harsh and ragged. He stared down at her in the dim light, his face shadowed, and he silently lifted her hand to his mouth to press a gentle kiss in the cup of her palm. Holding her eyes with his, he kissed each finger, and the fiery torment eased a bit as he pressed his mouth to her wrist.

Thank God he knew what to do, how to allay her silent fears. Slowly, with infinite patience, he worked his way up her arm, nipping gently at her skin until he reached her shoulder. He pressed his face against her neck, his breath warm and making her shiver as he teased her ear with the tip of his tongue.

He kissed her temple, then her brow, before working his way down the slope of her cheek to her mouth to linger a while. His mouth found the rapidly beating pulse in the hollow of her throat, then moved even lower to her breasts again until she was quivering with helpless anticipation.

Then he kneeled over her and pulled away the last vestige of modesty she wore, removing the silken shift and her stockings and tossing them to the floor. She wanted to cover herself with her hands but remained still, fists curled at her sides and her body afire.

"God . . . angel, you're beautiful."

The husky sound of his voice was a caress, and the sweep of his eyes as potent as the stroke of his hand, and she trembled.

Suddenly his hands moved to touch her between her thighs, gently but firmly, and she moved instinctively to stop him.

"Lie still, angel. I won't hurt you. You know I won't—"

She did know, but it was difficult lying there naked when he was still fully dressed, letting him explore the hidden valleys of her body with his fingers until she began to burn beneath his touch. The peculiar thrumming was in her stomach again, and her nerve ends were so sensitive she cried out when his hand swooped over her belly to come to rest on the nest of red-gold curls between her thighs.

His head was bent so that all she saw was his dark hair and his shoulders, his hands moving between her legs with fiery persuasion to explore that secret recess. She trembled when he stroked the inner folds, and a new fire ignited. He glanced up at her once, his face fiercely intent, and he dragged his thumb over the aching center of her need so that she cried out softly.

Elusive release hovered just beyond her reach, and she didn't know how to reach it as she quivered and strained toward him, toward the searing strokes that took her ever closer.

When the explosion came it was shattering, and she moved with artless ecstasy against his hand, barely hearing his murmured coaxing as her thighs clamped over his hand and delicious shudders undulated through her entire body.

A soft sob tore from her, and she whispered, "Oh, Jake, oh God . . . it feels so good. . . ."

"Yes, angel." He bent and kissed her, then said softly against her mouth, "And it gets better."

She laughed weakly. "I don't think it can."

"It can." He gave her a look that burned like dragon fire. "Oh, it can, sweet angel. This is only the beginning. Here. Touch me now— no, don't pull away. There's nothing to be afraid of, and it's too late to stop now anyway. . . ."

He was right, and yet it was so difficult to force herself to touch him. His shirt was unbuttoned, baring his chest, and he took her hand and pressed it against the warmth of his dark skin. Ridged muscle bunched beneath her palm, and she felt him tense when she spread her fingers over his belly. With one hand, he unbuckled his gun belt and unbuttoned his pants, and with his other hand, he dragged her hand lower. His skin was hot beneath her questing fingers, and after a moment she moved her hand away.

He laughed softly. "There, that wasn't so bad, was it?"

"No." She bit her lower lip.

Averting her face when he shrugged out of his vest and shirt, she heard the metallic clink of his buckle as he laid his gun belt on the small table beside the bed. Then he stood up, and she closed her eyes with something like panic as he kicked off his boots and pants.

Oh, God. Oh, God . . . it was moving so fast, and she didn't know if she was ready for this, didn't know if she could do what she'd been told was done. Oh, all these contradictory sensations inside her left her so confused, the coalescing need that had been gathering in her for weeks still so new and raw . . .

The mattress dipped with his weight, and she felt him move over her again, stretching out beside her like a great bronzed cat, his body like heated iron next to her. He was facing her, and took her chin in his palm and leaned forward to kiss her again. She didn't move, trembling when his hand moved to her breast in a light caress.

After a moment, his head lowered and his tongue flicked out to circle her nipple, raking across it in erotic strokes that made the breath catch in her throat. His hand continued to tease the tight peak of her other nipple, twisting it between his thumb and finger until she moved restlessly. The relentless throbbing escalated between her legs again, and she pressed her thighs tightly together to ease it. That only heightened the torment, and as if he knew what she felt, Jake drew her nipple into his mouth with a strong, rhythmic tug that sent a spear of heat through her and increased the ache to an unbearable pitch.

She moaned. "Jake . . . don't. I don't think I can—"

"Hush, angel. You can. You can. . . ."

His soft words were lost in a haze of new sensations, and she forgot what she meant to say. It was all so different from what she'd thought it would be, and the first flush of embarrassment at being naked with him had melded into this strange, overwhelming sense of urgency that made her want to explore it all, to test the limits of this newfound sexuality that seemed so wonderful and so frightening.

And now he was drawing her other nipple into his mouth, and the urgency grew higher and tighter, as if a silk rope were being twisted inside her, and she arched into him with soft little moans. Her body felt so heavy, so raw, that the lightest touch sent shock waves through her.

Just when she thought she would explode from the tension that gripped her, he paused and looked up at her, and his eyes were heavy-lidded with passion, glowing like hot embers beneath his thick fringe of lashes. Holding her gaze, he took her hand again and drew it slowly down over the hard, hot muscles of his chest to his belly. She felt his muscles contract beneath her palm, the dark curling fibers of hair tickling her as he dragged her hand lower until she caught her breath.

Oh, he was so different from what she had imagined, hard and hot, yet strangely soft, the texture like heated velvet beneath her palm. He held her hand on him, his eyes closed and a tautness making him vibrate with strain, then he slowly moved his hand away.

Her fingers curled around him, testing the length and width, slowly moving up and down in a light exploration that made the blood beat faster through her veins. He throbbed in her clasp, and she heard him draw in a sharp breath between his clenched teeth when she tightened her grip.

"*Jesus . . .*"

She looked at him from beneath her lashes, at the shadowed angles of his face that had always seemed so hard and forbidding. He wore an expression as if he was in pain, and his jaw was set, a muscle leaping as she moved her hand in a gliding caress.

Now she grew bolder, wanting to touch him, wanting to be as familiar with his hard, bronzed body as he was with hers. She explored his flat, muscled belly with her fingers, then up to his sculpted chest, fingers raking over nicks and scars, some small and others long and raised.

"God, Angie," he muttered in a groan when she moved back to clasp him again, and this time he stilled her motion with his own hand, holding it.

With a sudden, swift movement, he pushed her onto her back and moved over her, his knee shoving her thighs apart. In an act of arrant sensuality, he put his hand between them to position himself, then braced over her, a hand on each side of her as he looked down, and she saw the rapid rise and fall of his chest. His weight pinned her to the bed, and she felt the hard, impatient nudge of him between her spread thighs.

Heart clamoring, she knew from the intensity of his eyes that he would not wait any longer. Poised, his heated length slid inside that first little bit, until she felt an unbearable pressure and moaned. He bent quickly to stifle her moans with his mouth on hers, a hard, savage pressure that distracted her from the invasion between her legs.

He kissed her with ruthless possession, until she forgot for an instant what would happen next. And in that instant, he thrust forward, sheathing himself inside her with a swift, devastating intrusion. Her body arched upward and she cried out against it, but it was over so quickly the brief pain was a memory almost as soon as it was a reality.

Panting, she lay quietly when he lifted his head to look down at her. His features were sharp with tension, but his words were gentle.

"That's the worst, angel. I promise. No more pain."

Not quite believing, she closed her eyes, and in a moment he began to move inside her again, this time with slow, certain strokes that overpowered her halfhearted resistance. The exciting haze that had enveloped her earlier had been vanquished by that sharp, searing pain that had disappeared so swiftly.

Now he kissed her again, his tongue exploring her mouth as his body moved in and out of her with erotic friction. It was not the exquisite, thrumming pleasure of earlier, for it was still too new, too raw, to be pleasurable, but after a few moments the pain was gone, replaced by mounting expectation. Her hips arched to meet his driving thrusts, and she put her arms around his neck and synchronized her movements until they moved together in perfect rhythm.

How strange, to think that not long ago she had not even known he existed, and now they were as close as a man and a woman could be . . . had he done this with Eugenié? The unknown Anna? But of course, he must have, and she felt a sharp, blinding jealousy that they had known this with him, too.

No, she didn't want to think of that now, not when he was holding her so fiercely close. And he had made it all so wonderful instead of frightening, so he must care about her, maybe even love her, or he would not have been so careful and tender. . . .

Instinctively, as Jake's movements increased, she moved with him, until she thought of nothing but how he felt and that he muttered soft endearments in her ear, called her his angel, *querida,* darling—and then dimly, as if from a great distance, she heard his harsh mutter, felt him stiffen, and then slowly he relaxed atop her, lowering his weight on her briefly before he rolled to one side, still holding her in his embrace.

Angie lay quietly as her heart gradually slowed to a normal pace, but the strange restlessness still filled her. Was this all? Wasn't there supposed to be some—some grand finale? She felt his eyes on her and was suddenly shy. When she looked away, he laughed softly.

"I hope you don't think that's all there is to it for you, *pequeña,*" he murmured in a lazy tone, "for it isn't. It just takes time for you to enjoy it as well."

"How much time?"

A little disgruntled that the high expectations she'd held were so quickly dashed, she didn't really expect him to understand, but oddly, he did.

"Sweetheart . . . look at me." He pulled her face about with a finger under her chin when she did not move. A little smile tugged at the corners of his mouth, and he looked at her with something close to tenderness. "God only knows why, but women are made so their first time isn't that special. Not like this was for me, anyway. But next time, this will be much better for you, I promise."

Her heart clutched. *The next time!* Yes, there would be another time, and he was right—it would be much better. She knew it would. With a sigh, she rested her head in the hollow of his shoulder and arm, and he held her against him, his arms around her so that she felt safe and secure. It was somehow renewing to lie with him like this, as if they had been lovers for years.

Soothed by the regular thud of his heartbeat beneath her ear, she slowly relaxed. So this was what it was like to know a man, this sense of intimacy that was much more fulfilling than the physical act itself. It was nothing like she had thought it would be. Nothing Simone had told her had really prepared her for it. But then, perhaps it was so different because Jake was so different from Jean-Luc. Yes, that must be it. Why else would she feel so comforted? So relaxed and even sleepy? Though it was late and she knew she should go back to the hotel, she closed her eyes for just a few moments of sleep. . . .

It seemed like hours, but it could only have been a little while before he stirred, and Angie muttered a sleepy protest when he urged her awake.

"You need to go back to your hotel, Angie. Come on, angel. Co-operate with me. . . ."

She did, slowly and a bit clumsily, letting him wash her off with tepid water from the basin and pitcher in his room, blushing a little when he dragged the rough cloth between her thighs with tender care. He helped her dress, kissing her when she protested, and knelt on the floor to roll her white silk stockings up her legs.

When she stood up she was wobbly, and he steadied her with a faint smile. "I'll get dressed and take you back. God knows, I'd like to keep you here all night, but there would be hell to pay in the morning."

Morning. Yes, when light came, she would have to face him again, and she wondered how she would feel. How *he* would feel. Would he regard her more intimately now? Or would he do as Jean-Luc had done to Cousin Simone, and reject her?

She shivered, and he muttered that she should have known better than to come out without her shawl.

"It may be hot as hell in the daylight, but at night it gets cool."

Jake took her back to her hotel, telling the driver of the hack to wait as he walked her into the lobby. Thankfully it was dark, with only a single desk clerk on duty, and he had his back to them as they stood in the shelter of a potted palm.

Cradling her chin in his palm, Jake said softly, "Go straight to your room, Angie. No point in starting trouble."

But later, when she had slipped unnoticed into her room and into bed, she lay looking up at the darkened ceiling as the first pearly fingers of dawn brightened the room, and she wondered if trouble had not already started.

15

They were two days out of San Antonio, and Angie had to admit that though riding horseback was not as comfortable as traveling in a wagon, it was quicker. On a good day, they could make twenty-five miles. And she felt so much freer riding astride instead of perched off balance in a sidesaddle!

While in San Antonio they had purchased divided riding skirts and blouses of lightweight cotton, and she loved the relative freedom of these far more practical garments; at first, Maman had been a bit scandalized, but she was bearing up well under the changed circumstances.

Poor Bette, who had never ridden a horse before, found it difficult to walk by the end of the second day when they made camp in a small hollow.

"You'll get used to it," Dave Logan told her, and his eyes crinkled with amusement when Bette wailed piteously in French that she would die first. "Reckon I can get the gist of that without knowing exactly what you said, ma'am."

His eyes moved to Angie, and she shrugged wearily, too hot and tired and thirsty to comment. Riding in this arid land was much different from the pleasant jaunts she had been accustomed to in France, where they donned elegant riding outfits and paraded their horses in the park.

"After today, you ladies are gonna care for your own mounts," Logan said, looking at them a bit warily from the corners of his eyes as he pretended to study something on the horizon. "Tom Spencer and I can show you what to do, if you need us to."

Angie stared at him. "May I ask *why* we are expected to groom and tend our horses, Mr. Logan?"

"Well, ma'am, Braden seems to think that it's important for you to

know how, just in case you ever need to take care of them yourself."
He cleared his throat and looked down at his dust-covered boots. "No
telling what may happen, and if we ever got separated from one of you
ladies, it'd be pretty necessary for you to know what to do with your
horses."

"I see. Survival learned by feeding a horse or eating one?" Angie
said sharply, and almost laughed at Logan's quick, pained glance at her.
"Is this supposed to teach us self-reliance in the desert?"

"No, ma'am, but if you get caught out here without knowing anything about your mount, you'd be afoot before you could say gopher
hole." Logan's mouth twisted. "Maybe I picked the wrong time to tell
you, since it's the end of a long day."

"Maybe, Mr. Logan." Angie smiled, and Logan grinned back at her.
She threw up her hands, asking a little wryly, "Will tomorrow be soon
enough for these new lessons?"

"Yes, ma'am, I reckon it will." He touched the brim of his hat with
one finger, nodded at Mignon, and after a lingering glance at Bette,
moved away to join the men, who were setting up the remuda.

Angie watched him go, and saw Tempe Walker look up and in her
direction. When he met her gaze, he nodded, then looked away, and she
flushed. Had he told all the others, or kept it to himself, that he had
seen Jake return her so late to her hotel?

It was most unsettling, but Tempe Walker had confronted her late
that next day; his voice was bitter as he regarded her with brooding
blue eyes.

"If you'd just told me that you were trying to make Braden jealous,
Miss Lindsay, I wouldn't have made a fool out of myself trying to
protect your honor," he'd said.

For a moment she had not known what to say, then she managed to
ask if that was how he'd gotten the black eye and split lip.

"It looks so painful—was it a terrible fight?"

"Do you really care about me, or are you more worried about your
lover?" he asked harshly, then looked away. "If that's it, don't worry.
He looks a hell of a lot better than I do right now."

Chagrined, she'd put a hand on his arm to comfort him, but he'd
jerked it away, staring down at her with dark shadows in his eyes.

"Better not let Braden see you around me. I'm liable to end up scouting Apache country on my own if he gets his back up about it."

Since then, he had avoided her, and while uneasy, Angie was also
resentful. How dare he behave as if she had wronged him by preferring
Jake? He had no claim on her, and though she *had* flirted with him, she
flirted with many men. Out here, it seemed that men took things so

seriously, when a Frenchman would have shrugged his shoulders, smiled a wry little smile, and moved on to the next woman he fancied.

Maman did not know what Angie had done, of course, but Bette, who had slept in her room, often looked at her with a sly, knowing glance that made Angie wonder if the little maid had been awake after all when she had come in so late. Probably so. It was obvious to her that she'd changed, and she felt as if everyone must know she was no longer the naive virgin she had been only a few days before.

God, she felt like a completely different person. The mystery was gone, the wondering what was out there for her, and who. Yet there had been few words exchanged with Jake since that night, and those only pleasantries, as if he was a stranger instead of the man who had initiated her passage into womanhood.

That's how she thought of it: a passage from untutored child to experienced woman. She thought suddenly of Simone, and how happy she had been at first with her Jean-Luc, and wondered uneasily if her cousin had felt the same optimism before her love had been so cruelly betrayed.

But this was different. She was not betrothed to another man, and Jake Braden was definitely not a fortune hunter like Jean-Luc had been. No, he had been so gentle with her, so considerate, and she knew he would never do to her what Jean-Luc had done to Simone.

It was still very hot when she spread her blanket on the ground near the fire, and Angie wondered where Jake was and why he had not tried to see her again. Their only contact had been in the company of others, a fact she found frustrating, though he had not seemed at all bothered. Indeed, he had been as distantly polite to her as he had been to her mother—even inviting Mignon for a ride ahead of the others—and it infuriated her.

But perhaps he was only trying to protect her, and she thought then of Pablo Ortega and of how he had been so ready to draw his gun and fight over her. If Jake had exhibited the least weakness or reluctance, no doubt shots would have been fired. She knew that. She knew that the only reason Pablo had retreated was because Jake gave him no edge. His hard competence daunted all but the most obtuse of men, it seemed, and she could understand it, for he had frightened her that night with his cool nonchalance, as if he killed a man every day.

Perhaps he did. She'd heard rumors, and wondered if they were true. Sitting around the fire at night, when Jake was gone with Logan or Spencer or one of the other men, out scouting for Indian sign or doing whatever it was he did, the men talked among themselves, lightly for the most part, but sometimes about Jake, as they did this night.

Tom Spencer, a short, laconic man with a droll sense of humor, mentioned that Braden once rode with the Comanche.

"War paint and all, the way I heard it," he drawled, and leaned forward to spit a stream of tobacco juice into the dust.

"Aw, Spence, you're fulla"—Dap Higdon paused, glanced at the women, and ended—"buffalo dust. If Braden rode with the Comanche, he wouldn't be an army scout."

"No? There's plenty of Injuns riding scout for the U.S. Army these days. Takes one to find one, they figure, and since Braden knows 'em better'n most, he must have rode with 'em." Tom Spencer's eyes crinkled at the corners, and his leathery face creased into a broad grin. "Wouldn't be too surprised to look up one day and see Braden ridin' in to camp in a 'clout and feathers, scalps dangling at his belt."

"But surely he wouldn't do that," Mignon exclaimed in obvious shock, and Spence just shrugged.

"Ain't likely, but ain't impossible, ma'am. Don't get me wrong—Braden's no show-off. But he ain't the kind of man to back down from a fight, either. He's got a reputation as a fast gun, and I ain't never knowed one of them to back off from anything or anybody."

Angie shivered. She knew that well enough. Hadn't she seen him meet a challenge? Heard him say he wouldn't back down? And that man in Galveston was dead, just as Jake had said he would be if he kept pushing.

It was Bette who leaned forward with eyes wide and voice a little breathless to ask, "But is Captain Braden one of these so-savage Comanche?"

"Hard to say, ma'am. Looks like one. Acts like one when he has to—but I don't reckon he is at that. He's too blamed civilized to be part savage."

"That's just *your* opinion," Tempe Walker said quietly, and all eyes turned to him for a brief moment. No one said anything until Angie spoke up.

"I think it would be best if we changed our topic of conversation, Mr. Spencer. It seems to upset some of us."

Tempe didn't reply, but his jaw set and he got up to walk away from the fire.

I don't care! Angie thought angrily. Let him be angry with me. He is making it so obvious that there is ill will between him and Jake, and these men are not stupid. Neither is Maman! I will not be forced into a position that I may be compelled to defend—not yet. Not until I have a chance to talk to Jake . . . or should I call him Diego?

Diego—Spanish for James. Was he Spanish or Mexican? Despite

their intimacy, she felt as if she did not know him at all, as if she did not even know him well enough to ask such questions.

She didn't know whether to take Spencer seriously or not, but it wasn't too difficult to imagine Jake half-clad and wearing war paint, for he looked like an Indian with his dark, bronzed skin and thick black hair. She remembered that Henri Delacroix had said contemptuously that Braden was a half-breed, with a Mexican father and Comanche squaw for a mother. Was it true? And did it really matter to her if it was?

Restless, and filled with growing uncertainty, Angie wished she felt comfortable enough to really talk to him.

But there never seems to be the right time, she thought resentfully, for always there are people around. We have not been alone since that night at his hotel. How can I speak to him without betraying to others how . . . how *close* we have been?

It was too awkward, and Maman would certainly guess the truth. No, perhaps it was best to be discreet for now, though it was ridiculous that she must feel so dishonest.

Heat shimmered in the air, blurring the rocks that still reflected sunlight, but as the sun began to drop the air grew a bit cooler, and purple shadows settled over the vast, flat land studded with mesquite and greasewood. They were camped in the shelter of a cottonwood grove; a thin trickle of water cut through shallow banks and nourished the trees.

Mignon left the camp and moved toward the creek, the hem of her riding skirt lifted above the dust. She chose a flat rock at the edge of the water. Pickerel weed poked up through the shallows, the arrowhead-shaped leaves cupping remnants of the brush of blue flowers. The slender stalks swayed slightly as the sluggish current flowed around them. Night slowly settled on the land. It was dry now, but a rainstorm could swell this narrow stream to a torrent in shockingly short time, sending it crashing through shallow banks and sweeping along everything in its path. Flash floods were all too common, and terrifying, in this arid land.

Mignon had seen more than her share and had never forgotten them. Ah, it was all so long ago; she should have been able to forget the nightmares by now. But she had not, and Colonel Jim Patterson had not let her forget those she wanted most to put out of her mind.

Her hands clenched tightly in her lap, and for a moment she forgot her sore muscles, unaccustomed to so many hours on a horse, and the worries about Angelique—she remembered instead the terror of those months, when she had felt so alone and mortal. John should have protected her, should have listened when she told him how frightened she was, but he had thought only of his land, not their lives. It wasn't until she'd almost lost hers that he'd realized how fragile life could be, and then it was too late. By then, she knew that she could not remain in New Mexico one more day.

If not for Jim Patterson—Captain Patterson then—she might well have lost her life so long ago.

Closing her eyes, Mignon shivered. How raw and savage this land was, ruthless and merciless, taking everything if one was not vigilant.

Why had she allowed herself to be persuaded to come back here? Surely, she could have found a way to convince Angelique not to continue, but it had all seemed so hopeless once Monsieur Gravier and Governor Warmoth suggested she seek her inheritance. After they had promised to help, they had betrayed her, encouraging Angelique to risk her life to come out here. It was enraging! She knew how dangerous it was, while they sat safely in New Orleans, threatened only by their own greed and Warmoth's ill-advised political schemes. Never should she have consented to allow Raoul Gravier to handle their affairs, but he had presented her with a paper that seemed so legal.

It seemed as if Captain Braden had been right all along about him, and she should have listened.

A warm wind rustled the leaves of the cottonwood, and one of the scouts came down the sloped bank to the creek to fill a bucket with water. She watched silently. He looked tired, with dust covering his blue trousers and coating his boots in a thick film. She recognized him; Dave Logan, who seemed to be well acquainted with Jake Braden.

A faint frown creased her brow, and she pushed at a loose strand of hair in her eyes. Jake Braden—an enigma. She'd seen the way Angelique watched him—and worse, seen the way he watched her.

There was something between them now that had not been there before. She recognized the signs, the careful evasion, the swift glances Angelique gave him and the flush that colored her face so prettily when he happened to catch her eye. Dread seized Mignon, and she prayed that her daughter had not been so foolish as to yield all to that hardfaced man.

Ah, Angelique—so stubborn, so spirited and strong—all the things that Mignon had not been in her youth. Always, Mignon had been frightened, and now that she was older she was even more so, but not for herself alone.

She knew what waited at the end of their journey, for the Double X could not have changed that much since she was last there. In appearance, perhaps, with new buildings, a bigger house, thicker walls—but the land would be the same. There was no changing the wild, desolate land around the ranch, the bleak hills and miles and miles of stunted grass and mesquite . . . there would be no changing the hot, fierce winds that blew dust devils thick enough to choke a steer.

It was hard to think of her daughter risking her life to stay in such an inhospitable land.

Her mouth hardened, and she curled her long-boned fingers into tight fists in her lap. No, even if she had to deal with the devil, she would do everything in her power to get Angelique away from New Mexico Territory and back to France. Oh, if only John had not sent that last letter! Curse him. He'd known what he was doing. He had known quite well that a young, impressionable girl would be fascinated with the thought of adventure across the ocean, with an inheritance of an estate she had never seen . . . for a moment Mignon almost hated him.

And that made it easier to accept that she might very well have to involve Don Luis to get what she needed so desperately to have done. He was the only man with the power to change John's will, so that they could get the money they needed without having to stay in New Mexico.

It seemed so easy in theory, but she knew well that it would not be in fact. There were too many men who wanted the land, who would kill to get it, and that's what terrified her the most. She needed a strong power behind her to keep them safe until Angelique realized that it was not at all what she had hoped and would consent to leave.

But dealing with Don Luis would be like dealing with the devil, and she was afraid of that, too.

Mignon inhaled deeply, and the sharp scent of sage filled the air. With the setting of the sun, it was growing cooler. Already, a half-moon hung low in the sky, bright and shimmering against the purple shadows. Out on the prairie could be heard the high, lonely warble of a coyote, and she shivered. There were predators everywhere, and the human predators frightened her much more than the animal ones. Quietly, she returned to camp.

When Jake Braden rode in just after dark, Mignon looked up from her seat beside the fire and thought to herself that with his brown face and hard, lean body he looked very similar to the men of the plains, painted savages with no compunction about taking what they wanted.

Apparently she was not the only one who thought that, for one of the other scouts had grabbed for his rifle as Braden rode into camp in an obscuring cloud of dust.

"Hell, Braden," Tom Spencer said in disgust, lowering his rifle when the dust settled some and he recognized the rider, "you shoulda called out and let us know it was you comin' in. Good way to git yourself killed, ridin' in like that."

"I figured any man in this outfit who doesn't know an Apache from a man he's been riding with for two weeks doesn't need to draw pay from me.''

Jake dismounted easily, throwing one long leg over the back of his horse and sliding to the ground. His dark brow cocked at Tom Spencer. ''At least you could recognize the horse, Spence.''

His mount was lathered, a leggy bay with four black stockings and a white snip, easily recognizable. Spencer flushed a little and shook his head.

''It ain't Apache that I git confused with you. Hell, you're built too far from your corns to be mistook for one of those short-legged howlers, but not for a Comanche. All you need is some yaller streaks on your face and a rawhide 'clout and you'd make a damn fine Comanche brave.''

''*Ahó.*'' Jake grinned when Spencer scowled and shook his head.

''You even talk like an Injun. How was I supposed to know it was you?''

''Use the glass. That's why we have it.'' Jake pushed his hat back and dragged his sleeve over his forehead. ''Who's supposed to be standing guard tonight?''

''Wright and Jones.''

''Send a man to check on them. I didn't see either one of them out there.''

He moved to the water bucket and lifted the dipper, looking up over the bowl of the ladle as he drank. His eyes narrowed slightly when he looked toward the fire, and Mignon intercepted the glance he gave Angelique.

She sat near the low fire, looking cool in spite of the heat, her hair fastened on top of her head with a comb. Talking softly with Bette, she returned Jake Braden's glance from beneath her lashes, and he looked away.

Mignon frowned slightly. There were undercurrents in that glance that she did not care to examine too closely for fear they would bear out her suspicions. Oh, good God, it must be true. She had suspected as much, and the unexplained bruises on Tempe Walker's face only bore out her premonition that there had been much more behind the supposed ''accident'' he had encountered than she'd been told.

If she had not come upon them quite suddenly before they left San Antonio and seen for herself the two men with torn clothes and bunched fists, she might have believed the unlikely explanation that they were wrestling for diversion and Walker's injury was accidental. There had been no sign of amusement in either man's eyes, only frustration and fury. She had seen such spectacles before, but not since she had left America.

Instinct warned her it had to do with Angelique.

Past experience promised an unpleasant tension between the two men for the duration of the journey. She had been surprised to find Walker still part of their group, but he had shown up for duty with vivid blue-and-purple bruises on his brow and cheek, and a marked aversion to Jake Braden.

It was a most awkward situation.

Dave Logan felt the same way, and he kept Tempe Walker out of Jake's way as much as possible. No point in inviting trouble, and since Patterson felt the lieutenant was too great an asset to transfer to another post, he was still with them.

Logan looked up, a little startled when Angie Lindsay came to sit down beside him, spreading her riding skirt around her long slender legs with a feminine gesture that he found both enchanting and alarming. It was his experience that women like her didn't mind using their female wiles to whatever end they had in mind, and it always left him a bit nervous.

"Good evening, ma'am," he said politely when she smiled up at him.

"Good evening, Mr. Logan. I was hoping you might be able to give me some information."

"Were you, ma'am?" He flicked a faintly desperate glance toward Jake, who stood near the fire and talked in low tones with Dap Higdon. "I don't know about giving out any information. Captain Braden's better at that than me."

"Yes, and you don't need to repeat everything I say to him, so don't keep looking in his direction."

Caught between amusement and caution, he regarded her warily. She was very beautiful, with a thick mane of copper hair and the kind of pale, flawless skin that poets wrote about. A man could drown in her eyes, deep pools the color of violets set in a thick fringe of dark brown lashes. He didn't blame Jake for taking what she'd been so anxious to give him, but he sure didn't want to get in the middle of it.

Her lush mouth curved into a smile, and he found himself smiling back at her.

"You've been friends with Captain Braden for a while, I believe."

He nodded warily again, and knew immediately where she was going with her questions.

"Yes, ma'am. One thing we do for each other is not discuss our personal business. If you're curious about Jake, you need to ask him what you want to know."

"You're rather blunt, Mr. Logan."

"Yes, ma'am. Saves time."

A faint frown creased her smooth brow, and she blew out an exasperated sigh. "And what do you do with all the time you have saved, Mr. Logan?"

He grinned. "Count myself lucky to have it."

"I suppose you do." She slanted him another glance from her slightly tilted eyes, looking beautiful and exotic and dangerous. "Why do you do this? I mean, travel over the land like you do? It seems as if it would be too arduous, and after a while too monotonous to keep doing the same thing."

"Reckon it can get that way."

Leaning back, she lifted one leg and hooked her clasped hands around her knee, smiling a little. She looked relaxed and seductive, and her voice was a soft purr.

"But perhaps you feel safer with the familiar, is that it, Mr. Logan?"

"Don't know about safer. If we don't run across any hostiles, it's safe enough, but that ain't likely. They're always out there."

"Always?" She looked uneasy and sat up straight. "Are they out there now?"

"Yeah, but don't let that scare you too bad. The land's too flat here for them to sneak up on us. We would see 'em coming for miles. There won't be any danger until we get to the foothills, where there's rocks and arroyos that will hide a passel of 'em. That's when you've got to watch out. Before you know it, you've got a bunch of hostiles coming down on you, and you'd better be ready."

"Mr. Logan, are you trying to scare me?"

She looked angry, and he grinned. "Yes, ma'am. But no need to get mad at me about it."

Rising to her feet, she smoothed her skirt and looked down at him coolly. "I know what you're doing."

He stood up and pushed his hat to the back of his head, some of his humor fading. He should tell her what he thought and warn her not to mess with Jake Braden, that she'd only end up hurt, but it had been his experience that few women appreciated or heeded such warnings. So he shrugged and offered what advice he thought she would take.

"Ma'am, you're goin' about this all the wrong way. Jake's over there. He's the one you really want to talk to."

He half expected her to get even madder, but except for a furrowed brow, she only nodded agreement.

"But Jake is more difficult to approach than you are," she murmured with unexpected honesty, and he followed her gaze.

Jake did look unapproachable. He was squatting Indian-style by the fire, scooping up beans from a shallow tin plate, his face guarded and closed. Dave had seen that look on his face before, and it usually presaged trouble.

Automatically, he searched for Tempe Walker, but there was no sign of the lieutenant. The tension brewing between the two men was thick enough to slice with a dull knife. There would be trouble before too much more time went by. It was inevitable and unavoidable, and made for damned strained nights.

If trouble was coming, Dave thought grimly, he'd just as soon it get here before they reached those foothills, because he'd told Angie Lindsay the truth about the danger that awaited them once they neared the mountain pass. They hadn't even crossed the Pecos River yet, and there was already Indian sign.

It looked like it was going to be a dangerous journey in more ways than one.

16

The heat was oppressive. It bore down on them with relentless monotony as they moved across the plains toward the crumpled folds of hills now visible on the far horizon. It was hard to believe they were still a hundred miles away; the mountains fringing the rocky plateau they traveled were a thin blue haze that seemed much closer, yet it would take them several more days to reach the pass.

By now the routine was familiar. They rose early in the day before the sun was more than a faint, pearlescent glow and the air was fairly cool, and one of the men—usually Tom Spencer—cooked a quick breakfast of bacon and beans, always accompanied by thick, scalding-hot coffee. It had taken Angie several days to grow accustomed to the bitter brew, but she found if she drank it piping hot and quickly, it wasn't too bad.

That early nothing much mattered, because she was usually too sleepy to protest the lack of variety in their menu. The novelty of sleeping on the ground rolled up in their blankets had rapidly palled, and poor Bette bemoaned the absence of the wagon that had provided them a covered bed before.

"*Mon Dieu!* Even the hard wagon bed was better than lying on the ground like dogs!"

"But the wagon slowed us down, ma'am," Logan explained to her again with infinite patience. "Without it we can get through the mountain pass a lot easier. We've got what we need packed on the mules, and they're surefooted in the mountains."

Angie still quailed at the thought of crossing the mountains, but refused to let Dave Logan know that he had succeeded in frightening her.

A hot wind blew scouring sheets of grit over the riders all day, so that kerchiefs were necessary to keep it out of noses and mouths. Water was scarce, and they were reduced to rationing it out between the infrequent waterholes and the thin, dirty trickles that Spencer referred to as rivers.

"Looks more like buffalo piss to me," Angie heard Danny Wright grumble when they paused beside one of the muddy rivulets late in the day.

She agreed with him, but only smiled gratefully as she dipped her kerchief into the water and wrung it out. Tilting back her head, she drew the damp cloth over her dust-coated neck, then grimaced. It only made mud of the grime. She should have known better, but God, it was so hot and she was so miserable! Had she really ever longed for this heat? That seemed a dream now.

Taking pity on her, Danny Wright offered to tend her horse while she "cooled off a mite."

"Oh, thank you, Danny," she said with relief, and he took her mount's reins and led it into the water upstream.

She knelt in the hard-baked ground beside the sluggish water where it provided cooler relief from the ever-present heat. A brake of willows cast some shade along the bank, unexpected and a welcome respite from the sun.

She pulled off the low-crowned, wide-brimmed hat she wore to protect her head from the harsh rays of the sun, wincing a little at the dull, throbbing ache in her temples. Even her eyes hurt, baked dry by the sun's glare off humped rock and expanses of prairie studded with sagebrush and clumps of prickly pear cactus.

A hand on her shoulder startled her, and she jerked upright to see Jake Braden behind her; his eyes crinkled slightly against brittle light not even the brim of his hat could block.

"You might want to go upstream from where the horses are drinking," he said, and pointed. "It's a little cleaner, but not much."

She flushed. It was silly of her not to have noticed that she was downstream, but she'd been so hot and the water and willows were so inviting that she hadn't bothered to pay close attention.

"Yes. You're right." She managed a careless shrug. "Guess I was in a hurry. It's so hot."

His eyes were on her, shaded by his hat but openly staring, and she realized that her blouse was partially unbuttoned and her skin was damp from the wet rag. She didn't move, but stood there silently, her heart thudding erratically at the quick, hot flare in his eyes, and knew he was remembering that night in San Antonio.

No one was near; most of the men were with the horses, moving into the middle of the thin stream of water to hold their reins and let them drink slowly, standing in it to their boot tops and heedless of mud as they scooped water in their hats to pour over their heads. Maman and Bette were carefully upstream; they knelt daintily at the river's edge to wet cloths, preserving their modesty with cautious pats against face and wrists and on the napes of their necks.

Because he was still staring at her so intently, and because she could think of nothing else to say, she looked up at Jake with an awkward smile.

"I thought the horses needed to cool down before being allowed to drink water."

"Usually." His lips flattened into a slight smile. "A little won't hurt them as long as they're not too hot. In this heat and this terrain, the horses are our most precious possessions."

"Yes. So I heard Mr. Logan say." She pleated the folds of her gown between her fingers, feeling childishly shy all of a sudden—and angry at herself for letting him make her feel so awkward. "He also said that we could make better time on foot than with the horses."

"It's true." Jake looked away from her, his tawny gaze shifting to the distant hills, then back. "A foot soldier can make a good thirty miles a day in this land, but twenty-five is about all a horse can stand if you want to keep it fresh and healthy."

"It seems contradictory. I thought horses were supposed to be hardy."

"Fast is more like it. If a man needs to get somewhere in a hurry, a horse is likely to get him there a lot quicker than his own legs." He pushed his hat to the back of his head, his eyes narrowed against sunlight reflected off the shallow water behind her. "I'll be riding ahead of the others again tomorrow. Care to ride with me?"

Her heart lurched. She wanted to say "Yes!" but paused, unwilling to appear too eager.

"Won't it be dangerous to ride alone?" she said instead, and he shrugged.

"Not yet. Besides, we won't be that far ahead. We're almost to the old fort near the Pecos River, and we can wait there for the others."

"Oh." She was inexplicably disappointed. "We'll be staying at a fort tomorrow night?"

He grinned, a flash of white in his dark, tanned face. "Before you get too excited, I should tell you that it's been abandoned for the last two years. But some of the buildings are still in good shape. It's got a well, and the river runs close. Since one of the pack mules has pulled up lame, we'll take the opportunity to stop early and rest a spell, let some of the men do some hunting for fresh meat. Unless you prefer Spencer's salty beans.''

She laughed easily, and without thinking put up a hand to straighten a tangled thread of fringe on the front of his buckskin shirt. With her hand resting against his chest, she looked up at him through her lashes.

"I'll be ready in the morning."

When he met her gaze, his eyes were as unreadable as amber marbles, and he nodded. Then he walked away, and after a moment, she moved upstream to stand with Maman and Bette and wash as much of the dust off her as she could.

It was futile, and she longed for a real bath, though she knew there was no hope of that. But tomorrow she was going riding with Jake, and she wanted to be at her most presentable—her lips curved in a smile. It was about time they could be alone together, and she hoped Maman would not protest. But why should she? Maman had gone with Jake for a solitary ride, hadn't she? Yes, and she had not offered a single objection when Logan took Bette for a ride ahead of the group, and they had been out of sight of the slower caravan of pack mules and horses for a while.

Angie smiled to herself. It had not escaped her notice that Dave Logan paid particular attention to Bette; indeed, the tall, handsome scout always seemed to be hovering near her, and his light blue eyes often strayed to the dark-haired little maid. Of course, Bette did not mind at all, and why should she? She had said one night when they lay in their blankets beside the fire that she thought him very handsome, with his brown hair streaked blond from the sun.

"And he is so tall! Like a strong tree, do you not think?"

It would not surprise Angie at all if Logan and Bette became *very* close on this journey, and she laughed softly to herself. Perhaps it was inevitable, too.

When morning came, Angie rose before the others and went silently down to the edge of the water, taking a clean cloth with her. She scrubbed her face, and in the deep gray and purple shadows of predawn, washed as much of her body as she could reach without completely disrobing. She wore only a thin cotton dress and no underclothing, and stood in the shallow water almost up to her knees to wash.

Shivering a little in the cool stillness, she watched as the flat tableland stitched with ridges and humped hills slowly began to lighten. The growing light cast the plateau in stark shades of gray and black, but as the sun climbed higher, it took on a rosy hue. Lacy clumps of mesquite waved in a gentle breeze, and bluethorn shimmered.

It really was impressive. Barren and bleak only if one ignored the beauty of simplicity.

As she sat gingerly on a clump of grass at the edge of the water to dry her feet and slip on her shoes, she heard the camp begin to stir. Dap Higdon cleared his throat noisily as he did every morning, and Tom Spencer began to grumble about the lack of respect for his cooking; Dave Logan set out to check on the guards posted, and Tempe Walker roused men to tend the horses.

When she arrived at the fire, where coffee was already beginning to brew in an enameled pot and the familiar smell of beans filled the air, Spencer glanced up at her with a lifted brow.

"You go down to the river by yourself, Miss Lindsay?"

"Yes." She did not meet his eyes as she took the cup of coffee he held out to her, but she felt his disapproving gaze.

"Braden won't like it if he finds out."

The coffee was hot and bitter. She looked up at him over the tin rim of the cup. "Do you intend to tell him?"

He scowled and dumped more salt on top of the slowly simmering beans. "Maybe."

"Then I'm certain he'll have something to say to me about it when you do. If you put some onion in those beans, they'll taste better and you won't need as much salt."

Spencer's mouth tightened, and he muttered, "Everybody knows how to cook better'n me, but can't get nobody to do it."

Angie didn't comment, and after a moment Spencer grabbed an onion from one of the supply bags and chopped it into quarters, then tossed it into the iron pot. He shot her a quizzical glance.

"How's that, ma'am?"

Laughing, she said, "I'm sure you'll find it tastes much better now."

"Always a critic in the group." Despite his grumbling, there was humor in the look he gave her, and they talked amiably for several minutes before Angie rose to tend her horse.

Learning to saddle the animal had been more difficult than she had supposed it would be. Early in the day, the horses were almost always fractious and wary of the saddle and bridle, and she had hit upon the idea of using a lump of sugar to bribe the mount she had been issued. It worked quite well, and while the horse was nuzzling her for more of the treat, she managed to brush and saddle him.

When Jake reached her side, she had the sorrel saddled and ready to go.

"Have you eaten yet?" he asked, and when she shook her head, he said, "I've got some biscuits and bacon in my pack. We'll eat those on the way. Let's ride before it starts getting too hot."

She looked up at him, and her heart lurched with unexpected pleasure. Why did she always feel this way when he looked at her, as if she couldn't breathe for the strange fluttering in her stomach? Unbidden came memories of that night in his San Antonio hotel room, and of how he had looked at her, and of the slick, hot feel of his muscled body beneath her hands.

"I'm ready," was all she said, not quite trusting herself to say anything else when her senses were clamoring and she felt so peculiar.

Leaving the others behind quickly, she glimpsed her mother's pale face as a blurred oval when they rode away, and Angie knew that Mignon would be furious with her. But it's *my* life, Angie thought defiantly, and besides, what can happen that hasn't already?

They rode in silence for a while; the only sounds were the dry thuds of hooves on hard ground and the creaks of saddle leather. The sharp scent of sage filled air that smelled of dust, hot wind, and horse. Rocky mounds billowed like ocean swells around them, and buttes thrust upward as the land evolved from flat plateau into rugged hills.

Angie had eaten her biscuits and bacon and washed them down with tepid water that tasted like the metal canteen she carried on her saddle. The brim of her hat was flattened by the press of wind as they rode, but since they were riding toward the west now, the sun was behind them so that it did not glare directly into her eyes.

They stopped to rest and water their horses at a small seep, an underground spring Jake found beneath a massive boulder that hung over rocks and dirt. He knelt beside it to wet his kerchief and wipe his face and neck, one knee pressed into the dirt as he squinted into the distance.

"Not far from here are underground caverns. They're huge, with formations like ice on the ceilings and walls."

"Can you take me to see them?"

He flicked her a quick glance and shook his head, brows drawn down over his nose. "No. Not enough time. Even if there were, it's hard to see anything without plenty of torches." He stood up, dusting his hands against his cord pants. "We still have a ways to go to reach Fort Lancaster."

Angie sensed that he was restless and moody, impatient to move on. Perversely, she delayed, moving to seat herself on a flat rock and remove her bonnet. Fanning herself with slow, idle motions, she watched him from beneath her lashes, fully aware that he was observing her as well. What would he say? What did she *want* him to say? Oh, she didn't know exactly what she wanted to hear from him, only that she must have some kind of answer to this nagging confusion inside her.

He had been so infuriatingly polite on their ride, as if she were a stranger instead of the woman he had made love to in San Antonio, and he made no attempt at all to allude to any of that. Indeed, until now, their conversation had been as sparse as the greenery on this arid land.

Finally Jake crossed to her and held out his hand, his eyes hooded by his lashes and shaded beneath the brim of his hat.

"We need to ride on before we lose too much time."

"Do we?" She ignored his hand and stirred the hot air over her heated skin with another wave of her bonnet. "I thought they were supposed to catch up with us."

The corner of his mouth kicked up at one corner.

"If we want them to catch up, we have to be ahead of them. At this pace, they'll end up passing us."

"Maybe that would be a welcome change." The bonnet stilled, and she felt suddenly restless as well. "Enforced companionship can grow palling at times, don't you think?"

"Depends on the companion."

She looked at him more closely. There was a taut set to his mouth, and she wondered crossly why he had brought her out here where there was no one around for miles and miles if he didn't intend to *say* something or *do* something, for God's sake!

"What do you want from me, Jake Braden?" she heard herself demand, and his hand dropped to his side. "We're out here alone—can you not say something more personal?"

He watched her warily for a moment, then shrugged. "What do you expect from me?"

Exasperated, she stared at him, and the heat burned down with blinding intensity, shimmering on rough rocks and dirt.

"I don't know *what* I expect, only that . . . that you be honest with me, I suppose. Tell me how you feel. Or what you want from me, perhaps." She paused when he didn't respond, and shrugged helplessly, feeling the damp cotton of her blouse stretch across her shoulder blades. "I don't know why men always have to be too talkative or too silent. Can't there be something in between? Can't you tell me what you honestly *want* from me? I thought you were different, that you were a man who does what he wants and takes what he wants without caring what people say about it."

She sounded irrational and she knew it, but she couldn't stop herself, her words tumbling out unchecked as he just stood staring down at her with unreadable eyes.

"You're ruthless and not afraid of anyone else—people say you're a hired gun, a half-breed, and that you're too dangerous to provoke. Which man are you, Jake Braden—the brutal gunman or the passionate man I knew in San Antonio?"

"Christ." There was a harsh undertone to his voice, an almost violent note. He pulled her up from the rock with swift hands on her wrists, and her bonnet flew from her hands to skid across the rubbled ground. "Is that what you find so damned fascinating about me? Rumors?"

"No! That's just all I *know* about you—you won't tell me anything else and you don't like it when I ask questions, and we . . . we haven't even had a chance to talk without either fighting or—"

"Making love?" he finished for her when she jerked to a halt. He grimaced wryly and released her wrists. "You want honesty from me, Angie Lindsay? I'll give it to you—I wanted you that first night I saw you in the ballroom of the St. Louis Hotel, looking all naive and virginal in your white gown and lace. But I knew enough to stay away from you. You're John Lindsay's daughter, and he was a friend of mine. God, you were a virgin, for Chrissake, and I knew better than to get mixed up with you. I'm still kicking myself for letting you get to me, for being stupid enough to forget good sense and honor, but dammit—it's not too late to stop now, before you get in too deep."

Angie could hardly believe her ears, and felt the blood drain from her face at his words that were like the lash of a whip across her cheek.

"Damn you, Jake Braden! Do you think you can just take what you want and move on without thinking of the effects of your actions?" Her hand was trembling, and she shoved at a loop of hair the rising wind pulled loose from her braid, tucking it behind her ear. "It's already too late. There's no going back, no way to give me back what was taken— what I *gave* you that night. This isn't just your responsibility, it's mine, too. I'm a grown woman, with needs and emotions, and enough sense to decide for myself what I want. Don't you *dare* think it was all your idea and your doing, because by God, if I had not wanted you, you wouldn't have gotten near me!"

Breathless, hot and shaky with the desire to burst into tears of frustration and anguish, Angie glared up at him from violet eyes silvery with unshed tears. Her lower lip quivered slightly, and she stilled it with an effort.

She would *not* let him see her cry, would not let him know just how much he'd hurt her. . . . Oh, she'd been so stupid! She'd ignored the lesson she had learned from watching Simone and Jean-Luc, or perhaps she'd thought she would be much smarter than Simone . . . what a fool she was!

He hadn't brought her up here alone to tell her that he loved her or even to make love to her again—he'd wanted to tell her he didn't want her. And she had been so giddy with delight, so absurdly ecstatic at his careless invitation!

Angie pushed past him, and he stepped aside to let her go, watching as she scooped up her hat from the ground and tied it on her head again. Her hands were shaking, and it took several tries to manage the wide ribbons before it was secured.

Finally it was done and she turned to meet his hard eyes before he quickly hid them with half-closed lids.

"If you'll lead the way, Captain Braden, I'm ready to join the others."

"Angie . . . Christ." He jerked off his hat and raked a hand through his hair, looking angry and resentful. "You know what I said makes sense. It's my fault things went too far, and I don't want you to be hurt."

"Is this supposed to be some sort of apology?" Her brow lifted when his jaw clenched, and she laughed in deliberate derision. "Oh, that's right, I forgot—apologies aren't your style, I think you said. How foolish of me to forget that—and to forget that if more than one person says a man is dangerous and no good, then he certainly must be."

Sunlight glinted off his black hair, and his eyes were narrowed against the glare. He stood with taut anger evident in the tense lines of his body, sounding every bit as menacing as she said he was when he snarled at her. "If I'm so damned dangerous, maybe you should learn better than to mess with me, Angie Lindsay."

Before Angie could back away or protest he had moved swiftly to grab her, jerking her to him to jam his mouth down over hers in a harsh, brutal kiss that muffled her aborted cry and left her breathless. The tenderness he had exhibited that night in San Antonio was gone. This kiss was ravaging, plundering her mouth and rendering her weak enough to swoon as she hung helplessly in his arms.

Somehow her hat was gone, the ribbons ripped loose to free it, and Jake backed her toward the rock where she'd sat earlier, his long, hard body pinning her against the rock with fierce insistence. It was solid behind her, and his weight held her against it as his hands moved freely over her body, ignoring her struggles.

While his tongue explored her mouth his hand loosened her hair, then freed the top three buttons of her blouse. He cupped her breast, his hand sliding beneath the thin silk camisole to find the taut, sensitive peak and tease it with his thumb and fingers.

Her struggles grew halfhearted as the familiar heat ignited inside, and she closed her eyes, yielding to the awful need. The hard, tight knot deep in the pit of her stomach twisted tighter, until the burning urgency spread through her entire body and she arched against him in helpless surrender.

Overhead, the sun beat down, but their inner heat was all-consuming, flaring higher and higher as he pulled open her blouse and caressed her. Oh, God, it was so familiar and so alien still—this wild intensity that made her forget good sense and self-respect to leave her mindless in his embrace. What was she doing?

From somewhere, Angie found the strength to push him away, her hands coming up between their bodies to press against his chest and her fingers curling into his soft buckskin shirt as she wrenched her mouth from his.

"Stop it! Oh, God—I'm going to be sick."

Maybe she was, sick with revulsion at how foolish she'd been, sick at heart that she'd given herself to a man who did not cherish her.

Jake released her and stepped back, and there was a hot, fierce glitter in his eyes that warned her to silence. He was right, and it was that she couldn't bear facing, the knowledge that she had pursued him and *wanted* what he did to her . . . but now wanted more than he could give.

Straightening, she buttoned her blouse, then reached up to find her hair loose and waving around her face and her hat lost somewhere on the ground. She struggled for composure under his hard, relentless gaze, and was chagrined that he didn't seem at all perturbed.

"Have I made my point, Miss Lindsay?" he asked coolly, and she wanted to slap his impassive face so badly she curled her hands into fists behind her to stifle the urge.

"If your point was that you are a bastard, yes, you have succeeded admirably, Captain Braden."

There was a surprised flash of grudging admiration in his eyes, and one corner of his mouth tucked inward.

"Maybe we should ride on now. By the time we get to what's left of Fort Lancaster, Logan should have the rest of them there."

Silently, Angie allowed him to find her hat for her, and she tied it on tightly even though dark clouds had begun to scour the sky and the sun was obliterated. It was difficult, but she gathered the shreds of her dignity around her as she mounted her horse and followed him down the rocky slope to flatter land where the trail snaked westward.

17

The charred, crumbling walls of Fort Lancaster, deserted for over two years, stood in eerie silhouette against the darkening sky. The sun-baked mud-and-wood buildings provided a shabby shelter of sorts from the elements and stood as mute testimony to the harshness of the land.

A high, hot wind whipped loose boards into clattering banners, and the horses snorted restively as Dave Logan herded them into one of the roofless structures still left pretty much intact. After fashioning a makeshift gate across the single opening to keep them from bolting, he looked up at Jake.

"Ought to hold them a little while, anyway."

Jake nodded and looked away. Dave followed his gaze and saw Angie Lindsay talking with Tempe Walker as they stood in the shelter of a red-barked madrone tree growing against a soot-blackened wall. When she laughed and put her hand against Walker's chest, Jake swore softly under his breath. Then he looked back at Dave and shrugged.

"If Walker's smart, he'll end up married to her. That might end one of her problems."

"I doubt it."

"Yeah, you're probably right."

Dave hesitated, then said, "If the Double X goes up for grabs, there will be an all-out war over it. I wouldn't be surprised if Don Luis didn't end up owning it."

"Anything's possible."

As Jake walked away, Logan thought he seemed even more withdrawn than usual tonight, and wondered if his partner's sullen mood had been caused by Angie Lindsay. It was likely, but he hadn't asked questions and wouldn't. He didn't need to. He knew Jake Braden pretty well by now, had known him all their adult lives, and knew how he dealt with women. Women fell for him, but he never seemed to care much one way or the other about them. It wasn't that Jake was cruel, necessarily, for as far as Dave knew he was honest to the point of being rude with them, letting any woman in his life know from the outset that he had no intention of lingering.

But Angie Lindsay was different from Jake's usual kind of woman— she wasn't experienced and she wasn't wanton, despite being a flirt and as seductive as hell. What made her especially different was her independence and fiery nature, Dave mused as he watched Angie pointedly ignore Jake and continue her flirtation with Walker.

Whatever had happened between them out on that trail today was making for a mighty unpleasant evening.

Dave slanted a glance up at the sky and the lowering black clouds that rushed overhead. A storm threatened, but it wasn't as ominous as the one on the ground.

With the animals restless, everyone was on edge, and even the usually even-tempered Dap Higdon snapped at Spencer that he couldn't stomach any more damn beans.

Mignon and Bette were edgy as well, and a strange air of foreboding hung over the adobe walls of the crumbling fort. The women had their own quarters, makeshift shelter in the only structure that still had an entire roof, and had set about hanging blankets over the open doorway for privacy. Only Bette remained outside; Mignon had gone inside to lie down, and Angie had disappeared with Tempe Walker into a far corner of the parade grounds where weeds grew and a stunted mesquite had taken root.

A low growl of thunder rumbled, and the wind picked up to send a blast of grit across the ground. Dave considered going over to talk to Bette; she sure was pretty, with her dark hair and eyes, and rosy lips that seemed to always smile at him.

Indecisive, he stood for a moment in the shadow of the wall, a shoulder pressed against the warm adobe.

"Damn you, Dap Higdon, you don't know a friggin' thing about cookin'! All you know is eatin'!"

Tom Spencer's voice rose loud enough to be heard over the thunder, and Logan straightened up from where he'd been leaning against the wall. It sounded like trouble.

The two men faced each other over a black iron skillet and a blazing fire, bristled up like two dogs and ready to fight. Danny Wright stepped between them to avert a brawl, but Tempe Walker told him sharply to stay out of it. Angry, Wright turned to Walker in a furious exchange of words. Dave swore softly under his breath and started toward them, but before he got halfway across the open parade ground of the ruined fort, the quarrel had escalated into a furious fight.

Jake reached them first, and grabbed the first man he came to and gave him a shove. Tempe Walker whirled around, and the savage fury in his face flared higher when he saw Jake.

"If you were doing your job, *Captain*, I wouldn't have to be stepping in!"

"Any time you think you're ready to take it away from me, you're free to give it a try."

Logan heard the deadly menace in Jake's tone and came to an abrupt halt. There was more to this than the obvious. A flash of lightning cracked overhead, and the air vibrated with electrified tension. He looked away when he heard a woman cry out, and when he looked back, Jake and Tempe were fighting, fists slashing at each other with vicious fury.

Angie Lindsay came running up just then, and as a boom of thunder and another brilliant bolt of lightning followed one on the other, she put her hands over her ears and screamed at the men to stop fighting. Her voice and words were lost in the fury of the storm and the battle.

She screamed again, but no one paid any attention to her, and a sweeping glance at the men circled to watch was ample evidence that no one wanted to stop the fight. Only Jake and Tempe were fighting now; the others had stopped and were onlookers to the brutal spectacle.

Bette reached Angie's side, and her hand curled around Angie's arm with horrified strength. "Can you not stop them?" she cried in French, and Angie shook her head.

It was too late for that; they were past paying attention to anyone else, to anything but their own fury and bestial impulses. Oh, God, she had not thought men would fight like this, with the raw, vicious intensity of animals, heedless of anything but the desire to brutally punish an opponent. . . .

The sickening sounds of fists striking flesh, the grunts and snarls of rage were too animalistic, too frightening to bear, and she wanted to turn away, to run from the sight, but couldn't. She stood still as if turned to stone, only one of the avid witnesses who watched with mindless excitement. Her heart was pounding fiercely in her chest, and she could not turn away but stood staring as Jake and Tempe fought their way across the chewed earth and weeds of the old parade ground.

She was only vaguely aware that her mother had come up behind her, that her mother had asked a frantic question that Dave Logan answered with uncharacteristic roughness.

"But this is foolishness!" Mignon exclaimed. "Stop them or they will kill each other!"

"No, ma'am. Jake won't kill him."

Angie glanced at Logan, struck by the certainty in his tone, and said sharply, "What makes you think it's Tempe who is in danger of being killed?"

Logan didn't answer, but lifted a brow and gave her a look that said it all.

He was right. Angie turned back to see Jake shake Tempe as if he were a child's doll, saw his fist draw back and drive into him, and saw Tempe fold over in a suddenly boneless sprawl, then drop to the ground. He lay still, groaning in the hard-packed dirt, and did not try to get up.

Jake stood over him for a moment, fists still clenched, his breath coming hard and ragged and his eyes still bright with the fury of battle. When Tempe remained on the ground, Jake slowly straightened, then pivoted on his heels and stalked away without a backward glance.

Angie hesitated, all her instincts driving her to go to Jake but knowing that he did not want her.

So she went instead to Tempe, and knelt beside him in the dust and dirt while Tom Spencer ran for his medicine box. Tempe looked awful; his face had been battered so badly he could barely open his eyes, and the cut lip that had been almost healed looked like raw meat. He grimaced and tried to sit up, and Angie put out a hand to hold him.

"No, Tempe, be still. Oh, God, why on earth did you have to fight him? You could have been killed. . . ."

Through swollen eyes, he peered at her, and the sound he made resembled a rusty laugh.

"Thanks . . . for the . . . faith in me."

"Oh, don't talk now. Save your strength. It looks as if you'll need some stitches in that cut on your cheek."

Angie retreated when Spencer returned with the box, unable to bear watching as they helped Tempe to a blanket hastily spread under a shed of sorts and then set to work to bind his wounds. It was cowardly, but she could not endure the sight of blood, and had fainted the only time in her life she had cut herself badly. Just the sight of a raw wound was enough to make her queasy.

Mignon met her at the blanketed threshold of their quarters, and her lips were taut.

"What did they fight about, Angelique?"

"How should I know?" She sounded too sharp and knew it, but the tension had frayed her nerves to the point of breaking. "They're men— they don't need a good reason to fight."

"It was over you, was it not?"

Angie gave her a startled glance. "No! Why should it be?"

"You went riding with Captain Braden today, and now this evening you were with Tempe Walker, flirting like a shameless hussy."

Shocked, and uncomfortably aware of the truth, Angie said defiantly, "What if I was? Does that give either of them an excuse to behave like . . . like animals?"

Mignon's gray-blue eyes were dark with shadows, and her mouth set into a tight line as she regarded Angie. Wavering light from a lantern flickered over them in erratic patterns, and the wind blew in through the flimsy barrier over the door.

"No, of course it does not, but you must acknowledge that you are partially to blame for this. Angelique, what has happened to you? Since we have come to America you are so different, so . . . rebellious. Ah, it is this land, this savage land, that changes people. Please, reconsider your decision and agree to return to France. This is no place for you. It is uncivilized."

Her mother sounded almost desperate, and Angie stared at her helplessly for a long moment. How could she tell her what had changed her? It was not the land, or even their arrival in America. It was something far deeper than that, a longing for something she had never had and would never have if she gave up.

She wanted stability. Security. Independence. Only by pursuing the last did she have hopes of finding the first—it was obvious, even more so now, that if she depended on someone else to provide for her, she would lose all.

Drawing in a deep breath, she said simply, "I cannot go back. I will not go back."

With a soft cry, Mignon turned away, holding her closed fists to her mouth. Her shoulders shook, and when she turned back there were tears in her eyes.

"You ungrateful child! You do not know what has been done for you, and you will throw it all away! You are too stupid to see past the moment to what lies ahead, and now you risk everything! I will not allow it, do you hear me? I will *not*!"

Angry now, Angie faced her mother with bristling fury. "It is not your choice, Maman. Since I was a small child, I have heard that you suffered so for me, that you gave up your life for me, but I have never heard how. When I asked about my father, you told me nothing. When I asked anything, you told me *nothing*! What was I supposed to think? To *feel*? I have always been a burden, the cause of your misery, and now—when at last my father has left me a part of himself and I want to see it, to touch the things he touched and see the things he saw— you wish to deny me. I wish you had never come with me, that you had stayed in France, where you belong. As far as I am concerned, you can go back right now, for I do not need you here with me.''

Dangerously close to tears, Angie stood panting from the emotion of her outburst. Her mother's face was only a blur. And then Mignon stepped forward, and before Angie realized what her mother intended to do, Angie was rocked by a hard slap across the face.

The stinging blow galvanized her into flight, and with a soft cry, Angie turned and fled the shelter.

Heedless of direction and her mother's plaintive cry, she raced across the hard ground and past the abandoned walls, grief and anger driving her on.

Clumps of cactus and gray sagebrush snagged the hem of her riding skirt as she fled over rocks and dirt, and her throat and chest ached with effort and anguish. Thunder rumbled overhead, and another slash of lightning illuminated the blackening sky to a blinding white. She did not slow, but left the fort behind, her feet finding solid ground and pushing against it with growing force, as if the more she ran the more she could, the need to escape propelling her onward.

It wasn't until she finally slowed that she heard the relentless pounding like approaching thunder and stumbled to a halt to turn around. She should have known.

Jake Braden rode toward her, riding his big bay without a saddle, and when she stopped, panting for breath, he came up beside her and halted. There was one cut on his eyebrow and another on his cheek. The bay snorted, blowing, and pranced in the dust and trampled a clump of sagebrush. A sharp fragrance melded with the smell of dust and eminent rain.

"Going anywhere particular?" Jake drawled, and she shot him a furious glance.

"Just somewhere you're *not!*"

"Too bad. Looks like you're out of luck today." He held out his hand. "I'll take you back."

"I'm not going back right now."

Impatiently, he kneed the restive bay until it sidled around. Still holding out his hand to her, Jake said, "Take my hand, Angie. This damn storm is about to break and I'd like to be back before it does."

She saw now that she had run much farther than she'd thought. The fort was far in the distance, looking small on the horizon, a tumbled ruin with blackened walls like broken teeth against the sky. The wind whipped stinging dust clouds through the air to pepper her face and bare arms.

She would have to go back, of course, but she did not want to face her mother yet—or the others, who must think the same thing, that she was a shameless hussy to act as she had. It would do no good to try to explain what she didn't quite understand herself, and she shook her head.

"No, let me just stay here a while. I'll be fine."

Jake swore harshly, a Spanish curse that she only half understood, and she grew angry.

"You do not have to be the hero, Captain Braden! Go back and beat up on someone else, or—"

As if someone had dumped a bucket, a sudden onslaught of rain crashed down on them, drowning out the rest of her sentence and immediately drenching her to the skin. She gasped, and choked on a mouthful of rain. The rain was as violent as the land, pounding down in blinding sheets that made her feel as if she had fallen into a river, and she struggled for breath as she staggered blindly.

Then Jake was beside her, taking her arm and half dragging her with him, sliding a little in the slick dirt that was rapidly turning to sticky mud. She stumbled beside him, clutching at him, shaken by the sudden violence of the storm. It raged overhead with crashing reverberation and sizzling bolts of lightning, and she screamed once when it felt as if a thunderbolt had cracked open the ground at her feet.

She fell, and Jake hauled her back to her feet with a harsh, ruthless tug to propel her forward. Blindly, she did not resist. When he caught her around the waist and half carried her, she hung limply in his embrace and put her arms around his neck to hold on.

Then he slung her to the side, and suddenly they were out of the rain and beneath an outcropping of rock. For the first time since the rain had begun, she could breathe without choking. The first deep breath caught in her throat.

Weakly, she coughed, and sagged against the cool slab that smelled of wet dirt. Jake hunkered on his heels next to her; his black hair was plastered to his head and his shirt was sodden and clinging to his chest. She shivered with reaction and chill.

"You all right?" he asked

She nodded. When he looked at her, she saw his gaze drop to where her wet blouse molded to her breasts like a second skin. Her nipples were hard beneath the thin cotton. Unmoving, she recognized the quick, hot flare of light in his eyes before he looked away, and she flushed at how easily he could make her remember things she would have to forget. How could he sound so calm?

"Might as well get comfortable. This looks to be one of those storms that will last a while."

"I thought it never rained out here," she said, and sat up, covering her chest with her crossed arms. If he noticed, he did not comment about her reaction.

"It doesn't rain often. When it does, the land is so dry that most of the time there's the danger of flash floods that swell a river to more than twice its normal size. Takes everything in its path with it. When the rain is over, it goes back to a trickle."

He was staring out at the rain, and though his voice was flat, it was the most he'd said to her since their conflict that morning. She shivered again, and her teeth clattered as she hugged her knees to her chest.

Jake turned to look at her with a slight frown. "You can't possibly be cold."

Her chin came up. "Well, I am. I get cold easily. Maman says I have thin, delicate skin." Her voice broke a little on the last word, as she thought of her mother's harsh words and shocking blow.

Lifting a brow, a smile pressed at the corner of his mouth, he regarded her for a moment.

"I would have said you must be cold-blooded like a chameleon, but your mother's version is more polite."

"Yes, I certainly agree with that!" The last few words came out in a broken chatter as her teeth clacked together, and he looked amused.

Unbuttoning his shirt, he said, "Take off your clothes, Angie."

Disbelieving, she stared at him. "I beg your pardon!"

"Take off your clothes. You want to get warm, don't you?"

"Of all the most egotistical, conceited men I have—"

"Don't be stupid. This has nothing to do with sex, so you needn't think it does. You're wet. I'm wet. The rain is liable to keep up for a while. If you're so damn cold, we can share body heat until it slacks up enough to leave here. Unless, of course, you find me too irresistible to trust yourself with me."

"I'm not naive enough to fall for that little ploy, Jake Braden, and you needn't think for a moment that I am!"

"Angie." He met her eyes then, and she tried not to look at his bare chest. "It's not as if I haven't already seen you—all of you. When the rain lets up, we can walk back. But right now we're stuck here. If you're worried about anyone coming up on us, unless they've grown gills, they're not likely to brave all this rain, much less even know where we are."

She stared at him resentfully. He made it sound so logical, but she didn't trust him.

"Where's your horse?"

"I let him go. I couldn't manage him and you both, and I had the stupid idea you were more important at the time."

"I suppose I should be flattered."

"Yes, you should. That's the best horse I've ever owned. I'd hate to lose him."

Disgruntled, she looked away, still not trusting this cozy, concerned Jake who was so different from the earlier one. Another tremor racked her body, and the sodden weight of her riding skirt clung to her legs when she tried to stand.

"All right," she muttered, "but turn your back while I take this off."

"For Chrissake," he began, then paused and shook his head when her chin came up and she narrowed her eyes. "All right. All right."

It was awkward, standing beneath the low-hanging rock, and her head grazed the surface as she balanced on one foot and stepped out of the divided riding skirt. She draped it over a smaller rock without any real hope it would dry, and peeled off the thin cotton blouse. Her shoes were gone, no doubt lost in the sticky mud, and one stocking drooped around her ankle as she quickly removed them. Then, clad in only her silk camisole and pantalettes, she huddled on the rough floor with her bare feet tucked beneath her.

"Don't you have any way to make a fire?" she asked when the silence stretched, and Jake turned back around.

"In case you haven't noticed, I'm as wet as you are. If I did have something to start a fire, there's no wood. I'd have to burn your clothes. Come here. I can't get you warmer if you stay over there."

He patted the small depression beside him, and she rose to her feet to stand shakily for a moment before joining him. He'd taken off his shirt and boots, but still wore his pants and gun belt. She eyed the last warily, and he shrugged.

"It's probably too damn wet to fire properly."

Somewhat clumsily, Angie settled down beside him and let him pull her against him. He circled her shoulders with both arms and nestled her into the angle of his chest and thighs. His pants were damp but not drenched, and the heat of his body warmed her spine and hips as he held her.

She felt the regular thud of his heart against her back, and his gun belt pressed into her hip. She shifted, and he tightened his embrace briefly.

"Not so bad, is it?"

His breath was warm against the side of her neck. She shook her head.

"Not as bad as I thought it would be. Just don't move around."

"Where would I go? My options are limited here, though it's better than being outside in that downpour."

Angie listened to the noise of the relentless rain and the mutter of thunder that was broken occasionally by the loud crack of lightning, and silently agreed with him. Some of her tension began to dissipate as she lay there listening to the rain and the steady hum of Jake's breathing. He didn't talk, and she thought he must be asleep. The air shimmered with the smell of rain and wet earth.

Lulled into drowsiness as she grew warmer, she closed her eyes. Perhaps she slept, but when she opened her eyes it was still raining and Jake's arms had slipped from around her shoulders. She angled her head to look back at him and saw that he was awake, watching her through narrowed eyes.

"Maman must be worried," she said for lack of anything better to say.

"She should be. The two of you yowling at each other like a couple of barn cats didn't help anything."

She sat up with a jerk. "And I suppose you think that nearly beating a man to death did?"

He stared at her coolly. "Walker's a little bruised but not anywhere near death. If he hadn't thrown the first punch he could have just walked away."

"You didn't have to hit him."

"If you're so damned worried about your new love, you can hold his hand and weep over his wounds when we get back to the fort."

"You're despicable, and I think I hate you, Jake Braden!"

"Do you?" He stared at her with an inscrutable expression. "Sometimes you tempt me to find out just how much you hate me, Angie Lindsay."

"I can make it easy for you by telling you that I find you to be the most contemptible man I have ever met."

A faint smile curved his mouth but did not reach his eyes, and he leaned forward to grip her chin in his palm, holding it so that she could not look away. Trapped by his grip and her awkward position in his embrace, she stared back into his eyes helplessly as he held her gaze with his own.

"Am I?" His voice was soft, a menacing purr that should have warned her.

Stubbornly, she said in a whisper, "Yes. You are. I hate you. I really do."

His other hand moved to slide down her bare arm to her wrist, his fingers circling the fine bones to hold her as he leaned forward. She could feel the heat of him like a burning brand, and closed her eyes when he drew even closer.

His mouth covered hers, gently instead of with the harsh pressure she'd expected, and his lips were warm and soft and coaxing as he kissed her. She thawed gradually, and her lips parted to allow in his seeking tongue. Madness, to allow it and not resist, but there was something so intrinsically arousing about the way he kissed her that she found herself kissing him back.

A rattle of thunder shook the ground, and she leaned into him with almost desperate need when he kissed her throat and lower, his mouth hot against her chilled flesh as he blazed a fiery path from mouth to ear and back to the small, fluttering pulse in the hollow of her throat.

It was inevitable.

She had known somewhere in the small part of her that still hoped that if he touched her again she would melt, but had not admitted it even to herself. Now she dissolved beneath his caress, the sweep of his hands over her as he slid down her still-damp camisole and caressed her breasts with his hands, then his mouth. Her head fell back, and weakly she surrendered all to him.

He spread his buckskin shirt beneath her, and moved over her with lithe purpose, still kissing her as he eased her down onto the soft leather. She was shaking now but not from the chill, and he parted her thighs with insistent pressure, moving his hand through the open slit in the crotch of her pantalettes to stroke the soft folds of skin between her legs.

"God, Angie," he muttered against her cheek, "you're so sweet and soft there . . . open for me, love. That's right, like that."

With an emotion almost like despair, she realized that she had wanted this since the last time, wanted to feel again that rush to oblivion that he created in her and that, despite everything, only he could give. It was more than physical; there was an elusive passion that he could ignite with just a look, and no one else had ever awakened it in her until Jake Braden.

She gave herself to it, lost herself in the all-encompassing desire he kindled in her.

There was something so arousing about being half clad, with the rain and thunder enclosing them in this chamber of dry rock, that she felt safe and surprisingly secure, and every inch of her body was aflame with need.

"Put your arms around me," he whispered in her ear, and she obeyed, her hands sliding over his hot, damp skin to hold him as he moved between her legs, his body lifting over her.

He kissed her again, roughly, his mouth going from gently coaxing to fiercely possessive as he slid inside her, and she cried out at the hot, sweet ecstasy of it. Her cry was lost in his kiss, and she dug her hands into the taut muscles of his back as he began to move inside her with strong, relentless strokes.

"Do you still hate me, Angie Lindsay?" He lifted his head to stare down at her with tawny eyes like flames, and she arched upward into the hard thrust of him, moaning. "Tell me . . . how much . . . you hate me, love," he said between thrusts, and she tried but could not.

Jake charted her hollows and ripe curves with his hands as the taut feeling inside her grew tighter and tighter until she felt as if she would snap from the strain. He impaled her, filled her with his body as she arched up against him, seeking the sweet release that hovered just out of reach, until finally, as she poised breathlessly on the brink, it exploded into a thousand tiny pieces and there was the shattering sound of thunder that she wasn't certain existed outside her own mind.

This was so different than last time, when the pleasure had come before and not after; now it washed over her in hot, depleting waves that left her languidly replete.

Half sobbing, she clung to him as he held her, and she heard his fierce, harsh mutter in her ear, then a groan, and he rested his forehead against her cheek, breathing raggedly for a moment. Then he lifted his head to gaze down at her with veiled eyes.

"I don't know who's crazier, you or me."

Her lashes slowly lifted, and she stared up at him. A frown tucked his black brows together over his eyes, and the heated lights she'd seen earlier in their depths had faded so that his gaze was as cold and emotionless as a tiger's detached regard.

"Why do you say that?"

He rolled to one side but kept his hand on her hip to knead her flesh in a soft caress. "It must be insanity to do this when they're all waiting for us back at the fort."

"You said yourself that we couldn't get back until the rain eased, and it's still raining."

"Christ, Angie." He looked almost sulky, and his mouth tucked inward at one corner. "That's not what I mean and you know it."

"No, I don't know what you mean at all!" She pushed at him a bit angrily, and his hand fell away from her hip as he regarded her with wary eyes. "If you didn't want to . . . to *do* this, then you should have kept your hands to yourself. I certainly don't want you to do anything you don't want to do!"

He smiled faintly. "That's the problem. This is all I think about doing when I'm around you. You're like a fever in my blood, and don't tell me you don't know what you're doing when you look at me with those big purple eyes of yours. You know exactly how you affect me, and how you affect any other man, with that wild mane of hair like copper silk and the way you hold your mouth, so it looks as if you're waiting on some man to kiss you."

Slightly amazed, she stared at him without knowing how to respond. What should she say—that she was glad he admired her but it was too bad he considered her an immoral flirt? It was as dismaying as it was infuriating.

"If you're expecting me to be thrilled that you think I'm so desirable, I'm not." She sat up and reached for her blouse where it lay in a wet lump on the slab of rock. "I resent your inference that I deliberately flirt with *any other man*, and if you think that, then you don't need to come near me again. I would hate for you to be contaminated by someone with such loose morals when yours are so pure!"

Jake sat up in a lithe curl of his lean body. His eyes had gone hard. "As usual, you've managed to misunderstand. I'm not surprised."

"I'm sure you're not."

She stuck her arms into the wet sleeves of the blouse, shivering at the clammy cotton that clung to her skin. She looked away from him; he did not bother to cover himself, but knelt shirtless on the rock, his bare chest gleaming darkly in the gloomy light that came in through the narrow opening of rock. Why didn't he cover himself? His pants were still open and revealing, and dark hair arrowed down his hard, flat abdomen to disappear beneath the cord material. Her fingers fumbled clumsily with the buttons of her blouse. Must he look at her so closely?

"Angie."

"Just leave me alone!"

Why did she feel like crying all of a sudden? How absolutely *maddening* that the tears came so readily when she wanted to present a composed facade!

"Qué coño te pasa!" Jake swore softly, a fluid Spanish curse that hung in the close, musty air of the hollow as he reached for her, and Angie tried to jerk away but there was no room.

"Let go of me," she said furiously, but he held her tightly as he pushed her back against the rough wall.

"Listen to me for one goddamned minute, will you?"

"Why? So you can tell me what a horrible flirt I am? No, thank you. I'm ready to go back, and I don't care if it's still raining or not!"

"If you don't care about it, I do. There's such a thing as flash floods out here. We're on high ground, but the Pecos River is just down that slope and liable to be running over its banks about now. We're not going anywhere until it runs its course, unless you're in the mood for a long swim to the Gulf, because I can damn sure promise you that's what you'll get."

Shivering again, Angie collapsed in a sodden huddle when he released her, and she pushed a wet strand of hair from her eyes to regard him with a dark gaze. Why were her feelings always so raw lately? As if she wore them on her shoulders? It was the uncertainty of it all, of the newness of everything that had happened, how she felt about Jake and this land—about everything.

"Christ, Angie," he said roughly when she got up to kneel at the opening and watch the rain, "you make me crazy. Just listen to reason and stay here a little while longer. Don't make me chase you."

She stared at the rain-drenched prairie. Beyond the rock where they'd taken refuge it was deep in mud, and the river had already overrun its banks with a rush of muddy water. The wind was wet and cool against her cheek and where her arms and legs were bare, and she shivered.

"I could find my way back without you."

"You know I won't let you do that."

She looked at him over her shoulder. His mouth went flat and taut, and in the fading light that filtered through the rocky opening, she saw his frustration.

"Yes." She drew in a deep, shaky breath. "I know."

She wanted to tell him to go to the devil, but there was a part of her that yearned to hear him say more than just that he found her desirable. Oh, God, was it *love* she wanted from him? After all her vows to keep her heart inviolate, had she been foolish enough to fall in love with Jake Braden?

Trembling, she looked away from him. Perhaps that was why she provoked him so often, to wrest honest emotion from him, an admission that he cared. If she truly loved him, she needed to know that he wanted more from her than her body.

He put his hand out to touch her on the shoulder.

"Angie . . . *querida,* I won't let anything happen to you. Don't make this any harder than it is."

"Harder?" She laughed shakily and turned to look at him. Her throat almost closed on the words, and she cleared it before saying, "How could it get harder than it has been? When I don't know how you feel—how *I* feel?''

It was true. He called her *querida*—darling. And he whispered love words in her ear when they were intimate, sex words that she didn't quite understand as the vernacular was different from the pristine Castilian Spanish she had learned, but she caught the gist of them well enough. Yet how did he really feel? There had been no *real* words of love from him—other than the careless ''darling'' or ''my heart'' that he threw about far too casually, as he had done with that tawdry barmaid in San Antonio.

Had it been only a week or so before that she had so glibly declared to Bette that she would prefer being a mistress to being a wife? That it would be far better to be unmarried and take lovers instead of give oneself wholly over to a man's will and whims? Yes, she had, and now she cringed at how naive she had been. She had discounted the tangled emotions she would feel, not thought that it would be so overwhelming to completely yield all, body and mind—and heart?

It was so confusing, and she tried not to think about Jean-Luc and Cousin Simone, and how Simone had convinced herself of a love that wasn't there. Angie didn't want to do the same thing poor Simone had done, did she?

''Angie—'' Jake sucked in a deep breath and drew one leg up to prop his arm as he leaned back against the rock wall behind him. ''I want you. Isn't that obvious?''

''Yes, of course.''

She hugged her knees to her chest. No words of love. Had she really thought he would say them? Did she really want him to?

But when he reached for her again, this time with that intent look in his eyes that she'd come to recognize, she yielded without protest, putting her arms around his neck and lying down as he took her with no words of love, no promises, only a hot, fierce urgency that swept her along to that elusive release.

The storm outside eased, but the storm beneath the rock raged as Jake made violent, exquisite love to her, and Angie knew with despairing futility that if she was to survive with her heart intact, she would have to fight this lethal attraction to a man who would ruin her if she let him.

It was not the most encouraging realization.

18

Mignon stood anxiously in the mud near the wall to wait for them to return. What was taking so long? The rain had stopped at last, and Braden's horse had returned, dragging mud-coated reins along the ground, looking bedraggled and skittish, but unharmed. Three of the men had gone out looking for them, though Dave Logan seemed to think there was no need.

"Hell, Jake was raised in the desert and knows this land like the back of his hand. He's most likely curled up under a rock somewhere to wait it out."

"But does he have my daughter with him?" Mignon asked tartly, and was not comforted when Logan shrugged.

"Most likely. If he went after her, you can bet he caught her."

Which, of course, meant they were somewhere together—and quite, quite alone.

Mignon's head began to throb, and she thought longingly of the medicine she took at night to make her sleep. She used it sparingly most of the time, but lately she wanted more and more of it, needed it to ease the nerve-racking fears that assailed her with every passing mile.

"Madame?" Bette came to her side, looking up at her with anxious eyes. "I am certain that the so-brave captain has her safely with him. It is like Monsieur Logan says, that he knows this land well. Mademoiselle Angelique will be brought back to you."

"Yes. Yes, of course she will, Bette. You are right, and I am being foolish, but a mother worries."

"Shall I prepare you a small tonic to ease you? Your head must ache so from the worry."

"Yes, Bette, would you? Not much, of course, but I—I am so tense, and my head throbs unmercifully. A small tisane, perhaps."

"Yes, of course, I will make it just as you like it."

An unspoken message passed between them, for Bette knew quite well what Mignon required in her tisane. But the maid was a good girl and told no one. Not even Angelique knew.

Oh, what was the *matter* with that girl! Had she lost her wits? Been deceived by the handsome captain into giving herself? But no, Angelique was not at all foolish enough to yield what she did not want to yield, and if she and Jake Braden were intimate, it was because she wished it.

Mignon closed her eyes, pressing her fingertips to her throbbing temples. Her head ached so that it felt as if a hundred horses pounded inside. . . .

"Rider comin' in!"

At the cry she jerked her head up to stare anxiously across the undulating prairie, but the lone rider was unknown to her, and she slumped dejectedly against the rough surface of the wall again.

Dave Logan went out to meet him, rifle held casually in one hand, but apparently he knew the man, for they talked in low tones for a few moments before entering the compound at a walk.

When Logan saw her looking at him, he switched direction and came toward her, and Mignon asked when he reached her, "Is there trouble, Mr. Logan?"

"No, ma'am. No trouble. Look, I know you're worried, but I bet they'll be back here by dark, or right after. Since they're on foot, it will just be a little longer, that's all."

"Who is our visitor?"

Logan looked startled by her abrupt query, then gave a shrug. "One of Colonel Patterson's scouts. He's just passin' through."

"I see. How fortunate that he was able to find us out here in the middle of the desert."

Logan's mouth twisted into a sardonic smile. "Yes, ma'am, it is lucky he happened up on us, ain't it."

He touched the brim of his hat with a forefinger, then moved off in the direction of the campfire built under a low arch in the wall, and Mignon watched him go with a somber gaze.

There was much more here than met the eye, and she did not like it one bit.

It was no better when Angelique returned, accompanied by Jake Braden and looking defiant and curiously replete. She met her mother's gaze briefly, then looked away, and they did not mention the argument of the afternoon or the doubts and fears that both of them felt.

When morning came, they were greeted with the news that Jake Braden had gone in the night, leaving with the scout who had joined them after the late storm.

"But why did he leave us alone?" Angie demanded of Dave Logan, who pushed his hat to the back of his head and carefully avoided her eyes. "Who will guide us to New Mexico now?"

"Guess he thought it was best after yesterday's fight with Walker. The lieutenant knows the trails nearly as good as Braden, and what he's forgotten, I probably know. You'll get safely to your destination, ma'am."

That's not at all what bothered her, and Angie thought with rising despair that Jake had managed to leave her without a word of comfort or farewell—or the assurance that she meant more to him than just another casual woman. Oh, how infuriating! And worse—it was obvious from the way Logan would not meet her eyes that he knew what had happened between them.

But what *had* happened between them? She didn't know. Yesterday she'd thought she knew, when he'd been so tender and gentle, then fiercely possessive. Since then she had been confused by the contradictions of how she felt and how she was supposed to feel—why had he left so abruptly?

It was no consolation now that he had been so loving, if he only left her in so cavalier a fashion, and the hurt she felt at his indifference slowly evolved into a hard, aching knot of resentment. Damn him! It was difficult enough to confront her own insecurities without having to face the glances in her direction and the obvious public knowledge that she had been deserted as nonchalantly as any common street whore.

Angie forced herself to hold her head high, ignoring her mother's brooding glances and Bette's sly smiles. It was all she could do to keep her mind off Jake Braden while they rode away from Fort Lancaster, and she wished fervently that she had something else to occupy her thoughts so she would not repeat every word he'd said over and over in her mind until she thought she would explode with the frustration and distress.

After the storm, the day had dawned clear and bright, with a shimmering freshness of scoured land and skies. The wind was soft, and the ground dried quickly under the bright burning rays of the sun.

By noon of the next day, Jake Braden and Steve Houston were nearly at the mountain pass, their horses' hooves clattering over rock and hard ground. They had left early the day before, long before the others awoke and after Jake had left Tempe Walker in charge—with Dave Logan to keep them on the right track.

"He's next in the line of command," Jake had said to Dave, who shrugged his indifference.

"Hell, Jake, you know I don't give a damn about that. Walker means well, even if he just don't know no better at times." After a pause, he squinted at Jake against the light from the torch. "What do I tell the others?"

"Whatever you want. As long as they get where they want to go, there should be no problem. If it goes all right, I'll catch up with you at Fort Stockton or El Paso."

It was perfect timing that had brought Steve Houston to the ruins of Fort Lancaster. Jake knew that the tension between him and the lieutenant would only get worse. Any qualms he might have had about leaving were surmounted by the need to apprehend the men responsible for the selling of weapons to the Apaches, and because of the awkwardness of the enmity with Walker, it was best he leave quickly and without long explanations to anyone.

Including Angie Lindsay.

Inexplicably, he thought of how sweet and passionate she had been in his arms when he should have been thinking about how much trouble she had caused him. Not that it was all her fault. It was his own damn fault that he let her get under his skin as she had, for forgetting good sense and restraint every time he was around her. It didn't make sense that she could get to him as easily as she did, but it happened.

This was the best thing, to put as many miles between them as he could. If it distressed her, she'd get over it soon. He'd watched her enough to realize that she was like a cat, always landing on her feet, quick to recover.

"They're camped south of Fort Stockton about thirty miles or so, in a little canyon near Sierra Madera," Houston said when they halted to rest and water the horses at a small seep trickling into a shallow stone basin. He squinted up at the sky. "They must feel pretty safe, with only one way in and guards stationed at the mouth. They've been there long enough to build a shack, but I don't think they plan on homesteadin'."

"It must be a meeting place. Wonder who they're expecting?"

Houston grinned. "Let's hope we find out."

Rising rock ledges narrowed into gritty tunnels where brush studded the steep slopes and loose rock tumbled down without warning to skid across a narrow, hard track. Where they were going it was almost like a funnel guiding them into a single line.

Bleak shadows, cast by the high walls and the blazing sun, stretched across the trail when they reached the cutoff that led to the hidden canyon.

"This is it," Houston said, reining his mount to a halt and shading his eyes with one hand. "Stewart should be waiting for us up ahead. He'll make his way back here when I give the signal."

Houston angled a small piece of silvered glass against the sunlight to flash a reflected splinter of light against the high rock wall. He waited, then did it again.

It wasn't long before Jack Stewart showed up on foot, looking like an Apache with knee-high moccasins and a red headband circling his head. He ran crouched over, a rifle in one hand, until he hit the bottom of the gully and topped the rise to reach them. Then he straightened, and his gaze flicked from one to the other as he eased free of a bow and quiver of arrows he had slung across his back.

" 'Bout damn time you two showed up. Thought I was goin' to have to rout them by myself."

"If you got the itch, scratch it," Houston retorted as he slid from his horse. "Anything we should know about?"

"There's two more showed up. That makes seven of 'em now. Ugly sonsabitches, too."

"You ain't no prize, Stewart."

Stewart grinned. His bronzed skin was red from the sun and his black hair was thick and coarse, reaching to his shoulders. His mother had been Apache, and it showed.

"Comin' from you, Jake, I consider that a high-flyin' compliment."

Kneeling on one knee, Stewart took his finger and drew a map in the dirt.

"Here's the wash, and this here's the shack they built. A wall behind, and the trail in. Guards are posted here at the mouth. Looks like they can see us comin' for a ways unless we circle behind, but it's open and steep that way. Our only chance to take 'em would be to draw 'em outside. Otherwise, they'll pick us off if we try to form an assault."

Jake studied the map. "I've got an idea that will smoke 'em out. You boys feel like a turkey shoot?"

It wasn't as difficult as it had first seemed, and when Jake snaked his way on his belly along the harsh ridge above the shack, he calculated the distance and wind as he notched an arrow to the taut bowstring of Stewart's elm wood bow. The head of the arrow was thick with coiled rope and had been smeared with globs of animal fat so that it would burn.

Years ago, when he had lived with the Comanche, Jake had learned the art of shooting a bow and arrow with deadly accuracy and speed. It had been a while since he'd used the weapon, so he took his time. There wouldn't be too many chances. Surprise was a key element. He was in the open on the flat ridge, with no cover, a fine target if he was spotted, and he hoped grimly that Stewart and Houston had dispensed with the guards at the mouth of the canyon.

Finally the signal came, a brief flash of light that danced across the red rock walls.

Jake lit the end of the arrow and bent the bow as he drew back and sighted down the smooth wand. After adjusting his aim for the extra weight, he released the arrow with a humming *twang* and heard the solid thunk as it struck the wood plank roof of the shack.

He put three arrows into the roof before it caught and quickly flared up in the heat and windless swelter of the canyon. Flames danced across the dry tinder in spreading orange and yellow tongues, and a shout of alarm sounded inside the shack.

When the roof began to smoke and thick black clouds rose into the air, the door of the shack finally opened and three men stumbled out. Fire opened up on them, bullets spanging into the dirt at their feet as Jake grabbed up his rifle and waited. One of the men ducked behind a rock, firing back, while two ran for cover behind a low rock shelf ridging the canyon wall. Jake waited, eyes squinted against the bright glare of the sun reflecting off rock walls.

As the fire raged, two more men burst out, diving for cover behind rocks as bullets spat at them from the high walls in front. When the final two men emerged, coughing and choking as crackling flames completely engulfed the rickety wood shack, Jake pushed up to kneel on one knee, aiming his rifle down into the canyon floor. Heat waves shimmered up to dance eerily above the shack; the air smelled of burning wood. He watched and listened as they fired back at Stewart and Houston, the noise brittle and muffled by the walls.

When three of the men stopped to reload, Jake took careful aim. His first bullet caught one in the arm and spun him around, and another bullet slammed into the second man's shoulder. His third quick shot tore into a thigh. Deliberately, he did not shoot to kill—his fire was a warning. If they surrendered, it would be the end of it. Resistance meant a fight.

Gunpowder smelled sharp and acrid. Heat waves blurred the air and shimmered from the rock walls. The mercenaries below reacted with predictable panic, some whirling around to fire wild shots up toward Jake, the others wasting bullets by firing at the unseen ambuscade at the mouth of the canyon. Stewart and Houston held them down, pinned

by crossfire from ahead and above, and after a few more minutes of
fierce shooting three men lay dead on the rock floor of the canyon and
two were wounded. Only two remained crouched behind the rocks and
the sparse shelter of a bristlecone pine.

"Hold your fire!" Jake yelled when a staccato eruption of gunfire
spattered rock fragments over the two desperate men below. He wanted
at least one of them alive. There were questions that needed answers.

The two survivors were in fairly bad shape, both of them wounded
but still belligerent. One of them was a Mexican, with a sweeping mustache that covered his mouth. He glared up at his captors and growled
an obscenity.

"*Chingate!*"

Stewart promptly kicked him in his wounded leg, and the man howled
with pain.

"Tie 'em up, Jack, while we figure out how we want to do this,"
Houston drawled, eying the other man, who was more stoic though no
less hostile.

Stewart tied them with a length of rope and left them in the shadow
of the stunted pine. Smoke still boiled up from the burned shack, and
charred timbers emanated heat.

Jake surveyed the two captives dispassionately, then glanced at Stewart. "Which one might tell us what we want to know?"

"I know the Apache," Stewart said shortly, and jerked his head toward the two bound men. "His name is Six Feathers. He used to ride
with an Apache hostile named Gokhlayeh a few years back. They're all
renegades, and Gokhlayeh is one of the worst. Taught old Six Feathers
a few tricks. They hate Mexicans and white men 'most as much as they
like *pulque.*"

"I know that name," Jake said. "Gokhlayeh—he's called Geronimo
now. A Mimbreño leader who fights with Cochise."

Stewart shrugged and nodded.

"Do you speak Apache?" Houston asked with a frown.

Stewart grinned and moved away to hunker down in front of the
captive. They spoke a few minutes before he returned to say with a
shrug, "He might talk if we get him away from his *compadre.*"

Houston pulled a small flask from his pack and tossed it to Stewart.
"See if a little whiskey will help loosen his tongue."

While Stewart plied Six Feathers with whiskey, Jake took stock of
the camp. It was small, but provisioned too well to support only seven
men. A hidden cache, maybe?

Houston agreed. "Yeah, probably a base camp, which means there
ought to be some of 'em come back to get more supplies."

"That's what I thought." He stood up. "Looks like we may have to stay a while and see who else shows up to visit."

Grinning, Houston rose to his feet and stretched. "Might as well get ready for our company. I've got a feeling they won't be too happy to see us when they get here."

19

El Paso was nearly as civilized as San Antonio—why, work had even begun to bring in a railroad. It had the wide, mud-baked streets and the crude wooden buildings next to adobe structures of a frontier town, but also surprisingly modern conveniences.

Angie lay in the blissful comfort of a thick feather mattress while a hot wind belled out the lace curtains at the window of her hotel room. New Mexico was just across the border, and in a few days she would see the Double X for the first time.

It was about time.

She closed her eyes, relishing the rare comfort, and tried to forget the harshness of the journey. Only once had they been accosted by Indians, and because they were fortunate enough to be only a few miles from Fort Stockton, the running battle had been short. As they raced for the safety of the post, soldiers poured out to their aid, and the Apache raiders melted away as swiftly as they had come, taking a few horses with them but leaving behind no casualties. The incident left Angie shaken and grateful for a respite.

They lingered at Fort Stockton for several days while replenishing their supplies until she wondered if they were waiting on something— or someone. Dave Logan was very close-mouthed, inexorably polite until she wanted to scream with frustration, but not forthcoming with any news at all about Jake or why he had left so abruptly. Or even if he would be back. . . .

It had something to do with the sudden arrival of the rough scout, a tall, brawny man named Steve Houston. Like Logan, he had been silent and solitary, keeping to himself instead of mixing with the others, but at the time, Angie had not thought much of it. Not until she'd woken to the news that Jake had gone with him in the middle of the night and left behind no explanation or farewell.

During the long, tedious hours of riding, when simple conversation was next to impossible and they were too weary to try, she had plenty of time to think. She had come to the conclusion that it was for the best if he had gone. He left her too confused and turbulent, and it was apparent that he did not intend to remain in her life.

After making it through the pass in the Davis Mountains uneventfully, they had pushed on through rigorous days and nights of blistering sun, hot winds, and constant fear to reach El Paso at last. Guarded by Fort Bliss to the north, the town squatted on the boundary of Texas and Mexico, and was only about fifteen miles from the New Mexico border. A diverse blend of cultures invested the town with a mood of raw anticipation.

They were to stay in El Paso a few days to provision the rest of their trek, Dave Logan explained to her the next day when she went to the hotel restaurant for the noon meal.

"Shouldn't take too long, ma'am," he said laconically when she asked him how long they were staying. "Colonel Patterson made all the arrangements, and the commander at Fort Bliss already has supplies for us. We'll get fresh horses while we're there, too. And by the way, ma'am," he added, and looked at Mignon, "you ladies have been invited to join General Smith for dinner if you like."

Angie wondered if her mother was well acquainted with *this* army officer as well, but Mignon merely inclined her head politely and thanked Dave Logan for the invitation, saying she would consider it.

"We are still so weary from this arduous journey, you must explain to him, so will require rest before we can be proper guests, Mr. Logan."

"Yes, ma'am. I'll tell the general what you said. I'm sure he'll be glad to wait until you feel up to it. Don't get many ladies out here, especially not pretty ones."

After he departed, Angie eyed her mother with a faint frown. There was still constraint between them, an odd, aching sort of barrier that she wished had never been erected but did not know how to topple. *Why must Maman be so difficult? Could she not see how badly Angie wanted this chance to be independent?*

Mignon lightly touched the corners of her mouth with her napkin and looked up finally to meet Angie's gaze.

"We will soon be there, Angelique. I hope it is everything you want it to be."

"Yes, Maman. So do I."

"And if it is not?" Mignon smoothed her napkin back over her lap and lifted an eyebrow. "What will you do then, *ma petite*?"

"Why—I do not know. I have not considered that, but then, I expect to like it very much there." She lifted her glass of wine. "Whatever happens, however, I will have the comfort of knowing that I made my own decision, that I did not depend upon someone else's opinion to form mine."

It came out more sharply than she intended, and her mother's brow arched with delicate sarcasm.

"No? And Captain Braden—what is his opinion?"

Angie's fingers tightened around the stem of her wineglass. "I have no idea, nor do I care."

"Really. I thought perhaps you cared very much what he thought. You seemed very . . . close to him."

"Are you hinting of something more intimate, Maman?"

"I do not know, Angelique. You seem to have all the answers lately. Perhaps you can tell me what I mean."

"The circumstances of our journey have made me close to many of the people with us. I often share a blanket with Bette, but we have not tumbled in the dark."

"Angelique! That is an unnecessarily vulgar remark!"

Angie lifted her shoulders in a shrug, angry at her mother for being blunt enough to say what she felt, yet angry also at herself for being so vulnerable to the truth.

"What is the matter with you?" Mignon leaned forward, and her mouth was taut with suppressed anger, her voice low as she hissed at Angie. "Since we have come to America you have changed horribly! I do not even know you!"

"That seems fair, since I do not know myself any longer, either."

Angie's sudden honesty blunted her mother's anger as well as her own, and they stared at each other across the table with something like regret. Then Mignon pressed a hand over her eyes, and her tone was softer, filled with emotion.

"Ah, *petite*, what has been done to you? It is my fault, I fear, for I have not made wise decisions." Her hand fell away from her face and she sat up straight, as if suddenly conscious they were in a public dining room, though there were few people present. "Perhaps I should have allowed you to meet your father years ago. Then you would not have this overpowering need to come here."

"Perhaps, but I do not think it would have helped, Maman. Oh, do try to understand, though I cannot explain it very well—I have long yearned for just such a land as this around me, though I admit, it is more frightening than I had thought it would be. Still, there is opportunity here, and a sense of independence, and a freshness that I did not expect. It is as if . . . something calls to me.''

Mignon's face had gone white, and her eyes were like gray slate in her face, all the blue swallowed by dark pupils.

"Angelique—ah, it is an echo! You are so like your father at times. I can still hear him say almost the same words to me . . . that the land called to him. He never understood why I could not feel the same way. He never saw what I saw then, what I still see—the savagery, the danger, and the fear and the heat and dust and primitive cruelty that is all around us—the attack we suffered before we reached Fort Stockton, do you recall how you felt then?''

"Yes, of course. I was afraid.''

"That is how you will soon feel every hour of the day, as you wait and watch for them to come, to leave the hills and swoop down like hawks on you—it is a horrifying sight, Angelique, the screams like wild animals and the bestial, painted faces, and their vicious weapons. You will not be able to sleep for fear that you will not hear them when they come, and you will be afraid to do such a simple thing as walk under the trees or sit in the sunlight, for they might come out of nowhere and seize you. I know. I lived it every day until I could no longer bear the waiting, and began to almost *want* them to come and get it over with.'' She drew in a deep breath, and as if to herself, said softly, "It was the waiting, the dread of what I knew would soon happen, that almost destroyed me until I managed to escape.''

For several moments Angie could not speak, but sat still as she tried to visualize the depth of her mother's horror and fear. Yes, she could understand more now, for she had felt the same debilitating fear, the paralyzing terror that incapacitated her to the point of numbness, so that Tempe had been forced to ride close to her and grab her horse's reins to guide her in the right direction.

It had been over very quickly, and then they had been safe inside the fort, so she had not had the time to dread the possible consequences. But she understood the fear now.

"Maman—I do understand. But I cannot live my life fearing what may happen. I must deal with the realities instead of my fears.''

"And what happens if the realities become nightmares?'' Mignon was more composed now, and her brow lifted. "You are young. You think nothing will happen to you. I pray that you are right, but I fear that you are wrong.''

It was a conversation that haunted Angie's thoughts for quite a while, but even after they left El Paso behind and rode once more across the burning rocks that changed from red to brown and back, she could not bring herself to regret her decision.

The transition from Texas to New Mexico went almost unnoticed, for the land stayed the same, with wide expanses of sage and stunted mesquite broken by flat-ridged limestone hills or high granite buttes. The plains were cut by arroyos snaking in deep slices over the ground. Clumps of prickly pear cactus dotted the land erratically. To the west, the Guadalupe Mountains heaved northward from El Paso in rugged peaks that were nothing like the mountains of France and Germany. These were bleak, ridged peaks that were as harsh as the land around them.

Weary, hot, and aching from the constant riding, Angie was grateful when Tempe Walker came to tell her that they had only two more days on the trail at the most.

"We'll be in Las Cruces by nightfall, and after that, it's about thirty miles to the Double X. Fort Selden is midway between them."

"So. We're almost there." Angie stood on the rim of a rocky ridge that overlooked the Rio Grande River. It swept past only a few yards away, a shallow ribbon of muddy water slicing a path through sandstone rock. Pecan trees grew wild along the bank where she stood, and the wide gorge that was bisected by the river below sported a stand of young, green willows.

"Angie—Miss Lindsay." Tempe put a hand on her arm, then quickly removed it when she glanced up at him. His skin was reddened from the sun, and his eyes were very blue in his bronzed face. He looked uncomfortable. "I want you to know that I'm sorry for some of the things I may have said to you a while back. I get—got—kinda crazy. Hell, I never should have let Braden get to me, but he's so damn cocksure and arrogant that I did. Please say you forgive me."

Angie smiled. "Of course. There's nothing to forgive, Tempe. Captain Braden can be very . . . abrasive."

"Yes, he certainly does chap my hide." Walker gave a shrug when she looked at him quizzically. "I'm just as glad he left when he did."

"Yes, we all are." She bit her tongue to keep from adding that if Jake hadn't left, Walker might have found himself dead instead of just bruised. It was petty of her, and anyway, the journey was almost over and they would be at her new home.

Her home. It would be all hers, something of her very own that she would not have to answer to anyone to keep. All she had to do was live there, and she thought she could do that with no problem.

A hot wind blew, lifting her hair where it had loosened from the neat plaits. She untied the kerchief that held on her hat and swept it from her head. It was a relief to free her hair and let it down around her shoulders.

"Angie, your hair is so beautiful. Like a living flame when the sun hits it like this. . . ."

Tempe drew her from her reverie, and she ran her fingers through her unbound hair as she smiled up at him, enjoying his unbridled admiration. It was gratifying to her bruised ego to have a man look at her like that, to know that, even dusty and bedraggled, she could arouse his ardor.

"You have the soul of a poet," she murmured, and knew from his expression that he wanted to kiss her. Why not? Perhaps he could erase the memory of Jake from her mind, obliterate the passion she had felt when *he* had kissed her so ruthlessly, as if he was branding her. She turned, her hand stilling in the curve of hair draped over her shoulder and her face turned up to Tempe in open invitation.

He cupped her chin and whispered, "May I?" even as his head was lowering to brush his mouth over hers. He kissed her gently at first, and when she did not protest or push him away, grew bolder. He put his arms around her to hold her against him, trapping her hands between their bodies as he did, and deepened his kiss.

It was not unpleasant, but it did not stir her as Jake's kisses had, and she wondered despairingly if she was cursed by what would always be an unfavorable comparison. As if he sensed her withdrawal, Tempe released her mouth, but he kept his hands on her shoulders.

"You drive me crazy," he muttered in a half groan, and his fingers dug into her skin through the cotton blouse. "I know it's sudden, but I've watched you since that first day I saw you, when you were sitting on the patio in Galveston sipping orange juice in the shade of palmetto plants."

"You . . . you saw me that day?" She felt a little dizzy from the heat, for the brassy sun had hammered down with unremitting vengeance all day.

"Yes. You were the most beautiful thing I'd ever seen. You still are. Angie—say you'll give me a chance to court you. I'll come see you every chance I get. The fort isn't far from the Double X, and you know I'll make sure you're cared for and protected there."

Evading his question, she stepped back, and his hands fell away from her shoulders. He stood looking at her, and because she was uncertain and confused, not wanting to hurt him as she knew she would do if she gave him false hope, she blurted the first thing that came to mind: "Do you go often to the ranch?"

"I've been there once or twice, but now I'll have a reason to visit. Will you receive me?"

"Of course." She turned away, and wished she had not let him kiss her. "At first everything will be so new, and I imagine I'll want to get things in order. Why, I don't even know if my father has things like soap, and linens for the beds—men can be so careless about those things."

"I imagine Miss Lindsay insisted he buy them. She seems like she would appreciate scented soap and pretty things."

"Miss Lindsay?" Angie frowned. "Who do you mean? Did my father have a sister?"

Tempe looked startled. "I meant your sister. Or your half sister, I suppose she would be, since her mother—you don't have the same mother."

Angie stood as if turned to stone. Despite the heat, her blood ran cold and she began to shiver. Through stiff lips, she said, "I don't know what you're talking about."

"God, Angie—you mean you don't know? Oh, sweetheart, please forgive me . . . I didn't know—wait!"

Blindly, she walked away from him, crossing the empty ground to the camp to find her mother. Was she the only one who did not know? But how? Oh, this could not be true, for she had thought all these years that she was his only child and that was why he left her his land, so she could love it as he did, cherish it and learn to know the man who had carved a home out of the wilderness—could it be true?

But even though she wanted so desperately for it not to be true, somehow she knew deep down that it must be, or Tempe would not have mentioned it so casually.

Mignon was as shocked as she to hear this news, and even more upset than Angie.

"No! It cannot be true. You must be mistaken, Lieutenant Walker. I am certain I would know if there was another child. After all, there is no mention of her in the will that I read, and—"

"Mrs. Lindsay, I can understand your distress, and I wish it had been anyone but myself who had brought you this news." He looked wretched, and stole a glance at Angie, who stood a little apart from them under the shade of a scrubby pine. "I know only what I was told. It is very possible that I am mistaken."

"Tell me what you know, Lieutenant." Mignon's voice was crisp now, and her eyes burned in her pale face like twin brands. "If true, it certainly explains much."

"Ma'am, I can't tell you anything other than that I was introduced to a young lady by the name of Miss Lindsay, and I was given the impression that her father was John Lindsay. That's all I can tell you."

Angie stared across the vast land toward the granite needles and spires of the Organ Mountains that formed a long spiny ridge like dragon bones on the horizon. The earlier excitement she had felt was gone, vanquished by the shock of learning she had a sister. *A sister!* Perhaps it would not be so very bad to have a sister, someone who could tell her about their father. Or perhaps—yes, it was very possible that this Miss Lindsay had been adopted by John Lindsay, or even that she belonged to a relative.

Yet she heard the dismay in her mother's voice and knew that Mignon had not considered those options.

"Maman—there are other possibilities, you know. This Miss Lindsay may be a relative's child who came to live with him and took his name."

Mignon recovered a bit and nodded coolly. "Of course. I should not have become so distressed, but I was quite unprepared for this news. Someone should have thought to inform us before now."

Angie was struck by that truth, and then she thought with growing fury that Jake Braden had known all along and had never mentioned it to her. He *had* to have known. He had said he was John Lindsay's friend and of course he would know about this girl. Why had he not told her?

It was one more reason to loathe him, but it was hard to drum up the hatred. Right now, she was still too shocked by the discovery that she had a sister to think of anything else.

What would she be like? Would they like each other?

As Tempe promised, they reached the Double X in two days, and evening shadows cloaked the hills in deep purple when they crested a high slope dotted with grazing cattle. It was peaceful, the time of day when even the air seemed imbued with serenity and the disabling heat of the hot sun had melded into cooler shadows.

Riders, garbed in leather and guns but friendly behind their open curiosity, came out to meet them.

One of them, who said his name was Bill North, grinned at Angie and touched the brim of his hat with a finger in the customary gesture of respect and greeting.

"Glad you made it, Miss Lindsay. Colonel Patterson sent word that you should be gettin' here about this time, and we was gettin' a little worried."

"Is there reason to worry?" Mignon asked, and her voice had risen a little so that North glanced at her.

"No, ma'am, nothing in partic'lar. Just worried that you might miss supper."

That made Walker laugh, and as they accompanied North down the final slope, Angie saw the Double X for the first time. Her breath caught. Why, it was like a fortress! High stone walls enclosed a compound of scattered buildings, and it seemed to stretch for a mile, up and along the hill behind it until it disappeared. Treetops rose above the high walls, and red-tile roofs gleamed warmly. Patches of garden were visible, and fencing stitched enclosures around beanpoles and fruit trees. It looked to be self-sufficient, with windmills for water, and even a tank on high stilts.

"No, ma'am, we don't have much trouble gettin' water most of the time," North replied in answer to her question. "We're lucky enough to have a little spring that hasn't run dry on us yet. That's what makes this place so valuable."

Angie stole a glance at her mother, but Mignon's expression was impassive as they rode through the open gates and into the grounds. Was she thinking of long ago, when she had lived here with her husband? Did she really hate it so badly here, or was it John Lindsay she had hated? There were times when Angie wondered if Maman kept silent about it because she did not want to reveal how she had felt about her husband instead of the land.

But there was too much else to think about now that they were finally here, and Angie felt suddenly overcome with emotion at the long-awaited sight of her new home. Dogs barked wildly, scampering about the horses' legs in the dirt of the open yard as they came to a halt in front of the adobe-and-wood house. Dusty green vines wound up and over the long, low porch roof of the main house, tangled on trellises and heavy with white, fragrant blooms that were just opening in the deep dusk. Flowers edged one adobe wall, growing wildly over stones and a tile pathway, spicing the evening air with scent as they clambered over a small picket fence.

"It's beautiful," Angie said when Tempe Walker helped her down from her horse in front of the house, and her voice was hushed, as if she were in church, the wonder she felt at that moment like a knot in her chest.

The front door opened as she turned toward the house, and a large, smiling Mexican woman stepped onto the porch, followed by a young girl who *must* be her half sister Rita. They stood indecisively for a moment, until the Mexican woman came forward to greet them in accented English.

"Welcome, *señorita,* to your home. I am Concha Gonzales, and we are all glad you have safely arrived at last."

Angie moved forward with a smile of her own, feeling awkward and wondering if the girl—Rita—felt the same. Surely she must, for though she was obviously aware of the situation, she no doubt had known about it for some time. This was still so new, and just the thought of having a half sister was exciting and frightening at the same time. Perhaps they could be friends, and then Angie would not miss poor Simone so much. . . .

"Thank you, *Señora* Gonzales, for welcoming me," Angie replied, though her gaze shifted to Rita.

Light from a lantern hung from the porch roof flickered over the girl's face. She was unsmiling, with dusky skin and a black cloud of long hair worn loose over her shoulders. For a moment, Rita returned Angie's uncertain gaze steadily, then she turned slightly to speak to someone behind her, her voice a low, rapid flow of Spanish as she asked if this was the girl.

A man stood in the shadows, and Angie's heart skipped a beat even before he stepped into the light.

Jake Braden's tawny eyes met hers as he drawled, "Glad you made it, Miss Lindsay."

While Angie stood stiff and silent with shock, Rita laughed softly and slid her arms around Jake's middle to rest her head against his shoulder. A smile curved her mouth.

"Welcome, Angela. I believe you already know my *novio,* do you not?"

Novio—lover. Or betrothed . . . *Damn him!*

Later, Angie could only barely remember the reply she had made, vaguely conscious of Jake's admonishing denial to Rita and her own disdainful reaction as she acknowledged him with the barest of greetings and went into the cool parlor of the home that she had waited so long to see.

The constraint was evident, and while Jake and Tempe traded hostile glances, Mignon immediately appropriated the main bedroom, pleading exhaustion and a headache as she retired for the night with Concha scurrying at her heels. Tempe excused himself to tend the horses and the men, and that left Angie alone with Rita and Jake.

Angrily, Rita muttered to Jake in Spanish, "She took *my* room! Because she once lived here, she thinks she can come back and just take over again!"

"She is his widow," Jake replied softly, but his eyes moved to Angie, and he seemed to be waiting for something from her. An acknowledgment, perhaps? An explosion of anger at his perfidy? She really should blast him for his treachery, but she would not demean herself.

Nor would she betray that she understood them quite well, even though the dialect they spoke was a bit different.

Rita shrugged her disagreement, and the awkwardness grew heavy in the spacious room filled with heavy leather-and-wood furniture and sturdy tables. A stone fireplace stretched across an entire wall, and double doors opened onto a patio thick with greenery. An oasis in a barren land could not have been more unexpected or more appreciated.

"Well, Miss Lindsay," Jake finally said into the silence that was freighted with tension, "you must be tired. Rita can show you to your room if you're ready."

Ignoring him, Angie turned to Rita, furious that he would dare take it upon himself to act as a host, as if he belonged here—did he think his relationship with Rita gave him a right to play the host? She should tell him quite sharply that it did not, yet she did not want to insult her sister when she had only just met her. Nor did she want to try to become acquainted when Jake was there.

"I am very pleased to meet you at last, Rita. I am certain that we will have much to talk about tomorrow, but tonight I must rest. Would you mind terribly if I asked to be shown to my room now?"

A fleeting smile crossed Rita's lips, and her shoulders lifted in a shrug. "I had not thought you would be so tired, but of course, you are not used to the rigorous life yet. Shall I have Concha or Blanca bring you a tray?"

"Yes, please. It's been a long day, and you are right when you say that I am unaccustomed to the rigors of life out here. I am not, but I hope to soon feel at home."

Rita indicated Bette, who stood still in the arched doorway. "Does she sleep with you, or would she prefer her own quarters?"

"I am certain Bette would prefer her own room," she said, and turned to the dark-haired girl to include her in the discussion. "Would you not?"

Bette, obviously too weary to care about the subtle nuances of tension, only nodded. "*Oui*—I would like to have a small space to call my own, I think."

"Blanca will show you to the servants' quarters," Rita said then, and smiled at Jake. "Darling, would you be good enough to summon Blanca while I show our guest to her room?"

Angie clenched her teeth, refusing to glance at Jake when he said bluntly that he had work to do outside. "But I'll point Bette in the right direction. Good night, Miss Lindsay."

Angie ignored him and did not look at him when she left the main room to follow Rita down the long, cool corridor of plaster walls and stone tile. Her room was charming, with two wide windows that opened to the night and allowed in cool breezes rife with the fragrance of night-blooming flowers.

Moving to one window, she rested her palms against the broad window ledge to lean out. In the distance, the sharp ridge of mountains was black against the darkened sky, lit only by a thin moon.

"How beautiful," she murmured, and breathed in deeply as a cool breeze wafted through the opening to stir the light curtains. "With this view, I'll leave these open all the time."

"There are shutters you can lock in case of Indian attack," Rita said, and smiled when Angie turned sharply to look at her. "Sometimes they come down from the hills, but not usually at night. Not the Apache, anyway, because they don't usually want to anger their spirits by fighting at night. The Comanche are different. They love a night when the full moon is high and gives off a lot of light. It makes it easier for them to see their victims."

"Are you trying to frighten me, perchance?"

Rita grinned and looked suddenly very young, though she could not be much younger than Angie. Her dark eyes danced with deviltry. "Yes. Is it working?"

"Quite well, thank you!"

With a hand on the doorknob, Rita looked back at her. "I'm disappointed. You should not make it so easy. I'll be bored if you do."

"I'll try not to bore you. Tomorrow, I will be much braver—and meaner."

"Good. I love a challenge."

"I've been known to be quite formidable."

"So have I."

There was a definite challenge in Rita's eyes and tone, and even in the smile that curved her mouth as she eyed Angie with bold insolence. Yet Angie understood that, and would have felt the same if an intruder had come in as she was doing. With a flash of resentment, she wondered why her father had not arranged things more diplomatically, or why someone had not been considerate enough to inform her of what she would face when she arrived.

But perhaps no one had thought she would accept the challenge if she knew the difficulties it would present. They should have given her the choice, she thought then, instead of forcing her into such an awkward position. Not even Jake had bothered to inform her, yet she shouldn't be too surprised by that.

"Then we should both be well entertained in the future, don't you think?" Angie said casually as she turned to lean back against the window ledge and smile at Rita. "But I hope we can be friends as well. It would be wonderful to have a sister at last."

There was a long pause. Outside could be heard the murmur of men talking, and dogs barked. Cattle lowed, and a nightbird shrilled. Someone laughed, a soft, comforting sound of familiarity.

"I'll send Blanca with a tray," Rita said, and for a moment there was something like consternation in her eyes before she shrugged and turned away.

As the door shut with a soft click, Angie thought of Jake and Rita, and wondered if it was true that he was to marry her. Oh, God, how she absolutely *hated* him at this moment! All this time he'd known she had a sister and had not told her, and now to find out that he was so very close to her—what a fool she had been to ever give him a moment's thought or waste an ounce of emotion on him. It was obvious that Jake Braden had no morals or scruples at all, or he would not have made love to her while engaged to her own sister!

But still, when she lay awake in her bed and gazed out the window at the dark blue sky strewn with stars that night, she could not stop the overwhelming sadness that came over her, and she buried her face in her pillow to absorb the flow of hot tears.

More laughter drifted through the open window, a jarring reminder that she was in a completely different world from any she had known before. Here, nothing was as it seemed. Heat could form a mirage that looked like a lake on the hot earth, and Jake Braden could form an illusion that fooled her into thinking he cared. What a fool she was! Right now he was probably with Rita, whispering into her ear the same things he had whispered in Angie's, words he did not mean.

Angie was partially right. Jake was whispering in Rita's ear, but not the same things he'd whispered in hers.

"Dammit, Rita, what in the hell do you think you're doing?"

"I've grown up now. Didn't you miss me, Jake?"

She gazed up at him with teasing eyes, running her fingers over his chest in a light caress. He caught her arm at the wrist and held it away from his bare chest, frowning down at her. A soft breeze cooled his hot skin, sweeping across the yard in front of the cowhands' barracks, where he was staying.

"You only think you've grown up. You're acting like a silly child. Stop it."

"Why? You like it. I know you do. I used to watch you with Rosa, you know."

Amusement battled with irritation. "That was a long time ago. Rosa's married now."

"Yes, I know, but I'm not. I waited on you, just like I said I would."

"Rita, you know damn good and well I'm not going to marry you. What made you say that in front of everyone?"

She shrugged her shoulders. Lantern light revealed her mouth turned down in a sulky frown. "Oh, I don't know. Maybe because Angela is so pretty, and I saw the way you looked at her when she got here. You do like her, don't you?"

"Not that much. She's even more spoiled than you are."

Rita laughed, her good humor restored. "Is she? I might like her after all, then. At least she's not boring."

"No." Jake's lips twisted wryly. "She's definitely not boring."

Rita's eyes narrowed again. "Why did you arrive first? I thought you were supposed to escort them here."

"I did my part. Walker was capable of getting them here alive, and here they are."

"Walker—I know him. He comes to buy beef, just like you used to do. He's very handsome, and half the girls in Doña Ana sigh over him whenever he attends a fiesta or comes into town. Perhaps I shall get to know him better while he's here."

She was looking at him slyly, and he lifted a brow. "You might have trouble with that. I think he belongs to Miss Lindsay."

"Does he? Why would she choose him over you?"

"Maybe she has better taste than I gave her credit for having. Look, Rita, it's getting late and Concha will be out here looking for you. Go back to the house before someone sees you here and jumps to the wrong conclusion."

"I could stay, Jake." She moved closer and leaned into him again. Her breasts were firm and warm against his bare skin, and he felt her heart beating rapidly and the quick flutter of her breath against his neck as she gazed up at him. "No one will know about it unless you want them to. Do you remember the time you kissed me?"

"I remember the time you kissed me. It's a wonder your daddy didn't take my hide off with a bullwhip."

Rita laughed and made a wry face when he pushed her gently away. "He liked you. I heard him say once that I should marry a man like you."

"What he said was that a man like me would have no problem with taking a belt to your backside when you pull some of your crazy stunts. Go inside, Rita. It's late and I'm tired."

She pouted a little, but finally left, and Jake leaned against the support post of the small house occasionally used by visiting army officers. He built himself a cigarette and lit it, squinting against the curl of smoke that rose into the air.

Logan should be back some time in the night. Six Feathers had given up plenty of information after a few bottles of hard liquor. Between the Pecos and the Rio Grande was a box canyon where the renegades waited for another shipment of new rifles. Dave thought they might be up in the Malpais, where it was difficult to navigate the ancient lava beds unless you were familiar with them.

But Jake had another idea; it seemed more likely the renegades would stay closer to the source of their weapons. His mouth hardened. He hadn't been at all surprised to learn that it was his uncle who was involved in the ready supply of repeating rifles that were so lethal in the hands of the renegades.

It made his job easier—and harder. His uncle was no fool, and would guess why he was there if he showed up for no reason. But there was to be a fiesta soon, and it would cause no comment if he attended as he usually did. It was the only plausible plan.

No doubt Angie Lindsay would be there as well, and he thought cynically that she would probably ignore him again until he pushed it. Damn her soft white skin. He wished he could forget her, how she felt and how she tasted, but he found himself thinking about her when he should be thinking about more important things. She was like an itch he couldn't quite scratch, and he wondered impatiently when he would get over it. It was beginning to wear on his temper that even when he closed his eyes at night he saw her violet eyes and cloud of copper hair.

There had to be a way to put her from his mind, but he was damned if he'd figured it out yet. Worse, he hadn't even been tempted by another woman since Angie, and that in itself was unusual. If he wasn't careful, he might find himself moping around like a green youth in love, and that would be intolerable. He didn't have time in his life for a woman, save for brief physical encounters, and he sure as hell didn't have time for a troublesome woman like Angie.

He'd find a way to cure himself of this absurd need he felt for her. He didn't have much of a choice.

Part Four

The Crossing

July, 1870

20

Her first morning there, Angie awoke in a wide, soft bed, blinking at the broad streamers of sunlight that filtered into the room through open windows. Concha came in with a tray of coffee and rolls that were still hot, for steam wafted upward and filled the air with a delicious fragrance. She set the tray on a small table, then pulled drapes over the windows to shut out some of the light.

"Good morning, *la patroña*," Concha said cheerfully as she bustled about, as if the night before had not been an awful strain and awkward for everyone there.

Angie sat up against the fat feather pillows, still groggy from a deep sleep that seemed to have drained her.

"Am I the last one to wake?"

"*Sí*. Even the *señora* is up now, though she prefers to stay in her room. The soldiers are getting ready to leave, I think, and that handsome lieutenant has come to ask about you twice already this morning. Shall I tell him you will soon be available?"

"Yes, please. It won't take me long to dress . . . is there water in the basin pitcher?"

"*Sí, la patroña,* there is water, and clean cloths to wash and dry your face. Your gown is being pressed, and I will bring it to you as soon as the girl, Bette, has finished. Is there anything else you require of me?"

"No, thank you." Angie paused awkwardly. She plucked idly at the comforter spread over her, staring at the patchwork squares without really seeing them. She wanted to ask where Jake had gone, or if he was still there despite the constraint. Probably. It had certainly not seemed to bother him at all, and though Rita presented a bold front, behind the facade she sensed an uncertainty in her, as if she suffered the same sense of dispossession that Angie had always felt.

In some ways, their similarities should unite them, but at the moment a barrier was between them that would be difficult to surmount. Jake Braden was part of the obstacle. It made Angie so *angry* when she thought of how he had deceived her all this time when he not only knew about her sister but had been intimate with her as well! No, she could not mistake that look in Rita's eyes when she watched Jake, for it was uncomfortably close to how she had felt about him.

No more. Now he was just a hated part of her past, a mistake in judgment, but one that had taught her a necessary lesson. She had no intention of allowing him to fool her again or of allowing her to fool herself into thinking there would ever be anything more than physical intimacy between them.

It had been only that, after all, for he'd made it plain he had no use for her other than the use of her body. Hadn't he even said that to her quite bluntly that night on the steamer going to Galveston? Yes, and she had ignored it, as she had ignored so many other things she should have noticed.

It was all behind her now. She was here at last, and the world was fresh and new. As soon as she solved the problem of Jake Braden, she could get on with her life.

Outside the open windows were the noises of that new life: the crowing of a rooster, the distant lowing of cattle, and the muffled sounds of men going about their work on the ranch. The Double X was a productive business, supplying cattle to area forts and even to the Apache reservation at Fort Stanton. Who had told her that? Oh, yes—Jake.

Determined not to let anything spoil her pleasure at finally being here, Angie rose from the bed after Concha left. The coffee was hot and strong, the rolls flaky and very good. She had already eaten and started washing when Bette came in with the newly pressed gown, and the maid's eyes were bright as she chattered gaily.

"Ah, there are so many new things here! It was still dark, and that rooster woke me up, crowing under my window so loud! And the women, they are so calm, when all about them are men demanding food at a most unreasonable hour—I saw Captain Braden this morning, for all the men who work or stay here come into the kitchen to eat."

Angie dragged a wet cloth over her face, pretending an indifference she certainly did not feel in light of Jake's betrayal.

When she did not respond, Bette continued slyly, "Of all of them, Captain Braden is the most handsome, I think, though Monsieur Logan is very close. Do you not think so?"

"Mr. Logan is very handsome, yes. The sun has bleached his hair almost white in places, and with his dark skin and blue eyes, he is quite appealing."

Angie took the gown from Bette and stepped into it, foregoing cumbersome petticoats in favor of mobility and freedom. She had no intention of being hemmed in again—by anything or anyone.

"So true," Bette was saying in a dreamy voice. "Logan is most handsome."

"Speak English now, Bette. We are in America, and should conform."

"Conform?" The little maid tossed her head so that her dark curls bounced against her rosy cheeks. "Me, I can conform quite easily when I wish. But you—oho, you are not so easy to follow that suggestion! Do you think I have not noticed how you prefer being alone? Your own mistress? Yes, it is evident!"

An unwilling smile twitched Bette's lips as Angie turned to glare at her and saw the mischief in the girl's eyes as she grinned impudently.

"It is true, yes?"

"Yes, Bette, I suppose it is. Now, help me with my hair so I can be presentable when I meet everyone." She turned as Bette drew a hairbrush through her hair and pinned its copper lengths atop her head with a few combs, loathe to admit that she was nervous at the thought of meeting all the men who worked for her now. For *her*! Why not Rita?

As soon as possible, she intended to speak to Jake Braden and find out the details of her father's will. It would be too awkward to ask Rita, and there was no one else who could answer those questions. Jake would know, and by God, he would tell her the reason she had inherited the ranch instead of Rita, who had lived here all her life.

Renewed with determination, Angie stepped out into the hall and went to the parlor. She wore a lavender gown that hugged the curves of her body but fell loosely to her ankles to allow freedom of movement. It swirled around her legs as she walked, and when she entered the parlor, the men came instantly to their feet.

Dave Logan and Bill North nodded politely, but Jake leaned against the door leading to the patio with his arms crossed over his chest, his entire posture one of insolent negligence. He nodded coolly when her eyes met his, but there was a taut expression on his face that warned her he was not in the best of moods. Well, too bad! Neither was she, when she thought of how he had lied to her and tricked her.

"Good morning, gentlemen," she said as she swept across the room to a chair by the massive fireplace.

A chorus of greetings answered her, and she ignored Jake, who only stared at her with a strange, guarded tension.

"I trust you all rested well last night?" She seated herself, and by unspoken agreement they all took their own seats again. Except Jake, who remained where he was, silent and unsmiling.

For a moment she felt awkward, knowing they waited to see what she would say, and she wished suddenly that Maman would join them, for she always knew how to take charge of a situation. But wasn't this her home now? Her role to be in charge? Yes, of course, and she must start out being in command. She cleared her throat and stood up again, turning to face them.

"This is my first morning here, and of course, I will need to familiarize myself with the operations of the ranch for a while before I institute any changes or make any suggestions. So please pardon any questions I may ask while I observe you work that will no doubt seem foolish."

She had been looking at Bill North when she spoke. North was the foreman of the ranch, and he gave her back an appalled stare that made her falter a bit. It was Jake who spoke up, however, his voice abrupt.

"Don't come in here trying to change things, Miss Lindsay. It's working fine the way it is."

She turned toward him, angry at his audacity. "I was not speaking to you, Captain Braden. Mr. North is the ranch foreman, I believe."

"Maybe so, but he's too polite to tell you that you don't know a steer from a sheep and will only get in the way if you intend to stand around and observe."

"Are you suggesting I not attempt to learn the workings of this ranch?"

"Ma'am, I'm just suggesting that you take it easy. Listen a spell before you start handing out orders. These men won't take orders from a woman anyway, and if you start contradicting North, you're liable to end up punching cattle all by yourself."

"Must you call me ma'am, as if I am an old married woman?"

"Sorry," he said without sounding a bit sorry.

Angie was tempted to ask him to leave, but if he did, it was likely she would never find out what she wanted to know about this awkward situation. Not without alienating Rita, anyway, and she was strangely reluctant to do that.

"Thank you for your suggestion, Captain Braden," she said coldly, and turned back to Bill North. "Mr. North, I am sure you realize that I would never contradict any order or method of operation you have enacted."

North stood up awkwardly, twisting the brim of his felt hat in his big hands. "Yes, ma'am, I'm sure you won't. And you're welcome to look around at anything you like, but it'd be best if you have someone show you around. There's thirty thousand acres here, give or take an acre or two, and it'd be easy to get lost. Of course, you wouldn't want to ride out by yourself anyway."

"No? Perhaps not."

Nodding with relief, he said, "There's a lot of paperwork to go over, and of course, there's the mine shares you'll want to discuss with George Sherman, your father's attorney."

"Mine shares?"

He looked uncomfortable. "Yes, ma'am. Sherman can tell you all about it when he gets here in a few days."

"He means the Santa Rita mine, Angelique." Mignon entered the room in a cloud of perfume and confidence, and Angie turned with all the others as her mother crossed the parlor floor. "Is that not so, Mr. North?"

"Why, yes, ma'am, that's the one."

"This is a gold mine? Silver?" Angie's brow furrowed.

"Copper." Jake moved forward now, and his eyes were hard beneath his long lashes. "Once it belonged to the Spanish, and then to Franciso Elguca from Chihuahua, in Mexico. Of course, when New Mexico became part of the United States instead of Mexico, ownership transferred. The Mexicans say the mine still belongs to them, but the American government claims it belongs to us."

"Then who *does* it belong to?" Angie asked sharply.

"It used to belong to your father," Mignon replied in that same cool tone. "I assume he retained ownership."

Jake shrugged and looked at Angie. "I'll let Sherman discuss that with you ladies."

"It occurs to me that you know much more about my life than I find comfortable, Captain Braden," Angie retorted. "However, I would appreciate it if you would spare me a few minutes of your time."

"If you make it quick. I'll be riding out soon."

Angie wanted to scream with frustration. "I will be most happy to see you go; however, there is the matter of your pay and a few loose ends that I need to tend. Do me the favor of remaining here when the others leave."

"Since you ask so nicely, Miss Lindsay."

His mockery was abrasive, and she steeled herself for an unpleasant interview with him as the others took their cue and filed out the door, only Dave Logan pausing to hold out his arm to Mignon.

"Ma'am, I'll be glad to show you to the orchard, if you like. There's a bench out there just right for sitting in the shade."

To Angie's surprise, Mignon accepted his arm with only a slightly lifted brow to indicate her displeasure, then left the room without glancing again at Jake or Angie.

The parlor was empty now except for the two of them, and Angie turned to stare at him a bit angrily.

"You lied to me!"

"I knew you'd say that."

"If you knew it, why didn't you bother to tell me that I not only have a sister but that she's *living* here? Did you think I'd do something terrible if I knew?"

"What I thought doesn't matter. If John Lindsay had wanted you to know, it would have been made plain in his will." Jake shrugged. "Maybe he thought you wouldn't come out here if you knew about Rita."

"Why wouldn't I? Of course I would! That would give me even more reason to want to come. Especially now that he's dead. Who else will tell me about him?"

Her voice had quivered at the last, and his eyes narrowed a little when he looked at her.

"What about your mother?"

"She . . . she finds it difficult to discuss him at all. I thought—oh, I don't know what I thought would happen when I got here, but I suppose I thought I would find him alive and waiting for me, that it was all a hoax and he would greet me with open arms and I would meet him at last."

She saw in his eyes that he felt sorry for her, and she turned her back to him, suddenly unable to bear his sympathy. She'd rather have his hatred than his pity, and her words came out sharply.

"I'm certain you thought it would be quite amusing to be at your fiancée's side when I arrived. I hope my reaction did not disappoint you too greatly."

"Not at all. It was everything I thought it would be."

"You bastard!"

"Is that a question or an observation?"

"It's a character assessment!"

When she whirled away he put a hand on her shoulder, but she wrenched about to glare up at him, shoving hard with the flat of her hands against his chest. He caught her wrists and held them, his fingers digging painfully into her tender skin until she bit back a gasp.

"Don't," he warned when she lifted a foot to kick at him, and she paused at the menace in his tone. Then he laughed softly. "You're too predictable, Angie. Don't you ever give up without a fight?"

"Never. Let go of me or I'll scream."

"That ought to be interesting, but you've threatened me with that before, if you remember."

Oh, yes. She remembered. And she remembered how he had held her against his body and kissed her so ruthlessly, too.

"Damn you, Jake Braden! You are an immoral, licentious beast, and I should never have thought for a moment that you had even a shred of decency in you!"

"Your mistake." His hands fell to his sides and his lips flattened. A groove deepened in one cheek as he stared down at her. "You should have known better."

"Yes, I certainly should have!"

"Look, Angie," he said impatiently, "trading insults won't solve anything. I had my reasons for not telling you about Rita. Give her a chance, will you? She's taking this harder than you are, because John Lindsay was all she had left. Now he's gone, and she doesn't even have her home anymore. Think you can spare a little of that pity you're floundering around in for her?"

A clock on the mantel over the fireplace ticked loudly, the only sound in the room as they stared at each other. Angie was stricken. Did he really care that much about Rita, then? It must be true if he was trying to shield her, and she wished it didn't hurt so much to realize how little she mattered to him, after all.

To disguise her hurt and dismay, Angie shrugged with feigned indifference, and her voice was tart.

"If you'd thought so much of her feelings, you should have stayed away from me. Or do you intend to even let her *know* what happened between us?"

"I'll leave that up to you."

"Oh, I'm sure you'd like for me to do your dirty work for you, but I won't. You're the despicable beast who has caused this mess. You can explain to your precious Rita why you go from one of us to the other. But you can also tell her that I want nothing more to do with you while you're at it, because it's the truth. I prefer a gentleman, a man like Lieutenant Walker, who knows how to treat a woman."

"Then maybe you need to be talking to him, not me, Miss Lindsay. He's been waiting for you all morning. Shall I get him for you?"

Damn him! He was so coolly infuriating, staring at her with those eyes like chips of amber, cold and hostile instead of the warm lights she had once seen in them—why did it make her feel so terrible? Oh, and she knew she sounded shrewish, but she wasn't able to stop herself, wanting him to feel as badly as she did at this moment.

"There's no need for you to get anyone for me, Captain Braden. Unlike you, Tempe has been invaluable to me. I cherish his companionship and find that we have much in common. After all, he *is* a gentleman, well-bred and educated instead of an ill-kempt savage."

There was a lot more she wanted to say, but he didn't give her a chance. He pivoted on his heels and stalked from the parlor, leaving her standing alone in the room that smelled faintly of beeswax and lemon furniture polish. Tables gleamed, and a large rug covered the tile floor in front of the fireplace. She stifled the impulse to follow him and flung herself back into the chair she'd used earlier, confused and angry, and inexplicably hurt.

He had not denied that Rita was his betrothed. Nor had he offered any excuse for his actions. But then, he had warned her, hadn't he? Somehow, that did not exonerate him for making her think there was more to what had happened between them than just lust.

Her throat ached, and her eyes burned with unshed tears as she sat for a while, listening to the vague household sounds that were still so strange to her. Nothing had happened as she had once envisioned it would. And now there was this unexpected complication of a sister, as well as a mine the ownership of which apparently was contested. Her mouth twisted wryly. Maman would be most satisfied if she knew how at a loss Angie felt now, even to the point of wondering if she should stay.

But she had come all this way, and though the journey had not been too terrible, she was not eager to repeat it any time soon. No, she would stay, and perhaps if she could just *talk* to Rita, she could discover the things she needed to know if she was to be content here.

If only Jake Braden had not complicated things so, she and this new sister might have had a chance to be friends. Now she was not at all certain they would be friends, or even cordial to one another. Not if Rita knew or suspected about her and Jake.

As if summoned, Rita appeared in the parlor door then, and surveyed Angie with cool eyes.

"Have you seen my *novio*?"

Angie winced slightly at Rita's free use of the term, and nodded warily. "Yes, he was here a few minutes earlier."

Instead of leaving, as Angie expected, Rita lingered in the doorway. She wore a white cotton blouse with a gathered neck and short puffed sleeves, and a full skirt that looked cool and even more liberated than the one Angie wore. On her feet were simple sandals, such as the Mexican peasants wore. With her thick mane of dark hair and dusky skin, Rita looked exotic and lovely, and very young.

"How well do you know him?" Rita asked abruptly.

Taken aback, Angie fumbled for a tactful reply. "Do you mean Captain Braden?"

"Of course." Impatiently, Rita shook her head. "I've known him since I was twelve years old. I've been in love with him all these years."

"Oh." There didn't seem to be anything else to say, so Angie just looked at her. Resentment simmered inside her, warring with the inclination to bridge the widening gap that separated them. Jake promised to be a divisive wedge that would only complicate the situation, and she would rather not even talk about him. Not to Rita.

Rita ambled into the room, running an idle hand over a gleaming tabletop but watching Angie from the corner of her eye.

"Your mother is beautiful. My mother wasn't married to my father, but I suppose you know that."

"No, I didn't know that. I didn't even know about *you* until just before I arrived here."

"Really?" Rita's eyes widened almost ludicrously, and then she laughed. "I imagine that was a shock!"

"Well, yes it was. A happy shock, however."

"Happy?" Rita's eyes narrowed a little. "Hm. You say that now, but I have a feeling that you won't always be so happy about it."

"Why is that? You seem very nice."

"Oh, I guess I am." Hugging her arms to her chest, Rita leaned back against the stones that formed the fireplace wall and studied Angie seriously. "You're different than I thought you would be."

"Am I? What did you expect?"

"I don't know. Someone dainty, maybe. Like a desert flower."

"I would think desert flowers would be rather hardy."

"They don't live long. They're too fragile. If it rains they bloom, then die before the day is over most of the time."

"Maybe I'll be a cactus flower, then, and live longer because I'm prickly."

Rita grinned. "You're not so bad, I guess. I wasn't ready to like you."

"Because you're afraid I'll take over and make you leave?"

"Oh, you can't really make me leave, not according to the terms of my daddy's will. I own shares in the mine, so I'll always have an income, as long as I don't sell them. He gave the ranch to you because I don't want it."

She had come close now, moving to stand just in front of Angie, and

Angie could smell a light, powdery fragrance. At the moment, Rita seemed fragile and vulnerable as she stood gazing at her with dark, solemn eyes, and Angie found that she was growing ever more curious about this sister.

"Why don't you want the ranch, Rita?"

"I hate it here. It's too remote. I like to hear music and go dancing— *real* music and dancing, not the stuff the Mexican *vaqueros* play down by the bunkhouses at night. I want to see New Orleans, New York, maybe even Paris—have you been to those places?"

"Paris and New Orleans, yes."

"What are they like?" Rita came to sit beside Angie, and there was an eagerness in her now that made her entire body vibrate. She hooked her hands around one knee and rocked forward a bit. "Are there lots of people, and lights, and exciting places to see? Did you see anything wicked?"

"Yes, there are lots of people." Angie hesitated, then said softly, "I have never told Maman, but once when I was younger and went to Paris with my cousins, I visited a cabaret where the girls danced with short skirts and bare legs that kicked high into the air, showing much too much of their secrets to the men watching. It was very risqué you see, and we were not supposed to be there at all, for the men who watched were there to choose which girl to . . . protect from the others."

Rita laughed softly. "I know what that means. Were you shocked by it?"

"Yes, I was then."

"But you would not be now."

"Well, I am older now and have seen a little more of the world." Angie paused, then asked a question that had burned in her mind for years: "What was he like?"

"Who? Oh, our father? Big. Tall as a mountain pine, and just as tough." Rita smiled a little. "I've seen him wrestle a full-grown steer to the ground and not even get winded. He had eyes almost just like yours, you know. That deep shade of blue that turns purple sometimes . . . even your hair is like his in a way, though his was darker, with only streaks of red in it. I have my mother's hair and eyes."

"She must have been very beautiful as well."

Rita looked startled, then nodded. "Yes. She was, I suppose, though I don't really remember her. She died when I was only two."

"I'm sorry."

Shrugging, Rita stood up again, and seemed to draw a cloak of indifference around her. "I never really knew her. I suppose that's how you feel about our father."

"No, I feel . . . bereft. Cheated. I would like to have known him. I wish I'd had the chance to love him."

It was far more honest than she'd meant to be.

Angie was slightly surprised to realize that she meant it. There was something so vulnerable about this girl who was her sister, and despite the niggling feelings of rivalry that pricked her, she also felt a certain empathy. Had they not both recently lost a father?

Rita gave her an odd look and then turned away, moving to the parlor door before she paused to say over her shoulder, "When I marry, I shall leave here."

Then she was gone, with only the echoes of her cryptic remark left. Angie sank back against the cushions of the sofa. For a first conversation, it hadn't gone too badly. Barring open war, it might be all right after all.

21

It had changed in twenty years. Mignon sat on a bench in the shade of an orchard that had been only saplings when last she was here, and gazed past the gnarled, twisted limbs of apple and peach trees toward the distant ridge of blue-hazed mountains. In the mid-morning hour it was still and peaceful with birds twittering in the tree branches and the air still relatively cool. It seemed as if nothing could touch them here, no intruder able to penetrate the security of high thick walls that encircled the ranch.

Yet beyond the walls of the Double X, New Mexico was the same as it had always been—feral and deadly.

And deceptively cruel. All this time, John Lindsay had kept another woman, had another child, another life, while she lived alone in France. She should have divorced him, shocking as such an act would be. Why had she not known, or at least suspected, that he would take another woman and sire another child? If it had been a son instead of another daughter, would he have been so quick to summon Angelique to America?

Ah, God, it had been so difficult to regain her composure upon learning of it, almost impossible now not to demand answers from the dusky-skinned young woman who was John's youngest daughter. It was an insult, an affront to her pride and position as his lawful wife that heaped humiliation upon her head even after he was dead. He must have known how it would be, how she would feel, yet he'd never once hinted that there was another child of some illicit union with a Mexican peasant.

And no one had told her, not even Jim Patterson, who certainly should have mentioned it. It was an outrage. How was she supposed to deal with the girl? It changed everything.

Mignon drew in a deep breath. It was not, after all, the girl's fault, but she must know that there would be no compromise. The estate belonged to Angelique. She was John Lindsay's lawful heir, not a dark-eyed girl with flimsy garments and a sultry smile who claimed Jake Braden with much too exclusive an air.

A hot breeze stirred the green leaves of the apple tree closest to her and cooled her, and she smoothed the frown from her face to prevent wrinkles, then thought of her vanity and smiled. It was an old habit, foolish in ways, for she had never considered another man since John. Except one, of course, but that had been so long ago . . . he still thought her beautiful, if he was to be believed. Perhaps she was. If she stayed in New Mexico with the hot wind and burning heat, she would soon resemble a dried grape, with wrinkled skin and permanent frown lines between her brows from squinting in the relentless sun.

Ah, what did it matter? Soon it would be too late. She must worry about Angelique, must see her secure with a decent husband, not some-one like John—or Jake Braden, who watched Angelique much too closely, in her opinion. He was all wrong for her. He was too much like John, he was tough as this land, comfortable in it with his hard eyes and sun-bronzed face, the air of confidence that was comforting and frightening at the same time. And even more than John had been, this Jake Braden was dangerous in his way; a man who inspired fear in other men was always dangerous.

Was she the only one to recognize the danger? At times it certainly seemed like it. No one would listen, especially Angelique. But she had not really expected Angelique to, after all, for she was so headstrong and stubborn.

"Captain Braden is not a gentleman," she'd said to Dave Logan, but he had tactfully murmured a polite excuse, then left her alone in the orchard. She closed her eyes as she recalled planting some of these very apple trees, tiny twigs then, under a burning sun that seemed more likely to scorch them than allow them to grow. But they had.

Everything had grown and changed, altered beyond recognition. She had changed as well—had John changed before he died? She wondered. Angelique was unaware of it, but she, too, had received a letter from him, a most poignant reminder of what had once been between them as he penned words of persuasion to allow his daughter to come to New Mexico. But she had been afraid, not just of this untamed land but of John and of the feelings she had once held for him that she'd buried so deep. It was so much easier not to feel those stringent emotions that could tear at one's soul until any peace was shattered.

It was too much, too many memories gnawing at her soul with relentless persistence, and she rose abruptly from the garden bench. Fretful, Mignon turned toward the house. A hot wind sent up a small dust devil that swerved across her path, bringing along with it the smell of sage and creosote. How she detested that smell; it reminded her of the past.

And of John. . . .

Her throat closed. From the moment she had entered the house, she had seen him in every room and every item in the sprawling hacienda that had been only a three-room adobe house when last she had been here. Now it spread out into fifteen rooms, not counting the kitchen. There was even a room for the bath and convenience at the back of the house, a modern marvel that she would not have thought John would care about. No doubt, it was the girl, Rita, who had thought of it. The John Lindsay she had known would not have cared about such a convenience.

But she had to admit—to herself at least—that the red-roofed house with its gleaming white walls and carefully tended greenery seemed to be more a home than the primitive structure she'd remembered and expected. Small touches, like the fragrant flowers and herbs tucked away in corners and inside the picket fence, made all the difference. Inside the high, thick walls it was a small paradise.

Yet outside it was the same, with danger and death lurking in the ridged hills and arroyos.

How could she reconcile this place with the place of her memories?

As she drew near the house, Jake Braden emerged from the kitchens at the back. He strode toward her, his long legs closing the distance between them quickly. He wore heavy gun belts that crossed over his stomach, the holsters low on his thighs so that the butts of the twin pistols were within easy reach. He looked more like a gunfighter than an army scout, and Mignon wondered once again why Jim Patterson had sent him to New Orleans as their guide.

As always when she thought of Jim, she immediately pushed him from her mind, and she greeted Braden with a cool nod of her head.

"Good morning, Captain. You seem to be in a hurry."

"Ma'am, thought I'd let you know that I'll be riding out now."

"So you said. I thought you were to stay a while."

"No, ma'am. There are enough men here. You don't need me or Logan hanging around."

"What about the others?"

"Spencer, Higdon, and the others are riding out in the morning, but there are plenty of men left for protection. North is a good man; he's managed to keep the ranch intact and going strong. You'll be just fine."

"I see." Mignon hesitated. There was something else behind his decision. His deliberate indifference was too obvious. "Does this have anything to do with my daughter, Captain? I know Angelique can be ... difficult at times, and she does seem to have taken somewhat of a dislike to you of late."

The last was a shot in the dark, for it was far too plain that Angelique was very intrigued with Jake Braden, but it must be accurate, for his face changed subtly.

"If you'll forgive me for saying it, ma'am, your daughter is more than just difficult. She's headstrong and stubborn, and liable to get herself into real trouble if she ignores common sense. Someone needs to get a rein on her."

"Perhaps. But Angelique has always been willful. Since receiving John's letter and passage to America, she has been even more so. I do not really know her anymore. In the past weeks since we left San Antonio, she has changed a great deal."

If he was having an affair with Angelique, Jake Braden would not betray it, Mignon realized when he just shrugged and said, "Everyone changes."

"Yes, but my daughter seems more . . adult . . . now than she was when we came to America, Captain. I find it intriguing."

Jake slapped his hat against his thigh and looked past her, and she sensed his restless impatience to be gone.

"She's twenty-one years old. It's time she grew up, don't you think, Mrs. Lindsay?"

"Growing up and becoming experienced are two entirely different things, Captain."

"Not always." He looked directly at her now. "At times, it's a simultaneous event. Cause and effect, so to speak."

"You know, Captain, you rather intrigue me. At first I thought you merely a rough, crude frontiersman. Now I am not so certain. If you are trying to hide your education, it slips through at times in your speech and your views."

"Why would I hide an education, ma'am?" His drawling question sounded amused.

"I do not know, except that it must suit you for some reason. Yet you speak enough Latin to exchange gibes with another educated gunman, and you are fluent in French. You needn't tell me again that you learned it in New Orleans, for that is not true. The dialect is completely different."

Jake shrugged. "The girl I learned it from was born in the Loire Valley. We were close for a long time."

"No doubt, but I still do not believe that you are as uneducated as you like to pretend. And there are times that you seem vaguely familiar to me, as if I have met you before New Orleans."

"No, ma'am, we never met. Perhaps you knew some of my distant relatives, who are from this area. It's possible." He moved away, then turned to look at her again, and there was genuine concern in his eyes and voice when he said, "Be careful in choosing your friends, Mrs. Lindsay."

"I always am, Captain."

He nodded, then was gone, striding swiftly toward the stables and corrals, where she could hear men working with the horses. Yes, a most intriguing man, but she would swear she had indeed met him before.

Ah, well, it would come to her. Soon she would recall where she had met him, and when. Jake Braden had somehow become a part of their lives, as he was so obviously a part of Rita Lindsay's life. If she could, Mignon would keep him away from the Double X until Angelique had obtained her inheritance and they were gone. Life would be much simpler once he was gone. Yes, and she could perhaps *talk* to her daughter again, instead of the stranger she had become.

But now, she must see what she could do about this situation before it grew impossible.

Mignon picked her way down the broken brick pathway that angled up to the house, her skirts brushing against fragrant herbs that grew among the stones. Shiny green plants were heavy with red peppers among the garlic and onion stalks that thrust upward, and the fierce heat of the sun released their potent fragrance into the air.

Beyond the orchard a small garden provided beans, squash, and corn for the house, and in the kitchen could be heard laughter broken by occasional spates of Spanish from Concha as she directed one of the Mexican girls in the cooking. No, few things had greatly changed in the past twenty years. If she closed her eyes, it would all be the same.

In a few days, she would contact her old nemesis, for it was only he who could change things for her, and though she loathed the very idea of dealing with a man like him, she would do it. It was the only way.

Angie listened politely to Tempe, but her mind was on Jake. Did he really mean to leave? She could see him in the distance, saddling his horse and talking with Dave Logan and some of the other men, his movements spare and efficient. Oh, she did not care, she truly did not care if he left! Why should she still be thinking about him when he had made it so obvious he did not care for her?

"Angie," Tempe was saying softly, "I know this is a little early to ask, but do you suppose you would attend a fiesta with me in two weeks? It's an annual celebration, and there is usually lots of food and dancing.''

She dragged her attention back to Tempe and managed a quick smile. "Of course. That would be lovely. What are you celebrating?''

When Tempe grinned, he was really quite handsome, she thought with a sigh. If only . . .

"I never have figured that out, but it doesn't really matter as long as we have music and good food. One of the old-time locals gives the same fiesta every year. Most of the ranchers attend, and the women all dress up and look lovely to remind us lonely bachelors what we're missing by not being married.''

Feminine laughter rose into the air, and Angie saw that Rita had joined the men at the corral and stood very close to Jake. A lump squeezed her throat when Rita leaned against Jake and he dropped an arm around the girl's shoulders in casual intimacy. In only a moment, Rita had moved away from him, but nothing could lessen the impact of that gesture.

Angie stiffened when Jake glanced toward her, and she thought angrily, He better not try to talk to me now, not after what I just saw! Oh, he is so treacherous . . . I should never have been so foolish!

She turned back to Tempe, and a slow smile curved her mouth as she gave him a deliberately demure glance from beneath her lashes. Impulsively, she placed her palm against his chest and leaned closer, her voice soft.

"Are you hinting that you're lonely?''

His hand found hers, and he brought it to his mouth, turning it over to press a lingering kiss on her palm as his eyes held hers.

"I was until I met you, Angie.''

The husky intimacy of Tempe's tone made her uneasy, but she let him hold her hand a moment longer than necessary as she looked up at him with a gay smile, her tone light and flirtatious.

"How could you possibly be lonely with all these people around you?'' she asked glibly. "I cannot imagine that you would ever feel alone. Indeed, I would think you'd want solitude at times, when you are constantly surrounded by other soldiers.''

"A man can be lonely standing in the midst of a crowd,'' he said seriously, and there was such intensity in his blue eyes that she could not look away. "I'm tired of being alone. I want someone to share my life. I won't always be in the army. My father owns a shipping firm in Savannah, and I promised to go into business with him when I leave the military. We'd be well off, Angie. We could travel, see new places.

And Savannah is lovely, with miles of oceanfront and warm breezes off the water. You'd love it there. It's so green.''

Why must he be so earnest? Didn't he recognize when a woman was being only flirtatious? Angie fought a wave of irritation and guilt. Perhaps she should not so shamelessly flirt with him like this, for he was obviously more serious than she would ever be, and it wasn't fair to him.

Withdrawing her hand from his, she managed a nonchalant shrug.

"It sounds wonderful, Tempe. But I like it here. Oh, I know that may sound silly to you since you have been out here for a while, but it's still so new to me, so unique and wonderful—''

When she paused, he pulled a wry face. "I suppose it does seem unique at first. I remember thinking it was. Guess I'm just not as enthusiastic about New Mexico as I used to be. After a few Apache raids and chases through the hills and over desert sands, it palls.''

"Are the Apaches that bad out here?'' she asked to change the subject, and if he guessed her motive, he did not mention it.

"At times. Mostly renegade bands roam now, for others are either on reservations to the east or scattered about Mexico. But you have a few bands that are lawless and make their own rules, causing trouble when they can. It's those new weapons they're getting that make them so bold, I think, but we don't know where they're getting them or how to stop it.'' He frowned, and his blue eyes darkened. "The renegades have better weapons than we do most of the time.''

"Then it's more dangerous than I've been told.''

"At times. As with anything else.'' He smiled, and there was a warm light in his eyes. "I'll protect you, if you will allow it.''

Unwillingly, her eyes strayed past Tempe to the corral where Jake Braden was mounting his horse; he ignored the stirrups as he vaulted atop the animal in a graceful move that made her think of an Indian brave. He looked a part of the animal, a centaur of the plains, rough and capable.

Rita put a hand on his boot and he looked down at her, then bent slightly to kiss her on the brow. Angie's face burned with agitation and distress, and she wanted to look away but couldn't. Did he have to be so—*public* about his preference?

As Jake rode toward the gates he glanced over at them with an ironic smile and nodded coolly at Angie. Then he was gone, joining Dave Logan and disappearing through the gates without a single word to her, only that cool nod and an infuriating smile that left her with a lump in her throat and a feeling of overwhelming frustration and emptiness.

"Angie, aren't you coming to the fiesta?" Tempe prompted, and the insistence in his voice drew her attention back to him.

"Fiesta? Oh. Yes. Of course." The gate swung shut again, closing out the sight of Jake and Dave as they rode away. Her voice sounded strange to her as she murmured, "I am certain Bette and Rita will want to come as well, and perhaps we can persuade Maman to join us. She will no doubt know many of the people there."

"She may. It's been a long time since she lived here, and a lot more families have settled. She'll know some of them, though, those that have been here a long time, like the Riveras and the Maguires and the Holts. Some of those families have been here since this land belonged to Mexico."

Was she supposed to reply? She didn't know. Oh, she was so distracted now, her thoughts in turmoil as she struggled to regain the thread of conversation.

"Really? I thought the Mexicans had gone back to their homeland." Tempe shrugged. "For the most part they did, not always willingly. But a few stayed behind, became part of the United States."

"I look forward to meeting them, then."

Tempe lingered until Angie finally murmured a vague excuse about settling in and exploring her new home, then he took his leave with a promise to return in two weeks for her and was gone at last, rejoining his men, who were already mounted and waiting for him near the gates. This time as the gates opened and closed she felt only a sense of relief instead of the despair she had felt earlier, when Jake had gone.

Later, when she stood atop the thick wall to gaze out at the ridged mountain peaks that seemed to graze the sky, she wondered if she was doing Tempe a favor by encouraging his attention. She did not feel what he wanted her to feel, and it was unfair to let him hope.

Perhaps she should politely decline the invitation. It would be more honest than pretending an interest she certainly did not feel. But it would be an excellent way to meet her neighbors, people who had known John Lindsay, and she did not want to refuse. When she went to the fiesta, she would find a way to gently tell him that she wanted only to be his friend, and nothing more intimate.

It had nothing to do with Jake Braden, nothing at all.

22

Days passed slowly in a haze of dust and heat, but to Angie they seemed to fly. She savored the long hours as she explored the house, delighting in each find that defined John Lindsay a little more for her. He must have been a complex man, for the little bit Rita told her—grudgingly—about him was often at odds with what she heard from the men who had worked for and with him.

Slowly, she was piecing together a picture of John Lindsay that was both intriguing and ordinary. He was an enigma, rather like the land around her. Had he been a successful rancher but a lackadaisical father? If she chose to believe Rita, that was true. Yet he had managed to carve out of this wilderness a thriving ranch that supplied beef to military forts and even an Indian reservation, holding the land against great odds. Floods, bitter winter weather, Indian raids, and scorching heat often worked against the settlers in the area, yet they stayed, caught by the beauty and promise of success.

New Mexico was a land of surprising contrasts, some beautiful and exotic, other aspects mundane. She wished she could explore the surrounding area more fully, but every time she mentioned it, Bill North or one of the others dissuaded her.

"Ain't safe, ma'am," North usually said with studied courtesy and a thoughtful frown. "Them renegades have been kickin' up a fuss the past few months."

"But have they been in this area lately?"

No, they had not, North had been forced to admit, but that was no guarantee.

Angie's patience was waning. She was eager to see the land that was hers, to survey the beautiful ridged mountains and broad plains that fanned out beyond the walls of her prison. Yes, she was beginning to feel imprisoned, but would not admit it. Maman would only look at her with knowing eyes that conveyed her thoughts without her having to say a single word.

Mignon had become closed in upon herself, withdrawing to her room with a headache far too often. The visit from George Sherman, a local attorney, had much to do with it, Angie thought privately. For he had stated quite plainly that John Lindsay's will was iron-clad.

"He was of sound mind, Mrs. Lindsay, when he wrote it. Angela is to receive control of the ranch if she so desires and all the proceeds thereof, after having lived here for one year in entirety. If she chooses at any time to leave, ownership reverts to his youngest daughter, Rita Maria. Both young ladies share in his portion of the Santa Rita mine, and the benefits derived from the copper are to be divided between them, with Rita receiving the larger portion in lieu of her share of the ranch." Here Sherman paused, glancing up at Angie and Rita with an apologetic smile. "Should both young ladies refuse ownership or pass away, control of the ranch then goes to a conglomerate composed of three men, whose names are to remain confidential until such time as it should be necessary to reveal them."

"I see," Mignon said quietly after a long silence fell and Sherman began to gather up his papers and stuff them back into a battered leather case. "Can you tell me what option Angelique has if she does not wish to remain here?"

"Maman! There is no point in asking that, as I do intend to stay," Angie protested, but Sherman pursed his lips and chose to reply.

"She may return home to France with a small stipend from her shares of the copper mine, but that is all, Mrs. Lindsay. The ranch is very valuable, as it has contracts to supply beef to the army posts and reservations. Once the railroad gets this far, its worth should increase tenfold. Mr. Lindsay did not wish to see unscrupulous men gain control of these lands, and he has taken every precaution to prevent that. He loved this land, you see."

"Yes," Mignon replied with a touch of bitterness, "I know that only too well. Thank you for your time, Mr. Sherman."

She rose to her feet and the interview was over. Later, she refused to discuss it with Angie, but chose to remain in her room most of the time, writing letters and pleading a headache.

To Angie's surprise, she accompanied them into town several days later, venturing out with the protection of Bill North and several of the ranch hands to the nearby small town of Doña Ana. It was a brief expedition to buy supplies, and Mignon disappeared for a short time to the post office, where Angie found her sending a telegram.

"Who are you sending a telegram to, Maman?" she asked, but Mignon only shrugged and said that she had personal business of her own to take care of.

"Do you think you are the only one with business affairs, *ma petite*? You are not. I, too, have affairs of my own here, you know."

Maman had become estranged, secretive, and withdrawn since they'd arrived in New Mexico, and though Angie did not understand it, she did not pursue it. As long as Maman was content, that was all that mattered, and Mignon swore that she was quite content now that they were finally here.

"It has changed," she admitted on the way back to the ranch from Doña Ana, "and I feel safer than I did the last time I was here."

"Then you will stay in America with me?"

Hesitating, Mignon finally shrugged and murmured a noncommittal reply, saying that time would tell if it was the right thing to do. "Besides," she added, "you may not want to always stay yourself."

"Oh, I don't think I'll change my mind." Angie surveyed the land beyond their buggy, the rugged hills thick with brush, and in the distance, tree-studded mountains. "This is mine, and I hope to stay here."

Mignon did not comment, and when they returned to the ranch, she went immediately to her room, pleading a headache caused by the heat of the sun.

Early one morning several days later, Rita came to find Angie in the orchard. She stood awkwardly for a moment, stripping the leaves from an apple twig she'd broken off a tree before she asked, "Would you like to go for a ride?"

"A ride—you mean away from the ranch?"

Rita's lips twitched. "Yes, that's usually more interesting than trotting around the corral."

The suggestion was too tempting for Angie to waste time being irritated at Rita's sarcasm, and Angie surged to her feet and nodded. "I'm ready, but I'm surprised that Mr. North has changed his mind. He was so vehement yesterday that I not venture beyond the walls."

"Bill North is a fusspot." Rita pushed impatiently at a loose strand of dark hair in her eyes and watched Angie with a slight frown. "You don't intend to go telling him that we're going, do you? Because if you do, we'll end up peeling potatoes or crocheting a rug with old Juana instead of riding."

"Oh." Angie hesitated, a little deflated at this revelation. "Then it's not safe."

Rita snorted. "I was born here, remember? I've lived here all my life, and except for a time or two, the only danger I've run into has been an occasional rattler or a drunken cowboy. Well? Do you want to go or not?"

It was tempting. And after all, Rita was right. She knew this land well and would not endanger herself.

"Yes, but I must change into a riding skirt first."

"Hurry. I know a place where the water comes down over a pile of rocks to form a fall and there's a small pool beneath it that I like to swim in. Do you swim?"

"I can, but it's been a long time."

"Great. Meet me at the stables when you're ready. And don't talk too much or one of those blowhards will try to stop us from going. If you don't hurry, I'll leave you."

If this was Rita's best foot forward, Angie thought as she changed clothes, her congeniality left a lot to be desired. But at least she was making an attempt, and so Angie should try to meet her halfway. Since they were sisters—despite Maman's refusal to acknowledge it—they might as well be cordial, shouldn't they? It might alleviate some of the tension around the sprawling house lately, and hopefully end the barbed comments Rita seemed to enjoy using at meals in the dining room.

It was only when they met for the private family meal in the evening that Rita grew surly, making tart comments to Angie and Mignon. In the kitchen in the mornings, when they ate with the hands, she laughed and joked with the men, and it was then Angie had glimpsed the girl Rita must be when she didn't feel so uncomfortable.

She knew how Rita must feel, for she felt it herself. And why not? It was an awkward situation, and it mystified her that John Lindsay would have created it when he could so easily have eased things for all of them with a bit more information and consideration.

Angie slipped from the house, closing the front door behind her. It was still early enough to be fairly pleasant, and a cool breeze tousled the heads of flowers blooming alongside the short pathway to the front gate of the tiny enclosed yard around the house. An incongruous picket fence had been erected around the house, an attempt at a garden that had only half succeeded. But the plants that survived waxed beautiful, and she thought of Rita's efforts at making a "silk purse out of a sow's ear," as she had wryly referred to her garden.

It was quiet for the most part as she neared the stables, meeting Rita as she led two horses out to tie them at the corral fence. She swept Angie with a glance, and her smile was a little patronizing as she said, "Guess I'll have to saddle your horse for you."

"Not necessarily. Where's the tack?"

Rita's brow rose, and she indicated the small room with a jerk of her head, but the smile did not waver until Angie returned with a saddle, blanket, and bridle. It was a coup of sorts that Angie was able to bridle and saddle her own mount, and she felt Rita's eyes on her as she performed the task with slow but certain movements.

When she was done, she turned to look at her. Rita had already finished, of course, but the smugness had disappeared to be replaced with a grudging admiration that went unspoken except for a brief nod of approval.

"Most of the men are out checking on the cattle, but a few of them are hanging around here trying to look busy when they see Bill coming. Follow me and do what I do, and no one will ask any questions."

No one stopped them or even seemed to notice as Rita opened the front gates, then mounted her horse and motioned for Angie to follow. As they rode through, one of the hands came up and shouted, and Rita told him to shut the gates behind them. If he had any reservations, he didn't offer them, and instead moved to obey.

"That was easy," Angie said when they were a little way from the walls. "If I had known it would be so simple I would have done this last week."

Rita shrugged. "You couldn't do it alone. They'd know to stop you, but I do this all the time. They're used to seeing me ride out."

"Aren't you ever afraid?"

"Of what?" Rita tugged at the wide-brimmed hat she wore atop her head, pulling it lower over her face. Then she glanced at Angie as the horses settled into a brisk trot. "Where is your hat?"

"This is it." Angie touched the brim of her straw bonnet. "I wore it all the way from Corpus Christi."

"It won't be enough out here. I don't know how you've kept from burning and peeling as it is, with that dead white skin of yours."

Angie pressed her lips tightly together. If Rita wanted an argument, she would have to wait. It felt too good just to get away, to ride without restriction or someone looking over her shoulder. And really, she understood some of what Rita must feel.

"Maybe you're right," was all she said, and Rita gave a shrug and lapsed into silence broken only by the thud of hooves against the hard ground.

The sun beat down, burning her even through the layers of clothes she wore, and she wished she'd thought to bring her gloves. The backs of her hands were getting red, and her palms were sore from the chafing of the leather reins. But the air was clear and the mountains beautiful.

Strange plants dotted the landscape, and a shallow creek cut through rocky ridges. The plains swelled upward in graduated knolls scattered with mesquite bushes. Green leaves concealed sharp thorns on the slender branches, and the twisted, stunted shapes of the bushes often rose to the height of small trees. Yucca plants sprouted in clumps of ten-foot stalks, bristling on the rolling land like silver-green swords. Neither woman spoke as they rode along, crossing a meadow thick with tall grama grass to reach a creek. Here the ground rose sharply, becoming more barren in places. Prickly pear cactus and rabbit brush fanned over the land and grew in rocky crevices as they followed the meandering path of the creek.

Some time had passed before they reached the waterfall Rita had promised, and Angie dismounted gratefully.

"It's beautiful . . . however did you find this place?"

Water tumbled from a high ridge, bouncing off boulders to spill into a shallow pool below. Cottonwoods crowded the banks, providing sketchy shade. It felt cooler already, and the thought of dipping into that cool water was enticing.

"Jake's right," Rita said abruptly, "you aren't so very boring."

Angie stiffened. "I wasn't aware that Captain Braden was in the habit of discussing me."

"He isn't. I asked about you. Well," she said crossly when Angie glared at her, "how else was I supposed to find out anything about you?"

"You could ask me."

"Like you asked me?"

Angie didn't respond for a moment. She pushed her hands into the small of her back and arched to stretch her cramped muscles.

"You're right," she said unexpectedly, surprising them both. "Perhaps we should start over. If you have any questions you want to ask me, go ahead. And I will do the same with you."

Rita turned to loosen the girth on her saddle, and Angie began to think she intended to ignore the invitation, but in a moment she turned back, upending the saddle on the ground to dry as she said, "Fine. I will."

"Go ahead. What do you most want to know about me?"

"Are you in love with Jake?"

The question wasn't entirely unexpected, but it was much balder than she'd thought it would be, and Angie smiled ruefully. "You don't believe in subtlety, I see. Well, since I started this, I'll answer honestly—I have no idea what I feel for Jake Braden. At times I hate him. And at others . . . I just dislike him. Is this why you brought me out here? To ask me about Jake?''

"Is that your question?'' Rita asked slyly, and grinned when Angie frowned. "Never mind. Yes, I guess it is the main reason I wanted you to come out here with me. And maybe I just wanted to see if you really do like this land the way you say you do.''

"It would be rather difficult to tell that after a few hours' ride, I would think,'' Angie murmured. "Would it make a difference if I hated it out here?''

"Yes. Then you would leave.''

"Is that what you want me to do?''

"At times. I can't help but wonder why you really came all this way, why you would leave the city to come here where there's dust, tarantulas, rattlesnakes, and Apaches. It doesn't make good sense.''

"Yet you are here.''

"I was born here. I never had a choice. Even now I don't really have a choice.'' Rita paused and looked down at the ground, scuffing the toe of her boot over the yellow earth. "I may have money, but I still have no place to go.''

"Are you afraid to travel alone?'' Angie asked in some surprise. "You could, you know. Take one of the servants with you and—''

"I'm not afraid!'' Dark eyes flashed angrily. "It's not that at all. Besides, I'm going to marry Jake, remember?''

"Yes. I remember. He can take you where you want to go.''

"But he won't.'' Rita moved restlessly away from the horse and sat down beneath a cottonwood to tug off her boots. "He says he likes it out here. I don't know if I can get him to leave. I can't even get him to stay when I want him to.'' She laughed softly, cutting Angie a glance from beneath her lashes. "But he's always been that way. One day he'll come back and settle down. After all, he's already been halfway around the world, and he's seen everything I want to see. I used to think we'd see it together, then I found out he'd already seen it all. Funny, isn't it? He doesn't really care about it, and I do, yet he's the one who's seen France and England, and even India, and I'm still here in the middle of the desert.''

Angie didn't say anything as she sat down beside Rita and pulled off her boots and stockings. They both peeled down to chemises and pantalettes, and Rita went first, bending slightly to sweep a foot in a skimming motion through the water.

"Not so cold,'' she pronounced it, and jumped in without another word, disappearing beneath the surface only to bound back up again.

Clawing hair from her eyes, she eyed Angie, still on the bank. "Well? Are you coming in?"

Angie took a deep breath and plunged into the water, gasping a little at the shock of the cold water on her heated skin. She found her footing quickly, for it was fairly shallow here, coming up to her chest. It occurred to her that she would never be able to explain her wet hair and undergarments when she returned, but that didn't matter now.

She felt free, deliciously abandoned as she splashed in the pool. Rita floated nearby, her long dark hair drifting on the surface around her like a sable cape. Her eyes were closed, the wet cotton of her chemise clinging to her as it no doubt clung to Angie, concealing little. But it was desolate here, with no one likely to discover them.

Both of them drifted for a while, with the sun burning down from above and the cool water beneath. It was so quiet and restorative, and Angie watched through slitted eyes as a hawk circled overhead, wheeling through the pitiless blue of the sky in lazy loops, wings spread wide and an occasional cry piercing the air.

For the first time since she had arrived in New Mexico, she felt at home. She was suddenly grateful to Rita for giving her this gift. It was what she'd been searching for since receiving her father's letter, this sense of peace and belonging that had eluded her until now.

Perhaps it was only fleeting, but the emotion eased some of the sting she'd felt at Jake Braden's blatant rejection of her, his obvious preference for Rita. It should not have mattered to her so much, but it did—though she would not admit it to anyone else, of course.

It was so pleasant to relax like this and not think of anything else, especially Jake Braden, and she pushed him firmly from her mind. Water lapped around her body and filled her ears so that she could hear only the rhythmic thud of her own heart pumping, and she closed her eyes and tried to think of nothing.

Finally Rita spoke, her voice sounding as lazy as Angie felt as she suggested they sit on the rocks to dry out. "Or Concha will know where we've been. She probably will anyway, but there's no point in making it too easy."

Laughing, Angie stood up in the water and slicked her hair back from her face. "I take it you do this fairly often then," she said.

"Often enough. Since I've gotten older Concha doesn't dictate to me as much as she used to, but she still scolds enough that I'd rather avoid it if I could."

Rita waded through the water and clambered up the bank to perch atop a flat rock heated by the sun, and Angie followed her. Though the shade of cottonwood branches filtered the light, it was still hot enough to warm her, and she stretched out her legs and wiggled her toes as she began to pull her fingers through her hair.

"I imagine you've led rather a carefree life at times," she mused aloud, and was surprised when Rita snorted.

"A lot you know! It hasn't been easy. Just because you never knew him, you seem to think our father was wonderful. Oh, he was sometimes, believe me, but more times than not he was just irritable. I can remember doing things just to get his attention. He was always so busy buying cattle, rounding up cattle, selling cattle, fixing fences, or breaking horses that he often forgot about me."

A careless shrug accompanied this recital, and Angie looked at Rita curiously, compelled by a pang of sympathy to murmur, "I'm sure he loved you."

"Of course he loved me!" Rita threw her an angry glance. "Why wouldn't he? I was just trying to tell you how busy he was, that's all."

Angie's hands stilled in her hair, and she stared at Rita in exasperation. "I didn't mean anything by it, Rita. I never got the chance to know him, so I'm eager for anything you can tell me, I guess."

"Yes, well, I've told you all I can." Rita stretched out her long, brown legs and stared sulkily at her toes. "Why did you really come here, Angie? I mean *really*?"

"I told you. It's a chance to be independent and to learn what I can about the man who was my father. You may not want to hear it, but I do feel cheated by not having had the chance to know him."

"Yes, you said that." Rita drew her knees up to her chest and wrapped her arms around her legs to study her toes with fierce intensity. "You couldn't have been independent in France?"

"No. It's different there. I would be expected to marry a man I didn't love just for security. I didn't want to do that."

Rita lifted a brow. "So you came here to find a husband?"

"No, I told you that I came to America to meet my father. Until I arrived in New Orleans, I did not know he was dead. I came to New Mexico to be independent."

"You're liable to be disappointed." Rita plucked a long blade of grass from where it sprouted between two rocks, and began to chew on the stem, watching Angie. The sound of falling water was loud, and one of the horses blew softly and continued munching the sparse tufts of grass beneath the spreading cottonwood. "It's the same here as it is in France. Men expect you to be available or good, but not both. A Saturday night whore and a Sunday morning saint. I haven't met one I'd give a tobacco plug for. Except Jake." A frown stitched her brows over her nose, and she spat out the grass and shrugged. "The only other man

I've met who might be worth a nickel is that handsome lieutenant who hangs around you like ants at a picnic.''

"Tempe?'' Angie was surprised she'd even noticed. "Why do you say that?''

"I don't know. I guess because he's always so nice to me when he comes to buy beef. He has the job Jake used to have. That's how I met him, you know—I mean Jake . . . as well as Lieutenant Walker. Jake started coming to the ranch when I was only twelve to buy beef for the army. He was at Fort McLane then. It's gone now, abandoned about six or seven years ago, but it was close to the ranch. Closer than Fort Selden—and *much* more convenient, if you get my meaning.''

Angie intercepted her sly grin and knew exactly what she meant, but preferred not to acknowledge it.

"Lieutenant Walker has been very effective,'' Angie said. "When we were attacked by Indians before reaching El Paso, he fought so bravely I didn't even have time to be frightened. It was over quickly, and he saved my life by dragging me into Fort Stockton just in time.''

"Yeah, Jake saved my life like that one time.'' Rita slid her another sly glance and leaned back to brace herself on her arms, stretched behind her as she gazed up at the still, dusty cottonwood branches over her head. "It was a long time ago. I was sixteen, and old enough to know better, but we had been out to a line shack at Mimbres Canyon. I don't guess I have to tell you why. When we were coming back, a band of Apaches got after us. Jake rode right in beside me, shooting the hostiles off their horses to get me to safety. When I was inside the gates, he took off, and he came back later with one of their scalps as a trophy.''

She laughed softly when Angie made an involuntary sound of revulsion. "Didn't you know that he's supposed to be part Indian himself? That's the rumor, anyway.''

Angie looked away. "I'd really rather not discuss Jake Braden.''

"No? Why not?''

There was a definite challenge in her tone, and Angie shrugged. "I do not find him as intriguing as you apparently do, I'm afraid.''

Silence fell. Then Rita said tautly, "Liar.''

"I beg your pardon! What do you mean by that?''

"Just that I've seen both of you together. I'm not blind and I'm not deaf. I've seen the way you look at him.''

"If you think I'm intrigued by him, you're wrong. I find him to be despicable.''

"I know him better than you do, and he's not at all what you say!''

Rita surged to her feet and reached for her skirt and boots. The thin strap of her cotton chemise slipped down her bare brown arm, and she shoved it back up. "It's getting late. We should go."

Angie got slowly to her feet. The pleasant mood had been dispelled, but it was difficult to know what to say to Rita. She was so touchy at times.

She had dressed and was still braiding her wet hair when Rita moved to her horse and began to mount, and by the time she reached her own mount, Rita was reining around.

"Wait," Angie protested, "I'm not ready yet."

"Too bad." Rita paused, eyes narrowed beneath the brim of her wide hat. "You can catch up."

Alarmed, Angie grabbed for her mount's dangling reins as Rita drummed her heels into her horse's sides and took off at a gallop. But when she tried to mount, the saddle slipped to one side and she had to tighten the girth. By the time she was finished, the only sign of Rita was a faint, hazy dust cloud.

Angie drew in a deep breath to stifle the panic that welled inside. No, she would not let this frighten her! Rita was only being contrary. Surely she would not leave her out here alone.

Mounting slowly, she nudged her horse forward in the direction from which she thought they had come. No doubt Rita was just ahead, hiding behind a rock or a clump of mesquite and laughing to herself about how she had frightened Angie. As tempting as it was, Angie did not intend to betray her fear when finally she caught up with Rita, but would pretend a nonchalance she certainly did not feel at this moment.

She held a tight hand on the reins and kept the horse to the rutted track that led from the ridge to the flatter land above. They had come this way, hadn't they? The line of trees looked vaguely familiar, and the sun was behind her now, so she should be traveling east. Yes, the Double X was this way, and Rita was probably waiting not far ahead.

Damn her, does she think this is funny? *I* certainly don't, Angie fumed. Perhaps it is time I say what I really feel instead of trying to be so polite! This is ridiculous, and I shall tell her exactly what I think when she finally shows up again!

Ocher expanses of land swept around her in confusing similarity as she rode at a sedate pace, and when what seemed like miles had passed and Rita had not appeared to end her uncertainty, fear began to supersede her irritation. It was so desolate, with only the circling hawk overhead to mark her progress. Nothing stirred for miles. Nothing looked familiar, and no landmarks rose to point the way. It all looked the same to her.

Unbelievable as it seemed, it looked as if Rita had indeed abandoned her.

Angie began to grow afraid.

23

Mignon stared at Rita in disbelief. The girl looked wretched, with big dark eyes full of guilt and tears, and her lower lip trembled as she repeated again that she had only been teasing.

"I thought she could see me, I swear it! But she must have gone in the other direction, because when she didn't come after me and I went back, I couldn't find her. Oh, please believe me, I never meant to lose her like this!"

"No? Then how *did* you mean to lose her, if not like this?" Mignon demanded sharply. "You know she is not familiar with this country, and now your childish prank has probably cost Angelique her life."

"You sound as if you think I *meant* to do it!"

"Did you not?"

"No!"

Rita stared at her belligerently, and Mignon fought the almost overwhelming impulse to slap her hard across the face. It would solve nothing and only add to the tension between them.

She turned back to the ranch foreman, who looked miserable and awkward standing in the parlor.

"How many men are you taking with you to look for her?" she asked Bill North, and he seemed relieved that she was no longer talking to Rita.

"About ten or fifteen. We'll spread out. It won't be dark for a few hours yet. If she has sense enough to stay in one place, we should find her pretty quick, ma'am."

"But if she tries to find her way back?" Mignon could not help asking the question, though she knew the answer. How could she forget the time when she had wandered this arid land alone? Sunburned and frightened half out of her wits, stumbling over burning sand and rough rocks, she had been nearly delirious by the time an army patrol had happened upon her. It was only chance that had saved her, and now her daughter was out there and might not have the same luck. She felt sick with apprehension.

"If she gets close enough," North said, "we'll find her. If she goes the other way, she's liable to run into Doña Ana or even Fort Selden. I've sent a man to the fort to get help in finding her, just in case."

Mignon drew in a deep breath. "Yes, thank you. I am certain that with all this assistance, she will be found quickly."

When North had gone, Bette joined Mignon in the parlor, bringing a headache powder and holding it out anxiously.

"You will take this now, yes?"

"No, Bette. Not now. I don't want to sleep. I want to wait for Angelique to return."

Bette looked distraught, and Mignon turned away, unable to bear anyone else's distress when she was still so upset.

"I would like to be alone now, however, Bette. Please inform Concha that I will take my evening meal in my room, and I want to be informed the instant word arrives."

"Yes, madame."

Being alone was worse. She fretted, alternately cursing the fates and the wayward girl who had cruelly left Angelique to fend for herself in such a hostile land. How could Rita have been so malicious? And Angelique—to have left the safety of the high walls and ventured out bordered on insanity! What would she do if something had happened to her daughter? She would never forgive herself for allowing Angelique to come to this terrible place.

Her hands clenched into tight fists and she drew in a deep, shaky breath. A messenger had come today with a reply to her telegram. At first she had wavered. Now she knew what she must do.

If Fate was kind and returned Angelique unharmed, she would agree to Don Luis's first suggestion and do what must be done to protect her daughter and rid them both of this cursed land. . . .

"Rider comin'!"

The two words penetrated her fear and anxiety, and Mignon wrenched open her bedroom door and flew outside to stand on the veranda. Would it be her? Or one of the men returning without her? She murmured a brief prayer of hope.

Night shadows were lowering, turning the mountains to a blue haze and the air crystal clear, and as the heavy gates swung open, lantern light flickered over familiar copper hair in welcome glints. Mignon

sagged with relief and leaned against a support post as Angelique rode
alone into the compound.

She was safe . . . thank God.

One of the men took her horse, and another helped her dismount. She
slid from the lathered animal and accepted the offer of an arm, limping
slightly as she approached the house.

Mignon went to meet her, struggling to remain calm.

"Did Bill North find you, Angelique?"

"No." She pushed a damp, lank strand of hair from her forehead,
and her face was a hot pink even in the dim light. "I didn't see anyone
or anything except lizards, scorpions, and a rattlesnake that almost got
the best of me. I'm hot, tired, and thirsty, and when I've had my bath,
I'd like to talk to Rita. I assume she made it back just fine?"

"Yes." Mignon gestured toward the house. "She's waiting inside."

"How convenient."

As they came into the light from the lantern dangling from the veranda roof, Mignon saw streaks of dirt on her daughter's pale cheeks,
and recognized the set of her mouth. She was angry now, but she had
been terribly frightened. The tear tracks were ample evidence of her
fear.

"*Ma petit chou*—how did you find your way back without help?"

"Thank God the horse got hungry. It probably knew the way back
all along. I should have let it find the way hours ago, but I thought . . ."
She drew in a shaky breath and her lower lip quivered slightly as she
finished in a murmur, "I thought I could be so damned independent!
Oh, Maman, I was terrified out there!"

"I know. Oh, I know well how you felt." Mignon put a hand on her
daughter's shoulder, and as the door opened and Concha came to welcome them, she said softly, "Perhaps one day I will tell you—"

"*La patroña!*" Concha cried as she rushed out the door to enfold
Angela in her arms, "we were so worried! Ah, are you all right? You
must be hungry, and thirsty, of course, so come with me to the kitchen—
no, you will want to wash first, I see. Blanca! Maria! Come at once to
help *la patroña* get a bath and clean clothes. Do not worry, I shall see
that you have food and a cool drink, eh?"

Mignon smiled slightly as her daughter disappeared into the house
surrounded by Concha's frenetic affection and ministrations. In all these
years, the cheerful Mexican woman had not changed. Perhaps everything else had changed, but Concha was still comforting and sensible.
It was consoling to know that there were some things in life that did
not disappoint.

Rita appeared in the hallway as Concha escorted Angela to the huge bathroom at the rear of the house, staring after them with a strange expression on her face. Mignon lifted a brow when the girl turned and saw her there.

"She is home, mademoiselle. Are you disappointed?"

"Of course not!" Rita flushed angrily. "I told you I did not mean for her to get lost. If I wanted to get rid of her, I could think of other ways to do it. I could have drowned her, or sold her to the renegades, and then she'd never have come back."

"You seem to have considered it, to be so familiar with many options."

Moving closer, Rita said softly, "You don't like me, so you're not going to believe anything I say anyway. Maybe I understand why you don't like me, but that doesn't mean I have to let you talk to me that way. This is my home, not yours anymore."

"Ah, but you are wrong, little cat. I was married to John Lindsay and we never divorced. I have more right to this house and these lands than you do, so do not think you can take them away from my daughter or from me!"

Rita's laugh sounded bitter. "Is that all you care about? This house and these lands? I could save you some worry, because I don't care about them. I never have. Like you, I've always wanted to leave here. But unlike you, I have no intention of disregarding my father's wishes. Whether you like it or not—and you've made it quite obvious you do not—he was my father. My mother lived here after you left him, and I was born here. I'd burn down this house before I'd leave it to someone like you who hates it so terribly, and I think my father would approve of it!"

"Either you didn't know your father very well or he changed a great deal in the past twenty years," Mignon said dryly. "The John Lindsay I knew would never have allowed so much as a stick of wood to be burned without his approval. He loved this land and those cows more than he ever loved a human being. No, do not think I am unaware of what he wanted here. He wanted to leave it to Angelique because he hoped she would love it like he did—and God help her, he may have been right. But I am her mother, and I intend that she realize her place is not here, but in a civilized land where there is no threat of savage barbarians coming down out of the hills to loot and murder."

"Forgive me, but it seems that I remember reading about something called the French Revolution not so long ago, when your cities were destroyed by rabble and aristocrats were murdered in their beds and on guillotines. Or am I wrong?"

Mignon stared at her coolly. "I am not unaware of my country's history. It has nothing to do with this land."

"No? I think you are wrong. I do not know of a country where there has not been some kind of war. New Mexico is not so different."

"Are you now defending the land you profess to hate? It seems I am not so very wrong when I say that you would like to keep Angelique from having her inheritance."

"Why should she have everything?" Rita's dark eyes flared with hot lights. "She has the ranch and shares in the mine, and because she has such soft white skin and that stupid French accent, she even has the men following around after her like dogs after a bitch in heat. It's not fair that she gets everything!"

Mignon studied the girl's flushed face for a moment and began to understand a bit more. Perhaps it was not all about the ranch after all. There was much more to Rita's resentment than she had considered. Ah, how could she have been so blind, so isolated in her own distress that she had not noticed?

She had misjudged Rita—as well as Jake Braden. It might work to her advantage after all.

Mignon smiled.

Lieutenant Walker arrived at the Double X with a platoon a few hours after Angie had found her way back, and she could hear the dogs barking a welcome as the dusty, tired troopers milled in the yard. Angie sighed softly. She certainly did not relish the thought of dealing with him tonight, not after the day's ordeal.

"If you want, I'll tell Walker you're resting now," Rita said abruptly, and Angie's eyes narrowed.

She wanted to believe that her sister had not abandoned her to the barren emptiness, but it was difficult. It didn't help that Rita had offered only the lame excuse that she'd not thought Angie would ride the other way.

"I thought you had enough sense to follow my tracks," she'd added tartly, and that was as near to an apology as she had come.

Now Angie shrugged and rose from the chair where she'd been sitting on the veranda. "No, I'll see Tempe. He'll wonder why I'm avoiding him if I don't."

Rita didn't reply, but pushed away from the wall and left the veranda to disappear around the corner of the house. Gone to the orchard, no doubt, where she liked to escape beneath an old arbor covered with straggling rose vines.

"Angie!" Tempe vaulted over the low picket fence without bothering to open the gate and strode up the broken tile path to where she waited on the veranda. He grasped her by the shoulders and stared down into her face, searching it in the dim light afforded by the hanging lantern overhead. "They told me you made it back alone. Are you all right?"

"Don't I look all right?" She managed a smile.

"You're always beautiful." He cupped her chin in his palm and held her face up to his as some of the worried lines eased his brow. "I rode here as fast as I could after getting North's message."

"I'm glad I was here, then, instead of out on the prairie waiting for someone to find me."

Tempe looked startled, then smiled stiffly. "Without a knowledge of the general area you were in when you got lost, I could have gone in the wrong direction. I had to at least find out where you were going or where you'd been."

"Yes, I know. I'm sorry, Tempe. I guess I'm still a bit distressed by it all."

"I would think so, darling. Here, sit down again. You must be exhausted after your ordeal. How did it happen?"

She sat down in the cane-back chair, deftly managing to disengage her hands from his as she did, and leaned back. "I was out riding with Rita and we became separated."

"Good God, out riding! What were you two thinking to leave the ranch without an escort?" Tempe's brows drew down over his eyes, and his mouth thinned. "You could have been killed or worse. North should be firmly reprimanded for allowing you to leave as you did."

"Bill North had nothing to do with it. Rita and I just wanted to get away for a while and we did. If I hadn't gotten lost, no one would even have noticed. Besides, I don't see all the fuss about it. The worst thing I saw out there was a rattlesnake, and it slithered off in the opposite direction when it saw me."

He took her hands again and knelt down in front of her to say earnestly, "Please promise me you won't do that again, Angie. It's too dangerous."

She snapped, "I will promise nothing of the kind! I do not intend to while away my days here walking the walls like some medieval princess shut up in a tower!"

Tempe stared at her in obvious distress, and perversely, Angie wished he would not kneel there in front of her as if a supplicant for her favor but stand up like a man and say what he had to say. He looked so . . . weak.

"Angie, I understand, I really do. But you must listen to those who have been out here longer than you have. If something happened to you, I couldn't bear it.''

There was quiet desperation in his voice, and Angie wanted to flee from his pleading eyes and clinging hands. It rankled that she could not bear *his* touch but melted when Jake Braden—a thorough bastard—came near her.

"Tempe, please—it's late and I'm exhausted. Perhaps we can discuss this another time." She stood up, and he rose to his feet immediately, reaching for her again before she could avoid him. He grasped her hands and held them tightly.

"Of course. I'm a beast not to have thought of that. I'll still be here in the morning. Since the fiesta is two days away, I might as well stay so I can escort you through the pass."

"The fiesta? Oh, yes . . . I had forgotten. Where is it to be held? I thought it would be at Fort Selden."

"Oh, no. This is an annual event, held at the Rivera hacienda every year. He always invites the officers from the fort as well as the neighboring ranchers. This will be only my second year to attend. Last year, I was posted at Fort Davis until I was reassigned to Fort Selden right before the fiesta. As an officer, of course, I was invited."

"Of course," she murmured. An insect buzzed close to her face, then flew toward the lantern hanging above her. A dog began barking furiously, and laughter came from the direction of the barracks where the ranch hands slept. She tried to remove her hands from his clasp but he held them too firmly.

"Tempe, please let go of me so I may go in," she said sharply, and he drew her toward him. She turned her head as he bent to kiss her, and his lips grazed her cheek instead of her mouth.

He did not pursue it, but dropped her hands and stepped back to allow her past. "Good night, Angie darling."

"Good night, Tempe."

"I want you to save all your dances for me," he called after her, and she turned in the open doorway to gaze at him with a faint smile.

"Perhaps I will. But you might grow tired too easily, and I will have to dance with others."

"Never. For you, I will dance all night."

"We'll see." She laughed. "We'll just see about that!"

24

For miles before they arrived, the hacienda could be seen across the flat expanse of land. It was nestled in a grove of towering oaks with branches as big as a man's torso spreading out to shade the red-tile roof. White adobe walls glistened with a powdery sheen beneath the searing sun, a blinding white that hurt the eyes. Rancho de Tesón sprawled in inviting grandeur, an oasis in a barren land.

The journey had been uneventful as they traversed the San Augustin Pass through the Organs. Ahead lay the Jarillas, a rugged mass of granite-and-limestone peaks rising nearly three hundred feet above the valley floor and situated halfway between the Organ and Sacramento Mountains. The desolate range of hills was nearly ten miles long and half that wide, and broken into several sections dissected by narrow passes or defiles. The Rivera hacienda was nestled in a strategic valley with a commanding view of the ridged range enclosing it.

As their buggy jolted over the rutted track that led down the slopes toward Rancho de Tesón, Angie only half listened to the chatter of Bette and Rita, who seemed to have become the best of friends. Their dark heads were frequently seen close together, their laughter shared over some jest or observation.

Bette had been Angie's confidante for quite a while, and Angie viewed her burgeoning friendship with Rita as a defection. How could she confide her mistrust and worries to someone who might very well repeat them—however innocently—to the very object of her concern? She could not, and so she had withdrawn little by little, until now she kept her qualms to herself. It was just as well. Since Rita's treachery of two days before, she would trust no one.

"Oh, you will enjoy this," Rita said to Bette, and indicated the sprawling hacienda with a careless wave of one arm. "Everyone comes. It is his annual birthday fiesta, and he invites the entire region. There will be soldiers—only officers usually—ranchers, politicians, all the people who are even the least bit important are invited. It lasts for two days or more, with dancing and music and much food. I think you will enjoy it as well, for you must join us."

Bette hesitated, and Angie saw her quick glance at Mignon. "I do not think it is allowed, for I am only a maid, after all."

"Don't worry about that. You are French, and no one will know. Is that not right, Doña Mignon?"

She had begun calling Mignon by that title—more as an irritation, Angie thought, than out of respect. Maman turned her head slightly to regard Rita with a lifted brow.

"I am not in the habit of considering servants as equals, but here in America it is different, I perceive. I suppose because so many Americans come from peasant stock."

It was a definite snub, and Rita's face flamed. "If you are referring to my mother, she was not my father's servant!"

"No? Yet I recall her working in the kitchens when I was here. Perhaps it was another Mexican." Mignon smoothed her gray silk dress over her knees and turned her head to gaze at the passing landscape again, apparently dismissing Rita.

Angie stepped quickly into the breach. "I enjoyed helping Concha in the kitchen. She showed me how to fry beans and make tortillas and create something edible out of almost nothing. It was interesting."

"If you enjoy such bourgeois food, I imagine it would be," Mignon replied calmly, and Angie felt like shaking her mother.

Although Angie didn't view Rita in the best of lights right now, she could almost understand her. Wouldn't she feel the same if she was in Rita's shoes? Defensive and apprehensive about the future? Yes, in all fairness, she had to admit that she would. It still didn't change the fact that she did not trust her, but she understood the girl's emotions.

Lieutenant Walker rode close to the carriage, and though he spoke generally, his eyes lingered on Angie. "We will reach the hacienda soon, so I will not see you again until later this evening at the fiesta. I insist that each of you ladies save me a dance and make me the envy of every man there."

It was Rita who answered, laughing huskily as she replied, "We will be honored, Lieutenant, but it will be the other ladies who are envious, I think."

Walker laughed, and touching the brim of his hat with a finger, cast a last glance at Angie and joined his men again to ride in front of the carriage down the road to the Rivera hacienda.

Rita watched him go with a fading smile, and scowled when Bette said with a giggle, "He makes it obvious who he likes, does he not?"

"I think Lieutenant Walker is just being polite," Rita snapped. "Not everyone falls in love with Angie the minute they see her."

Bette lapsed into silence with a startled glance at Rita, and Angie looked away. Tension stretched between them, unbroken as they rolled down the long, curved road.

Arriving guests were shown to their rooms at once when they reached the hacienda, and Angie found that she was to share a room with Rita as well as several other young ladies. Huge beds draped in netting filled the room to capacity, and servants with armloads of dresses and items of apparel bustled about busily.

Because there were six girls in the room—two to a bed—it wasn't as awkward as it could have been to share a room with Rita right now, and Angie found the others friendly and curious for the most part.

"I heard that you had finally arrived," a brown-haired, freckled young lady with a saucy smile and the unlikely name of Natasha observed candidly. "My mother wondered if you would even come—or stay once you got here. Are you—staying, I mean?"

"I intend to stay, yes." Angie tucked her feet up under her as the other girls had, cushioned by a thick carpet spread over the tile floors. A soft breeze blew through open doors that led onto a private veranda, and music soared in the distance. It was the middle part of the day, time for the prerequisite siesta customary here as well as in Mexico.

"And your mother? I don't remember her, of course, for I was too young, but my mother recalls her being here for a short time. She left right after that nastiness with the Apaches and hasn't been back. We thought she'd never return."

"Apaches?" Angie flicked a quick glance toward Rita, but her sister's expression was blank. "Oh, you must mean the raids."

Natasha nodded. "It was a terrible time then, but now is not much better. I overheard my father say that there's a new band of renegades threatening all the outlying ranches and smaller homesteads. A band of them even attacked Doña Ana a few weeks ago. They took horses mostly, but some supplies from the general store as well."

"But what is being done about all this?" Angie shivered as she thought how close she had come to disaster a few days before. "Can the army not stop them from raiding towns and homes?"

One of the other girls, Linda, laughed. "If they could, New Mexico would have more people in it than New York does. It's the threat of

Indian attack that keeps so many settlers from coming here, and I think the politicians like it that way. It gives them more land to steal.''

''Now you sound like my father,'' Natasha observed wryly. ''He says the same thing. In fact, isn't the governor supposed to attend the fiesta?''

''No, just some senator. I think Don Luis has political ambitions. At least he certainly has a lot of important connections. Why, there might be lots of rich, ambitious young men attending the fiesta! I certainly hope so. That's why I came,'' the dark-haired Linda added with a sly smile.

''To listen to politicians?'' Natasha teased, and they all laughed.

Rita stretched out like a cat, her smile mysterious. ''Perhaps his nephew Diego will attend the birthday fiesta. Do any of you know him?''

One of the girls heaved a huge sigh, and they all broke into laughter again.

''Know him? I wish I did,'' Linda moaned. ''He is so very handsome—''

''And so very *macho hombre*,'' another girl added. ''I danced with him last year, but he did not stay long. As usual, Diego and his uncle are quarreling.''

''My father says it's because Diego feels his uncle has stolen his inheritance.''

''There seems to be a lot of that going around these days,'' Rita remarked with a careless shrug, and before the moment could become uncomfortable she added teasingly, ''Perhaps Diego will not come this year and we will all have to sigh and pine for him.''

''He always comes.'' Linda sat up and made a face. ''At least he makes the other men jealous if he dances with us, and then we can pretend we do not care and they will try harder to please us, eh?''

Everyone laughed again, and more tales were shared about Don Luis's nephew before the conversation turned to other eligible young men.

There was a festive air in the room, one that Angie did not share. These were young girls, still sheltered, still enamored of flirting with many young men, while she had progressed beyond that stage. It left her feeling out of place, as she found them pleasant enough but a bit silly at times.

Later, when Bette came to help Angie and Rita with their gowns, she told them that the hacienda was full of guests, with more coming every hour.

''So many! Handsome men are everywhere, it seems, and the gowns some of the women wear are quite exotic. They look very Spanish, with mantillas and lots of lace, and many of the young ladies have chaperons called *dueñas* with them at every step. Here, Doña Rita, this is your gown. The ivory silk is for—"

"No." Angie rejected the gown firmly and ignored Bette's wide-eyed dismay. "I will not wear this again. Give it to someone if you like, but bring me the dark blue gown. I put it in the trunk myself, so I know it is here."

Bette shifted uneasily. "Madame had me remove it, I fear. Oh, do not be angry with me, please, for I told her you would not like it, but she insisted!"

"You could have told me this before we left, you know. Now what am I to do!"

Crestfallen, Bette lifted her shoulders in a shrug, and Angie stared at her angrily. "You will have to find me a suitable gown, Bette. That is all there is to it. I will not wear that ridiculous piece of fluff again. I feel absurd wrapped in yards of lace and ribbon like some candy box!"

"But where shall I get another gown?"

"I don't know, but you've always been resourceful. You will manage it before tonight's festivities, I'm certain."

When Bette scurried away, Rita looked at Angie with a lifted brow. "Is it that bad of a gown?"

"Worse. Have you seen it?"

Rita grinned. "Yes. It is rather . . . frilly. I'd feel ridiculous in it."

"I certainly do. Yet Maman insists that I wear it, while she wears stylish, sophisticated gowns that are very flattering. I wish to look lovely tonight, not childish."

"Is there someone here you hope to see?" Rita stood in her chemise and pantalettes, her hair in dark ringlets around her face and shoulders. Bare toes curled against the thick carpet on the floor. "Or would you like to meet someone new, perhaps?"

"Neither. I just want to look my best. These people are my new neighbors—and I hope they will become my new friends. I'd like to feel comfortable with them." She looked directly at Rita. "I hope you don't have any more surprises for me tonight."

"Surprises? I don't know what you're talking about."

"Yes, I think you do." Angie stepped closer, so the girls across the room wouldn't hear. "Maybe you don't like me being here right now, but I'm here to stay. And since I will be here, you and I might as well be friends and not enemies. Think about that the next time you want to play a joke on me."

It was a declaration of war and an offer of peace. After a moment, Rita nodded and shrugged her shoulders.

"I will if you will."

"Do you think I have not?"

"I think you and your mother look at me as an obstacle or an inconvenience. You've made it clear that you don't want me to stay in the home where I was born."

Angie bit back the sharp retort on the tip of her tongue. She wanted to remind Rita that it was *she* who had declared war that first day by meeting her at the door with an obvious claim on Jake Braden, but did not.

Instead she said calmly, "I was born there, too. While I may have inherited the house, it is still your home. Can't we share it?"

"That's up to you." Rita picked her way across the floor, strewn with petticoats and discarded shoes, and said over her shoulder, "You can let me know later what you decided. If you're still speaking to me."

Angie stared after her. She had the distinct feeling that Rita was up to something.

Music soared from guitars, small drums, and brass horns that filled the night with melody. Chinese lanterns were strung over open patios and verandas, and light streamed from the hacienda's doors and windows, flung open to the cool night air. Groups of people gathered in knots beneath huge trees or strolled the grounds, and small bands of mariachi players roamed through the throng. The faint warble of an Italian opera singer occasionally rose above the constant hum of conversation and laughter.

Old Spanish families mingled with settlers newly come to the region. Spanish was spoken as freely as English, weaving a collage of dialects. There was laughter and long tables filled with food, and several spaces had been cleared and wooden floors laid in them for dancing.

Angie smoothed the folds of her skirt with one hand, waiting for the moment when her mother saw her. Spanish combs held her hair off her face, and a lacy veil draped down over her loose hair in a gauzy drift. She wore not the white gown Mignon had brought but a fitted gown with ankle-length black skirts and a scoop-necked bodice that hugged her form. It was not revealing in itself, but the way it fit her left no doubt that she was a full-grown woman. It was a gown that would not meet with her mother's approval. And although Maman was too well-bred to create a scene in public, she would certainly have plenty to say later, Angie was sure.

But it is her own fault, Angie thought defiantly, for trying to dress me as a child! I am a woman, and even if she does not wish to face that fact, it is the truth.

Bette had traded Angie's other gown for one that was far less expensive, but this was a flattering gown that fit her well, and there were other girls dressed very similarly.

Taking a deep breath, Angie left the shelter of the arched iron doorway and crossed the crowded room to her mother's side. She saw Mignon's eyes grow wide. Yet Mignon did not betray by any other reaction her distress as she greeted Angie with a faint smile and a cool nod of her head.

"You join us at last. Angelique, I would like you to meet Don Luis de Rivera, whose feast day we are celebrating this evening. It is he who owns this lovely hacienda."

Angie dipped in a light curtsy, and the tall, silver-haired gentleman smiled. He was very distinguished, with dark eyes beneath silver brows, and a luxuriant mustache that was neatly trimmed. His skin was the lighter color of the criollos instead of the mestizos, who were much darker, and his French was perfect.

"Good evening, mademoiselle," he said in French, and bowed with a flourish. "I am honored to have you visit my home. May I say that you are as lovely as your mother, though she does not seem old enough to have such a beautiful young woman as her daughter."

"You are too kind, monsieur," Angie murmured.

Don Luis's gaze shifted, and his smile widened. "But how gracious you are to wear a gown of my country. I am honored that you would be so thoughtful."

Angie did not look at Mignon, but only smiled coolly. "I am glad that you appreciate my small effort, Don Luis."

"But of course. Such thoughtful consideration could not go unnoticed. I trust you are having a lovely time while you are here. If there is anything you require, you have but to ask and it will be given you. My house is your house."

"I appreciate your kindness to a stranger, Don Luis."

"Ah, your mother and I have been acquainted a very long time, though I had thought never to see her again. I am glad to discover I was wrong in that belief." He paused, stroking his mustache with one finger, and his dark eyes were grave.

"Don Luis, if you will be so kind, I wish to speak to my daughter a moment," Mignon said with a cool smile. When they stood apart, she leaned close to Angie and, with the smile still on her face, hissed, "This is not the gown I brought for you to wear!"

"Yes, Maman, I know that. But it is the gown I wish to wear."

"So I see." Mignon's smile thinned. "We will speak of this later. Tonight, I wish for you to be very polite to Don Luis and to his guests."

"I am always polite."

Mignon stared at her in frustration. Did Angelique not see how difficult this might be? Though Don Luis was very encouraging, he might not be so helpful if he thought she would cause trouble. After all, it was a delicate matter, but one that could be resolved to the satisfaction of all if things went well. Angelique would have money instead of this ridiculous inheritance, they could both go back to France, Don Luis would have the lands he coveted, and Rita would still have her shares of the mine and could go wherever she pleased. Yes, it would work out so well if only Angelique would not be foolish!

Nothing was as she had hoped it would be. Ever since they had learned that John Lindsay had died, things had gone awry. What should have been a brief visit was turning into a nightmare. Did Angelique not see that she was in danger here? Had being lost in this savage land not taught her anything? Ah, she was so stubborn and willful, and despite everything, was maturing into a woman who would not need her mother at all anymore. It was shattering to perceive that one was no longer needed. Not even Mignon's husband had really needed her, for he'd had this terrible love for his land that superseded everything else, even her love for him . . . but it must have been only infatuation, or how else could she explain even to herself how easy it had been to leave him behind?

Mignon took a deep breath. There were more important matters to think about now instead of those lost days. Don Luis promised to help her wrest control of the land away from her foolish daughter, and in turn she would sell it to him for a great deal of money. Angelique might not understand her reasons at first, but she would soon see that Mignon had been right, and one day she would be grateful for her mother's interference.

"Yes," she said to Angelique, "you are always polite, it is true. But I wish you to be gracious as well this night, for Don Luis is an old friend of your father's."

"Is he?" She glanced at Don Luis, who was standing by an arbor festooned with flowering garlands, and there was a spark of interest in her eyes that Mignon had guessed would be there once Angie learned he had known John Lindsay well. It was true that they had known each other, but John had always detested Don Luis, calling him the scourge of the earth and a buzzard who would pick clean the bones of New Mexico if he wasn't stopped. Both men had their own ambitions, and they were in constant conflict. But Angelique need not know that now.

"The Riveras are one of the oldest families in New Mexico, Angelique, having come here when it still belonged to Spain two hundred years ago. Don Luis knows everyone in the territory. In fact, I believe your father purchased his land from Don Luis, though the facts are a bit hazy to me now, since it has been so long. If you ask, I am certain he will be glad to tell you whatever you wish to know about John.''

Angie's eyes lit up, and she smiled. "Thank you, Maman.''

Mignon was watching when Angie turned toward Don Luis, and saw her eyes widen and her face pale, and knew who must have arrived. It was inevitable, but she regretted that he had come when she had plans of her own.

Turning, she sighed as she recognized the man standing beside Don Luis and wished again that he had stayed away. His presence would only complicate matters.

Then Don Luis came toward them and with a smile said, "Doña Mignon, you remember my nephew Diego, do you not? He has come to help me celebrate my feast day.''

Angie burst out, "Diego! This man is your nephew?''

Jake Braden, garbed in a short Spanish jacket and snug-fitting pants and looking very handsome and very Spanish, sketched a brief bow before his eyes came to rest on Angie and his mouth curled into a mocking smile.

"Miss Lindsay and I have met before, Tío.''

The tension between the two of them crackled like summer lightning, and Mignon thought with something close to despair that she should have connected the small boy she had seen only once long ago with the arrogant young man who had escorted them to New Mexico.

How could she have been so blind? Ah, now it would be even more difficult to arrange matters, for the feud between Don Luis and his nephew was infamous and long lasting. Never had she thought Diego Rivera and Jake Braden were one and the same man. Bon Dieu! What a mess!

25

Don Luis must have felt the same crackling tension in the air, but he merely smiled blandly and regarded Angie and Jake with something like complacence as he spoke of the lovely night and the music and the importance of family. His eyes were hooded, his smile constant, and Jake thought with cynical amusement that his uncle had not changed in all these years. Unless it was to become more greedy, more devious in his schemes.

But he knew what was expected of him, and he bent slightly from the waist, rather enjoying the dumbstruck surprise in Angie's eyes as well as that in Mignon's. He had wondered at times if Mignon remembered meeting him as a child. Now he knew she had not.

Angie recovered quickly, as he'd expected. Her violet eyes darkened to almost black, and her mouth compressed into a thin line as she glared at him. The black lace mantilla and fitted gown suited her, framing her pale skin and brilliant hair. She really was a beauty. No wonder Walker wanted her so badly. He'd bet a gold eagle the lieutenant wouldn't like it when he saw him with her tonight, and that should make it quite an interesting evening.

"I was unaware that your nephew traveled in such elegant circles, Don Luis," Angie said sharply, and if the older man noticed her sarcasm, he did not betray it.

"I am not surprised that you have met Diego before, Doña Angela, because he is known to be quite active in this area, as in others." Don Luis smiled, but his eyes were cold when he glanced at Jake. "He visits only once a year now, when not long ago he came often to see his old uncle."

"You don't want to bring that up," Jake said in Spanish, and when his uncle lifted a brow, he added with a matching smile that felt stiff, "Not unless you want to tell them why I don't come to see you more often."

With a shrug, Don Luis offered his arm to Mignon and asked for the pleasure of a dance with her.

"If my old bones will tolerate it. I shall leave the livelier dancing to the young ones and beg your patience, Doña Mignon. It is inconceivable that you are the mother of a grown daughter, for I recall you at that age as if it were only yesterday." He smoothed a hand over the fingers she curled atop his forearm, still smiling. "I am not at all certain who is the more lovely of the two of you."

Jake eyed Angie, who stood with rigid resentment evident in her face and her posture as her mother walked away.

"I don't suppose you want to dance."

"You needn't regard it as an unpleasant duty, *Diego*, for I am quite capable of filling my dance card without your assistance."

"The ever-present Lieutenant Walker, perhaps?"

She glared at him. "Do you think he is the only man who will ask me to dance?"

"No. I'm asking, aren't I?"

"Is that what that was? An invitation to dance? You could make an invitation to heaven sound like drudgery, if that is the case."

He grinned. "I'd forgotten what a termagant you are, Angie. Do you know, I think I've missed you."

"Oh, I'm certain you have!" Her eyes narrowed, and the combs in her hair caught the light from the Chinese lanterns hanging overhead, reflecting sparkles in her bright hair. "I suppose you've forgotten you have a fiancée?"

"Christ, Angie, you know damn good and well that's not true." When her eyes widened a little, absorbing light, he shook his head. "Don't tell me you believed that? I've known Rita since she was just a kid. I care what happens to her, but I'm not ready to get married. To anyone," he added when she opened her mouth.

He watched her, and after a moment she shrugged.

"Then it's cruel to let her continue believing that you mean to marry her."

"She knows better. I imagine she was just trying to get a rise out of you. I see it worked."

For a moment Angie wavered, then she laughed shortly. "I should have known better, especially after some of the things she's pulled on me. What a dimwit I must seem!"

"Rita can be pretty convincing." He cocked his head to one side.

"As much as I hate agreeing with my uncle about anything, maybe we should dance. It's not exactly proper for us to stand here alone talking without having a chaperon for you."

"A little late for that, isn't it?" she asked tartly.

But she allowed him to take her to the dance floor, where other young couples stepped in time to a waltz under the watchful eyes of *dueñas* and parents. Jake saw Angie's mother standing with Don Luis across the room; both of them were too engrossed in their own conversation to pay any attention to what Angie was doing, and he wondered just how well they had once known each other.

Pretty well, from the looks of it. He frowned, his mind on his uncle more than Angie for a moment as he thought of Jim Patterson's recent warning:

"Don Luis will do anything to get his hands on not only the Double X but the shares to the copper mine. If he can control both of those, he practically owns all of New Mexico Territory. Watch him, Jake. He's ruthless and determined, a dangerous combination."

"Selling guns to renegades is one thing, but he'd have to kill both heirs to gain control, and that would be too obvious, Jim. My uncle may be ruthless, but he's not stupid enough to risk being caught and going to jail or hanging."

Patterson had raised his eyebrows.

"There are many ways to get rid of inconvenient heirs without raising suspicion, Jake. He'll have someone else do his dirty work for him. You should know that well enough."

It was true. He should and did know how his uncle worked. Was he trying to recruit Mignon Lindsay into being an unwitting pawn for some devious scheme? It would be just like him.

The waltz ended, and Jake halted, his attention returning to Angie. She looked uneasy, and he forgot for the moment that he was supposed to be watching Don Luis. Instead he watched her, the way the light fell across her face and graced her hair with a hazy glow. He thought of how she had felt against him the last time as his hand smoothed over the soft flesh of her arm. He didn't want to linger near her too long, or he'd start thinking again of how she felt beneath him, and how her excited little moans affected him, and the way her pale skin flushed with release—

"Do you want something cool to drink?" he asked abruptly, and she turned her violet eyes up to him with a strange expression.

"Jake—what are you doing here? I mean *really* doing here?"

"It's my uncle's birthday. I told you that. He expects me here every year."

"Yet you aren't on good terms with him. I heard some of the others talking about you, only I didn't know it was *you* they meant at the time. They said you have a long-running feud with him. Do you?"

He cursed inwardly.

"Yes. But it's my business, not yours."

"You know all of my business, why shouldn't I know some of yours?"

"If you don't mind, I'd rather not discuss my private affairs in the middle of a crowded room, Angie. Christ. Don't look at me like that."

As they were talking, he led her into the shadows and turned her with her back to a towering, vine-covered column that held up the gallery above. He pressed her against it, his hands on her shoulders, and she looked up at him with a startled expression.

"Jake, what are you—"

Surprising himself, he bent and kissed her, his mouth smothering her soft gasp of protest. A bolt of desire shot through him, and he knew he'd made a mistake. It was too easy to think of Angie's soft, perfumed body rather than the real reason he was here, too tempting to forget for a time that he was supposed to observe certain guests and decide which of them his uncle sanctioned.

He gathered her closer despite his self-admonitions, and when he felt the swell of her breasts against his chest, the importance of his mission abruptly faded. Her eyes were spangled with mysterious light, and her lips were parted as she leaned into him and looked up.

"Jake, I—"

"Not now," he muttered thickly, and kissed her again, harder this time, until he felt her breath quicken and knew he must stop.

When he lifted his head, she whispered, "Why did you come back here?"

Dropping his hands, he took a step back, staring down at her ruefully. "Don't make me think right now, Angie, when all that comes to mind is the inclination to make love to you. It would be a bit embarrassing to be caught in flagrante delicto here under the gallery. Unless you're willing."

"You say the most terrible things," she began indignantly, but he caught her to him again and gave her a swift, hard kiss that stifled her indignation.

This time when he released her, she did not speak but stood quietly in the shadows of the gallery, her mouth soft and slightly swollen from his kisses. Music from the house began to penetrate again, and he recognized a Spanish ballad he had often heard as a boy. Guitars throbbed, and the horns sobbed the melody of lost love and languishing fate, and he was jolted back to reality with regret.

"Angie, right now I've got someone I must meet, but I'd like to talk to you later, if you think we can exchange more than three words without fighting."

"No guarantees." She lifted a hand and tugged at the lace mantilla that had been knocked awry. "Perhaps it would be best if we waited until tomorrow."

"No. I may not be here tomorrow. I'll meet you by the fountain in the back garden before midnight. If you're not there, I'll understand."

"Will you?" She gave him a strange look. "Perhaps I will be there, and perhaps I won't."

Impatiently, he said, "Angie, dammit, I don't have time to explain now, especially since I see your stalwart protector heading our way, but there are some things I have to tell you. Will you be there or not?"

"Yes, I probably will. But if you don't show up, Jake Braden—"

"I'll be there. I might be late, but I'll be there. Wait for me."

Then he was gone, slipping away in the shadows and leaving her standing alone beneath the low roof of the gallery that stretched along the entire side of the sprawling hacienda. Angie stared after him uncertainly, and when Tempe reached her, she saw from his face that he had seen Jake as well.

"What is Braden doing here?" he demanded abruptly, and the accusing tone of his voice set her teeth on edge.

"For an answer to that question, perhaps you had best ask his uncle, Don Luis," she retorted sharply, and Tempe's brows rose at her tone.

"I thought Braden and Don Luis were at odds."

Exasperated, Angie muttered, "I don't know why I am always the *last* person to learn these things! Why did you not tell me that Jake Braden is related to Don Luis?"

Tempe shrugged, and his blue eyes were wary. "I didn't think it would matter to you. You didn't know Don Luis until today, and rumor had it that Braden went to Arizona, and it didn't occur to me that you would want to know of his relationship to Don Luis. Does it matter?"

"Not for the reason you seem to think," she lied. "I just get tired of always being the last person to know anything."

Relaxing a little, Tempe smiled down at her, and she thought how handsome he looked in his blue cavalry uniform with its bright brass buttons and yellow stripes. If things had been different, perhaps she would have been attracted to Tempe instead of Jake, but it was too late now. Her course had been set, and no matter how she fought against it, when she saw Jake she melted into his arms without a thought. It was quite maddening, really.

"So, have you saved me a dance, Angie?"

"At least two." She put her hand into the crook of his elbow and allowed him to escort her into the brightly lit parlor where the furniture had been moved aside to accommodate the dancers. Maman was still here, talking with Don Luis and another man she did not know, standing apart from everyone else in a small alcove across the room. No one seemed to have missed her, and most of the faces here were unfamiliar.

As she danced with Tempe—a lively reel instead of the slower, more intimate waltz—she saw Rita at last, laughing and flirting with a dark-haired young man garbed much as Jake was. Rita's gown was a deep rose, with flowing skirts and a scooped neck and puffed sleeves, very flattering with her dusky skin and dark hair.

It wasn't until the reel brought the couples together in a passing step that Rita seemed to realize Angie was there, and her brow lifted and her mouth curved as she asked breathlessly, "How did you like Don Luis's nephew?"

Angie managed a careless shrug, her feet automatically finding the steps of the dance as she said, "I feel as if I have met him before."

Rita laughed and took Tempe's hand as they crossed partners, leaving Angie with the dark-haired young man. They joined hands and skipped down the middle of the lines formed by the other dancers, then skipped back, where they parted again, stepping around the end of the line to stand and clap their hands in rhythm. Somehow, Angie was now partnered with the dark-haired young man, while Rita danced with Tempe.

He shot her a quick glance and shrugged his shoulders, grinning as Rita laughingly took his hands and danced him down the lines again. Some of Angie's resentment eased; Rita was at least distracting Tempe, though no doubt she would not do so if she knew that Angie was going to meet Jake later.

And later, when she finally stole away from the noise of the music and laughter and the heated oppression of the crowded rooms and verandas, she was relieved that the back garden with the fountain was almost empty of people. Only a few whispered words that drifted on the wind gave any evidence of visitors, and those came from secluded spots that could only mean lovers wanted to remain hidden.

A perfect spot for a rendezvous.

Angie wandered the tiled paths of the garden, wondering at the lush vegetation that climbed walls and looped over trellises. Water splashed invitingly in the stone fountain, and a stone fish spewed a small stream upward to land in a tinkling patter in the carved pool.

Intriguing, that a land so barren and bleak, with burning deserts and dry arroyos, could magically provide enough water to furnish fountains. But perhaps this land also had an underground spring, as the Double X did. It was the spring that saved the ranch in times of drought, Bill North had told her, for it kept the worst of it at bay. Some of the cattle might be lost, but most could be saved with judicial rationing of the water supply. In this land, such a spring was more valuable than gold.

Frowning, she ran her hand lightly over the carved stone of the fountain. She had been here for over two weeks, and nothing yet had dissuaded her from remaining. What had so terrified and repulsed her mother? Oh, she had been frightened when she'd been lost, true, but she had found her way back, hadn't she? And though there were constant rumors of Indian depredations, she had not talked to anyone who had actually been *attacked* lately. The threat had been abolished for the most part, it seemed, as more forts were built and manned and the Indians were put onto reservations.

It was becoming civilized, with more and more people with the tenacity to stay arriving to settle the land and build towns. One day conduits would conduct water to the towns, and there would be gaslights and all the trappings of civilization.

Oddly, she dreaded seeing that day arrive. It was wild here, yes, but unspoiled. She didn't know quite why, but the difference between New Mexico and the tiny village of Saint-Dié, where she had spent so many years, was enormous. Perhaps because there was an excitement here that was not felt in France, where most people had lived on the land all their lives and knew that when they died their land would be given to their children, as they had inherited it from their parents.

Yes, finally she knew how her father had felt and why he had stayed here: It was the sense that every day was worth the risk.

The night air was cool, whisking over her skin and lifting the corners of the lace mantilla. Discordant notes drifted on the wind as two mariachi bands vied for attention with guitars and horns. The sounds were subdued, as she was some distance from the main house.

She began to think perhaps Jake had decided not to meet her as time passed, and wondered where he had been the rest of the evening. She had not seen him again, though she had been surprised to see Dave Logan there as well, his tall frame clad in a three-piece suit that did not suit him at all. He had spoken to her briefly, looking ill at ease and miserable as he asked if Bette had come with them, then taken his leave.

Had he gone to find Bette? He had certainly seemed interested in her on the journey, though he had kept a safe, respectable distance away. It had frustrated Bette enormously.

Angie smiled at the thought, and then gave a start as a shadow detached from the darker shadows to come toward her in long, lithe strides that she recognized as belonging to Jake.

"You scared me," she accused when he reached her, and he shrugged.

"It didn't seem polite to shout at you."

"When did you start worrying about being polite, may I ask?"

"When I saw how rude you were. I didn't like it," he drawled, and she gave him a hard stare.

"Is this why you asked me out here—to insult me?"

"No." Without warning, he jerked her to him, and his mouth came down over hers in a fierce, hard kiss that made her knees buckle and the blood run faster in her veins.

After a moment he released her, and she sagged against the rim of the fountain and gazed up at him. Faint light from a quarter moon was reflected in his eyes and cast the harsh angles and planes of his face in silhouette.

"I asked you out here to warn you," he said abruptly, and she just stared at him blankly.

Finally she asked, "Warn me about what?"

"Without being specific, you're in danger because there are unscrupulous people who want your land at all costs."

Angie didn't speak for a moment, then shook her head. "That's ridiculous. What are they going to do—steal it?"

"Yes. Dammit, Angie, don't be obtuse. There are ways to steal ownership of land and you have to know that. Dishonest men have always found ways to get what they want."

"But who would want to steal my land and why?"

"When John Lindsay filed claim to that land, he knew it had a lot more than just plenty of space for cattle. There is the Santa Rita mine to the northwest, and there are rumors of gold up in the foothills. More important than that, the Double X just happens to have a deep natural well that provides more than enough water for cattle and people. That's worth more than the land itself out here, for without water, everything else is worthless."

"That still doesn't explain—"

"Look, I don't really have time to argue with you, Angie. I have to leave, or I'd take you home myself. Get Walker to escort you and Rita and the others back to the ranch as soon as possible, but do it without arousing too much suspicion."

"You make it sound as if they are—"

"Here?" he supplied when she halted. "They are. If the information

I discovered is correct, all hell is about to break loose in New Mexico. Some of the people here tonight won't make it home alive. Don't be one of them.''

"Jake—if this is true, shouldn't you be telling everyone inside about it?''

"It would be a waste of my time. I've already told those I know will listen to me, but the rest will have to find out the hard way. You and Rita are in real danger, Angie. Listen to me, dammit! You are John Lindsay's heirs, and if you both disappear or die, then the land will be up for grabs to the highest bidder or the man with the most guns on his side.''

Angie started to push past him. "I need to tell Maman at once and see what she thinks we should do.''

"No.'' He caught her arm and swung her around, and in the fitful light of moon and clouds, she saw the set, hard expression on his face. "Tell your mother you are sick and want to go home, but don't tell her what I just told you.''

"Why not?''

His mouth flattened, and a deep groove etched one cheek as he stared down at her, and Angie suddenly realized that he thought her mother was somehow involved. She jerked her arm free of his grasp.

"That is ridiculous! Maman would *never* allow anyone to be hurt just to get rid of this land! How dare you even suggest it, Jake Braden? Oh, I should never have been so foolish as to think you had something worthwhile to say to me, and wasted my time coming out here—''

He grabbed her again and swung her around to face him, his voice harsh. "Your mother is being used, Angie. Just like you are, and just like Rita is. You can ignore me or believe me, but you'll be the one to regret it if you don't.''

She stared at him for a long time, racked by an agony of indecision. She had no good reason to trust him. Although he had never lied to her, he had also not told her the whole truth about things since she had met him. He deliberately evaded the truth at times and omitted it at others. Why should she believe him now?

As if he knew what she was thinking, he said quietly, "I can't give you details or facts, but trust me on this, Angie. I won't let anything happen to you if I can stop it.''

She wanted desperately to believe him. But he had not exactly filled her with confidence in the past, and she had no guarantees that he would not tell her this for some dark, mysterious reason of his own.

As she gazed at him silently he reached for her again, but instead of holding her, he pulled her against him and said against her mouth, "You'll just have to trust me."

She closed her eyes, and then her arms were around his neck and he was kissing her, pressing her back against the stone fountain until it cut into her thighs. His hand moved to the nape of her neck to hold her head still, and he kept kissing her as his other hand caressed her breast through the lacy bodice of her gown. When she heard the soft rending sound of ripping cloth, she sighed and thought that it was just as well she had not worn the Paris gown she loved.

Half lifting her, Jake carried her with him to the deep shadows at the end of the garden and through a leafy hedge to a small, secluded gazebo built of redolent cedar. It spiced the air with fresh scent as he shut the door of the little structure behind him and turned to look down at her.

Moonlight checkered the floor in tiny squares as it shone through the latticework sides and made shifting patterns on her gown and Jake. He knelt in front of her and held her gaze.

A square of light made his eyes gleam like molten gold as he said softly, "If I had any sense, I would take you back to your mother and leave."

"Yes. If you had any sense." She smiled, a slow, seductive curve of her lips meant to tease and tantalize him, and with a low mutter of resignation he pulled her to him and folded her into his embrace.

There was something so erotic about making love on the floor of a gazebo, cushioned by only her clothing and with the faint sound of a fountain tinkling nearby. Jake caressed her slowly, taking his time, removing her mantilla and unfastening the few buttons of her gown as swiftly and efficiently as Bette. When she lay only in her white silk shift, he sat back on his heels to gaze at her in the fitful light.

"God, I've seen you like this in my dreams," he said softly, and he smiled a little. "This is better, for I can touch you and stroke your soft skin—hear the little sounds you make when I touch you there . . . and there. Yes, *amante*, like that."

His hands moved over her with consummate skill, knowing just where to touch and caress—and when to stop so that she yearned for more . . . she reached for him and he came to her, his body blotting out the light of the checkered moon as he stretched over her, and she thought as he entered her with luxuriously slow strokes and arrant friction that she must be as mad as he was to do this. Yet it seemed inevitable whenever they were together.

"Querida . . . te quiero. . . ."

His husky murmur brushed past her ear as his mouth found her earlobe, then her cheek, capturing her lips in a lingering kiss that made her forget everything but the moment and the man who wanted her.

It was elemental and primitive being out here with him like this, with the soft wind around them and the moon and stars overhead, the faint sound of music in the distance and the rushing sweep of ecstasy that he ignited in her.

Angie gave herself up to it and arched against him, half sobbing, all too conscious of the pressure of his long, hard-muscled legs against hers, and the feel of his bare chest against her naked, tingling breasts, and the crisp feel of his hair beneath her clutching fingers. The cadence of his breathing quickened as he moved against her, thrusting with increasing rhythm so that she felt the familiar heat and throbbing in her loins as he took her to oblivion.

Afterward, she drifted in the half-world of repletion and held him against her as his own breathing slowed, warm in the curve of her neck and shoulder.

Then his head lifted sharply, and as he stared into the darkness beyond the gazebo she felt his body tense again.

"Jake? What is wrong?" She felt languid, lazy, but the beginning of alarm stirred in her when he swore softly under his breath and rolled from atop her.

In the shadows, she heard him grope for his clothing, and his command was terse: "Get dressed, Angie. Stay here until I come back to tell you it's safe."

"What . . . what do you mean?" Truly alarmed now, she sat up and tugged at her gown, slipping the black lacy garment over her head again and fumbling with the buttons.

"Don't you hear that?"

She did hear faint pops and shrill voices, but there had been fireworks earlier as part of the festivities and she did not see cause for alarm.

"The fireworks?"

"Christ, Angie." Jake stood up, stomping his foot down into his boot again. "That's gunfire, not fireworks. Unless it's part of the entertainment—which I doubt—we seem to have attracted some attention from uninvited guests tonight. And me without my guns. . . . I should have known better than to listen to my uncle, and worn them anyway."

Angie lurched to her feet, abandoning her stockings and mantilla to clutch at his arm. "Don't leave me out here!"

"For the moment you're safer here than in the main house if it's an attack. Just stay inside and don't come out until someone comes for you, do you understand me? Keep quiet and no one will know you're here."

"Is it Indians?"

"I can't tell just by the gunfire," he said wryly, and opened the door to the gazebo to peer out.

"Jake—"

He grabbed her and kissed her again, hard and quick, then left the gazebo at a run, blending into the shadows in his dark clothes. Only the silver gilt pattern on his jacket could be seen in the night, and Angie huddled on the floor of the gazebo and watched through the latticed walls as he disappeared.

Good God, what was she to do? Oh, she prayed that Maman would be all right, and Rita—*was* it Indians? She thought of some of the stories she'd heard, tales of atrocities and terror, and shivered with dread.

But I will not give in to the crippling fear, she thought with grim determination; no, I will not!

It was more difficult to hold to that resolve than she had planned, for she started at every noise and cringed at the distant clamor of gunfire and screams. Crouching in the dark, she shivered with apprehension for herself and those she cared about. Was Maman all right? Bette and Rita? Oh, if only she could see what was happening, know if they were safe—

"Angie!"

She moved forward on her hands and knees to peer out the latticework, straining to see in the dark. A tall form approached, but it did not look like Jake. Heart pounding, she crouched with her fingers curled through the holes in the wooden walls and tried to discern the identity of the approaching man.

"Angie, are you out here? Answer me, for God's sake!"

When the man paused, moonlight flickered over his head and she recognized the pale glimmer of light hair and moonlight reflected off brass buttons. Tempe.

"Yes!" Half sobbing with relief, she struggled to her feet and stumbled to the door of the gazebo to wrench it open and tumble out almost into his arms. "Oh, yes, I'm here, Tempe . . . is it over? Are they gone? What happened?"

Catching her against him, Tempe held her for a moment, so close that she could feel the rapid thud of his heart and hear his labored breathing.

"God, Angie, I've been looking everywhere for you! If Don Luis had not suggested you might be here—are you all right? And what the devil are you doing out here alone?"

She had no intention of telling him the real reason she was out here, so she shook her head. "I've been hiding. Who has attacked us?"

"It seems to be one of those lightning raids the renegades are famous for, but they got more than they counted on, I think.'' He sounded grim. ''The gates were shut, and the fire arrows started only a few small fires, though enough to keep us busy. It's taken a little bit to get organized because half the men are near drunk by now—it could have been worse, I guess.''

''Maman? Bette and Rita? Are they all right?''

''They were close to the house and got to safety all right. I'm glad you had enough presence of mind to stay hidden out here instead of trying to make it back. A few of the renegades made it to the walls and picked off some men before they were seen and shot. It's impossible to guard all the walls, and I'm surprised that Don Luis did not post more sentries tonight. Guess he figured that with all these guests, no renegade would dare attack.''

''It seems he was wrong.''

''Yes.'' Tempe squeezed her tightly against him. ''It does. Come on. Let's keep to the shadows and get back to the main house. It'll be safer there than out here.''

She sensed his urgency, and with shaking hands, clung to his arm as he held her close to him. He had his pistol out, and held her to his left side as they moved along in the soft black shadows of the wall.

As they reached the tiled path that led to the fountain, there was a sudden noise behind them, and Tempe turned swiftly, lifting his pistol at the same time as he shoved Angie to her knees against the wall. There was the soft sound of a thud, a cry, and Angie watched in disbelief and horror as Tempe crumpled to the ground.

An arrow protruded from his chest, and his pistol had skidded across the ground almost to her feet. She moved toward him on her hands and knees.

''Tempe! Oh, God, Tempe . . . can you speak? Oh, please don't be dead, please don't . . .'' She knelt beside him, and when she curled her fingers around the shaft of the arrow and tugged, she heard him groan, a heart-rending sound but encouraging, for it meant he was still alive. ''Lie still, Tempe. I'll go for help.''

Weakly, he floundered, his legs kicking aimlessly as he tried to hold her, and she was pushed backward. Her hand grazed the pistol on the ground, and automatically her fingers closed around it.

''An-gie . . .'' Her name came out in a hoarse moan, and as she bent close to listen she heard a noise behind her and half turned, screaming as she saw the form leaping toward her.

Without pausing to think she brought up the pistol and fired. It bucked wildly in her hand and put her off balance, and she fell backward. A hoarse cry rent the night. Another form leaped atop her at once, knocking the pistol from her hand and sending it flying as she fought desperately to kick free. Guttural phrases and harsh grunts filled the air as she scratched and kicked, her legs tangling in the long folds of her skirt.

Panicked, Angie thought wildly that she was about to be murdered and they would find her body beside Tempe. Her hands slid on slick skin, and panic escalated as moonlight revealed the painted face and bare chest of an Indian.

He drew back and slapped her hard across the face, snapping her head back and sending the world into a reeling blur, and she was only vaguely aware of being pulled up from the ground. There was the dizzying sensation of being lifted, and she knew dimly that she was being taken back over the high stone-and-adobe wall and was being roughly handed to another man.

Then there was the hard, familiar jolt of a horse beneath her, and the blurring haze of grass and dirt in front of her eyes as she hung head-down over the back of a horse. Her captor's hand pressed hard in the middle of her back, and she could smell untanned leather and dirt as she was borne away into the night.

26

Voices escalated and receded. Laughter sounded nearby, and the soft keening wail of a woman rose and fell with annoying regularity. Jake tried to open his eyes, but it felt as if he had been slammed in the head with a hammer. He winced involuntarily at the pain and tried to remember what had happened.

When it came to him, he opened his eyes with a jerk and focused upon the person nearest him. Rita's dark eyes were wet with tears, shiny in the lantern light. She leaned forward to peer at him anxiously.

"Are you all right, Jake?"

He grunted and struggled to a sitting position, rolling his body to one side on the long wooden bench where he had been placed.

"No. I never have liked being shot." He looked at his uncle, who stood across the room regarding him with opaque eyes. "Especially not by friendly fire."

"It was a mistake, Diego." Don Luis strode across the room, and there was a touch of impatience in his tone as he gazed at his nephew. "In the excitement, my *vaqueros* shot wildly. But you are unharmed, save for a crease on your head."

"If that *crease* was an inch lower, I'd be dead." Jake rose to his feet, albeit a bit unsteadily. As his eyes regained their focus, he glanced around the room, then looked at Rita. "Where's Angie?"

Rita's quivering lip and ashen face answered his question well enough, and he swung around to face his uncle with a ferocity that sent Don Luis backward several steps.

"By God, if she's been harmed, there will be hell to pay! Where is she?"

"Gone, I fear. Diego, lower your voice. It will not do to distress her mother any more than she is already upset. You see that she has not taken the news of her daughter's abduction well at all.''

Mignon had collapsed in a corner, and several ladies were with her, soothing her, while Bette brought a cup of the soothing tisane she liked and held it out with a shaky hand.

"Drink, madame," she said in quavery French, "and perhaps when you wake, she will be returned to us."

Jake turned away with the intention of leaving, but the sudden movement made him reel dizzily. He clutched at the back of a chair to let it pass, and fixed his uncle with a cold gaze. "Where is she, *Tío*?"

"Really, Diego, you shame me with your insinuation that I would have any knowledge of the fate of the lovely Doña Angela. Why would I hurt her or allow her to be hurt? What could I hope to gain from such a heinous act?"

"You tell me."

"Diego, I must protest your attitude." Lifting a brow, Don Luis beckoned, and two of his *vaqueros* came to join him, ammunition belts draped across their chests and rifles in their hands. "These men will tell you that I gave orders to protect all within these grounds, and they fought valiantly to rebuff the men who attacked us."

"Maybe you can explain why there were no guards on the walls tonight, no sentries posted to warn of attack."

"There were guards, Diego."

"Then they chose not to give warning."

"*Callate!*" one of the guards snarled, and took a step forward, halting only when Don Luis held up a hand. Black eyes smoldered at Jake, and the man subsided with a final threat—"*Te voy a mandar pa'l carajo!*"—that made Jake's eyes narrow.

"If I don't send you to hell first," he replied softly, and Dave Logan came up behind him and put a warning hand on his shoulder.

Dave nudged Jake with an elbow and murmured, "Come outside with me. The fresh air should clear your head."

Once outside, Dave said urgently, "You know who is behind this."

"Yeah." Jake squinted against the pounding pain behind his eyes. "Tell me what happened while I was unconscious."

"After you were shot, I got to thinking about where you had been and went in the direction you came from. I figured you might have had a reason for taking off like you did when we were staking out Don Luis."

Dave paused, and Jake grimaced. "It seemed like a good idea at the time."

Grinning, Dave continued in the same low tone. "When I got there,

Lieutenant Walker had an arrow stickin' out of him and there was blood everywhere. He's still alive, so he can tell you the rest when they're through diggin' the arrow out of him. If he survives it. He did tell me that Angie shot one of the men, but he couldn't help her. They were after her all the time, because they waited until he found her in the gazebo and was bringing her up to the house. Jake, the arrows that were used tonight have Comanche markings.''

"Comanche? A bit convenient, I think.''

"Me too. A bit too convenient.'' Dave scrubbed a hand across his jaw. "Don Luis has been shouting outrage and drumming up a posse to go after the Comanches over this. He wants an all-out war.''

"He might very well get it, though he'd soon wish he hadn't. Listen, Dave, I'm going after her. If the Comanche have her, which I doubt, they'll give her back to me. If they don't have her, I'll take her back from who does.''

"Sure you don't want me to go with you?''

Jake shook his head, a careless act that sent splinters of sharp pain knifing through his skull. "No. I'm more likely to get close if I'm alone.''

"Yeah, I forgot you used to live with the Comanches.''

"That was a long time ago, but I think they'll still trust me enough to tell me what I want to know. Will you see that the ladies get back to the Double X safely? And try to keep an eye on Angie's mother. I don't think she meant for this to happen, but I do think she knows more than she'll be willing to let on. Send word to Patterson.''

Within an hour, Jake was riding away from Rancho de Tesón—Settlement of Tenacity. A suitable name, for the Rivera family had not yielded a foot of land willingly in the past two hundred years. Maybe he shouldn't fault his uncle, for Don Luis was only following a long-held family tradition of retaining a stranglehold on their land by fair means or foul.

All indications pointed to Don Luis as the man behind the selling of weapons to the renegades to keep the fires of war burning hot and high, a trick to keep settlers away. He wanted it all, the land and the mines, as well as complete control.

If Angie Lindsay had been hurt because of his uncle's greedy desire for more land, more power, more money, he would find a way to take it all away from him.

Right now, the most important thing on his mind was finding Angie before the men who had taken her could hurt her. They might not kill her, but there were worse things that could befall a woman taken by renegades. Far worse.

* * *

Would they ever stop riding? Angie wondered numbly, and yet dreaded the moment they did. So far nothing had happened as the stops had been few and brief; a moment alone in the bushes, a hurried drink of water that tasted of the leather bag it was carried in, then they were on their way again, chewing tough sticks of jerky for nourishment.

There were six of them, riding hard. Where could they be going? And—oh, God—would anyone be able to find her?

It was cold, and she shivered in the mountain air, her clothes still damp from splashing through shallow streams that wet her thoroughly. Sick with fear, she did not protest when her hands were bound in front of her and she was set upright on the horse, but kept her head up and tried to recognize landmarks once the sun rose to turn the land from pitch-black to a shimmering gray. They rode fast through strange country that looked all the same, a repetitious blend of humped rock and twisted trees like eerie ghoulish figures squatting in the dirt. The terror was bone-deep.

One of her captors was the man she had shot, and he rode close to gesture at her and snarl something in that strange incomprehensible language. She shrank back against the man holding her as he answered him roughly, and with a fierce glance at Angie, the other man drummed his heels against his horse's sides and moved ahead.

When she began to shiver with uncontrollable tremors, the man who held her said something sharp and made a sound of disgust.

"Then get me a blanket!" Angie flared despite her fear—and knowing that he probably didn't understand a word she said. But to her surprise, after a moment he reached behind him and came up with a rough blanket that he threw over her. She accepted it gratefully, clumsily drawing it around her with her bound hands as the horse stumbled over rocks and down an incline.

It was lighter now, and the jumbled mass of rocks rose on both sides of a barely discernible trail that was littered with more rock, forcing the horses to a slower pace. Blearily, Angie tried to commit to memory the way they were going, but she realized how futile this effort was when they topped a rise and she looked with dismay at more terrain that looked exactly the same.

How did they ever find their way over such monotonous ground that seemed indistinguishable from where they had been? Yet they did, riding with a grim purpose, pushing their labored horses over almost non-existent trails hardly wide enough for a dog, trails carved into steep walls on the edges of deep canyons far below. She longed for and yet dreaded the inevitable end of the journey, not knowing what awaited her.

It was inconceivable that the raiders had managed to breach the walls of Rancho de Tesón and snatch her up, and she thought of what Jake had said not long before the raid began:

"You are John Lindsay's heirs, and if you both disappear or die, then the land will be up for grabs to the highest bidder or the man with the most guns on his side."

It was true. Oh, God, that must be the reason these men had taken her, though she had not thought renegades would care about the ownership of land. Unless they had been hired to do this . . . with chilling clarity, she realized what Jake had been trying to tell her. She was not so much in danger from the common perils, but from the hazards of greed and the lust for power. As terrifying as that was, it also gave her hope that she might escape alive. For if she had been taken to gain control of her land, she had bargaining power. Her life for the land. It was simple. And she would do it to save herself and her family.

Bolstered by this, Angie endured the hours of riding with more calm, and when they finally stopped in a protected arroyo for the night, she planned carefully what she would say. It was a last, desperate hope, but one that might well work, for if they had wanted to kill her, they'd had plenty of chances to do that rather than to drag her with them on this grueling trek.

She was pulled unceremoniously from her horse, but her cramped legs gave way when she was set on the ground and she sprawled ignominiously on her face. Some of the men laughed as she was yanked upright again, and she bit her lip to keep from saying something unwise. The man holding her shoved her forward, not roughly but as he would have herded a cow, and she was pushed down to sit on a blanket tossed over rock and dirt.

Conversing in their guttural language, occasionally one of them would look at her with something like speculation, and Angie quaked with terror that she was wrong and they did mean to kill her. She sat numbly, her bound hands hidden in the tattered folds of her skirt. It was ripped in places and hung in shreds over her legs, torn by thorny branches that had scratched her legs and arms as well, and she realized that every muscle in her body ached. Her hair hung in her eyes, the combs lost somewhere and her mantilla left in the gazebo.

She thought then of Jake, and prayed that he was alive and looking for her. Had Tempe lived? Oh, Maman must be frantic with worry about her! She hoped Bette had brewed her a tisane that was very potent, for despite their warring beliefs, she knew that her mother cared deeply for her. It was a two-edged sword, that love, cutting and comforting at the same time.

Yet uneasily, Angie recalled that Jake did not trust her mother either. Ridiculous, of course. Maman would never try to hurt her, though she knew her mother well enough to know that she would do almost anything to achieve what she thought was right and best—had she not attempted to convince Jake to terrorize Angie into remaining in New Orleans instead of coming out here to claim her inheritance? Yes, and it did not help to think that her mother had been right, for now Angie *was* in peril.

Cautiously twisting her hands, Angie tried again to loosen the rawhide strips binding her wrists, and succeeded in slackening them just enough to ease the painful pressure that cut into her circulation.

Loud voices snared her attention, and she looked up with alarm as some of the buckskin-clad men began arguing. It was a heated quarrel, and she realized with sinking dismay that she was part of the dissension when the man she had shot gestured toward her with one hand. A bandage was wound around his upper arm where the bullet had grazed him, and though the wound did not seem to have affected him, he still gave her dark, furious glances far too often to make her confortable.

Heart pounding, Angie watched as they argued, and the man who had carried her on his horse finally shook his head and shrugged, then squatted beside the low fire. He looked over at her, then looked away, and she knew with sudden dread that whatever the quarrel entailed, he had yielded his position. Did it involve her? It must, for the man she had shot came close to regard her with grim satisfaction in his black, pitiless eyes and said something in his harsh tongue that made her shiver. Maybe she did not understand the words, but she certainly understood the intent in his expression.

But they did nothing for a while. They gathered around the low fire and seemed to have forgotten her as they drank from leather pouches. After a while, they grew louder and more boisterous.

Silent and terrified, Angie worked surreptitiously at the leather strips binding her wrists, tugging to loosen them. Even if she managed to escape, she would probably be lost in this savage wilderness, but even that seemed better than suffering whatever fate they had in mind for her.

Before she had the strips unraveled, the man she had shot rose from beside the fire and came toward her, his face set into a grim line of savage pleasure as he grinned. He whipped out a knife, and Angie shrank back as he knelt quickly beside her, but he only lifted her arms and severed the rawhide strips that bound her wrists.

Then he grabbed her by the hair and hauled her upward, ignoring her angry, frightened cry. Dragging her toward the fire, he said something to his comrades and they all laughed. More wood was fed to the fire, and it blazed high.

Angie's heart thudded with dread, and she twisted in his tight hold with growing desperation as she looked toward the man who had brought her with him on his horse.

"You speak English, don't you?" she asked shakily. "I know you do! You understood me when I said I wanted a blanket so I know you can understand me now. If this is about the land my father left me, I will sign whatever you want me to sign. You can have it. Let me go, and I will sign whatever it is you want."

Dark eyes stared back at her, and the man's face did not change except for a subtle shift of his mouth. Then he slowly shook his head and looked away from her, and Angie wanted to weep with terror and frustration.

Instead she stiffened her spine, ignoring the harsh hands on her as she said bluntly, "Only cowards would treat an unarmed woman this way. If you intend to kill me, at least give me a weapon so I can have a chance. Or are you so afraid of a woman that you dare not risk your lives?"

Her taunt earned her a surprised glance, and the man holding her laughed harshly.

"You are fool woman to think we give you more chance to shoot." He snarled. "You already shoot me once."

"Is that why you're so afraid of me? No wonder you hide from everyone, then, for you are cowards."

Growling something in his own language, he swung her around by her hair, and Angie bit back a cry of pain.

"We no kill you," he said then, "but we have fun now, eh? Like you have fun in little house."

Gripped by terror and panic, Angie could only think that they had been watching and listening to her and Jake in the gazebo, and for some reason had waited to attack. God, she could not bear it if they assaulted her, could not stand the very thought of being touched by these men who stared at her with hot, lusting eyes!

Pushing her down to her hands and knees, he laughed hoarsely as Angie tried to escape. Dirt and rock scraped her palms as she scrabbled away from him, and he hauled her back roughly by the hair, jerking until tears sprang to her eyes.

To her horror, she heard the rending sound of tearing cloth and felt cool air whisk over skin bared by the ripping away of her dress. Black lacy material was tossed into the air, and when she struggled, kicking and screaming, two of the others came to hold her by the arms while her tormentor finished stripping her of her clothes.

Shame flushed her skin and made her struggle harder as she was pulled to her feet, and the last vestige of modesty vanished with her white silk shift. She was held, shivering in the cool night air, her body bared to their eyes and hands. Harsh fingers stroked her quivering flesh, pinching her nipples, delving between her legs to touch her there, and Angie tried again to kick them.

They spread her legs roughly with hands gripping her thighs, then lifted her in the air. She bucked and heaved, and firelight danced over the scene in bright erratic light, illuminating painted faces and bronze skin in horrific glimpses like the blurring terror of a nightmare.

Hoarse laughter filled the air and black eyes glittered with lust as the men explored her squirming body with growing excitement. One of the men tugged at the red-gold hair between her legs and made a comment that earned him more laughter from his comrades, and Angie thought that she would rather die than be subjected to such degradation.

Somehow she managed to free one arm and brought her nails down in a slashing strike that dug furrows into the cheek of one man, and his howls of outrage filled the night.

A hard hand slammed against her head, and lights exploded behind her eyes. Dimly she felt her body being lowered abruptly to the ground. She was pinned spread-eagle, with two men holding her hands above her head and two men gripping her ankles with bruising force. The man she had shot knelt between her thighs, and as her vision slowly cleared, she saw with choking anguish that he was staring down at her obscenely spread thighs and open body with grim satisfaction.

"You see now that you helpless, eh? Yes, you do. Now you pay for shooting me."

Revulsion filled her as he touched her breasts again, pinching her nipples hard enough to make her bite her lip to keep from screaming. When she squirmed he laughed. Then his hand moved between her legs to prod at her with humiliating thoroughness, a painful invasion that made her body arch. Panic choked her, and humiliation and shame and fear blended into an agony of apprehension as he continued to stroke and touch her, as if he knew how degrading it was for her to suffer his touch and his laughing comments to his companions.

Then he sat back at last, his face creased with hot intent as he fumbled at the cord that tied his breechclout around his waist. He said something in his guttural tongue, and the men holding her wrenched her over so that she was on her hands and knees, still holding her down though she struggled to free herself. Her hair hung down over her face and dragged the ground, and her breasts scraped rock.

Somehow, this was even more humiliating, for she could not face her attackers. Straining against their grip, she felt herself lifted by two hands on her hips and her thighs spread even wider. One of the men holding her arm reached beneath her body to grasp her breast and squeeze, and he muttered a hoarse comment as he toyed with her nipple. Rough fingers tugged at it and rolled it between thumb and finger in an obscene parody of a lover's play, and Angie moaned.

As another man fumbled for her other breast, her loose hair was gathered in a hand and her head was pulled back so that her neck arched painfully. Oh, no, they meant for her to watch them after all, to see what they intended for her, to see their faces as they took turns raping her.

Through eyes blurred with tears of pain and despair, she glimpsed the man who had remained aloof come toward her, saw the hot lights in his eyes and knew that he intended to join them in their cruel game. He halted in front of her, and as the man behind her said something else in their crude language and they all laughed, he began to unfasten the loose pants he wore.

With her head tilted painfully back, she caught his eyes and managed to say through dry, stiff lips, "I did not think you an animal as well."

His hand paused on the buttons. Something like chagrin flickered in his dark eyes for a moment, then he shook his head grimly.

"I cannot save you."

"You could if you wished."

"No." His eyes narrowed. "You will not be killed. Is that not enough?"

"Would it be enough for you? For your mother or sister, perhaps?"

When he wavered, staring at her, the man behind Angie said something else in an abrupt, harsh tone, and she felt his hands between her legs again. Desperately, she said softly, "Do not listen to him!"

But he shook his head, and she knew that she was lost.

They would rape her, and there was nothing she could do to save herself. Fingers dug into her thighs with a firm grip, wrenching them far apart. Angie squeezed her eyes tightly shut and screamed aloud her misery and despair. The wailing cry rose into the air like the howl of a wolf, vibrating with anguished intensity.

27

As her cry faded, a shattering explosion suddenly freed her from the imprisoning hands, and Angie sprawled on the ground as another quick shot followed. The renegades moved quickly, then came to an abrupt halt when several men leaped down from a shelf of rock to confront them. One of them stepped forward, gesturing with a rifle as he spoke to them in the same harsh language. Through the tangled curtain of her hair Angie saw that it was another Indian, wearing only a breechclout that left his long legs bare. White paint covered his face, streaked with jagged lightning bolts that made him look as fierce and feral as the men who held her captive.

Was she to be captured yet again by new raiders? She eased to her hands and knees, balancing on the balls of her feet as she waited tensely for the chance to flee. They were arguing in their rough, abrasive language, and the man with the rifle pumped the lever again and fired, the bullet spanging into the rock over their heads and splintering into fragments that showered over them.

She cringed involuntarily, half expecting the next bullet to strike her. All her attention was focused on escape as more harsh words were exchanged, and she thought fiercely that she hoped they all killed each other. Inching sideways, her bare feet slid over rubble and rock. She felt so vulnerable and exposed, as naked as the day she had been born, as she scuttled across the rough ground.

Then she was grabbed by the hair and hauled backward, slamming against the rock in a painful fall. Tears of despair slipped down her cheeks, but she pressed her lips tightly together, refusing to give them the satisfaction of pleading again. She had seen that appealing to their warped mercy only amused them, and if she could not change her fate, she could at least cheat them of that.

Steeling herself for the worst, Angie waited, but to her relief, they seemed still to be quarreling over her. Perhaps they would kill each other after all, and she would be able to escape in the confusion.

Naked and shivering with cold fear, she crouched with rocks digging into her knees and waited; the man with the rifle snarled guttural comments at the others. After a few minutes of this, there seemed to be some kind of agreement, and Angie shuddered as the painted Indian slung his rifle to the ground and unsheathed a long, lethal-looking knife.

The man who had been about to rape her first had his own knife in hand, and they circled one another for a moment as the others watched, each side cheering on its comrade. She wanted to look away but could not, and watched with terrified dread as they lunged and grappled, their shiny blades reflecting firelight in sharp sparkles along honed edges.

The renegade's hair was long and greasy, but the challenger's hair was shorter and was held back by a strip of cloth wound around his head. It was almost the only way to tell them apart as they locked in a silent, gasping combat. They parted, clashed, and parted again, circling one another and calling obvious taunts in that oddly harsh language. Blood flowed freely, dripping down bare bronzed chests in steady streams.

Despite the drumming fear that filled her, she was caught by the primitive fascination of the two men fighting with knives, their bodies taut with the desire to spring at one another, but cautiously circling before one of them lunged forward and his blade flicked out like the tongue of a serpent to draw more blood.

There was a sudden harsh grunt as they clashed, and she watched as the renegade paused with a strange expression of disbelief, then slowly crumpled to his knees. The other man straddled him, and even as she cried out "Oh, God!" the blade of his knife flashed down and there was the sudden sickening sound of it striking flesh.

Nauseous, she buried her face in her palms, uncertain what would happen to her now, if she would be given to this new man or if they would just all share her. Perhaps she would be killed, for despite what she had been told, it was obvious this new band had taken charge of the renegades.

She looked up; he stood panting over the still body between his outspread feet, and apparently challenged those watching. No one accepted his challenge, though the man who had given her the blanket said something in a flat monotone.

The victor nodded and sheathed his knife, his lean body straightening as he came toward Angie. She cringed away from him, repulsed by the smell of fresh blood and the savagery she had just witnessed.

"No! Don't you dare touch me . . . oh, God, I'd rather you kill me than do this. . . ." She grabbed wildly for his knife, and he brought the edge of his hand down hard on her arm, numbing it. Panic overrode reason, and spurred to near hysteria, Angie began to fight him, not caring if he killed her but hoping for death as a quick end to the fate they had in mind.

Screaming insults in Spanish, French, and English, she resisted with all her might, and heard the sound of laughter at her struggles. She fought until she was exhausted, panting with fear and debilitating apprehension as he countered her every move with almost contemptuous ease. She clawed at his eyes, but he caught her wrist and twisted her arm to bend her backward, forcing her to her knees on the ground. He made some remark to the others, and they laughed again as he hauled her to her feet and held her in front of him, her spine pressed against his bloodied chest.

Boldly, he splayed a hand over her naked torso and said something to the renegades, and they nodded.

It was an obvious claim of victory, and through the haze of fear and desperation, Angie thought dully that she was doomed to suffer the worst at the cruel hands of this bloodthirsty savage who had fought and killed another for the right to rape her.

Even while her mind told her to submit, that submission was better than harsh retaliation, her nature by instinct was to resist, and when he dragged her with him toward a clump of sagebrush at the edge of camp where the firelight dimmed, she began to struggle. Weakly, she pushed at his inflexible arm where he held it around her middle, but his muscles tightened to hold her hard against his chest, half lifting her off the ground as he took her with him.

With his free hand, he threw down a blanket, kicked it open, and tossed her atop it, then used his body to pin her to the ground. She brought up a knee between them to wedge him away, her bare foot kicking wildly enough to catch him in the groin, and he gave a harsh grunt.

"*Zut alors!*" he snarled in French, and she went still at the sudden familiarity of his voice. Still in French, he muttered, "Keep fighting me or they will wonder why you do not."

No, it could not be—but was it? She tilted back her head and peered through the tangled mess of her hair at his face, and saw that his eyes were not black or even brown, but a molten gold like the eyes of a tiger. Jake? Beneath the thick war paint, could it really be him? Oh, God, if it was—then why was he doing this?

In French, she whispered, "Is it you?"

He spread a hand over the bare mound of her belly, and with his other, shoved aside his breechclout. Gold eyes held hers with a steady gaze, and there was no mercy in them as he grated, "Scream. Loudly. We have to make this good."

"But what—no!"

Roughly, he shoved her thighs apart and without warning plunged inside her in a harsh thrust that wrenched the scream he wanted from her. Bending his arm, he held it across her upper torso, taking her swiftly and roughly, and she screamed again, yielding to the emotion and fear that had driven her for the past twenty-four hours. She screamed until her throat was raw and Jake muttered an oath, then he relaxed his hold on her at last and braced his body over hers to look down at her with a wry smile.

"Convincing enough, I think."

Sitting back on his heels, he straightened the leather flap he wore and flipped the edge of the blanket over her, then looked toward the men gathered by the fire. Their faces were impassive as he said in Apache:

"K'adi. Déduudí—énáguudi."

No one argued with him, and he left Angie by the sage clump to stride to the fire and squat beside it, fixing the Comanche renegade with a narrowed gaze.

"Hakani unu nahá-nu?"

The Comanche looked away, scowling at being spoken to in his own language, and shrugged.

"Nothing happened to me," he replied sullenly.

"Yet you ride with men who do not respect the Comanche way." Jake indicated the others with a jerk of his thumb. "I know you do not like what they do."

"I do not like what the white man does. We must find ways to fight him instead of among ourselves, or we will be destroyed."

Jake went quiet a moment. Then he said, "It is true. But this is not the way."

"Do you know another way that will succeed?"

"I know that there are more white men than Numu, that if you fight them with bullets and fire, they will always win."

A bitter smile greeted his ambiguous answer, and Jake wished he could give him the answer he sought. He rose to his feet.

"We will go. I take the woman with me."

Rising also, the Comanche nodded. "You won her. She is yours. If you take her to Don Luis de Rivera, he will give you much for her."

"I will remember that."

It confirmed his suspicion, but still he burned with silent rage as he took Angie with him and they left the camp behind. She was still shaking but quiet for the most part, not protesting when he flung her atop his horse and mounted behind her. Though he did not expect pursuit, he wasn't about to risk it, and he rode swiftly into the night.

One by one, the Comanches with him departed, riding away by silent consensus to fade into the dark shadows, until finally it was just him and Angie riding alone through the night. If they were followed, there would be several trails instead of just one.

When morning dawned, Angie was slumped in his arms with exhaustion, the blanket around her slipping away so that he had an excellent view of her soft white breasts. He thought of how she had fought the renegades with surprising bravery and persistence, and felt again the cold anger at their violation of her.

He'd wanted to kill them all. It wasn't enough to have killed just the one who had nearly defiled her. If the situation had been different, he would have killed him in the Apache way, appropriate in light of his crime. When he thought of how he had almost missed them in the night until he heard her scream and saw the faint flicker of their fire among the rocks, it made him shudder. With six of them on her, she might not have survived the night.

And his uncle was responsible.

Above all else, he wanted to see Don Luis pay for his perfidy, but he would require proof. The word of a known renegade would not be sufficient. Nor would the oblique statements of men who held grudges against Don Luis, even though they told the truth. He needed more. He needed something solid, and he needed a witness who would be believed if charges were brought against an influential man like his uncle.

In all these years, no one had been able to prove charges against him, and one day he would grow overconfident and careless. One day . . .

"Where are we going?" Angie stirred enough to ask. "I need to go home, to see Maman and let her know I'm alive."

Clubbing her tangled copper hair into a clumsy braid that hung down her back, Jake reached around her to tug the blanket up over her breasts.

"We can't go back there just yet, Angie."

"Why not?" She turned sharply to look at him, and he saw in the growing light a vivid bruise on her cheek. "I am *not* going back to Rancho de Tesón!"

"No," he agreed, "you are not going there. But I can't risk taking you home, either. If this happened once, it could happen again."

"Do you mean the renegades—or am I truly in danger because of the land?"

Instead of answering, he reined the horse to a halt beneath the shelter of an overhanging rock on the steep slope of Dog Canyon. Flat-topped mesas were crimson-edged in the reflected glow of the rising sun behind them. The canyon sliced through solid rock to the top of the mountain, the mile-high west wall of the Sacramentos, twisting in convoluted trails between huge, multicolored cliffs. The precarious track clung to cliffs and wound upward until it broke on a pine-thick summit, and a thin river of water meandered a refreshing path among the boulders and pooled in rock basins along the way to the desert floor below.

This canyon—Cañon del Perro to the Spaniards—was a frequent camping place for the Mescalero Apaches. More than once, Mexicans had followed cunning Apache raiders into this canyon by way of a narrow path that traveled an almost vertical track to the summit, never seeing until too late the Apaches lurking behind rocks above to pelt them with stones and arrows and send them crashing to their deaths below.

It was a perfect spot for an ambush.

Jake swung off the horse and pulled Angie down with him, standing her on her feet in the shadows of the boulder. Still silent, he took the blanket she wore from her clinging hands and, despite her protests, slashed a hole in the center of it. Then he tugged the makeshift serape over her head and, using a twisted leather thong, tied it around her waist.

"That will do until we can get you some decent clothes to wear," he said shortly, and slid his knife back into the beaded sheath at his waist.

She eyed him narrowly. "I thought you were one of them at first."

It was her first reference to the night before, and he regarded her gravely. "I know. I couldn't chance being recognized as Don Luis's nephew. If one of them or you had recognized me, I would never have been able to take you from them."

Her chin set, and her mouth thinned into the rebellious line he remembered so well. "You could have let me know sooner that it was you."

"You know I couldn't."

After a moment, she sighed and looked away. "Yes. You are right. I don't know what I might have said or done if I thought . . . if I knew that it was you."

A faint flush rode her high cheekbones. Shadows darkened her violet eyes to deep purple, and her lower lip quivered slightly. He reached for her, but she shied away.

"No! Please—don't touch me, Jake."

His hand fell away, and he frowned. "Christ, Angie. You know I wouldn't hurt you."

She stared over the canyon floor that was littered with boulders and stunted brush. "I know. But you saw. You saw what they did—"

He hesitated before asking, "Did they hurt you?"

Astonishment filled her eyes with tears and outrage. "Of course they hurt me! Not, perhaps, as you mean it, but they touched me in places only you have touched me, and it was so . . . so *shaming*. Ah, God, I wanted to die, or kill them, or both." She drew in a shaky breath. "I feel so—*dirty*. And I wonder what I could have done to make them stop, or to keep it from having happened—maybe if I hadn't met you in the gazebo, or if I hadn't run out to meet poor Tempe, or—"

"Angie, nothing that's happened to you is your fault. You had no control over what they did, and you could not have stopped it. That's what I've been trying to tell you, without scaring you too badly or making it sound unbelievable, but now maybe you will understand. This has nothing to do with *you*. It has to do with the land, with the Double X and water and copper, and maybe even gold. Rumors run rampant. Some are true, some aren't. But men will kill for the chance at riches, and they don't care who they hurt in the process of getting what they want. You both just got caught in the middle, you and Rita."

"Is Rita all right?"

"Yes. She was in the house when the attack occurred, and two of the army officers came to her rescue. A stroke of luck for her. It was you they wanted first, because once they had you, I guess they figured Rita would give up quickly enough and abandon any claim to the land or mines."

"Who is this *they* you keep referring to?"

He met her clear gaze steadily. "My uncle and your mother."

Ashen-faced, she shook her head. "Your uncle, perhaps, but not my mother. She would not."

"Angie, I told you she is involved, though I don't believe she knew what my uncle intended."

She shuddered, and her voice was low and furious. "I will not believe my mother would risk me like that!"

"She wouldn't." When Angie gave him a baffled, angry look, he added, "If she knew about it."

"Maman is no fool."

"Neither is my uncle. Greedy, devious, dishonest, yes, but he is not a fool, and he knows to say what people want to hear. I am certain he told your mother that he would get you to a place of safety and persuade you to sell him the land, and then give you both an enormous amount of money so you could go back to France and live in luxury. Once you signed, he would renege, of course, and what could your mother do then? Nothing.''

"That's dishonest!''

"If he was honest, he'd make a damned good politician, but as it is, he only purchases them. If he can gain ownership of not only the Double X but the mines that go with it, he'd own most of southern New Mexico. He could get anything he wants from the political machinery that runs this country.''

"Just what is it he wants? Money? All the land in New Mexico?'' she snapped testily.

"Maybe. But I don't think that's what he's really after, though those foolish politicians think they can fob him off with a few grants here and there, some political favors.''

"What's so important to him that he would commit murder to get?''

"Independence.''

Angie looked at him strangely, and a smile tugged at one corner of his mouth.

"Not the kind most people want, but freedom from the very government he's using. I think he wants another revolution, Angie, a war between the United States and Mexico, and this time, the outcome would be very different if he had a strong foothold on this land. When the French were in Mexico, he tried to use the conflict with the Juaristas to drive a wedge between Mexico and the United States, but he failed. Now he's stirring the Indians to revolt, setting renegades on the settlers and burning them out, taking over their lands with promises to the renegades he doesn't intend to keep. He's funding it all, selling them rifles at cheap prices and beef at even cheaper prices. And the whole time he's sending his cattle north to the army posts and reservations along with whiskey and weapons, and using the money to negotiate a new war with Mexico.''

"Did . . . did my father know all this?''

A frown knit her brow, and Jake shook his head. "Not all of it. Hell, I didn't even know until lately the extent of his plans. It's been a long time since I've spent much time around him, for obvious reasons.''

"Why would my father allow me to come unprepared into this sort of conflict, Jake?''

"I guess because he was desperate, *chica*. He told me once he wanted his own blood to have his land, and he knew that Rita was itching to get away from here. Maybe he thought you would be the kind to fight for it.''

''I see.''

She was very quiet after that. They rode down into a sleepy village tucked into the shadows of the Sacramentos the next morning. After washing off the white paint and changing into his usual clothes, Jake bartered some new clothes for Angie, explaining to the suspicious Mexican woman that they had been assaulted by renegades and barely escaped with their lives. That had thawed her a bit, and she grudgingly agreed to trade a plain white cotton *camisa*, a red skirt, and some *huaraches* for the silver conchos he offered. When she saw the size of the conchos, she broke into a grin and added a black *rebozo* and some fresh tortillas.

''Muchas gracias, señora,'' he said as he tucked them under his arm and left.

After Angie put on her new clothes and threw away the now dingy, tattered serape, they went to a small *cantina* on the sleepy village's main street to eat. Delicious, tempting odors wafted out the open door, and they ate until they were full on beef and beans and fried bread.

Sitting back on the small stool drawn up to the wooden table, Angie fixed him with a steady gaze. ''Where are we going, Jake? You never have answered me.''

He hesitated, then shrugged. ''To be truthful, I'm not quite sure where you'll be safe, Angie. Once Don Luis discovers that you've escaped, he'll realize you're a danger to him as a potential witness. He may reason that it would be your word against his, but I wouldn't count on it. He'll want to shut you up at all costs.''

''Witness to what?'' Her eyes were wide and slightly unfocused, and he recognized the fear in her. ''I did not see anything or even hear anything but . . . but those horrible men who tried to—''

''He won't be sure of that. By now he'll know that you were not taken to the rendezvous spot where he planned to 'rescue' you, and that you've been taken by someone else. I hope that he does not figure out I was the one who took you, but I wouldn't count on that, either. He's not stupid. He knows I used to live with the Comanche, and when he can't find me . . .''

She sat with her hands tightly clenched in her lap and stared across the small room with its low beams and scattered benches, her gaze opaque. Refracted light glinted off her copper hair, hazing it to a soft glow like a halo. Even though they rode mostly at night now, her skin had taken on a peachy tint from the bright burning sear of the sun. She looked thinner, her cheekbones higher and her eyes larger; it only enhanced her beauty, and he noticed that several of the men across the room glanced at her far too often for his liking.

Slowly, he eased back the rawhide string that held his Colt in the holster, a surreptitious move. If Angie noticed, she said nothing, but remained lost in thought.

Jake rose to his feet and held out his hand, and she looked momentarily startled before she put her hand in his and stood.

"Cover your hair with the *rebozo*, Angie," he murmured, and she gave him another odd look, but she did as he asked, pulling the dark cotton over her head and draping the long ends down her back as the Mexican women did.

They moved to the door and stepped out onto the long wooden porch that stretched in front of the *cantina*. Three horses were tied to the hitching post in front, lathered and dusty, heads hanging wearily. He moved past them, his hand in the middle of Angie's back and his stride unhurried.

When they reached the alley where he'd left his horse, he heard steps behind them and shifted slightly so that Angie was on his left side, away from his gun hand. His horse was still there, tied to a post at the edge of the alley, and he put Angie up first and handed her the reins.

Then he turned the animal's head to the mouth of the alley and walked it to the street. As they reached the wide dirt expanse, two of the men from the *cantina* were waiting, and his hand dropped casually to the butt of his gun as he came to a halt.

"You waiting on me, gentlemen?"

"Maybe." The speaker leaned over and spat into the dust, then eyed Jake for a moment before looking up at Angie. "Maybe we're waiting on the lady."

"She's with me."

"She don't have to be." He grinned, but it didn't reach his eyes, and the man with him took a single step to one side and let his hand brush against a pistol in his belt.

Before either man could make another move, Jake's gun was drawn and pointed at them, and he drawled, "Yes, she does have to be. It's kinda personal with me—I don't like sharing."

He heard Angie's faint gasp, and his horse snorted and sidestepped with a jangle of bridle bits and curb chains that sounded loud in the sudden, hot stillness. He thumbed back the hammer of his pistol.

"Anything else, gentlemen?"

The speaker took a cautious step backward, but the other man's eyes narrowed with belligerence.

"Shit, mister, ain't no call to throw down on us! We just wanted to talk to the little lady. Been a long time since we seen a white woman out here. Ain't nothin' around but squaws and Mexicans to look at.''

Jake's brow rose but he didn't say anything, and after a moment they backed away, both moving warily. Spurs rattled as they retreated, and when they were out of sight, Jake swung up behind Angie and rode back down the alley to skirt the village and leave by way of the hills behind.

"Was that necessary?" Angie inquired when the village lay behind them.

"Not if you wanted to go with them. What, did you think they only wanted conversation?"

"No, but now they may follow us."

"I doubt it. They looked too lazy to go to any trouble. Keep your hair covered and next time we won't have to worry about it."

Irritated by her perception, he spurred the horse to a steady lope, his arms around her as they rode at a ground-eating pace for a while. The hot, searing sun beat down, and as it finally eased into evening shadows, he headed down a rocky slope to a string of lights glittering in the dusk. He followed the creek down into La Luz, nestled on the west side of the pine-cloaked Sacramento Mountains. The *malpais*—a massive jumble of volcanic rock formed eons before by lava flows and solidified for eternity into ridges of slick, hard rock—lay beyond.

"Can we stay here tonight?" Angie murmured wearily. "I'd like to sleep in a real bed for a change."

"Maybe." He didn't mention that someone was following them. No point in alarming her until it was necessary. "We need another horse, or mine will play out before long. I'd hate to be left afoot."

Instead of staying in the small hotel, they bedded down in the straw of the livery stable. He didn't want to be too obvious should the men they'd met up with earlier be on their trail, but Angie protested vehemently.

"I don't know why we can't stay at the local hotel and sleep in real beds! I've slept on rock for days, and I've got bruises all over my body."

His eyes drifted over her, and he smiled lazily. "Let me see them and I might change my mind."

"Damn you, Jake Bra—Ouch!"

He grabbed her hand harshly. "It might be better if you don't call me by name, *chica*. Never know when the wrong man may be listening."

Sullenly, she rubbed at her arm where he'd grabbed her and regarded him in the faint light of the lantern hanging from a hook on the stall post.

"It might be a lot better if you'd tell me what's going on, too. I'm tired of being kept in the dark like a child. Maybe if you'd told me the truth in New Orleans, I would have reconsidered coming to New Mexico."

"Would you?"

She sat quietly for a moment, then shook her head. "No. I would have come."

"Have you found what you're looking for out here?"

"Have *you*?" Her head tilted to one side, and she eyed him with a faint smile, her pale face rosy in the reflected glow of the lantern. The white *camisa* was low on her creamy shoulders, and she sat with her feet tucked up under her, the red cotton skirt fanned out in the sweet-smelling straw. "I don't know much about you, not really. Tell me what you want from life."

He shifted uncomfortably and leaned back against the thick wooden post behind him. "A dry roof and a warm bed and a woman to share it with, I guess."

"One woman or several?"

He grinned and stuck a stalk of straw in his mouth to chew on. "That depends on the one woman. If she's enough for me, she'll do."

"I suppose you mean in bed," Angie retorted with a curl of her lip. "You're too predictable."

He laughed softly at her mimicry of his stinging gibe her first day at the ranch, and saw that she knew he'd remembered his taunt. Shifting the straw stalk to the other side of his mouth, he drawled, "Well, that is an important part of it for a man. If I was a marrying man, I'd want someone who could be all of it."

"Wife, nursemaid, housekeeper, and whore, perhaps? A Saturday night whore and Sunday morning saint?"

"A little experience in bookkeeping wouldn't be bad, either." When she scowled, he spit out the straw stalk and leaned forward to cup her chin in his palm. "Truthfully, I never thought much about it. I just always figured I'd never live long enough to get married."

"Looks like you were wrong."

Startled, he stared back into her violet eyes, struck by her husky voice and faint smile. Her long lashes shadowed her cheeks, and in the rosy light he could see the flutter of the pulse in her throat. An unwilling smile tugged at the corners of his mouth.

"Yeah, looks like."

As if she'd been expecting it, she closed her eyes and leaned into him when he bent to kiss her, and the sweet hot fires of passion that had always existed between them flared high. It was late, and the stable was empty except for the animals, and Jake took his time with her, soothing her tremors with a gentle hand, whispering soft words to her as he slowly undressed her atop the blankets spread over cushions of straw.

At first she was reluctant, stiff with the memories of the last time he had taken her, and he coaxed her out of her fear and erased the bad memories with more patience than he thought he'd possessed.

When he entered her and she cried out softly against his ear, he felt a surge of tenderness for her that startled and disturbed him. He shouldn't let her matter so much, but she had haunted his waking thoughts ever since he'd met her. God, it wasn't fair to want her, to care about her, to . . . love her? No, he couldn't. He didn't want to love her, because it would make him vulnerable. The only reason he was still alive was because there was no one to use against him, no family to use as leverage, and he knew his uncle would not hesitate to do such a thing if he thought it would bring Jake to heel.

Slowly, rocking against her, shuddering at the exquisite thrust and drag of his body in her velvety warmth, Jake knew that if he gave in to the emotion they were both lost.

28

Jake woke her before first light, and she murmured a sleepy protest, snuggling deeper into the blankets made warm by the heat of their bodies. With his mouth against her ear, he urged her awake.

"We've got to go, Angie. Now."

There was an urgency in his tone that penetrated at last, and she came fully awake, sitting up and reaching for her clothes. She dressed quickly, shivering at the faint chill in the air, putting a hand over her horse's nose to keep it quiet as he instructed. She didn't ask why, but just silently obeyed, trusting him to keep them safe.

They were being followed. Two men, probably the ones they had met in the small village, and keeping well behind them, stayed on their trail. Jake did not seem perturbed by it, but stayed on the main road that led south toward Las Cruces, circling Chalk Hill and Wildy Well, traveling with apparent leisure and unconcern.

It wasn't until they neared the San Augustin Pass that he changed tactics, doubling back to retrace their steps and come up behind the men.

"Stay here," he told Angie tersely, and left her in the shadowed protection of a boulder. She napped and tried not to worry, but when she saw him return what seemed like hours later, she could not keep the relief from her eyes and tone.

"Is it all right?"

He nodded but did not divulge the details, saying only, "They were hired to find us. Apparently, I'm a fugitive from justice."

"Why?"

"Abduction and kidnapping." His teeth flashed white in the bronze of his face. "Your mother has filed charges against me."

"That's ridiculous!"

"Maybe. But I'm not taking any chances. It's a 'shoot on sight' offense, and with my uncle behind it, I'm liable to be dead before anybody bothers to ask questions. This complicates matters a little. Guess I should stop playing a waiting game and make plans of my own."

"Jake, what will you do?"

Instead of answering, he pulled her to him and kissed her with fierce desire, and after a moment she melted as she always did, returning his passion. They stayed the rest of the day in the small cave beneath the boulder, alternately sleeping and making love. That night, they rode out again, and Jake had no trouble finding their way in the dark.

A half-moon shone down, turning the land to silver and the sky to an icy glitter, and Angie thought that she had never seen so many stars before. They seemed to just hover in the sky, filling it with crystalline light.

In the days that followed they rode mostly at night when it was cooler, spending daylight hours beneath the cool, damp shadow of a granite boulder or tucked into a thicket of pines atop a mountain. Several times they stopped in villages or at homes he trusted, and they ate beans and tortillas with the Mexican inhabitants Jake knew.

"Some of them I'd trust with my life," he told her, and smiled slightly when she said she hadn't thought he trusted anyone. "I don't trust just anyone. These are people I do."

Late one afternoon, before dusk settled on the land, they crossed a small, shallow stream and rode up a hill. As they topped the rise, armed *vaqueros* rode out to greet them, and Angie's first alarm was allayed when they grinned and waved wide-brimmed hats in greetings.

"More friends of yours, I suppose?"

"Something like that."

"Don Diego!" one of the men shouted as he drew near, "we did not know you were arriving!"

Grinning, Jake greeted them, and they rode alongside for a while, exchanging news. Angie felt a little awkward at first, but the *vaqueros* treated her with respect. She was silent as they talked between them, in Spanish now, and her eyes widened when she realized that they had been riding for some time on Jake's land. It shouldn't have surprised her, but it did.

"It's been in my family for two hundred years, just like Rancho de Tesón." He shrugged away her questions and said only, "My father left this to me alone. It's the one thing Don Luis cannot have."

"But if you have this, why—"

"Don't I stay here? I will someday."

He didn't elaborate, and she didn't ask any more questions, but as they neared a grove of ancient trees with huge spreading branches, she heard the barking of welcoming dogs and felt a sudden pang of longing. She thought of the village of Saint-Dié in France, where she had spent her childhood, and knew that never again would she consider it home. America was her home now, for when she visualized the word *home*, the sprawling ranch her father had built came to mind.

Lights gleamed in the distance, visible through the trees as they drew closer, and Jake gestured. "*Casa en Paz*—House of Peace. It has been that for me at times."

It was a small house by some standards, but beautiful, with the familiar white adobe walls and tiled roof, set in a thick grove of trees that shaded it from the harsh summer sun. The heavy scent of moonflowers filled the air, and the thick vines of heart-shaped leaves looped and spilled over low stone walls in a rambling profusion.

A shallow porch stretched the length of the two-story structure, covered with more vines and fragrant flowers, and a light gleamed in the windows. As they rode into the yard flanked by the *vaqueros*, the front door opened and a stout, smiling woman emerged.

"Don Diego! You are home," she called in Spanish, and he grinned as he dismounted and flung his horse's reins to a waiting groom who also took Angie's horse.

"*Sí*, Maria, and I have brought someone with me." He took Angie by the hand, drawing her with him, and she saw the woman's brows lift with polite inquiry, and flushed.

What would she think of her, all dusty and travel-stained, with bare feet thrust into sandals and her clothes all wrinkled? And here she was, unmarried and with no *dueña* in a world where it was a requirement, in the company of a man and obviously more to him than an acquaintance.

But if Maria had any reservations she did not betray them, for she greeted Angie courteously as they entered the house. The house boasted a spacious parlor with gleaming mahogany furniture that was sturdy and functional as well as attractive, but Angie soon found herself wilting with exhaustion, and she was grateful when Jake had Maria show her to a bedroom.

The bed was huge, with a bright handwoven spread over snowy linen sheets. Heavy draperies were pulled back over a set of double doors that led onto a small terrace, and the sweet scent of more flowers filled the air. There was even a bathroom off the bedroom, and she had a long hot soak in a real tub for the first time in weeks, sinking down to her chin in a tower of bubbles. The tub was different from any she had seen, sunk into the floor with tiled sides and surrounded by greenery.

Later, lying drowsily in bed after eating a light supper of fruit, cheese, and cold chicken, Angie thought sleepily that if she were Jake, she would never have left this small oasis that was like paradise.

She slipped into a deep slumber, relaxed at last in the comfortable bed, and barely knew when he came to join her, slipping in beside her to pull her against him, fitting her in the angle of his belly and thighs.

It was sweet bliss, peaceful and safe, and she snuggled against him with a sigh of contentment.

In the weeks that followed, Angie found herself in a pleasant rut of long days spent in the cool house or on the patio, sipping chilled drinks or just gazing at the ring of blue-hazed mountains in the distance. Jake had spent only two days with her before leaving again, kissing her fiercely and promising to return as quickly as he could.

With his forehead pressed against hers, he'd murmured, "I can't sit and wait for them to make a move, I need to do it first."

"Jake—I don't want anything to happen to you."

"I know. Nothing will. Promise me you'll stay here, Angie. If I don't come for you, I'll send Dave Logan. Don't trust anyone else."

"Why?"

"Just listen to me for once, will you?"

And in the end, of course, she had promised, but she missed him terribly now that he was gone.

At first the days passed in a dreamy haze, one into the other in a blur of peace and serenity, but as her equilibrium was restored, so was her energy, and she grew restless. She began taking short rides, always accompanied by armed *vaqueros* who looked and were fiercely protective of her.

It was beautiful here near the foothills of the San Andres, green and lush in places, with the gentle hump of the mountain peaks a constant reminder that New Mexico was deceptive. Those same hills could be deadly, and if she had not been with Jake, she was not at all certain she would have survived them.

Perhaps Maman was right after all about this land, but that did not mean that Angie should give up her dream. Once she returned, she would find a way to fight Don Luis and the men who wanted to take away her inheritance. Was that where Jake was now? He had told her so little, except that he had to see to the charges laid against him.

She fretted on occasion, and Maria soothed her with the assurance that Don Diego was very capable of taking care of himself.

"Since he was a boy, and his parents were killed so brutally in a raid." Shaking her head, Maria looked sad, and delicately, Angie pressed her for more information.

"Tell me about him when he was a child, Maria. Did you know him then?"

"Oh, yes, since he was only four. His father was Don Diego y Sandoval Rivera, once the vice mayor of Santa Fe. But that was until the raids began, and it was said that he was responsible for some of the depredations." Maria looked sad, and her round dark face worked with emotion. "It was not true, of course. But Don Diego y Sandoval Rivera—Bah! Luis is bad, that one, and I have never trusted him. He took over the lands when Don Diego was found murdered by Apaches, as well as the lovely Sarah. That was a love match, *señorita*, for never have I seen such a love before or since. Perhaps it is just as well they died together, and it is only by the grace of God that Diego was spared the same fate. They found him hiding under the overturned carriage, for the Apaches had overlooked him in their haste. Usually, they will take a child and raise him as their own."

"Yet Jake—Diego—said he lived with the Comanches for a time."

"Oh, yes, he did. Always he was so wild after his parents died, rebelling against Don Luis, refusing to stay at the Rancho de Tesón and running away to come here. When Don Luis had him whipped for it, he ran away again the first chance he had, and went into the hills to stay with the Comanches. It was the only place Don Luis could not go to bring him back, and even so young, Diego knew it."

Angie thought of the boy Jake had been, and of how he had witnessed his parents' brutal murder so young. Perhaps it was no wonder he showed so little emotion, for having an uncle like Don Luis must have only intensified his grief.

Bit by bit, she learned more about Jake's early life from Maria. It helped her to understand the man he had become, and she wondered what she would say to him when she saw him again. That she loved him? Should she tell him how she felt, how she had felt for some time if she had only realized it?

Once, she could have discussed this with Simone; now, she did not have anyone. For a while she had thought Rita might fill Simone's place, but it was too late for that. Oh, it was so hard to know what to do, and she thought longingly of her mother.

Jake had been gone for two weeks when Maria came onto the patio off her bedroom to tell Angie that visitors had arrived and were asking for her.

"I did not know what to say, Doña Angela, for they are army officers and insist upon speaking to you."

"I will see them." Angie rose from the chair where she'd been drowsing instead of reading the book she'd chosen from the small library, and after smoothing her hair, went to greet the visitors.

"Ma'am," Sergeant Lopez said gravely, "we are sorry to disturb you, but Colonel Patterson has requested your presence in Las Cruces."

"May I ask why?"

"A man by the name of Jake Braden has been arrested, and Colonel Patterson insists that you can clear up any misunderstandings."

"Arrested! Oh, no—when?"

"Last week. If you'll pack a light bag, we'll escort you to Las Cruces and Colonel Patterson."

"Of course," Angie said distractedly, and sent Maria to pack a small cloth bag for her.

"Doña Angela, you are not to leave with those men," Maria insisted with a worried frown. "Do you not remember what you promised?"

"In light of the changed circumstances, I think I should go, Maria. Besides, I know Colonel Patterson, and he is an honest man who is friends with Jake. Please, pack my bag for me. I must hurry and get these charges against him dismissed."

Despite Maria's pleas, Angie went with the men, once again mounting a horse to ride with them.

This time the route was a direct one instead of the circuitous route she had traveled with Jake, and in two days they were in Las Cruces. She went at once to the hotel where she was told to meet Colonel Patterson, and was shown to a room off the main lobby. Pacing the floor, she fretted when time passed and the colonel had not arrived, then realized that he must be on his way. If he was coming from Fort Selden or Fort Fillmore, it would take him a little time to meet her.

When at last the door swung open, Angie turned toward it and was startled to see her mother.

"Maman! What are you doing here? Oh, I am so glad to see you at last!"

Mignon closed the door behind her and moved toward Angie with a smile, though her eyes were guarded.

"It is good to see you, too, Angelique. I have worried so about you."

"Did you not get the message I sent?"

"Oh, yes, I received word that you were alive and unharmed, but then you did not return, and—well, here you are now."

"Yes. Have you seen Colonel Patterson? I am to meet him here—they have arrested Jake, Maman!"

"I know, *ma petite.*" Mignon moved to a small settee and seated herself, regarding Angie with grave eyes. "Did you expect him to escape unscathed after abducting you?"

"He did nothing of the kind!" Angie frowned. Her mother was acting so strangely, for though she seemed normal, there was an underlying tension that was disturbing. "You must know he did not, Maman."

She remembered Jake's insistence that Mignon was involved in the raid in which she had been taken, and his admission that it was possible Mignon had been duped by Don Luis.

Moving to sit beside her mother on the settee, Angie said urgently, "Maman, I hope you have not been talking with Don Luis. He is not at all what he seemed to be, and—"

Mignon put a hand on her arm, fingers closing around it with gentle pressure. "Do not alarm yourself. All is well."

Relieved, Angie nodded. "I should have realized that you would not be foolish enough to trust him."

A faint smile curved Mignon's mouth, and she said nothing for a moment as she gazed at her daughter. Then, softly, she said, "We will go home now, Angelique."

"Yes. I am anxious to return. Is all well there? Is Rita all right now?"

Mignon's lips twitched. "Rita is more than well. She is married."

"Married!"

"Yes, to Lieutenant Walker. She nursed him to health after his unfortunate injury, and apparently, love blossomed between them."

Angie didn't know what to say for a moment. She was truly stunned by the news, but then she smiled. "I am happy for her," she said, and meant it. "I hope she will be very content."

"I think she will be. She has a husband to tend her, and it seems they will go to Lieutenant Walker's home in Savannah, where his parents own a shipping firm. First, they will travel to all the places she wants to go, just as soon as he completely recovers."

Angie sat in silence for a moment. Then she shook her head. "It won't seem the same without her there. But I will have you and Bette."

"Yes. You will have Bette and you will have me."

"Are Rita and Tempe still at the ranch? I would like to see them before they go."

An odd expression flickered on Mignon's face, and she looked away, then back, and something like determination set her mouth into a thin, taut line.

"Angelique, the ranch has been sold."

Angie did not move or speak, but stared blankly at her mother for what seemed an eternity. When finally she spoke, it was with incredulity.

"That is impossible!"

"No, it is true."

"But . . . but it is mine! No one can sell it without my permission or without my signature. How did this happen?"

Awful suspicion ignited even before Mignon said calmly, "I sold it when you were taken and thought dead."

"But the ranch was to go to Rita if something happened to me, and—"

"And she refused it. She said she did not need it and did not want it. Our passage has been booked back to France, and we leave in the morning, Angelique. We have enough money to live well now, for—"

"Who bought it?" Angie's voice was hard. "Tell me who you sold it to, though I think I can answer that myself."

"Don Luis de Rivera made a handsome offer, and as we thought you dead and I am your sole survivor, I accepted on your behalf."

Stunned, Angie tried to reconcile her mother's words with what she had been told by George Sherman. She shook her head, frowning.

"Maman, it is not legal. If you sold it, you had no right. It is mine. Mr. Sherman said it was irrevocable, and that there were others who would inherit it if Rita and I did not want it."

"There were three other people, Angelique, and two are dead."

"And the third person? Where is he?"

A faint smile touched her mouth again, and she said with slight irony, "In jail for treason, the selling of weapons to renegades, and your abduction. It is expected that he will be executed in two days."

Angie stared at her in disbelief, and suddenly she knew that Don Luis had won after all.

Taking a deep breath, she knew what she must do.

29

It felt as if he had been confined in this small jail cell forever, and Jake stared out the tiny barred window at the beckoning freedom of the mountains. Since being arrested at Fort Selden, he'd had a lot of time to think and reflect on his life. He thought again of Chabhi, the East Indian sage who had said it was not the destination in life that was important but the journey.

If that was true, he had made a mess of all of it.

Maybe he deserved this, for he had killed his share of men, though never one who hadn't drawn on him first. Still, perhaps Chabhi was right when he had said life was a circle that never ended, and one deed affected another, until it all came around again.

It was ironic that Johnny Ringo should have shown up in his life again, testifying against him at the trial that was far too short and far too prejudiced against him, but it had not been that unexpected. The gunman swore that he had seen Jake sell guns to mercenaries, and the jury believed him.

Only when he glanced at Jake and their eyes met did Ringo hesitate, then he looked away again and his testimony didn't falter. Jake was easily convicted of treason.

For some reason, Angie stuck in his mind, and Jake regretted that he had never told her how he felt. Lust and love were wildly different emotions. He should have told her. He would have if he had recognized it earlier, but it had taken tedious hours spent with only his own company to bring that realization.

Dave Logan had been allowed a single brief visit, and brought the news that Angie had sold the Double X to Don Luis after all.

"Her mother signed by proxy first, but Angie agreed when she returned."

He should have been surprised, but he wasn't. It would be nearly impossible for her to hold out against his uncle when few men could do the same. A woman alone—and essentially she was—would find it far too frightening and difficult. He didn't blame her, but he wished she had stayed on his land,where he'd left her.

"Watch out for her, Dave," he'd said, and Logan nodded soberly. "Any luck finding the renegades?"

Again, Logan shook his head. "No. But you know how damn hard to find they can be, hiding out in *rancherías* somewhere and watching while we beat the brush lookin' for 'em."

Jake nodded. He knew well enough how elusive they could be.

"I've set your Comanche friends to lookin' for them," Dave said. "Maybe they'll have better luck than me and Steve Houston have had."

But the day set for his execution drew closer, and still there was no word. If Colonel Patterson didn't show up in time, he'd end up dangling at the end of a rope. A jury had convicted him swiftly despite the lack of evidence, and he suspected his uncle had a hand in that, too. He'd need him out of the way, of course, as a witness and heir to the Double X. The other witnesses were dead, and he was the last one who stood in Don Luis's way. Once he was dead, it would not matter whether or not Angie had a right to sell the ranch, for there would be no others to lay claim to it.

Days that had dragged by with excruciating slowness seemed to fly by now. The evening before he was to be hung, he asked for pen and paper, and tried to write Angie a letter.

For a long time he stared at the blank sheet of paper, then finally wrote her just three words before signing it. She deserved to hear them. Folding the paper, he sealed it in an envelope and gave it to the jailer, then neatly arranged his personal effects on the small three-legged stool in his cell. It was all he had left, save the Casa en Paz, and once he was dead, that would revert to his uncle as well. Don Luis had won it all. Damn him.

Just before dusk, he heard an uproar in the outer portion of the jail, and he sat up on his cot at the unmistakable sound of a female voice. When he saw not Angie but Rita, he tried to hide his disappointment as he stood up to move to the bars.

Tears streaked her face, and she was sobbing as she looked up at him with drowned eyes. "They will not listen to me, Jake," she wailed. "I've told them you could not possibly be responsible for selling guns to the renegades, but they say they have evidence!"

He put a hand over her fingers where they curled around the iron bars, and he smiled. "Don't worry about it, *chica*. It's all right."

A harsh sob tore from her, and she hiccuped. "No, it's not all right. Tempe won't listen to me, either, and I wish I had never married him!"

She said it fiercely, taking him by surprise, and he said wryly, "You're married to Lieutenent Walker?"

She nodded bleakly. "Yes."

"I take it he survived his wound, then."

She grinned. "Yes, of course he did! Oh, Jake, I didn't mean that I don't love him. I do. But where you're concerned he's just so bull-headed!"

"Married—John would be proud of you, Rita."

"Would he?" Her eyes widened. "Because I'm married?"

"No, because you've grown into a beautiful, strong woman. I guess you'll be leaving New Mexico."

"You heard about the ranch." Her face darkened. "Maybe I should have fought him, but I've never wanted the ranch anyway, you know. And Tempe is taking me on a trip around the world once he's well enough. I'll see Paris, Rome, New York—places with people and—"

"Linen tablecloths," he teased, and she laughed.

Then she sobered, and pressed her face against the bars again. "Is there anything I can do?"

"See that Angie gets the letter I wrote her."

"I will, Jake. But maybe you can give it to her yourself. I sent a telegram to Colonel Patterson, but I had to go to Tularosa to do it. I hope he makes it here in time. I know he can stop this if he does."

After she'd gone, Jake lay back on his bunk and folded his arms behind his head. Shadows filled the cell now, crawling across the hard floor with slow precision. He thought of the mountains, and the blue haze of night that cloaked them in mystery and beauty. He'd miss it all. Most of all, though, he would miss Angie Lindsay. There were times when he shut his eyes that he could almost see her, smell her, taste her, and if he regretted anything in his journey through life, he regretted not telling her that.

The sun had just topped the Organ Mountains when Jake was led from the jail to the wooden gallows built just for his execution. The town was crowded, with people lining the streets and even on the tops of the buildings, and he squinted against the light as he was led toward the scaffold. A thick hemp rope swung gently in an early morning wind.

It was hushed and still, and he was surprised that so many good folks had turned out to see him die.

His gaze swept the crowd, looking for a familiar face, one that cared, and he saw to his surprise Maria's round face creased with worry and wet with tears. He frowned. She should not be here, should not even know about it until it was over. It wasn't often she left the safety of Casa en Paz, and he was sorry she had done so for this.

As his gaze moved over the crowd, he saw Don Luis standing to one side, and fierce hatred washed over him in a bitter tide. Don Luis had come to gloat, to be certain the last obstacle to what he wanted was removed, and Jake wished he had a weapon, for he would take his uncle to hell with him.

Behind him, the sheriff prodded him forward, and Jake moved across the expanse of dirt to the steep stairs leading up to the gallows platform. When he reached the top he turned to look out over the crowd. More spectators were arriving, with lathered horses pushing through those already lined up.

When the hangman positioned him atop the trapdoor, Jake steeled himself and stared over the crowd as the noose was settled around his neck and tightened. He should be more frightened than he was. Maybe it just hadn't hit him yet, and that sense of disbelief that had engulfed him since he'd been tricked at Fort Selden just hadn't dissipated.

A shout rang out, and Jake blinked as the rough rope grew taut around his throat. When the hangman held out a black hood, he shook his head. He didn't want anything to obliterate his last look at the world.

Another shout came up, and then there were curses in the crowd and a shot rent the air. Jake's muscles tightened, and he saw Colonel Patterson approach on a lathered horse, but he could not hear him for the sudden roaring sound in his ears. Dave Logan appeared, looking up at him, his face grim. Below, pandemonium broke out, and Jake saw in a haze his uncle's face reflect first outrage, then shock, as he was surrounded by the blue uniforms of soldiers.

A reprieve—that thought was quickly dashed as he felt the wood floor give way beneath his feet and a sudden sense of weightlessness before he began to drop, and he braced himself for the moment when the rope would tighten and snap his neck like a brittle twig, his mind racing toward a single sweet memory:

Angie . . .

The surging crowd moved forward as if one, and more shots were fired as Dave Logan watched in horror. Jake dropped through the gallows floor like a stone. Dave was too late after all, and he wanted to throw back his head and howl his frustration.

It was little consolation that the Comanche renegade had been found and had verified Jake's claims, too late now that three more men had testified that Don Luis had corresponded with Mexico about stirring a new revolution that would wrest New Mexico from the United States and return control to Mexico City. Don Luis was under arrest for the very crimes he had accused Jake of committing, and Johnny Ringo had fled Las Cruces, but it mattered little now if Jake was dead.

Dave fought his way through the press of soldiers and spectators toward the gallows, expecting to see Jake dangling from the end of a rope. Instead, he found him sitting on the ground, the rope snaking behind him in thick loops and the hangman peering down through the trapdoor.

"Jake . . . God, are you all right?" Dave knelt beside his friend, caught between disbelief and delight.

"Not sure. I think I broke my ankle when I landed. Damn fool hangman—somebody should have told him he has to tie the other end of the rope to something if it's going to work right."

Despite Jake's light words, there was a faint gleam in his eyes that Dave understood, and he grinned.

"Always complainin', ain't you?"

"Shut up and help me stand."

Dave complied, and by the time Jake hobbled to sit on the bottom step of the gallows, Jim Patterson was there. He regarded Jake with a lifted brow and slight grin.

"That was close, Captain."

"Too damn close for me. I quit. Find yourself another scout and spy. I've got something else to do."

Part Five

The Destination

October, 1870

30

A soft wind blew. Soon it would grow colder, with winter winds gathering in the mountains and blowing down canyons and valleys to bring snow and ice.

Jake rode up the last hill and reined his horse in at the top, gazing down at the small house nestled in the ancient grove of trees. Casa en Paz—home. A light shone in the window, and the house was quiet and serene under the glow of the moon. Usually the first sight of it stirred him, but all he felt now was a draining weariness.

Ever since being almost hung at Las Cruces, almost a month ago now, he had spent most of his time on horseback. He had gone at once to find Angie, but the Double X was nearly deserted except for Bill North and a few more ranch hands. Rita had already left with her lieutenant, and Mignon and Angie had gone as well, back to France, Bette told him, smiling shyly when he looked from her to Dave and asked why she was still here.

"Ah, I think you know, monsieur."

Yes. He did know, and Dave Logan only grinned and shrugged as he put his arms around Bette and held her against his side.

It had been a long ride to Corpus Christi, but when he'd arrived, the boat to France had already departed.

For a few days he'd lingered, hoping maybe Angie had decided not to go, but finally he had realized she was gone. It was for the best, he decided. New Mexico was still primitive, still fraught with tension and hostiles. After her terrifying experience with the renegades, it was no wonder she had given up and left America. He couldn't blame her, but he couldn't quite shake a lingering feeling of disappointment in her.

He'd thought she was stronger than that—hadn't she been the one to find the Comanche renegade who could clear him of the trumped-up charges his uncle had brought against him?

It must have taken a lot for her to go with Dave Logan, riding into *rancherías* to look for him, searching until she found him and convinced him to return with her. The lone Comanche would not have been enough to clear Jake, for, times being what they were, the word of an Indian was hardly proof against a solid citizen like Don Luis, but with the other proof against him, it had held. His uncle was convicted of treason and had been hung from the very gallows he'd had built for Jake.

Justice of a sort, he supposed, but he couldn't quite bring himself to feel much satisfaction.

Dogs barked wildly as he rode into the small yard that bordered his house, but no one came out to greet him. It was late now, the moon high overhead, a full moon that gleamed like old Spanish coins in the sky. As he dismounted, a sleepy-eyed stable boy came running to take his horse, and Jake ruffled his dark hair with a murmured greeting.

He let himself into the house, wondering if Maria had gone to visit her sister again. She had stubbornly insisted upon traveling back without him, though she had allowed Colonel Patterson to escort her on his way back to the post in San Antonio.

It was quiet, and he moved through the house without bothering with lights, his steps sure in the familiar rooms as he skirted furniture. The doors to the patio were open in the bedroom, and he paused in surprise. The room was occupied. His eyes narrowed, and then he recognized the bright copper sheen of hair that streamed across the fat white pillows. She turned, and he saw her eyes glisten.

Half angry that he had ridden all the way to Corpus, yet relieved she was here, he narrowed his eyes at her.

"What the devil are you doing here?"

Angie gazed up at him with a smile. "Waiting on you. What took you so long?"

"I went all the way to damn Corpus after you, that's what took me so long!"

"Did you?" She laughed softly and sat up in the bed, and he saw the high, creamy rise of her bare breasts as she held out her arms to him.

Stubbornly, he remained where he was, folding his arms across his chest and leaning against the door frame. "Where is your mother?"

"France, or close to it by now, I would think." Angie lowered her arms but still smiled. "I sold my shares in the mine and gave the money to her. Now she has enough money to do what she likes. I thought it was more than fair in light of the fact that she worked against me as she did." She paused, then said softly, "I learned some things about Maman that I did not know before. Jake, when she lived here long ago, she was taken captive. My father did not rescue her, but Colonel Patterson—he was a captain then—was able to find her. It was a terrifying ordeal, and one that I can fully understand now. All that she has done, she did for me, though you were right that she had no idea your uncle meant for me to be abducted by those renegades. She thought only that I would be kept to myself until I saw 'reason,' as she said it. She was horrified. But while I may understand it, I don't have to accept her fear as mine."

"No," he said, "you don't."

Angie's smile returned. "I have a feeling that a certain colonel will be visiting France in the near future, for I have it on good authority that since one of his best men has quit, he's retiring from military duty and government work."

Jake's mouth quirked upward. "That's just an excuse. He wanted to quit."

"I saw Rita. She came to visit me. For the first time, I feel as if I truly have a sister. I think she's happy, and I know Tempe is."

"I saw her. She came to visit me in jail—while you were out risking your fool neck!"

"Are you sorry I did?"

"No."

"Would you have come to France after me, Jake?"

He paused. Then he nodded as he crossed the room to the bed, shedding his clothes as he went.

"Oh, yes, *querida*. If you hadn't come to your senses, I would have come after you. I would go through hell and high water if I had to just to get you back. Don't you know that?"

She reached under the pillow and brought out a slim square of paper and held it up. "Rita delivered this letter to me before she left for Savannah. Shall I read it to you?"

"No. I know what's in it."

He waited, and in a moment, she sighed softly. "I want to hear the words, Jake. Tell me how you feel. Tell me . . ."

He did, in Spanish and French and English, telling her that he wanted her, needed her, loved her, and when she answered him, it was in fluent Spanish, the soft words flowing into the close air between them as he made love to her.

"*Alma mía, te llevo en el alma* . . . My heart, I love you deeply."

He whispered back to her, "*Eres toda mí vida*—You are all my life."

It was true. One destination had been reached, another journey only begun, and he knew that all the rest of the days of his life would be spent with Angie.

For both of them, it was enough.